THE
BRIARS

ALSO BY SARAH CROUCH

Middletide

THE
BRIARS

A Novel

Sarah Crouch

ATRIA BOOKS

New York   Amsterdam/Antwerp   London
Toronto   Sydney/Melbourne   New Delhi

ATRIA
BOOKS

An Imprint of Simon & Schuster, LLC
1230 Avenue of the Americas
New York, NY 10020

This book is a work of fiction. Any references to historical events, real people, or real places are used fictitiously. Other names, characters, places, and events are products of the author's imagination, and any resemblance to actual events or places or persons, living or dead, is entirely coincidental.

Simon & Schuster strongly believes in freedom of expression and stands against censorship in all its forms. For more information, visit BooksBelong.com.

For information about special discounts for bulk purchases, please contact Simon & Schuster Special Sales at 1-866-506-1949 or business@simonandschuster.com.

The Simon & Schuster Speakers Bureau can bring authors to your live event. For more information or to book an event, contact the Simon & Schuster Speakers Bureau at 1-866-248-3049 or visit our website at www.simonspeakers.com.

Interior design by Jill Putorti

Manufactured in the United States of America

1 3 5 7 9 10 8 6 4 2

Library of Congress Control Number: 2025013930

ISBN 978-1-6680-9188-3
ISBN 978-1-6680-9190-6 (ebook)

 Let's stay in touch! Scan here to get book recommendations, exclusive offers, and more delivered to your inbox.

For Michael,
who is, among other things,
the only left brain I'll ever have.

Good hunting!—aye, good hunting,
And dim is the forest track;
But the sportsman Death comes striding on:
Brothers, the way is black.

—PAUL LAURENCE DUNBAR

Man is not what he thinks he is, he is what he hides.

—ANDRÉ MALRAUX

PROLOGUE

Thick fog pressed down on the valley, snaking ghostly fingers between the foothills and leaving breath on every leaf. It stuck to the ferns in tiny droplets and hung bridal veils over the pines clustered around the shelf of rock jutting out over the gorge.

Ben Gannon sat on the stony outcropping, his gaze fixed far below on the patches of mist gliding along the narrow river like phantom schooners with torn sails. With a sigh, he pried open the lid of his water bottle and took a sip before passing it to his daughter, Layla, who sat at his side.

"Anytime now," he said as Layla chugged.

Ben angled a finger at the spirals of mist ascending the side of Mount St. Helens. "See there? Lifting already. Twenty minutes from now, it'll all be burned off."

Layla tucked the bottle in her backpack and twisted the strap of her pink binoculars with impatient fingers. "Can I have some jerky?"

Ben nodded and a moment later felt her prying into his pack. He held out his hand as Layla unzipped the bag, and she pressed a piece of jerky into his palm. Popping it in his mouth, Ben closed his eyes and filled his nostrils with the honeyed scent of May-morning air. A few minutes passed, and when he opened his eyes again, the other side of the gully was appearing between patches of mist.

"This is it," he said, rising and kicking out the pins and needles in his left leg. Layla scrambled to her feet beside him, lifting her binoculars.

A mild gust of western wind rippled their clothes and the sun broke through, bathing the valley in warm, weak light.

"Spectacular," Ben murmured, his hands on his hips.

This particular vista, even half shrouded in fog, never ceased to take his breath away. It was a dramatic view of the rolling foothills that flowed around the base of Mount St. Helens like thick green batter poured over a mold. Green, at least on *this* side of the mountain.

Odd, that. The contrast between the southwest side and the other, blown to smithereens twelve years before in 1980 and still bare and ugly as a newborn baby bird, while this half of the mountain and their quaint little town of Lake Lumin remained virtually untouched, not a pine tree out of place. They'd had their fair share of ash rain down from the black cloud that covered the entire state, ash that was now compressed into a single, fine layer several inches belowground, but other than that, you'd never know that the town had been a stone's throw from an eruption the magnitude of Mount Vesuvius.

Just plain dumb luck that the mountain had blown in that direction, Ben supposed as he gazed at the verdant foothills, each brimming with streams, and old-growth firs, animals, and birds.

The fog was higher now, just kissing the upper rim of the valley, and Ben lifted the binoculars from around his neck. Today was the day. He could feel it.

In perfect synchronization, father and daughter scanned the gully from left to right.

From up here, Ben could just make out a slice of Lake Lumin far below, a little crescent of blue-green water behind the pines in the late-morning sun, with a corner of the old boathouse peeping out around a dark grove of firs.

Ben's gaze left the lake and swept the vista toward the mountain.

Adjusting the focus on his lenses with a finger, he scanned a shadowy pocket on the far side of the gully.

There it was. A massive nest at the very top of a gnarled snag amid the living pines. He'd found it weeks ago, but had yet to catch sight of the bird that built it. One of these days. Maybe today.

For several minutes, Ben kept the binoculars trained on the tip of the snag, where large branches and piles of brush had been twisted into a nest the size of a golf cart.

"Bald eagle," he said under his breath. "Gotta be."

"She's not gonna show." Layla lowered her binoculars and popped another piece of jerky into her mouth. "There'd be hatchlings in the nest already if she was gonna lay this year."

"Hon, don't talk with food in your mouth."

Ben slid the binoculars away from the snag and grazed his sight left along Lewis Ridge, where a hiking trail ran atop the cliff on the north side of the gorge.

"She might lay late this year," he said. "Happens all the time."

Layla gave a derisive little snort as she zipped the baggie shut and tucked it into her pack.

When Ben's line of sight reached the end of the hillside that dropped down toward the lake, he started back again, slowly, patiently scanning the forest in the direction of the nest. If she was out there somewhere, he wouldn't miss her this time.

Sudden movement on a shelf of rock caught his eye, the glint of sun against feathers, and he whipped his binoculars toward it, shifting the focus with his index finger in a practiced motion that brought sharpness to his vision.

Ben's heart skipped a beat.

There she was, and she was a stunner. Huge, the most gorgeous eagle he'd ever seen in his life, standing there against the naked rock in perfect profile, her posture proud, white and auburn feathers fluffed in the wind.

"Layla," he whispered, nudging her with an elbow. "Honey, look."

Layla followed his line of sight.

"Oh!"

Ben turned to beam down at his daughter, open-mouthed in wonder behind her binoculars.

"Daddy, what's she doing?"

Ben lifted his lenses and found the bird again.

"Looks like she caught some critter for breakfast."

"Oh." Beside him, Layla's shoulders fell.

"Every animal has to eat, Lay," he said softly. "We talked about this, remember?"

Layla nodded, binoculars still at her eyes. "What's she eating?"

Ben adjusted the focus, squinting. What *was* that? It was finer and longer than fur. Silken, and floating, somehow.

Wind caught the shelf of rock, sending long dark strands dancing out over the cliffside, and realization washed over Ben in an ice-cold wave. Slowly, he lowered the binoculars a few inches. He swallowed, blinked twice, and raised them to his eyes again, magnifying the thing beneath the eagle that seemed to be waving in their direction.

No. He hadn't imagined it. It was crystal clear. The wind was lifting glossy strands of long brunette hair. A woman was lying face down on the rocks.

Instinct kicked in, and Ben's hand shot out, pushing Layla's binoculars away from her eyes.

"Hey!"

"Honey, don't look."

His voice was harsh, and Layla blinked up at him in confusion, but Ben was already bringing his lenses back to his eyes, frantically seeking the spot again.

Heart racing, he located the eagle, then angled upward, higher, higher, until he found the trail. The slender wooden fence that guarded hikers from the edge was unbroken and unoccupied, and there was no one standing at the top, screaming down to the woman who had fallen. He would have heard it from here anyhow.

Ben swore under his breath and dragged his binoculars back down, praying that somehow, some way, his eyes had been playing tricks on him, but there she was beneath the bird, and though her hair still swirled in the air like a ghost with each breath of wind, she had not moved.

"Dad?"

Layla's curious voice sounded far away, though she still stood next to him, her fingers tugging at the loose elbow of his flannel shirt.

"Hang on, baby."

"But—"

"Please," Ben said urgently. "Please just hang on."

"Hey!" He shouted across the gully, one hand on the binoculars, the other waving above his head, "Over here! Can you hear me?"

At his echoing shout, the eagle took slow, exaggerated flight, soaring west with the wind and dropping out of sight behind a row of scraggly pines, giving Ben a clear view of the woman on the rocks.

"Who is it?"

Ben didn't answer as he ran the math. It would take an hour to hike back out the way they'd come, plus there was the several-mile drive to town or the nearest phone. Too long. If the woman was badly hurt and needed help now, he was her only hope. Judging the distance, he could be across the gully and climbing up to reach her in less than twenty minutes, if he and Layla hiked fast.

Ben turned to his daughter, stooping to bring them eye to eye as he gripped her hard by the shoulders.

"Listen to me, Layla. Are you listening?"

She nodded.

"We've got to get over to the other side of the gully. There's someone in trouble over there and I need to see if she's all right. Just follow me and do as I say, understand?"

He kept his voice as steady as possible, but the fear that had blossomed in some small place beneath his rib cage was reflected in his daughter's eyes as she nodded.

Ben straightened. "Let's go."

There was no path down into the steep gully, save a rutted and ferny switchbacking trail carved into the hillside by deer and other forest animals. Ben nearly turned his ankle twice on the descent to the river, while Layla, for her part, flew between the tree trunks, scrambling downhill like a mountain goat and hopping on his back with a giggle when they reached the rushing stream at the bottom.

The water was ice-cold but mercifully shallow despite the recent rain, and Ben made it across soaked only to midthigh. He lowered Layla to the muddy bank and eyed the near-sheer climb ahead, finding the woman about sixty feet up, those wispy strands of windblown hair still dancing out over the edge of the rock.

Ben brought both hands to his mouth and gathered his breath.

"Hey!" he called again. "Can you hear me up there?"

A gust of wind ripped through the gully, but in the silence that followed it, there was no cry of distress. No groan of pain.

Ben pressed a hand to Layla's shoulder. "Stay here, okay? Please don't move."

There was an edge to his voice, and Layla nodded.

Ben forced his lips into a half smile. "It'll be okay."

Layla nodded again, and Ben turned to face the cliff.

It was slow going, with footholds that were narrow and slick with dirt, and more than once he slipped, catching himself with a loud grunt and a white-fingered grip on the rocks. It had been a while since he'd rock climbed, and muscles he hadn't used in a couple of years were screaming in protest, but he continued upward, making gradual, steady progress.

A quick glance down through his boots showed Layla thirty feet below. The drops of sweat beading along Ben's hairline raced into his eyes as he inched his way closer to the outcropping, growing more and more certain by the second that the woman on the rocks was either dead or unconscious. Surely she would have heard his ragged breaths by now and peered down to investigate if she was lucid.

Ten more feet. Five. Three.

Neck and back screaming, Ben stretched his right arm up and grasped the lip of the rock. He sought one last foothold for leverage and pushed hard, popping his head and shoulders above the ledge with a grunt.

Dead.

She was dead.

For a split second, Ben almost released his grip and tumbled backward, but he held fast to the rock as a wave of adrenaline overcame him, setting his limbs trembling.

The woman's head was twisted at an impossible angle, one brilliant eye the color of bright caramel wide open and staring straight up at the sky. Her face was untouched, but he could not say the same for the rest of her body.

Ben looked over the corpse, his mind fighting back against the horror of it. The eagle hadn't done this to her. Something else had. Something bigger and deadlier, with claws like switchblades.

The back of her shirt and pants were torn to ribbons, as was the skin underneath, flayed in deep gashes that spoke of long claws and sharp teeth. Some predator had torn her apart.

Ben forced himself to take a deep breath, and another, pulling oxygen into his lungs as he stared down at the young woman. She was barely twenty years old, if that, with a face he didn't recognize. Someone that looked like her, as pretty as any of the women on the covers of the teen magazines that Layla was starting to leaf through, would have been well-known in the tiny town of Lake Lumin.

Ben glanced up at the ridge, high overhead. In some tragic hiking accident, some stupid mistake, this woman must have slipped past the wooden fence guarding the cliffside and tumbled to her death.

"Who's up there?"

Ben swore. He had forgotten that Layla was at the bottom, waiting for him. Watching.

"It's . . . it's a woman," he called down after a beat. "I think she fell."

There was a moment of silence before Layla called up, "Is she okay?"

"Baby, I . . . I don't know." The lie tasted bitter in his mouth, and Ben shifted his grip on the rock. He had to get down before his arms gave out. The first thing he had to do was just get his feet back on solid ground, and then he'd figure out what came next. As he adjusted his fingers for a better grip, preparing his muscles for the arduous descent, the wind lifted the woman's hair again, exposing her neck and the black and purple bruises that ran the length of skin from ear to collarbone.

A curse passed Ben's lips in a shout.

"What?" Layla called. "What happened?"

For long seconds, Ben stayed frozen to the rock, muscles tensed and straining as he tried hard to blink, to look anywhere else, to come up with something, *anything* to explain away the ugly bruises that looked like . . . like . . . fingers.

But there was no other explanation. Big, rough hands had been around this girl's neck.

"Daddy?"

Ben flinched at the sound of his daughter's voice. He had to get down, had to get to a phone, had to tell someone else, someone who would know what to do and could bring the proper equipment to get this poor woman off the rocks.

Limbs trembling, Ben descended. The footing was far worse on the way down, and his eyes were useless, burning with sweat that just wouldn't quit.

It seemed hours before the heels of his boots touched the ground and he found himself standing before his daughter again, her small face creased with concern and fear.

"What's wrong with her?" Layla's voice was high, frightened, but inquisitive with the morbid curiosity of all ten-year-olds.

"She's . . . I saw . . . she's . . . she's up there." Ben reached for the water bottle in the side pocket of Layla's backpack.

"Is she dead?"

He pulled the top off the bottle and drained it in long gulps, as though he could wash it down, the painful twist in his throat reaching right through his belly into his guts. When he'd finished drinking, he handed the bottle back and bent at the waist, supporting himself with his hands on his knees.

"Yeah," he said, unable to meet his daughter's eyes. "She's dead."

Chapter 1

ANNIE

Four weeks earlier

Annie Heston mashed the toe of her boot against the gas pedal, pressing it harder than was strictly necessary to slingshot the Wagoneer around a green Jetta and whip it back into the fast lane. A moment later, the angry dual flash of high beams flickered in the rearview mirror, but Annie ignored them as she pressed the pedal harder, giving the V-8 more gas.

It was reckless, driving like this. Reckless and stupid and rash, and she knew better, but still, the speedometer stayed well north of eighty as she flew past dark fir groves and rolling acres of velveteen farmland. It felt good, speeding like a lunatic, fleeing north as though putting as many miles between her and Bend as possible would somehow lessen her heartache, even though the rational part of her brain knew it wasn't so.

Ahead on the horizon, a low, gray city ringed with emerald hills was rising up to meet her, and Annie glanced at the half-folded map on the passenger seat. Portland. Good. She was almost to the border. Once she was through the city, she would cross the Columbia River and enter Washington State, and from there, it was just ninety minutes farther on a remote highway that led northeast to the blink-

and-you-miss-it mountain town that no one, including her, had ever heard of.

Annie flicked the lever that spritzed the windshield with fluid and cleared the constellation of bugs from the glass with a sigh. She had to quit doing that, mentally tearing apart her new hometown before she'd even set foot there. No more framing it negatively. There was no going back now, so she might as well make the most of it. After all, she'd asked for this, outright, marching into her supervisor's office and slamming her hands down on his desk.

"I'm putting in for a transfer," she'd said without preamble or hesitation.

"What do you mean?" he asked, flabbergasted. "A transfer to where? Why?"

She ignored the first and last questions, but answered the second through clenched teeth. "Timbuk-flippin'-tu, Allen. I don't care. Anywhere. Anywhere that has a game-warden position open."

Allen, somewhat bewildered, had fired up the Macintosh on his desk and scrolled through the listings in the database, reading out the first one in a tone that was more question than recommendation.

"Lake Lumin, Washington?"

He looked up from the computer with his eyebrows raised. Nope, she hadn't heard of it either.

"Perfect," she said, and drove straight home to pack.

And now here she was, three hours into the drive with Portland rising swift and leaden around her, small houses in muted colors giving way to the brick and concrete of old downtown.

A mile before the river, northbound traffic snarled into a jam, and Annie rolled down the window, draping an arm onto the sun-warmed wood paneling of the Jeep. After a few minutes, the crawling cars ceased moving forward in short spurts and came to a complete standstill, leaving Annie parked next to a green exit sign that she stared at with a depressing case of déjà vu. How long had it been since she was right here, stuck in Portland traffic, staring at this very same sign?

HWY 26
ASTORIA, OR

Annie gazed at the seven-letter word with a lump in her throat.

It was almost six years since she'd stood on the balcony of that old faded-green Victorian house in Astoria with the train of her wedding dress wrapped around her body in the wind blowing off the ocean. Brendan had found her there like that, fresh tears in her eyes as she looked down at the beautiful rows of white chairs on the rain-soaked lawn below, each holding a puddle of water the size of a dinner plate. The storm had been unexpected, and the pink roses she'd woven so carefully through the archway were drooping and limp in the downpour. Brendan had found her there, and he'd married her there, on that terrible, wonderful gray afternoon. He'd squeezed the pastor and the six-person wedding party onto the creaking balcony in a little circle around the two of them, while the guests crowded in behind the glass door and gathered at the open kitchen window to witness nuptials that were barely audible over the sound of raindrops peppering the porch roof.

Annie's eyes burned, and she blinked furiously as the flow of traffic picked up. When the congestion was behind her and the engine humming again, she risked a look at her reflection in the visor mirror. Her eyes were red and her cheeks were flaming. Add that to the waves of copper hair spilling over her shoulders and the golden freckles sprinkled across her skin, and she looked red all over. Annie flipped the visor shut and shook her head. No. She would *not* cry again today. Twice was enough. There would be no more tears spilled over that two-timing—

Beeeeeeeeeeep.

Annie jerked the wheel right, swerving around a shredded piece of blown tire and narrowly missing the Subaru next to her, whose driver directed her back into her lane with both horn and middle finger.

"Sorry," she mumbled, lifting a hand in apology as the Jeep bounced onto the bridge that spanned the wide river. It sang under the Wagoneer as Annie shot across it, toward the sign that announced WELCOME TO WASHINGTON. The moment she passed it, she blew out the breath she'd been holding. So long, Oregon.

Far below in the water, two speedboats raced west toward the bridge, twin streaks of white foam spreading in their wakes. Beyond them was the open river, lined in frilly green cottonwoods, and the great, impossibly blue hills of the gorge. One after another, they folded into the distance beneath the sharp, white steeple of Mount Hood, and Annie drank the view in greedily as the tires bumped over the end of the bridge and landed back on solid ground.

She left the interstate for the narrow highway, and mile after mile passed beneath the tires of the Jeep. Around every sweeping curve, Annie expected to come upon a town, or at least a rural home or two, but this road seemed determined not to acknowledge mankind at all as she flew alone through the deep green corridor with tall, unbroken forest on both sides.

It was darker here, where the woods shadowed the highway, leaving just tiny patches of sunlight winking like stars on the pavement. Annie looked left and right, peering through the host of fir trunks flashing by. They were endless, thousands and thousands of evergreens that stood like a silent army, their pointed tips high out of sight no matter how she craned her neck to peer through the window.

No wonder. No wonder Dad had always laughed whenever people claimed Bend was the most beautiful town in the Pacific Northwest. He had known better. He had grown up near here, just west of the mountain.

Yes, Bend was beautiful, and they had their fair share of pines and waterfalls and stony mountains, but this . . . she had never seen a wilderness quite like this. The only word that came to mind was *exquisite*.

A hawk swooped from bough to bough across the road, and Annie blinked her way out of hypnosis, the spell broken. She'd lost herself for a minute there, a glorious minute in which her troubles had slipped from the front of her mind and she had managed to forget. But there it was again, worse than before, that blasted lump in her throat that just wouldn't go down.

Annie stared at the steepening grade of the empty road ahead. The engine was starting to whine, and around the next curving switchback, her ears popped. This must be it, the ascent toward the mountain.

Up ahead, a sign promised a scenic overlook, and Annie tapped the brakes, swinging the Jeep around the curve and pulling it off the road onto a wide gravel shoulder edged by a guardrail, beyond which lay an alpine meadow and the snowcapped summit of Mount St. Helens.

Annie eased to a stop, turned the key, and withdrew it from the ignition. For a long, silent minute, she sat with her hands on the steering wheel as the engine creaked and settled. Four hours. She'd put four hours and two hundred miles between herself and Brendan, but she hadn't managed to put one inch of distance between her heart and the pain of his betrayal.

Without warning, the sob she had been fighting burst out. Tears sprang into her eyes, and Annie wept like a child, furious and without restraint, slamming the heels of her hands into the steering wheel again and again, until her palms sang with pain.

When the tears were spent and all that remained was the empty ache, she leaned back against the headrest and closed her eyes, drained by her outburst.

She was tempted to stay right there, to cave into exhaustion and fall asleep in the Jeep, but she forced her eyes open. She needed to get to town, settle in, and get her bearings before starting the new job tomorrow.

A throaty engine rose in pitch on the road behind her, and Annie watched in the rearview mirror as a log truck rumbled past, the gust of wind in its wake rattling the windows of the Jeep. When the sound died, she unbuckled her seat belt and stepped out of the car.

With the tears still wet on her cheeks, Annie walked to the guardrail and rested her hands there, the metal cool against the tingling skin of her palms. She pulled in the first truly deep breath she'd taken that day, crisp and clean and faintly scented with the white feathery blossoms hanging out here and there over the guardrail on spindly limbs. Dotting the field before her were the first of the spring's wildflowers, red and purple, just now breaking like butterflies through their green cocoons, and beyond them, the majestic, ruined summit of Mount St. Helens.

Annie lifted her burning eyes to the hills. Somewhere in that wilderness was the tiny town of Lake Lumin, the place where she would attempt to put herself back together.

The woods had brought her to life once before, and they could do it again. Someday, perhaps when she least expected it, she would feel that familiar flicker, the pilot light sparking into being somewhere under the deep dark hole that Brendan had left in her chest.

Hope.

Chapter 2

ANNIE

A nnie stopped on the sidewalk, blinking up through the drizzle at the rain-streaked sign swinging from the lintel over her head.

LAKE LUMIN MUNICIPAL DEPT.

She glanced down at the note in her hand, double-checking the address written in Allen's dark scrawl, then looked back up at the sign just as a hanging drop of water fell, missing the brim of her hat by centimeters and landing squarely between her eyes.

401 Hughes Street.

It was the right address, but the building didn't look like any visitor center she'd ever seen. It was small and indiscriminate, with just one mirrored window bouncing her reflection right back at her. Maybe Allen had been off by a digit or two.

Annie took a step back, swiping at her forehead as she glanced at the storefronts left and right of 401. Bigfoot Pies & Pastries, and a nondescript bookstore. Neither looked remotely like a business that would serve as headquarters for a game warden, so, with a sigh, Annie pushed through the door of 401, sending a silver bell tinkling as she stepped into a warm office.

A sandy-haired young officer sat alone behind a counter, spinning slow circles in his desk chair. He caught himself by the lip of the counter and straightened out to face her with bright blue eyes. "Can I help you?"

Annie pulled her hat from her head without bothering to smooth the flyaways beneath it. "Maybe. I'm new in town, and I think I'm a little lost."

The officer's gaze slipped from Annie's face, traveling to her toes and back as confusion creased his brow.

"Well, I'm Jake." He offered a wide smile with a noticeable gap between his two front teeth. "Where are you trying to get to?"

Annie glanced down at the stitched name on his uniform that read OFFICER PROUDY.

Jake.

Apparently, this was the sort of town where people didn't bother with last names.

"I'm looking for the visitor center. I'm the new game warden."

"Oh!" Jake shot out of his seat and thrust his hand across the counter. "Right, of course. They told me someone would be coming in to replace Bud this week, but they didn't say . . . they didn't tell me . . . I mean, no one said you'd be . . ."

Annie pressed her lips together, enjoying the embarrassed flush working its way up his neck.

"A woman?" she supplied after a beat, and Jake nodded gratefully.

"Not that there's anything wrong with that," he said quickly, "we've just never had a lady officer of any kind here."

"I'm Annie." She took his offered hand and shook it more firmly than necessary. "It's nice to meet you, Jake. So, where's the visitor center?"

"This is it." He grinned as he spread his hands wide to indicate the small office.

Annie scanned the room. There was a filing cabinet with a crooked top drawer in the corner, a massive map with the mountain at its center

pinned to the back wall, a watercooler bubbling cheerfully in the opposite corner, and a vending machine with a buzzing blue light that
illuminated a few candy bars and bags of Frito-Lay's.

Annie tapped two fingers against the brim of the hat at her hip. "I
don't understand. The sign over the door—"

"Well, yeah." Jake plopped back down in his chair and gestured to the
second seat behind the counter, empty and crooked, with a tear across
the cushion. "We don't have a whole lot of personnel in the way of law
enforcement here, so we make the most of the space. Bud Griffith was
the conservation officer in town whose job opened up, and we shared
this office. Actually, you'd be surprised how many businesses double up
here in town."

Annie's eyebrows shot up and Jake went on, gesturing at the window
behind her, "Oh, you know, Sally at the bed-and-breakfast gives hair-
cuts downstairs, Doc Porter is also the coroner, and the third Saturday
of every month they clear the horses out of the Ward family stable and
hold the flea market there."

"Ah." Annie nodded. "I wondered why Sally was sweeping up hair
clippings when she checked me in last night."

Jake's brow furrowed. "You're not planning on staying at the B-and-B
long term, are you?"

Annie shook her head. "Just until I find a place to rent."

"I've got one." Jake reached for the phone. "Fully furnished and ready
to go. It's where Bud was living, just gimme a second."

Annie opened her mouth to protest, but Jake pressed the phone to
his ear and held up a finger. "Hey, it's me . . . Good, good. Listen, I've
got the new game warden here and she's looking for a place to rent so
I offered the room over the garage . . . Yeah, I figured that. Have you
cleaned it since Bud left? . . . Okay, I'll let her know . . . About six-ish.
Lasagna sounds great, hang on."

Jake cupped a hand over the mouthpiece. "You're not a vegetarian or
anything like that, are you?"

Dazed, Annie shook her head.

"Okay, great." He held the phone to his ear again. "No, she'll eat it. Thanks, Mom, we'll see you then."

Jake hung up the phone and scribbled out a note, whistling as he passed it across the counter to Annie.

"They live kinda far out there, way up in the briars, but my guess is you're used to the woods." He chuckled at his joke before going on. "You're gonna take the turn for Lake Lumin Road, it's unpaved, and you'll drive about a mile and a quarter up, past the Boyd place. You'll know that one by the peacocks in the front yard, then you'll see the mailbox for my parents' house, it's shaped like a trout. You can't miss it, but if you hit the lake, you've gone too far."

Annie was struggling to keep up. She had a place to live, with this scatterbrain of an officer's mom and dad, something about peacocks and a trout mailbox. She glanced down at the note in her hand.

"A hundred twenty-five a month?" She shook her head. "That's nothing. I couldn't possibly—"

"Take it," Jake insisted with another boy-next-door smile. "Dad's a quiet guy, and Mom likes the company."

"I . . . well, thank you." Annie tucked the piece of paper into her pocket. Despite herself, she returned his smile. "No, seriously, thank you. The bed at Sally's had about thirty embroidered cushions too many."

"Yeah, well"—Jake came around the desk—"my mom likes to knit so I can't promise there won't be afghans stacked up to the ceiling."

Annie drummed her fingers on the brim of her hat again. Officer Friendly was standing about four inches too close. "I guess I'd better walk back to the bed-and-breakfast to check out, unless there's anything urgent I need to do here before I go?"

"Call came in yesterday, actually." Jake reached for a set of keys hanging from a nail on the wall. "You know what, I'll tell you about it on the way. I better head over there with you and help you find the house, just in case. It's about time for lunch anyhow, and Mom's baking a strawberry-rhubarb pie. It'll be the best thing you've ever tasted, I guarantee it."

Jake strode to the door and held it open with an arm. Annie stepped past him, pulling her hat back down over her hair with a stiff tug. She didn't want to be prickly, but just about the last thing she needed right now was a man, *any* man, sidling up to her like they were best buddies.

Outside, the drizzle had lightened into mist, and Annie turned toward the north end of town where filmy tendrils of fog were scraping the dark pines that topped the foothills. The mountain was cloaked, but she could feel it there, pulling her awareness beyond that last, hazy ridge of firs.

"So, where are you from?" Jake asked as she fell into step beside him.

"Bend."

Jake's shoulder brushed hers, and Annie took a sideways step, clearing her throat. "You said a call came in yesterday?"

"Yeah, Austin Smith, buddy of mine. He's the sheriff up in Landers. He called to let me know about an active cougar up there. It's working its way south along the mountain, and he figures it's maybe five miles north of us now. Couple of campers up near Warner Lake lost a blue heeler to it Sunday night. He said they heard the dog scrapping with it, but by the time they got their flashlights on, it was gone. Great big prints left behind though." Jake held up both index fingers to indicate the size.

"Is it tagged?"

Jake shook his head. "Fish and Wildlife up there tried, but they couldn't manage to trap it. Austin said it's south of the 504 now, so if it's gonna get done, it's up to us."

Annie nodded, already running down the mental checklist of preparations she'd need to make for tracking the big cat. This was good. It was something to do. Something to occupy her mind and keep her thoughts here in town and out of the black hole of her memories in Bend.

"No human attacks reported?"

Jake shook his head. "Nothing fatal, but I guess a hunter up there claimed it charged him before he fired his rifle and scared it back into the trees. Given that, Austin said the sooner it's tracked down and tagged, the better. Hey, how you doing, Mr. Lindgren?"

Jake stopped for a handshake with a white-haired man sitting on a bench outside the Lake Lumin General Store, and Annie stood on the curb, waiting. With growing unease, she tried to ignore the curious eyes sliding in her direction as a few patrons passed in and out of the door.

Thanks to Sally at the bed-and-breakfast, Annie now knew that Lake Lumin had a population of 836, a number that instantly stuck fast in her head due to the absolute absurdity of it. There had been almost double that number of kids in her high school alone, and even then, the school had seemed far too small, a petri dish of students who knew too much about one another. Every embarrassment, every rumor, every secret, had been shared with the collective whole, but this was a town, an entire *town* of less than nine hundred, and she, with her five-foot-ten frame, long copper braid, and crisp uniform, was sticking out like a sore thumb. She'd lived in Bend for twenty-eight years, her entire life, and now, for the first time, she was the outsider.

Jake patted the man's stooped shoulder and started moving down the sidewalk beside her again. When they reached the bed-and-breakfast, he waited at the front desk with Sally while Annie jogged upstairs to gather her things. Even with the door closed, she could hear the cadence of his quick speech and ready laughter, and Sally's answering chuckles. Annie rolled her eyes. The guy was a cartoon.

Packing didn't take long. Most of her belongings were still in the Jeep. Actually, *most* of her belongings were in a storage facility in Bend, but the bulk of what she'd brought with her—clothes, her pack, some equipment, and a few framed photographs—were still in the Jeep. Annie tucked her nightclothes into her duffel and met Jake downstairs. Together, they walked down the hill to the car.

The morning mist was lifting, and small patches of bold, blue sky shifted in the haze overhead as they drove through town. Annie had to admit, the place had charm. Quaint shops in faded hues of green, brown, and blue squatted beneath towering Douglas firs, and the entire length of Main Street, less than half a mile as she'd measured it by the

Jeep's odometer yesterday, looked as though it had grown spontane-
ously in the forest, popping up like a ring of mushrooms after a rain.

Jake talked so constantly that Annie wondered how he managed to
breathe as he pointed toward buildings and people and rattled off a brief
history of each. Mountain Fountains and Chimes had several colorful
birdbaths for sale out front and was owned by a married pair of bird
enthusiasts named Ben and Delores Gannon. The Lake Lumin Zoomin' Go-Kart Track, which weaved a pretty, kidney-bean-shaped loop
through a patch of woods tucked back from the street, seemed to be the
popular hangout for high schoolers this spring, though Jake was sure
they'd migrate to the community pool when the weather got warmer.

He told Annie that the pool was drained for most of the year, and
that his primary duty as the town's lone police officer was to check it between the hours of midnight and 3:00 a.m. for teenagers huddling over
bottles of Olde English or making out. Annie nodded along, following
his rambling train of speech, but just barely.

When they reached the end of Main Street, they left the buildings
of town behind and turned north onto a thickly wooded two-lane road
that snaked toward the mountain. Two miles later, Jake angled a finger
at a tilted road marker.

"Lake Lumin Road," he announced.

Annie was grateful that he'd pointed it out. She would have flown
right past the green sign half hidden behind the arm of a leafy maple.

She slowed the Jeep as they jostled over uneven dirt, the motor revving up stairstepping hills that rolled with the land. The higher they rose,
the denser the woods that pressed in alongside the road. The forest here
seemed older, and it was even lovelier than the wilderness on the drive in.
Annie had the sudden sense that she was at the heart of it, the flawless
center of the diamond, with the last vines of fog still lingering at the edges
of blue shadows, and shafts of sunlight breaking through the canopy.

"What *is* this place?" she breathed.

Jake turned to her, smiling. "This is the briars, Annie. Most beautiful
pocket of land in this corner of the state, if you ask me. I haven't been a

whole lot of places, but I've never seen anything to rival this road right here. The whole other side of the mountain used to look like this, too, before it blew. We used to camp over there when I was a kid, but now it's completely brown and bare. The blast didn't spare so much as a blade of grass, but it'll grow back in time. Honestly, though, if she had to blow, that was the direction to do it in. Least amount of damage as far as human life was concerned."

Annie nodded. Eventually, she'd want to get over to see the ruined side of the mountain, too, but for right now, she was content to just look at the undisturbed beauty around her. It was pristine. Untamed. And already, just bouncing over the potholes on this remote road with the Washington wilderness surrounding her like an embrace, the sharp edges of her broken heart seemed a little less jagged.

"Roll your window down," Jake instructed, still smiling.

Annie lowered the window and fresh forest air, impossibly green and sweet, filled the Jeep. In an instant, she was back in her childhood home, dragging a sleeping bag into the living room to spend the night beneath the Fraser fir her father brought in, fresh cut, every December.

Annie inhaled the evergreen scent and turned to Jake, surprising herself with a laugh.

"If you could bottle that, you'd make millions."

"Right?" He nodded. "I can't really smell it much anymore, but whenever I leave and come back, it's strong as perfume for a day or two. Best smell in the world, isn't it?"

He was looking at her with that smile again, the one Annie was already starting to think of as his signature grin, and she smiled back. Despite her best efforts not to, she could feel herself thawing toward him. It might be nice to have a friend in town.

"Right here, this is the place." He nodded toward a driveway on the left marked by a mailbox that was indeed shaped like a trout, wide-eyed and gaping.

Annie pulled the Jeep in next to a blue sedan parked beside the detached garage and killed the engine. The garage door was open, and inside, a man with silver at his temples stood bent over a humming table saw.

"My dad, Walt." Jake reached over to tap the horn and lifted a hand when his father looked up. Walt offered a quick wave, then turned back to the board he was sawing.

Annie stepped out of the car, gazing open-mouthed at the fir trees towering around the white house. They were gigantic. Monstrous. Each one surely hundreds of years old, their great boughs moving in the wind with a sound like rushing water, and Annie was struck by the sudden, unpleasant thought that just one of these trees toppling in the wrong direction could smash the entire house and everyone in it to bits.

The front door opened, and a woman wearing an apron patterned with sunflowers came out onto the stoop.

"Come on in!" she called. "Pie just came out of the oven."

Annie followed Jake toward the house, where he introduced his mother, Laura Proudy, who wiped her hands on her apron and took both of Annie's with a squeeze.

"It's real nice to meet you, Annie," she said, vowels curling with the hint of a leftover Southern accent. The fine lines on her face spoke of mirth and patience, and Annie warmed to her immediately, thinking that she looked something like her own mother might have, if she'd lived into her early fifties.

Laura led them into a messy, inviting kitchen and pulled out a chair for Annie at the table, while Jake claimed the one beside it.

"I bet you're hungry after all your travel."

Annie nodded, though it wasn't true.

She hadn't been hungry in weeks. There were moments when she felt empty, or when the growling of her stomach propelled her in search of food, but nothing had truly tempted her appetite since the moment that her life fell out from under her like a trapdoor.

This morning at the bed-and-breakfast, she'd woken to a knock and discovered a wicker basket sitting in the hall outside. Her name was written in Sally's looping cursive on a pink place card, and beneath the linen napkin were two Swedish pancakes, rolled and stuffed to bursting with lingonberry jam and vanilla-scented whipped cream on a silver-lined plate. They were beautiful, but Annie sat alone at the little table in her room, cutting precise bites with her fork and forcing them down without tasting them.

She ate as a means to keep moving—as fuel, as a necessity to push forward. She had seen what sadness could do to a person's body, and she would not lose one ounce of her hard-earned strength over Brendan. She would cling to it like a bulldog, sinking her teeth in.

"Go ahead and have a seat, honey, I'll serve the two of you up," Laura said, pressing Annie into her chair with a hand on each shoulder.

Annie sat, the corners of her mouth lifting. It was blatantly obvious where Jake had gotten his bubbly personality and complete disregard for personal boundaries.

Laura plated two heaping slices of pie and topped them with generous clouds of canned whipped cream before setting them on the table.

"Thank you," Annie said, blowing on the steam before taking a bite.

She turned to Jake, whose brows were raised in expectation, and nodded. He hadn't lied. It was easily the best pie she'd ever tasted, tart and sweet and bursting with summery flavor.

"This is delicious," she said.

"It really is, thanks, Mom," Jake managed around an enormous mouthful.

Laura smiled and stepped back to the counter to gather the dishes.

Annie glanced down at her plate. Something in this pie elevated the strawberry and rhubarb. Orange zest, maybe, or lemon. Something that set it apart from the only other strawberry-rhubarb pie she'd ever tasted, the one Brendan's sister had made on the beach trip the whole family had taken down to Brookings.

No. She wouldn't think about that right now. Even the happy memories were unsafe. Maybe especially those.

Annie turned to Jake. "You mentioned the cougar was heading south from Warner Lake. How far is that from here?"

Jake slid his fork across the plate with a screech, gathering crust and berries. "Not far. Maybe eleven or twelve miles as the crow flies."

Annie ran the math. An active male would cover that distance in a day or two, especially one migrating to seek out new territory, but they tended to linger around areas with fresh water, so she'd have to account for that.

"Are there any lakes between Warner and here?"

"Maybe some smaller ones up near the summit." Jake lifted the last of the crust with his fingers and popped it in his mouth. "But the nearest one of any real size is Lake Lumin, up at the top of the road."

"Jacob, be a gentleman and carry this poor girl's bags up to her room," Laura said, stepping back to the table with a flour-dusted rolling pin in her hands. "I'll bet she's tuckered out and might like a nap. I just changed the linens."

Annie rose from her chair. "Oh no, that's okay, I can—"

But Laura put a hand on her shoulder and lowered Annie back into her seat. "Don't you trouble yourself. What you need is an hour of sleep, and you'll feel like a new woman."

Jake carried his plate to the kitchen, offered his mother a quick peck on the cheek, and disappeared through the front door, closing it softly behind him.

Laura slid the rolling pin into the sink and Annie cleared her throat in the sudden quiet. "I guess I'll start looking for tracks at the lake to-morrow, then. I just take the road all the way up?"

Laura flipped on the tap and started scrubbing. "You should prob-ably drive up along the service road north of town. You can park at the gate and hike down along Lewis Ridge."

Annie's head tilted. "Doesn't . . . doesn't this road go right to it?"

Laura's hand paused in its washing, and she nodded, but did not turn to meet Annie's eyes.

"So, couldn't I just drive up and park at the end?"

"Honey, I wouldn't."

"Why not?"

Jake's mother turned at last, hazel eyes hooded. "The man who lives at the end of the road, he's not . . . well, he's . . ." Laura's voice trailed away and Annie watched her with interest as she turned back to the sink to resume her scrubbing. "He's not the friendliest neighbor on the road, I'll say that, and we can leave it there."

Annie was most certainly not leaving it there. She needed access to that lake. Nine times out of ten, migrating cougars hopped from body of water to body of water, and it was the only lead she had. She wasn't about to be scared into hiking miles out of her way just because some grump in the woods wasn't exactly Mr. Rogers.

"What do you mean?"

Laura sighed and turned to face her again. "Honey, I don't believe in gossiping, but if you want just the plain facts, a guy no one had ever heard of moved in a few years ago, claiming to be a relative of the folks who owned the place that burned down up there, and frankly, he hasn't had much to do with folks in town ever since. Jacob managed to get friendly enough with him to fish in the lake on the weekends and swears he's harmless, but he doesn't give anyone else the time of day—always driving by with his head down, never so much as a wave or a hello."

The tap was flowing over the dishes unnoticed, and Laura went on, her wet hands dripping as they flapped with her speech. "And goodness knows why a young man with no family would choose to live way up there in an old boathouse at the end of a dead-end road with no one to talk to. Something's just *off* about him. Yes"—she nodded firmly—"that's the word. *Off*. Everyone thinks so. And if I were you, being a female officer and all, I'd hike around on the trail instead or, at the very least, take Jacob up there with you, just in case."

Annie could feel her indignation rising, and she shoved one last forkful of pie in her mouth to stop it.

People had a habit of doing that. Underestimating her. And it grated on her nerves every single time it happened. If she had a dollar for every warning she'd gotten about something completely routine and well within the bounds of the job, she'd have a pretty formidable bank account by now.

It was usually well-intentioned enough. People who didn't know her took note of her lean frame, and the fine, delicate mouth and chin she'd inherited from her mother, and made all sorts of incorrect assumptions about her capabilities.

Every now and then the warnings had been warranted, when Annie had been led into barns or sheds to face cornered animals, half rabid with panic and ready to lash out with quick claws and teeth, but some grump who lived at the end of the road in an old boathouse? No problem.

"Thanks," she said, rising from the table and setting her empty plate in the sink, "but I'm sure I can handle him."

Chapter 3

DANIEL

Glass shattered—a singing starburst of sound that broke with it the night silence and the dreamless sleep of the man on his back in the boathouse.

Daniel opened his eyes, his heart thundering with the quick, uneven beat that accompanies sudden fear, but the splintering crash was over as quickly as it had come, and quiet once again filled the room. A few seconds passed, and he lifted his head, turning over the possibility that he had dreamed it—a jolting prelude to yet another nightmare, but the silence was ripe. Full.

Daniel sat up. It was pitch-black in the windowless room, and his panic was thickening it. Already, he could feel his body responding, his breath growing shallow and his pounding heart sending blood rushing past his ears.

Slow down. Use your head. Think.

Daniel forced a full breath into his lungs, and another. He inched backward until his shoulder bumped the wall, then slipped his arm behind the mattress, reaching down for the length of copper pipe he kept under the bed.

He withdrew it and held it in his lap, waiting.

As his eyes adjusted to the darkness, familiar shapes in the room appeared one by one. There was the chest of drawers in the corner, and the straight-backed chair beside it, the low bench at the foot of the narrow bed, and the dim mouth of the open doorway. Daniel fixed his gaze there and waited without blinking for the sweeping beam of a flashlight, or the creak of a footstep against floorboards, or some other sign of whoever had finally tracked him down.

Whenever he'd pictured this moment, whenever he'd run through the possible scenarios in his head, it had never been like this. He'd imagined a sharp knock at the door, or the sound of a gun cocking somewhere behind him in the woods, or the cry of a siren, far off at first, wailing through the trees and growing louder and louder until he could hear the gravel popping under the tires of some federal SUV. He had always assumed he would hear the sound of the other shoe dropping—the sound of his past coming for him—but he'd never once pictured it like this. A surprise. A broken window in the dead of night.

For a minute that felt like an hour, Daniel sat motionless on the bed with the pipe gripped in his hands. Nothing appeared in the doorway, and all was quiet in the dark boathouse beyond. He dropped his legs over the side of the bed and rose to his feet. Every step on the warped floorboards ran the risk of creaking, and he moved toward the door with painstaking slowness, treading as lightly as a man of six feet can tread. Halfway across the room, a board groaned beneath his feet and Daniel froze.

For several seconds he stood rooted to the spot, all five senses humming, but there was no noise from the hall beyond. He wondered again if he had dreamed the sound of shattering glass, if maybe he was dreaming still.

He risked another step forward. A few more and he'd have a view down the hall into the main room.

He was probably overreacting, creeping around like this. It was probably something he'd feel foolish about in the morning. Probably. It was entirely possible that the wind had torn a branch from one of the alders and whipped it into the window, or that an owl or bat, chasing an insect, had flown into the pane and shattered it. But no matter the cause, he had to see for himself. He had to be sure. He'd never find his way back to sleep until he ruled out the worst-case scenario.

Daniel took a cautious step forward, and another—then he heard it. *Crunch.*

Glass underfoot. It was soft, but unmistakable. He was not alone. Someone was inside the boathouse. The last, foggy whisper of denial was swept away, doused by a cold surge of adrenaline, and Daniel gripped the pipe tighter, raising it over his shoulder as he stepped through the doorway into the hall.

Empty.

Broken glass was scattered across the floor, and something else, something dark and viscous. Small drops of blood.

Daniel's brows drew together, but he did not lower the pipe. A creak sounded from the dark space beyond the hall, the room that served as both kitchen and living area, and was followed by a soft, shifting rustle, like the sliding of fabric against furniture.

So quiet. The movement of someone who had done this before.

There was an image swimming forward from the back of Daniel's mind, a face threatening to come up like bile, and he shoved it away, refusing to see it as he gripped the pipe tighter, the hard copper a comfort against the calloused skin of his palms and fingers. No. Not tonight. Not any night.

Daniel shifted. Pressing his back to the wall, he moved sideways down the hall with his breath held, praying feverishly that the boards under his feet would keep quiet. He drew even with the window. It was thoroughly broken. Only a thin rim of sharp glass remained in the upper corners like jagged teeth.

Through the empty frame, Daniel scanned the dark woods to the dirt road beyond. There was no car parked outside, SUV or otherwise. Whoever had come was on foot and did not have the law in mind.

Daniel glanced down. The scattered circle of glass on the floor reflected the crescent moon outside, and he stared at it for a moment, his mind spinning.

He crouched, adjusting the image in the glass by tilting his head at an angle. Farther. There. Just barely, he could see around the corner into the dark kitchen using the glass as a mirror.

For long seconds he waited without moving, his eyes fixed on the shards.

A minute passed, and another, and his confidence in reality began to soften and slide. *Was* he dreaming? This silence had the clotted quality of a nightmare, and there was a sense that time was not moving quite as it should. A tense waiting for a bad thing to happen.

A breath of wind whispered through the broken window, and a handful of cherry blossoms fluttered into the hall, falling like snow and dancing across the fractured glass. As the last blossom twirled across the sharp edge of a lethal-looking shard, Daniel saw it, an inky shadow slithering across the glass.

The dam of fear inside him broke, flooding his slumber-heavy mind.

Monster. Demon. Something evil and awful was moving toward him, and Daniel did not think as he launched himself forward into a run, jerking the pipe back as he rounded the corner and bringing it down with all his might.

He made contact with forgiving flesh and unforgiving bone. There was a yelp of pain, a feral cry, and Daniel shouted, too, raising the pipe high over his head and bringing it down again and again on the crumpled intruder until the copper sang in his hands.

He struck blindly, savagely, without mercy, until his strength was spent and all that remained was his rasping breath and the broken body of the intruder heaped at his feet.

Chest heaving, Daniel raised the pipe over his head one last time, eyes wild, jaw muscles tight and bunching as he waited for any sign of movement, any sign of life, but there was only stillness and the cool night breeze behind him, carrying the scent of cherry blossoms through the broken window.

Inch by inch, Daniel lowered the pipe. Every muscle from his neck to his thighs was trembling with adrenaline and exertion, and his fingers stung from the vibration of the blows. He needed to see what it was. Who it was.

There was no way to stop the image from coming now—the face he'd seen in his nightmares, the pale blue eyes of the man he'd been looking over his shoulder for every day of these last seven years.

Daniel moved backward toward the light switch at the end of the hall, careful not to take his eyes from the body, half fearing that the lifeless mass would rise up at any moment and start fighting back.

His fingers fumbled with the switch for what felt like an eternity, and then he had it, and the light was on—the single hanging bulb overhead bathing the hall in a warm, yellow glow.

Daniel blinked once, staring at the blood-matted heap at the other end of the hall, eyes open, jaw cracked and hanging at an angle.

It was not a man or a monster he had beaten to death, but an impossibly large fox.

Chapter 4

ANNIE

Annie nudged the Jeep door shut with a boot and hiked her pack up onto her knee, shouldering it as she scanned the vista that dropped away before her.

She was on St. Helens now, about a third of the way up the mountain on the Forest Service road that cut a treacherous gravel path into the steep, piney grade. The road was poorly maintained in some places and downright dangerous in others where the land fell away beside it, but it was obvious why avid hikers risked the drive up.

The view that was spread out before her was breathtaking, with Lake Lumin far below, held like a sapphire in the palm of the foothills, and the town that bore its name beyond it, miniature from this distance and still appearing somehow organic in the forested hummocks that surrounded it.

It had taken four days to get out here—three days longer than she had hoped, due to near-constant rainfall in the latter half of the week. Not that she minded getting wet, but trying to track anything in the rain was foolhardy, unless she had a fresh sign to begin with and was hot on the trail from the start. Today, the ground would still be damp, but prints would hold, and all things considered, it had been nice to spend a few days getting settled in the little room over the garage at Jake's parents' place.

Annie consulted the map, then set off down the trail that bisected the road, leaning back to compensate for the abrupt downhill grade.

She had followed Laura's advice to drive up by way of the service road, not because she was nervous about confronting the hermit in the boathouse, but because she'd spent the entirety of yesterday at the station poring over the maps in Jake's desk and realized it was her best possible chance of crossing the cougar's path, if he was indeed migrating due south between the two bodies of water.

Annie raised her knee high to step up onto a boulder and hopped down the other side, where her boots slid out from beneath her and she landed hard on her backside in the mud with a grunt. Moments later, she fell again—the muck making it impossible to gain traction on the precipitous downhill, but this time she rode out the fall, catching at the trunk of a young spruce as she stumbled by and righting herself with a jerk.

She blew out a frustrated breath and kept hiking. It was hard to imagine anyone choosing this trail for a casual jaunt through the woods, but that was good. Preferable. It meant there would be fewer tracks to weed through.

For an hour, Annie stutter-stepped downhill between the trees, following the barely there path over raised roots and uneven boulders, sliding on the rain-slick mud from yesterday's downpour, until, finally, the terrain leveled out and the narrow trail deposited her onto the wide, even floor of the valley. She swept her sweat-damp hair out of her eyes. Ahead was flat ground—a dark, mossy forest studded with tree trunks and cut through with a pretty woodland path, choked here and there by patches of lacy blue forget-me-nots.

For a split second, Annie almost turned, almost looked over her shoulder to say something, and a stab of loss, sharp as a razor's edge, tore through her.

This was the moment she would have turned to Brendan, laughing and making light of the grueling trail they had just come down. He would point out the mud splattering her legs up to the seat of her shorts, and she would joke about the sweat soaking his shirt from collar to navel. But Brendan wasn't here. She was completely alone, and the novelty of it was excruciating.

That was one luxury of a place like Bend. Not a city by any stretch of the imagination, but a fair-size town that was outdoorsy to its core and supported a large group of wildlife officers, three dozen in all, from park rangers to game wardens to wilderness guides. There was no shortage of company, and almost every expedition into the wild was done in pairs. That was how she and Brendan had met, during a search-and-rescue mission late one November that was, in retrospect, the hardest week she'd ever spent on the job.

Brendan was a park ranger, and she had known him as a casual acquaintance, but had never been paired with him on an outing until then. She'd found him to be the perfect partner out in those snowy woods, quiet and steady, keeping her spirits high when their boots soaked through, freezing their toes. He was patient and dependable, everything Annie valued in a work partner and, later, a husband.

Search and rescue was one part of the job that Annie did not relish. It didn't happen often that game wardens were called in to assist in locating a missing hiker, or a child who had wandered too far from a campground, but once in a blue moon—in particularly bad conditions or when the search range was broad—it did.

On that particular operation, after three days of single-digit temperatures and continual snow at seven thousand feet, with limited daylight hours and gale-force winds to contend with, what had started as a rescue mission quickly became a recovery mission, and despite all odds, despite the hundreds of officers and volunteers combing the mountains, Annie and Brendan had been the team that found the body.

Just before sunset, as they pitched their tents for the night, Annie's gaze had snagged on a corner of yellow canvas flapping in the wind in a little nook between boulders, and she and Brendan had snowshoed over to find the missing hiker's tent half buried in the snow. Her hands had never trembled so badly as she fumbled with the zippered door, one thought racing over and over through her mind.

I didn't sign up for this.

Brendan had noticed her unsteady fingers and insisted that he be the one to open the tent instead. He had—and instantly tried to shield Annie from the gruesome and heartbreaking scene inside, but she had seen it, the dead hiker clothed in only his underwear, the telltale sign of someone who had succumbed to hypothermia. He was face down on top of his sleeping bag with the contents of his pack spread out around him, including a photograph of a smiling young woman with a baby in her arms.

Afterward, Brendan kept her talking and drinking from his thermos of hot coffee, the waves of shock and adrenaline threatening to set her body shaking uncontrollably as they waited for the snowmobiles to come pick them up.

It had bonded them, those bitterly cold days and nights in the wild. Bonded them for better or worse, and while Brendan had bounced back from the experience fairly quickly, Annie had struggled.

The thing that stole sleep from her, the thought she just couldn't get past, was the hiker's proximity to the trail. He had been less than a hundred feet away from the path that would have led him in a straightforward kilometer down to the nearest road, but covered as it was in snow, he might as well have been a hundred miles away for all the good it did him. The injustice of it gnawed at her, and she battled crippling insomnia for weeks.

Brendan had stayed up with her during those sleepless nights, coming over when she called him, and putting on pot after pot of tea as they talked it through. Tragedy. Tragedy and trauma, Annie knew, had the potential to be the strongest adhesive in any relationship, if they didn't splinter it first. Brendan became her best friend, her most trusted ally in the woods, a partner who had her back out there. And when he asked her to marry him a year later, bending his knee during a cliffside hike at the coast, of course she'd said yes. He was perfect for her, on paper at least, and she'd believed with her whole heart that he was the one.

Well, she was paying for it now, the high cost of her blind faith and misplaced trust in the person she'd chosen to be her companion. She paid in moments like these, alone in the woods without him; moments that stung like snake venom.

Annie shrugged out of her pack and sat down on a mossy log. Sliding her right foot out of her boot, she dumped the loose pebbles that had gathered there, then repeated the motion with her left. She lifted a granola bar from the pocket of her pack beneath the tranquilizer gun and tore it open with her teeth, looking around at the pleasant, wooded valley as she ate.

Her gaze skipped from felled log to felled log in the forest, at least a dozen of them here at the bottom of the hill. A landslide must have torn down this ravine at some point in the last century, toppling pines as it went, leaving logs that were now home to countless creatures and species, their very death and decomposition essential to new life. Destruction and rejuvenation walked hand in hand in the woods. The wilderness was like that, as was, Annie suspected, the human heart.

She popped the last bite of her granola bar into her mouth, telling herself that the woods were just as pretty when she was alone as they would have been with someone seated beside her. She dwelled on the thought with as much conviction as she could muster, though she couldn't quite manage to believe it.

Jake had offered to accompany her on the hike this morning, but Annie had declined. Jake was a golden retriever, and being lovable and chatty were acceptable attributes for an officer who thrived on the sidewalks of Lake Lumin or parked himself on the bench in front of the station, but she needed absolute silence in the woods if she was to have any chance at all of tracking the cougar, and absolute silence seemed about as foreign to Jake Proudy's nature as his nonstop rambling was to hers. And beyond that, while Jake was a casual outdoorsman, fishing and hiking on the weekends, he didn't have the first clue about what her job entailed. When she'd told him yesterday that back in Bend she had once used dogs to track a cougar, Jake had offered up his buddy's yellow Lab, as though that would have done her any good at all. A trained dog, she explained, would know how to scent a cougar and tree it, although tranquilizing the cat from the ground generally resulted in a fall through the branches and was often deadly for the animal, so all things considered, she was probably better off alone.

Annie tucked the empty wrapper back into her pack and stood, shaking her legs out one at a time. With the sun high above the treetops as a guide, she hiked forward into the pines. Here in the valley, the damp earth was fresh and dark. The heart-shaped tracks of rabbits and the slender indent of deer hooves crisscrossed the trail here and there, but nothing larger. Yet.

The bark of a nearby tree trunk was marred in gashes, and Annie left the trail to inspect it. Cougars often sharpened their claws this way, but so did bears. Up close, the mark was high and deep, the bark peeled away to show the yellowed skin beneath it, and Annie lifted away a short dark hair from the trunk with her fingertips. Black bear. It had peeled back the bark to get at the sweet sap underneath. Though it wasn't the sign she was looking for, it still felt like progress. A piece locking into place in the picture puzzle of these woods that was forming in her mind.

As Annie walked back toward the trail through the undergrowth, the toe of her boot caught on an unseen limb and she stumbled forward, snapping the branch beneath her as she regained her footing.

Sudden movement in the trees caught her eye, and Annie watched two deer, startled by the sound, as they darted in leaping bounds deeper into the forest. Annie stared after them, unnerved. She hadn't even known they were there. It wasn't often that she was surprised by wildlife, but this was the sort of woods that hid anything that did not want to be seen.

The forests of Bend gave up their secrets easily. They were drier than these woods, airy and more spacious, and it wasn't difficult to spot animals far off through pines that were sparse and thin, but here, with dense, wide trunks, and firs whose lower boughs scraped the ground, she could be mere feet from a bear or cougar and not know it until it was too late.

Annie straightened and scanned the trees around her, muscles tensing. There was an awareness tainting the edges of her mind with fear, the dawning realization that it was entirely possible for any creature out here who thought of itself as the hunter to easily become the hunted.

Keep quiet, Annie girl, and the woods will come alive around you. Threats always show themselves if you're silent for long enough.

It was her father's voice in her head, drawn forth from memory in the only place she ever heard him anymore—out in the woods.

For long minutes, Annie stood in the forest, warmed by the light of a sunray falling through the canopy. Only her eyes moved as they jumped from trunk to trunk until, at last, satisfied that nothing else was hiding in the trees, she stepped back onto the trail and moved deeper into the woods.

The vast majority of cougar attacks came from behind. Cougars were a predatory species that thrived on stalking slowly and silently, with patience and persistence. They caught their meals by surprise, and surprised was the one thing that a game warden, or anyone else who dared to walk into these woods alone, could not afford to be.

Dead ahead was the sound of flowing water, and Annie came upon a wide stream that split the forest floor. She dropped her pack, knelt down, and plunged her water filter into the cold current, filling her hydration bladder with her eyes on the woods. She drank her fill, then tucked the mouthpiece away.

Folded into the front pocket of her pack was the map of the mountain she'd borrowed from the station, and Annie lifted it out, unfolding it and running a finger down from Lewis Ridge to where she now stood. The designated trail continued on the other side of the stream, but she wouldn't be taking it. From here to Lake Lumin, roughly a mile if the map's key was accurate, she would be bushwhacking northwest through the forest in the hopes of crossing the cougar's tracks.

For several minutes, Annie walked with the current, stooping often to inspect marks on the soft bank, but the week's rainfall had swollen the creek and muddied the dirt, and though it was evident that animals had visited the stream, the prints were nondescript.

As soon as the land started to slope upward again, she left the stream and hiked back into the forest, stepping high over ferns and the barbed coils of rambling wild blackberries. When something on the ground caught her eye, she stopped.

A sizable pile of scat lay half hidden under an arching bracken fern, and Annie knelt beside it, lifting the plant with a finger. She stared at the waste, a thrill of discovery running through her, then grabbed a stick from the ground and poked at it, breaking it apart to inspect the contents.

Fur. A good bit of it, too, inch-long hairs that were tawny at the root and black at the tip. Annie remembered that Jake had said the campers up near Warner Lake had lost a dog to the cougar. A blue heeler.

She sat back on her heels, inspecting the scat with her head tilted. No flies buzzed around the pile, and no moisture gleamed in the sunlight. It was at least twelve hours old, but not much older than that, or the rain from yesterday would have partially washed it away. Annie poked at it for another minute as a memory ran through her mind.

Lion sign, the instructor of her tracking course had called it, gesturing with his wooden pointer to the pull-down screen that projected a pile of scat magnified to twenty times its original size on the wall.

A couple of guys in the back of the class had snickered, and Annie herself had barely managed to hide her giggle. The instructor was a distinguished conservation officer who often wore bow ties clipped to his pocketed shirts. Annie suspected that he considered it well beneath his dignity to speak to a group of twentysomethings on the subject of poop.

Still, it had been an informative lesson, and by the end of the course, Annie could match just about any droppings to the animal that had produced them, as well as identify how long they had been on the ground and what the animal's last meal had been.

Annie pushed back and rose to her feet, scanning the ground. Here, the forest floor was carpeted in a thick layer of sweet-smelling pine needles, and any tracks would be mere indents, telling her nothing, but just ahead the pines gave way to a patch of slender deciduous trees, and Annie moved toward them, her heart racing.

At first, she saw nothing. The dark ground between the trees was clean and slightly pocked from the rain. But a few feet farther in, her breath caught at the sight of a print, perfectly preserved in the soft dirt.

Eyes bright, Annie crouched over it.

The four toes were shaped like teardrops, with the lead mark that belied the symmetry of a canid. There was a gentle divot at the top, ever so slightly asymmetrical, as though the animal had been limping, but just barely. There was no doubt about it. This was a cougar. And unless there were two cats stalking these woods on the same day, this was the male she was looking for.

Annie stayed crouched for a minute, gazing at the print. It was a thing of beauty. The biggest she'd ever seen at nearly four inches across. She placed a fingertip into the leading toe mark. Due northwest, right toward Lake Lumin.

There were no marks above the toes, the sharp, slender gashes that indicated a cat in a hurry, gathering speed by using its retractable claws. This cougar was walking, not running. Annie searched the forest floor around the print and found another partial, the pad well-defined in the mud, the toes lost on the upraised root of a tree. A few feet farther in, another. She began tracking in earnest, walking through the woods with her eyes glued to the ground.

The cougar had left quite a trail of breadcrumbs for her to follow, soft piles of scat and fresh prints that weaved a lazy path through the forest as the land climbed west toward the lake. He was roaming, skirting the valley in an ambling circle, taking his time and getting to know the terrain. Twice Annie caught the telltale scent of urine and found thin streaks staining the lower feet of tree trunks. That was it, then. He was assessing the valley as new potential territory. Marking it out and exploring the different nooks and crannies. He was settling in.

The thrill of the hunt propelled her forward, though the growing sense of fear that accompanied it tainted her eagerness, and when the tracks deviated, angling sharply uphill, she paused.

This was what cougars did at the end of the night, when they were ready to bed down. They found high ground where they could see and not be seen, where they were safe and had the advantage over anything that came up the hill after them.

Annie unclipped the tranquilizer gun from her pack and loaded it, slipping a second dart into her back pocket before retrieving the canister of bear spray from a side pouch and tucking it into the empty firearm holster on her hip. The dart would do the trick if she caught sight of the cougar from a distance, but just in case, the bear spray was there as a more immediate resort. Her Ruger was locked in the Jeep's glove compartment. She didn't need it today. Usually, it rested on her hip as a method of persuasion against bullheaded hunters and fishermen, neither of which she anticipated out here.

With silent steps, Annie followed the cougar's trail up the hill to a soft bed of dead pine beneath a rocky lip on the sharp hillside. A den. Empty.

The tracks came and went, leading both to and away from the crag. The cougar had slept here, and it was the one place in these woods that she absolutely should not linger. Later on, she could come set snares here if she had to, but for now, she'd keep tracking to learn the boundaries of the cat's new territory. Annie walked back down the hillside, following the outgoing tracks into the forest. They led due west, where she caught her first glimpse of Lake Lumin, a far-off glint of blue-green water on the other side of the trees.

Annie's stomach rumbled, and she glanced at her watch. She'd been out here almost three hours. She should probably call it quits for the day and get back to the Proudys', but the last thing on earth she wanted to do was turn around and face the grueling, slick climb back up to the Jeep. It had been a hard enough descent, but with the slimy mud it would take twice as long to hike back up.

Annie contemplated the shimmering water just visible through the trees. She could save herself hours by making her way around the lake and walking back down Lake Lumin Road, where she could grab a bite to eat at the house, then ask Walt or Laura for a ride back up to the ridge to get the car.

Decision made, Annie moved forward into the trees, gaze snagging on an orange NO TRESPASSING sign nailed to the trunk of a hemlock ahead.

She had seen her fair share of private-property warnings: cracked signs hanging from rusted nails on fence posts, signs peppered with BB's, even homemade signs scrawled in black permanent ink warning trespassers that if they could read the words, they were in range. She was used to marching right past such signs in pursuit of hunters and fishermen who thought they'd slip onto private property unnoticed. It was the same story every time.

Private property? Really? Gosh, I must have missed the sign.

This was often accompanied with a scrunched brow and an actual head scratch, at which point Annie would walk the offenders firmly out the way they had come and point to the obvious warnings they had stepped right past to get there. In all honesty, she was doing them a favor, being the one who arrived to escort them away. Most men preferred a polite redhead to a butt full of buckshot from an unseen rifle in the woods.

If there was one thing she'd learned in her years as a game warden, it was that she need not fear the men who ignored the NO TRESPASSING signs, but the men who posted them. Those were the ones who meant business, the men who strode out of their trailers and barns and shops with twelve-gauge shotguns pressed to their shoulders, locked and loaded.

Annie reached up to touch the sign, inspecting the thin layer of dirt that came away on her fingertips. It hadn't been up for more than a few years.

She moved around the tree, taking another few steps forward, then saw the other signs.

The one on the hemlock had not been a lone warning, but the first soldier who appeared with his sword drawn atop a hill, followed a moment later by the rest of the army.

Two, three, five, a dozen. They were everywhere. Every third or fourth tree seemed to have one, growing denser as she moved toward the lake.

Who on earth is this guy?

Annie risked another thirty feet forward, but the closer she came to the water, the tighter her chest felt until she could not take a deep breath. Finally, she stopped altogether, scanning the forest ahead, her eyes jumping from sign to sign nailed on the thick trunks between her and the lake.

They were a statement. Unmissable. The man who had posted them was not just marking a boundary, but sending a message, loud and clear. Through her apprehension, resolve stiffened Annie's spine.

Who do you think you are?

A great big part of her was tempted to stride right past the militia of warnings and keep moving toward the lake. There was a lethal-looking firearm in her hands, a badge pinned to her uniform, and she had a perfectly lawful reason to be here.

As Annie stood still, teeth working away at her lower lip, she heard it: a faint sound coming from beyond the trees.

Scrape . . . scrape . . . scrape . . .

Her heart lurched into her throat.

This was not a sound of these woods. Something was moving. Shifting. Dragging. And underneath the murmur of the firs and the birdsong floating high overhead in the boughs, the sound kept coming.

Scrape . . . scrape . . . scrape . . .

Annie held her breath, her eyes wide and unblinking and fixed on the trees as she turned possibilities like pages in her mind.

A boot sliding with every other step. A man with a limp. A bear scratching itself on the bark of a tree. A beaver pulling a limb toward the water. Or maybe, just maybe, a cougar, dragging a large kill along the forest floor one foot at a time, back to its den to devour it in peace.

With deliberate slowness, Annie lifted the tranquilizer gun into fire-ready and took a deep breath. Then with equal, painstaking slowness, she positioned her boot over a dry, dead twig on the forest floor.

POP!

The stick snapped beneath her boot, and breath held, Annie whipped the gun left, then right, then left again.

Nothing came running through the trees, and after a minute of silence, with even the birds in the branches halting their songs to watch the woman below, Annie lowered the gun. She listened for the scraping sound, but it had ceased, and in its sudden absence, the silence was thicker, even more suggestive of a dangerous presence than it had been before.

A knot of fear, deep and instinctive, tightened in Annie's gut. The forest around her was still. Not a breath of wind stirred the fir boughs, but all at once, every single hair on her forearms rose at the same time.

She was being watched.

Slowly, she turned in a full circle, every muscle tensed and ready to fly to her defense at the first hint of danger, but she could not locate the source of her fear. No eyes peered at her from beneath the brim of a camo hat half hidden behind a tree trunk. No hunter was perched high in a blind, looking down at her through a rifle's scope, but the chill that traveled from the nape of her neck to her tailbone and back again whispered that she was not alone.

Her father's voice came again—soft with warning.

Go back, Annie. Turn around.

Annie took a single step backward, and another. She had confronted enough of these men in her line of work, the particular brand whose signs warning trespassers away had been ignored. They were a special breed, those men, with dark, bearded faces and hooded eyes that held something more threatening than any ordinary man's.

No. She wasn't risking buckshot to the butt, or anywhere else for that matter. She needed access to this land, and part of her job was to warn citizens in the area when a wildlife threat was present, so one way or another, she would have to confront the man who had posted these signs, but not like this.

As with encountering a predator in the woods, some men were better approached face-to-face. She would hike back out the way she'd come and drive around by the road up to the boathouse instead. It would take the rest of the afternoon, but if she made good time, she could be up to the lake by sunset, armed with her Ruger instead of a tranquilizer gun, to warn the man at the end of the road about the cougar and insist politely but firmly that she be given access to his land.

Annie turned her back on the signs and walked away, replaying in her mind that odd conversation she'd had with Laura Proudy, the glint of warning in her eyes when she'd told Annie about the man in the boathouse. The strange outsider who had chosen isolation over community for reasons known only to himself.

Chapter 5

DANIEL

S unlight fell through the alders, dappling the rust-colored heap of fur on the stump, and the man who sat in the old Adirondack chair, staring at it.

Daniel tracked the dancing patches of light as he made swift, sure strokes with his pencil on the sketch pad. He had carried the fox outside late in the morning and draped it over the tall pine stump before heading into the woods to dig the grave.

He'd walked all the way around the lake to the firs that bordered the southeastern shore and dug the hole there; far enough away that he might forget about it in time, where the briars grew wild in the summer, and it would be hidden under leafy blackberries.

When he returned from digging, he'd taken his seat next to the stump, and in the two hours since, he had not moved, his brows pulled together in concentration as he sketched the animal's likeness. When he was finished with his drawing, he would carry the fox around the lake to the grave and fill in the dirt around it, then put the memory of last night out of his mind for good.

The tip of the charcoal pencil snapped against the paper, and Daniel brushed his hand over the mark it had left. He was pressing too firmly, trying too hard to get the face just right. He had once heard that the aim of art was not to represent the outward appearance of a thing, but its inward significance, and that was proving easier said than done.

The trouble was the eyes. Those extraordinary red-brown eyes just a shade deeper than the fox's fur were foggy now, flat, like the false glass eyes of a taxidermied animal. No matter how hard he tried, he couldn't seem to give them life on the page.

He wanted them to be as deep and lucid as they had been at the moment he turned on the light. He wanted to remember the look that met his gaze from the other end of the hall, so that every time he flipped to this page in his pad, he'd have a reminder to not lose control in the heat of the moment. The truth was, he couldn't afford to.

It could have been a person—a human being, lying there dead on the floor. It could have been a burglar or, far worse; a kid, some runaway in the same trouble he'd been in at sixteen. And, sure, maybe he hadn't broken a window while seeking shelter, but close enough. What if the place hadn't been empty when he showed up? What if someone had been waiting for him on the other side with a copper pipe?

Daniel leaned forward in his chair, adjusting the fox so that its face fell into shadow.

There was some sort of justice in it, or penance, maybe, sitting for hours on end, staring at the creature he'd killed. He brought the tip of the pencil back to the paper and traced it around the outside of the eye again, darkening the feline markings that gave the pointed face that clever, cunning look.

Daniel reached for the plastic sharpener on the arm of the chair and gave the pencil a few quick twists, glancing up at a familiar sound coming from behind the trees.

Clear, musical notes were floating on the wind, the whistling preceding the man walking up the road, and Daniel scanned the pines that flanked the clearing.

Jake climbed the gate with ease and emerged with his hands in his pockets, sandy hair curling out beneath a Mariners cap that shaded his eyes in the open sunlight.

Daniel raised a hand in greeting and Jake returned the gesture, his gaze falling on the fox as he approached with a long, low whistle.

"You kill that thing so it would sit still for a portrait?"

Daniel forced air through his nose, the closest thing to a laugh he could muster, then nodded toward the animal. "You ever see a fox this size?"

Jake chuckled. "Of course not. That's not a fox."

Daniel looked up from his pad as Jake lowered himself into a squat beside the animal, reaching out to lift one of its dark paws.

"You ever seen a fox with legs this long? It's a maned wolf." Jake released the paw, and it fell softly against the stump. "Ronnie Boyd down the road got it into his head to open an exotic zoo on his property. He's been buying animals illegally from all over the country, then has the nerve to come down to the station a couple weeks ago to tell Bud and me his maned wolf got loose and it's our responsibility to find and trap it for him."

Daniel laughed in earnest this time. "Protect and serve doesn't cover that?"

Jake chuckled. "Sure doesn't."

A moment passed as Jake inspected the animal, a line appearing on the smooth skin between his eyes. "You really did a number on this thing," he said quietly.

Daniel turned back to his drawing pad, busying his pencil in shading the dark fur beneath the animal's chin.

"It broke into the boathouse at two in the morning. Smashed through the window. Spooked me, I guess."

Jake's gaze flicked to the boathouse, then returned to Daniel, white teeth appearing in a lopsided grin. "Brother, you got nothing in there worth more than a Pearl Jam CD."

Daniel nodded and rested the pad in his lap. "In broad daylight, I know that. But at two in the morning, it's another story."

"You get any sleep after that?"

Daniel shook his head.

No, he hadn't slept. There was something about the idea of being an instrument of life and death that kept a man awake after killing something that didn't deserve to die.

Jake pushed himself upright and clapped Daniel on the shoulder. "Well, come on. The fish aren't gonna catch themselves."

Daniel left the pad on the chair and followed Jake to the corner of the dock where the small aluminum skiff was tied. The identical Normark rods they used every Saturday were lying on the warped dock boards, and Daniel stooped to grab them, flinching at the pain in his left hand. He climbed into the skiff after Jake and propped the poles against the narrow bench seat.

He'd strained some muscle or tendon in his wrist the night before, swinging the pipe over and over like a maniac, and had worsened it digging the grave. The pain was an unnerving reminder of how out of control he'd been.

He couldn't go off the rails like that again. If the maned wolf *had* been a person, how on earth would he have explained a dead body in the boathouse? Jake could have walked right in through the door without knocking—as he often did—and it wasn't as if Daniel could have invited him to sit down and calmly explain why he'd gone ballistic in the middle of the night. Jake was trusting enough, but things were different now, with the badge and all.

They'd been fishing buddies for five years, and the guy was loyal to a fault. Sure, Daniel had been less than thrilled when Jake got it into his head last summer that he wanted to be a cop and left for the Police Academy, but he came back six months later, and Daniel was relieved to find that the academy hadn't changed him much. If it came down to it, Daniel was willing to bet that Jake would be just as likely to help him bury a body as to drag him down to the station for questioning. But he couldn't risk it. If the law ever came between them, or if Jake ever found out the truth about Daniel's past, there was no telling what he'd do.

Jake reached for the oars and pulled them through the wind-rippled surface of the lake as Daniel looked over his shoulder, watching the animal on the stump shrink into the distance.

"Ronnie thought he'd make a fortune, I guess," Jake said, "charging folks to come look at maned wolves and peacocks and wild boars in chicken-wire cages, but way up here in the briars? Fat chance. Once everybody in town had a look, he'd be a thousand dollars richer and straight out of business again. The guy's always thinking he has the next million-dollar idea. Last year it was growing rare mushrooms in his basement."

"Gotta admire a man with vision," Daniel joked, but Jake's face sobered.

"Not when he's got a wife and daughter to feed."

Jake rowed to the middle of the lake, stopped, and rested the oars across his lap. The skiff spun in a slow circle, and for a moment neither man spoke.

It was sacred, this spot, this quiet center of the lake. From the boat-house, the summit of Mount St. Helens was hidden behind a dark ridge of pines, but out here, the mountain showed its rounded top above the hills. The peak was still covered in a blanket of winter snow in defiance of the blooming valley below, and around the lake, deep-green firs as proud and thick as a front line of soldiers stood grandly, their lower boughs rising and falling in the wind.

Daniel scanned the untamed shoreline. Out here in the middle of it all, a man could shut his mind off. There were no responsibilities. No obligation beyond the simple act of being.

Jake pulled a can of snuff from his back pocket and wedged a pinch of it into his lower lip. He offered the can to Daniel, who shook his head. Jake shrugged and tucked it back into his pocket before resting his elbows on his knees and smiling at his surroundings.

Daniel watched him as he worked the tobacco back and forth with his tongue. Innocent. An all-American boy, raised on Sunday school and Little League. In many ways, they were polar opposites. Jake was fair where Daniel was dark. Jake was an eternal optimist and Daniel a skeptic, but somehow their friendship worked. They balanced each other out, and their Saturdays—reserved for fishing rain or shine—were the only dependable thing Daniel had to look forward to in the insulated life he'd carved out for himself.

"You're a lucky son of a gun, you know that?" Jake's voice interrupted Daniel's thoughts.

"You say that every Saturday."

"'Cause it's true." Jake spit into the lake. "I'd give my left arm to have inherited a place like this."

"It's as much yours as it is mine."

It was what Daniel said every Saturday in reply, to rid himself of the guilt every time Jake mentioned the "inheritance." Jake trusted him, and anytime their conversation ventured into the past, he accepted Daniel's glossed-over answers with the candor of someone who had been raised to believe what others told him.

Daniel reached for his pole and passed the other to Jake. They baited their hooks from the tackle box beneath the bench without conversation, and Daniel cast his line out first, wincing at the pain in his wrist.

A wide, black shadow crossed the skiff, skimming along the surface of the lake like a skipped stone, and Daniel nudged Jake with a knee. Both men glanced up to watch the massive bird soaring past on the breeze.

"Bald eagle," Jake said.

"She's getting ready to lay, I think," Daniel murmured, watching the bird as she rose on the draft with a long, pronged tree branch clutched in her talons. "She's been going back and forth over the lake for days."

Without warning, the fishing pole jerked in his hands, and Daniel gripped it tight, wrenching it back. There was a fish on the line, a big one, and he pulled hard, grimacing. Beside him in the boat, Jake whooped and abandoned his own rod as he scrambled to look over the side.

"Bring him up!"

Daniel battled with the fish, ignoring the sharp discomfort with every turn of the reel.

"You're losing him!"

Wrenching the pole, Daniel leaned forward, peering over the side of the skiff into the lake. Pearly lances of sunlight sliced through the gray-blue water, dancing with the rocking of the boat, and his fishing line cut a straight path through them into murky depths with no end in sight. How far down *was* this thing?

Daniel leaned back again, propping his feet against the bottom of the skiff and jerking the rod with all his might, muscles straining. Without warning, the line snapped free, and he fell backward with a grunt, striking the back of his head on the thin lip of the boat as silver fireworks exploded across his field of vision.

"You okay? You all right?"

Jake's voice sounded far away, underwater, and Daniel tried to nod, which worsened the pain at the back of his skull.

"I'm fine," he managed.

"Turn, let me see it."

Daniel turned his head slightly, and true to form, Jake whistled. "Bleeding, but not too bad. We'd better get you back. Put some ice on it. I can drive you down to Doc Porter's—"

"No." Daniel cut him off with another shake of his throbbing head. "I'm fine. I just need to lay down for a minute."

Jake looked doubtful, but he reached for the oars and pulled them through the water with swift strokes, angling the skiff back toward the boathouse. When Daniel looked up, Jake offered him a half-hearted smile that didn't clear the concerned look in his eyes.

"It's really not your day, brother."

Daniel nodded grimly. He was beyond exhausted, and both his

head and wrist were throbbing. Jake dragged the oars backward as they reached the dock, and the skiff nudged it gently.

"Too bad about the fish," Jake said as he looped the rope around the piling, and Daniel nodded again, but didn't answer as he climbed onto the dock and staggered toward the door.

He couldn't care less about the fish. He'd taken enough life for today.

Chapter 6

ANNIE

Lake Lumin Road was rougher up where it burrowed into the foothills, and the Jeep teetered and bounced over large rocks and gaping potholes as Annie drove to the lake with a tight-fingered grip on the steering wheel.

The last of the day's light was falling sideways through the trees, brassy and tired, and a violet dusk was spreading outward from deep pockets of fir and fern, but Annie's eyes were not on the loveliness around her. Her gaze was fixed on the road ahead as she scanned the trees for the first NO TRESPASSING sign that was sure to pop up at any moment.

She was sore and tired from the long hike back up to Lewis Ridge, and the dense forest outside the Jeep only made her warier about the confrontation ahead.

The Wagoneer swung around a gentle curve and Annie's fingers tightened on the steering wheel.

"Here we go," she said as the first NO TRESPASSING sign appeared, nailed to a crooked post leaning out over the road. The second was fixed to a tree trunk, as was the next, and the one after that. For a quarter of a mile, she passed sign after sign as the road climbed upward toward an unseen peak.

In her head, Annie ran down the list of bullet points she'd need to cover with the man who had posted these signs. The cougar near his property. The access she needed to his land. What he should be looking out for, and instructions to contact her if he came across any trace of the big cat.

The terrain leveled out at last, and ahead a brighter swatch of land appeared through the trees, flat and open with the glimmer of sunlit water beyond. This had to be it.

The road took a final turn around a narrow bend and the Jeep went with it, Annie slamming on the brakes at the sight of an aluminum gate blocking the way ahead.

The tires juddered on gravel like the grinding of teeth, and her entire body tensed up as she skidded over the road, slowing, sliding, finally screeching to a stop less than a foot from the gate.

Annie slumped back in her seat, blowing out a relieved breath before killing the engine and taking in her surroundings. Beyond the gate was a large clearing, ringed in firs. The lake rippled like pink satin in the light of the setting sun, and on the shore closest to her, a grove of slender trees, alders, if she was guessing right from this distance, pressed close to a small wooden building with a rust-colored roof and a sagging dock jutting out over the water. The boathouse.

Annie climbed out of the Jeep, slamming the door loudly enough to give the man somewhere behind the gate ample warning that she was here, but the boathouse was dark, and the clearing empty, except for a dinged-up forest-green Ford Ranger, parked at an angle beneath the trees.

Annie cupped her hands around her mouth and called, "Hello?"

Her shout echoed across the clearing and faded out into the open air above the lake. Only the wind answered, stirring the alders, setting their leaves murmuring.

Annie opened the door of the Jeep and leaned inside, pressing her palm down on the horn and holding it there for five full seconds, the sound blaring across the clearing and reverberating around the foothills like a phantom bugle.

That ought to do it.

For a minute, no one emerged, then a shadow moved in the grove of trees behind the boathouse. Someone was coming out of the woods.

Annie straightened the collar of her uniform and took her professional stance behind the gate: feet slightly apart, shoulders squared and hands clasped at her waist, firearm on full display in its holster.

A man stepped through the trees and into the clearing, his face angled toward the ground, white T-shirt bronzed in the golden light.

Annie's mouth popped open in surprise.

He was young. Very young. She had somehow imagined the "loner in the boathouse," as she'd come to think of him, to be in his forties or fifties, but this man was younger than she was; mid-twenties at the most, and built like a jaguar, lean and muscled in the taut, springy way suggestive of power.

Annie's mouth stayed open as he crossed the clearing with the sure gait of an athlete. His hands were in his pockets, and closer up, she saw that his shirt and face were dirty, his jeans torn across the thigh. He looked like he had stepped straight out of an ad for some edgy new brand of denim, the exact opposite of the scruffy and cantankerous middle-aged men she was used to dealing with on the job. Still, given the circumstances—and the small fortune he had spent on NO TRESPASSING signs—she wasn't about to let his appearance disarm her.

"Can I help you?" he asked as he approached, eyes on the ground. Annie bristled at his tone. She'd heard it before, countless times, the four words that were spoken as a question but sounded more like a threat.

You better have a good reason for being here is what he meant, and both of them knew it.

Annie lifted her chin. "You live here?" she said by way of introduction.

He gave a single nod.

"I'm Annie Heston"—she extended her hand through the gate— "the new game warden in town."

Still, he did not look up. A shadow of hesitance crossed his face, but he slowly withdrew his hand from his pocket and took hers, shaking it without offering his name in return.

Annie glanced down. His fingers were filthy, caked with dirt, the nails black and soiled as though he had spent the better part of the day digging in the earth. When she looked up again, eyebrows raised, he quickly dropped the handshake.

"I'm here because there's a cougar in the area," she said, resisting the urge to wipe her hand on her pants. "We've had a couple of sightings from folks farther north who lost pets. It's an active male. Big one. We'd like to get it tagged, but so far, we haven't been able to track it down."

The collective *we* she spoke of was just her, but the more authority she could squeeze into her little spiel, the better. He nodded along slightly as she talked, but his gaze roved. He looked at the ground, at the Jeep, and, finally, at the Ruger on her hip.

"Now, my best guess"—Annie nodded over his shoulder in the general direction of the mountain—"is that he came down from Lewis Ridge a day or two ago, and I think he has a den just southeast of your lake here."

For the first time, he lifted his eyes to meet hers directly. "The cougar wouldn't happen to belong to Ronnie Boyd down the road, would it?"

Annie's reply stuck in her throat.

His eyes were older than he was. Much older. Apple green with warm brown around the pupils, and just the suggestion of blue flecking the iris, but it was not their color that was so jarring. In that young, lineless face, the eyes were an utter contrast. They wore the same pained look she'd seen in her father's eyes during the dark and desperate months after her mother died. The same look she'd seen in her own eyes in the rearview mirror on the drive up here. They were the eyes of a man who knew with certainty that his best days were behind him.

"No, sir," she said when she found her voice again, "it doesn't belong to anyone."

He blinked, as though the *sir* had caught him off guard, and when he spoke again, it was with a casualness that sounded forced.

"Right." He nodded. "Of course not. It's just . . . he had this maned wolf . . ." The nod turned into a headshake. "It's not important."

Annie gazed at him curiously, and his Adam's apple bobbed. When he said nothing else, she nodded past him toward the lake.

"Anyway, I was able to track the cougar from the ridge down to the south side of the lake there, but it sure would be a whole lot easier if I could get in and out by way of the road. I know it's an inconvenience to have someone coming and going on your land, but the sooner I get him tagged, the sooner I'll be out of your hair."

He brought one dirty hand to the back of his neck and scratched at the skin there.

"I don't . . ." His throat bobbed again. "I don't know. I'll have to think about it."

Annie sighed. *Here it comes.*

"Then let me be frank," she said, keeping her voice steady, though her nostrils flared with irritation. "A federal wildlife officer has the right to enter any land or water, public or private, in the performance of their duty. I don't need your permission, but given the thousand signs you've posted, I gather that you're keen on keeping your privacy up here, and I thought I'd do the decent thing by asking first."

She had his attention now. He was gazing at her as though she herself were the cougar, crouched back on its haunches, tail flicking as it prepared to pounce.

For a moment, neither of them blinked. A three-second chess match. And then he cleared his throat quietly.

"All right. If I don't have a choice, I guess I'll leave the gate unlocked." He angled his chin toward the lake. "There's a trail on the west side. You can take that all the way around."

Annie nodded, and it struck her suddenly that there was something familiar about this man. It was in the way he had looked at her, startled, when she told him she would be using his property whether he wanted her to or not. She'd seen that look before, those bright eyes and the dark brows that hooded them, though she couldn't put her finger on when or where. She had never met him, she was sure of that, but where had she seen him? In town? No, that look was catching at something further back in her memory. Something from years ago.

As though he felt her trying to place him, his gaze dropped to the ground, and he scuffed at the gravel with the toe of his shoe. "You said you're new in town. You like it so far?"

Annie's brows rose at the unexpected question. The attempt at small talk.

"I do." She nodded. *Loosen him up. Compliment his land. Show him you're not a threat.*

She gestured to the lake behind him, the sunset light gone now, the water deep and amethyst with dark forest on all sides. "I'm still getting used to the woods up here, to be honest." She laughed. "They're incredible, really. The exact sort of place where you lose your mind, but find your soul."

"John Muir."

Annie's eyes flew back to his face. "You know that quote?"

"Yeah, John Muir. You know, 'Into the forest I go, to lose my mind and find my soul.'"

For a second, Annie stood gaping at him as he scuffed the ground with his shoe again.

"Who are you?" she asked finally.

"Does it matter?" he asked with a too-casual shrug.

He was clamming up. Shutting down. He didn't want her to know his name, and in response Annie pushed back harder.

"Not strictly speaking, but we're neighbors." She smiled. "I'm staying at the Proudys' down the road. I just transferred up from Bend."

At the word *Bend*, his nostrils flared, eyes widening for a split second.

Bingo. Bend. At some point, they must have crossed paths back in her hometown.

"You ever been down there?"

"No," he said with a tight smile. "No, never. I've heard it's beautiful though."

He was lying. This man was lying straight to her face.

If there was one thing the job had taught her, it was how to spot when someone wasn't telling the truth. Annie's gaze slid upward, to the tiny beads of sweat rising along his hairline.

For a minute she said nothing, letting the silence swell between them, then she looked over his shoulder at the boathouse again. His home. Even from this distance, she could see the tanks of propane lined up along the dock, the firewood stacked up to the eaves behind the house, and a broken window that had been patched with cardboard.

What are you hiding back there?

"Quite the place," she said.

He gave an unnecessary glance over his shoulder. "Thanks."

"It's a boathouse?"

"Used to be. Converted now."

Annie swiped an insect from her forearm without looking down. "Well, you seem good and ready for the apocalypse up here." Her tone was light, but her eyes were serious, and he gave a stuttering laugh in reply.

He wants me out of here.

Another beat of silence passed between them, then he said, "Well, I'll keep an eye out for the cougar."

It was an obvious attempt to steer the conversation back to why she'd come, to wrap it up. The first drop of sweat was sliding down his temple, and Annie watched it all the way to his jaw before she nodded toward the forest again, launching into a list of things he should be on the lookout for. As she used her fingers to show the size of the animal's tracks and detailed exactly what its scat looked like, he nodded along, his expression mildly interested, nothing more.

When she was finished with her lecture, Annie cleared her throat and fished a small white card from her shirt pocket. On it, she'd written her name and the number of the landline in her room at the Proudys'. She offered it to him through the gate.

He took it, his fingertips smearing the edges with dirt.

"That's my number. If you see any tracks or if you hear him, and believe me, you'll know if you do, give me a call." She reached out and double-tapped the card with a finger. "Annie Heston."

She waited, eyebrows raised, for him to offer his name in return.

"I'm Daniel," he said after a pause. "Daniel Barela."

"Daniel Barela," she repeated, and he nodded once. "It's nice to meet you, Daniel. Give me a call if you hear the cougar. Day or night."

He flipped her card over, and back again.

There was nothing left to say, and Annie turned toward the Jeep, reaching for the door handle.

"See you around," she said as she climbed inside.

"See you," he muttered, and she closed the door with a bang.

It took several minutes of inching forward and reversing before she managed to turn the Jeep around on the narrow dirt lane. As she backed up for the final time and pulled away, she took one last look in the rear-view mirror at the man on the other side of the gate.

He had not moved, but stood tight-jawed where she had left him, turning the soiled card over and over in his hands.

Chapter 7

ANNIE

B rought you something."
Jake shouldered his way through the station door and stepped inside. In one of his hands was a crinkled paper bag emblazoned with a Sasquatch giving a thumbs-up, and in the other, a steaming styrofoam cup, both of which he placed on the desk in front of Annie.

Annie looked up from the stack of forms in front of her. "Really?"

He nodded.

"Thanks"—she reached for the coffee—"that was nice of you."

"Well, it wasn't my idea, exactly. Mom called. She said you didn't eat breakfast before you left this morning, and she was worried."

Annie laughed and took a sip. "That sounds about right. What's in the bag?"

"Maple bar from Bigfoot's next door. I know I said Mom's strawberry-rhubarb pie was the best thing you'd ever eat, but just wait until you try that."

Annie lifted the doughnut from the bag. "Want half?"

"Nope. Already had two. Riding a crazy sugar high right now."

Jake walked around the counter and dropped into his seat, propping both feet up on the desk with a contented sigh. "What do you have going on today?"

Annie took a bite of the doughnut and set it on a napkin. "Paperwork. I need to finish the rest of these illegal-exotic forms."

A few weeks had passed since her meeting at the gate with Daniel, and she had been back to the south shore of Lake Lumin a handful of times, but hadn't found any fresh cougar tracks there.

She must have been wrong about the cat claiming the valley as his territory after all. He had probably continued migrating south, she'd figured, and she had thrown herself headfirst into the next task instead, dismantling the exotic zoo that Ronnie Boyd had set up on his property.

Annie had spent the last several days taking apart makeshift habitats and driving the animals down one at a time to a rehabilitation center in Portland. Normally, it would be a job for Animal Control, but in a town as small as Lake Lumin, she effectively *was* Animal Control.

So far, she'd transported two wild boars, a capuchin monkey, three lemurs, and a box full of venomous snakes that she'd eyed over her shoulder the entire drive down. Ronnie had also caged a family of squirrels and two large black crows, which she'd released on the spot with a stern warning. His wife and teenaged daughter, Jamie, for their part, seemed relieved to see the animals go. The place was starting to stink, Jamie confided in a whisper when Annie left with the snakes.

Jake folded his hands behind his head, watching Annie as she scribbled her signature at the bottom of one of the forms.

"I hate paperwork," she grumbled as she flipped the page over and started at the top of the next.

"I don't mind it," he said amiably. "It's like raking leaves or doing dishes. I like seeing progress in a quantifiable way."

"Well, I hate it," Annie said. "If I had my way, I'd spend every single second of my work week outside."

Jake watched her for another minute. "You know, I believe you," he said finally.

Annie smiled at him, then turned back to her forms, aware of his eyes lingering on the side of her face as she wrote.

"Tell me something," he said after another pause. "How'd you end up with this job?"

Annie looked up. "What do you mean? I transferred here."

Jake dropped his feet down from the desk and leaned toward her. "No, I mean, why this job in the first place? Why become a game warden?"

Annie opened her mouth and closed it again. She'd learned during this first month on the job with him that Jake was a master of distraction, always leading her astray from her duties down inane rabbit trails of conversation that rambled for an hour or more before she snapped back to reality and chided him for interrupting her work.

She turned back to the forms. "I was raised by wolves."

"Oh, come on." He leaned forward. "There's a story in there, somewhere. Let me hear it."

It had been a long while since she'd been asked the question directly. Comments were made from time to time, surprise expressed at her being a woman officer in such a male-dominated field, but no one ever asked her flat out why she'd chosen the job in the first place. No one since Brendan.

Annie scribbled her name on the bottom of the next form, then placed her pen down with a sigh and leaned back in her chair. Jake was still gazing at her, his blue eyes bright with curiosity, and she wondered how on earth she could possibly put into concise words everything that had led to this career choice.

The truth was, she was a game warden because there was nothing else she could be. She would die behind a desk—just wither and die— like a wildflower brought inside to live in a pot. It wasn't in her. She needed the woods the way she needed food, and the longer she went without them, the deeper and more desperate her hunger grew. They were her home. Her calling. Her savior. The plain fact of it was, they had brought her back to life.

"You really want to know?"

Jake's head bobbed. "I do. So do Mom and Dad, actually. They drink their coffee by the front window and think it's pretty weird that you disappear into the woods every morning when the sun comes up."

Annie laughed and Jake grinned back at her.

"Have you always been like that? Miss Outdoorsy?"

Annie shook her head. "No. Not at all, actually. Back when I was a kid, my life was mostly spent inside. You know, neighborhood friends, Disney movies, maybe the occasional trip to the park." She hesitated. "And then . . . when I was nine, my mom got sick. It dropped a bomb on our family. I guess something like that always does. It was stage four breast cancer. Completely unexpected, and within the span of an afternoon, every single thing in my life changed."

All trace of humor had gone from Jake's face, and Annie avoided his gaze. If she looked at him, the words wouldn't come out, so she stared down at the forms as she told him. The cancer was aggressive, and within four months it had ravaged her mother's body to the point that Annie didn't recognize her anymore. She'd lost her curves, and her hair, and the glow of her skin. The only thing it didn't touch was her eyes, which were too bright at the end. Annie had been afraid to be alone with her, scared of the gray, sunken face on the pillow, and those bright eyes that stared and stared, like she wanted Annie to know some secret she wasn't able to tell.

The pain was still there, deep down in Annie's chest, threatening to well up, but she pushed back against it, turning at last to face Jake. His face was full of understanding, and she latched on to it, taking strength.

"Afterward, once they'd boxed up everything in the room and closed the door for good, it was like my dad couldn't stand to be in the house anymore. When it was the two of us alone at home, he just . . . wandered through the rooms like a ghost. Neither of us knew how to be around each other in that house with our grief, so, we got out. It was once in a while at first, and then every day, driving to different trails around town for hikes, swimming in the cold lakes up in the mountains. He even bought a mountain bike, but one good crash landed it in the shed permanently. He took me along on his adventures—mostly, I figured, because I was too young to leave behind. But after a while we changed toward each other. Our relationship grew into something more than it had been before. Something that can only be forged out there in the woods, I think."

Jake nodded for Annie to keep talking.

"At first, it was an escape, a sort of distraction, but after a while the wilderness became his passion. He came alive again in the woods, and then some. He joined a group that maintained the trails, then signed up as a volunteer with search and rescue. He took a handful of survival courses and led some, too. Then, when I was twelve, he told me to load my pack, and he dropped me off at the base of South Sister Mountain. It was a Saturday afternoon, and he told me to summit the peak over the weekend and he would pick me up first thing on Monday morning."

Annie laughed at the memory. "I was standing there next to the truck, absolutely terrified, but he just told me to figure it out and left. And I did. They were the scariest two nights of my life, but I made it through."

Jake smiled, but said nothing.

"Afterward, we didn't talk about it to other people, and I had a feeling that I shouldn't—like no one else would understand why he had done it, or maybe they'd think that it was some bizarre form of child abuse or something, but the truth was that those two days changed my life for the better.

"During that weekend, I learned more than I ever would in a classroom. I walked back into that campground about five pounds lighter and proud as a peacock, with my legs torn up from sliding down scree slopes. Dad was waiting in his pickup, and I threw my pack in the back and climbed in. That's when I saw the dark circles under his eyes. I doubt he slept for one second that weekend. Anyway, about a year later I found out there was a job that fit the description, that the government actually pays people to spend all day in the woods, and I was all in.

I chased my wilderness degree with a fury, and the proudest I ever saw my dad was when he was beaming up at me from his folding chair as I walked across the stage with my diploma."

Annie smiled sadly. "He's gone now. Three years ago. And the woods make me miss him sometimes, but the feeling isn't only sad. Being out there brings me closer to his memory than anything else could, and this job, it's more than work. It's who I am. I couldn't have been anything else."

Jake sat back in his chair and folded his arms across his chest, still wearing that gentle smile as he gazed at her.

"Well, say something," she said, suddenly embarrassed at the sweeping range of emotions she'd put on display in the last ten minutes. It had been a long time since she'd given another person such an uninterrupted look at the inside of her head.

"I'm just processing. I mean, it's more words than you've said all put together since you moved to town." He lifted her doughnut from the napkin and took a bite.

"And I'm glad you told me," he said around the mouthful, "but that last part isn't exactly true, is it?"

Annie snatched the doughnut back. "What do you mean?"

"I mean that bit about you not being able to do anything else. You could have been anything you set your mind to, Annie." He gestured toward her with a hand. "I mean, look at you. You're smart, and funny. And tough as an old boot." He laughed. "But to be honest, I haven't met many girls who prefer to spend their days out in the woods, getting muddy and torn up out there, tracking animals or going head-to-head with guys hunting and fishing where they're not supposed to be. It's, uh . . . it's kind of intimidating. In a good way."

Annie's cheeks flushed with pride. It was a compliment she'd been paid before, one that she always heard as *You're just like your father.*

Jake folded his hands together on the desk. "So, you left Bend because . . ."

Annie took an unsteady breath and condensed the months of heart-ache into one word.

"Breakup."

"Yeah?"

She nodded, looked away. "Oldest story in the world. My husband and a younger woman."

Jake's mouth fell open. "You serious?"

"Yeah."

"Are . . . are you okay?"

Annie shrugged. "I don't know. I guess I'm still in that early phase where it feels like you're at the bottom of a great big hole and you don't know if you'll ever be able to dig yourself out."

Jake's reply was quiet. "You will. As soon as you figure out how to put down the shovel."

Annie turned to meet his eyes, and in them, she saw hurt. Old and deep, perhaps mostly healed, but hurt nonetheless. She leaned back in her chair and looked at him then, *really* looked at him: the young, handsome face, the slender cross tattooed on his forearm, the fingers interlaced on the desk. With a lump in her throat, Annie realized that the happy-go-lucky man beside her had once had his heart broken, too.

"You?" she asked quietly.

Jake's shoulders rose and fell. "Long time ago."

Annie waited.

"High school sweetheart," he said after a beat, looking away. "Bought a ring and everything. Found out about the other guy the day before I was planning to propose." He coughed and sat a little straighter in his chair. "I don't know. Time goes by and you figure maybe everything really does happen for a reason. I was just a kid. A selfish kid. The breakup forced me to reflect on a lot. I realized I wanted to live life for something more than myself. My faith got a whole lot more real, and this"—he waved a hand around at the small office—"best job I could think of to do some good for the town."

He smiled, but there was sadness in it.

"I'm sorry," Annie said.

Jake stretched a hand across the desk, as though he might cover hers with it, but he seemed to think better of it at the last second and dropped it instead.

"Thank you," she said, to cover the awkward silence that followed. "I guess neither of us meant to air all our baggage at once like that."

The phone on the desk chirped loudly, startling them both.

Jake snatched it up. "Yello?"

Annie watched as his expression grew serious, then crumpled completely into slack-jawed disbelief.

"Ben—Ben, slow down, tell me where you are . . . Okay . . . And, and you're sure? You're absolutely positive she's dead? . . . No, you drop Layla off with Delores and meet me back out there, we'll park up at Lewis Ridge and hike down to the spot . . . All right, I will, and, Ben, don't breathe a word of this to anyone else, you understand? I'll take a statement from you when we get up there."

Jake hung up the phone and stood, grabbing his jacket off the back of the chair and sliding an arm into it.

"I need your help." He turned to Annie again. "Can you identify claw marks on a body?"

Annie's voice failed her, and she nodded.

"Then I need you to come with me. Ben Gannon just found a dead hiker down below the eastern Lewis Ridge trail. He thought she fell, but when he got up to her, he said her body was all torn apart. He thought maybe a bear or cougar had gotten to her, but then he saw . . ." Jake hesitated with one arm in his jacket.

"What?" Annie asked, though she wasn't certain she wanted to know.

"Bruises. Bruises around her neck. Like . . . like hands."

Annie's breath caught in her throat.

Again came the thought she had carried with her through the snow. *I didn't sign up for this.*

Jake zipped his jacket and nodded to the back corner of the room. "Grab my camera, will you? It's there in the filing cabinet. I need to give Doc Porter a quick call and have him clear his schedule for an autopsy."

Annie found the Nikon in the bottom drawer and slid the strap around her neck with her eyes on Jake. The phone was pinched between his ear and shoulder as he relayed details and curt instructions to the doctor while scribbling out a note on the desk.

She'd never seen him like this. Restrained. Assured. In control. This was a completely different Jake Proudy. This was the officer who had graduated top of his class at the academy, the lovable, goofy boy-next-door shoved aside by the man of action.

"You ready?" he asked over his shoulder as he hung up the phone.

Annie nodded, though she wasn't sure she would ever be ready for what they were about to see at Lewis Ridge.

Chapter 8

ANNIE

The poorly maintained Forest Service road was not kind to the low-bottomed police cruiser, and Annie gripped the handle above the window as they climbed up and around the mountain.

She was doing her best to avoid looking at the sheer drop-off just feet from the spinning tires of the car and watched instead the slate-gray clouds at the top of the windshield, their dark edges roiling inward, threatening rain.

Jake's foot stayed on the gas as they bumped and jostled their way over the uneven gravel, engine whining loudly against the steep grade.

"Hang on." He whipped the wheel left, and Annie squeezed her eyes shut as they skidded around a tight curve, gravel spitting behind them. When she opened her eyes again, there was a black 4Runner parked on the side of the road ahead with a man standing beside it, waving his arms in the air.

"That's Ben," Jake muttered, swinging the cruiser in behind the SUV and shifting into park.

Ben, his mostly gray hair tousled, blue track jacket rippling in the wind, jogged to the driver's-side window of the cruiser.

"It's bad, Jake," he said when Jake opened the door. "Really bad. You're not gonna be able to get her out of here."

"That's okay," Jake said, zipping his jacket and climbing out. "County has a recovery team. I radioed on the drive up. They're on the way, but I gotta get down there and take some pictures of the scene first. You didn't touch anything, did you?"

Her. Annie made the correction in her mind as she climbed out of the car, bracing herself against the stiff wind. *You didn't touch her, did you?*

"No, no, I just climbed back down and hiked out of there as fast as I could."

Jake nodded. "Good. You show me where she is, then you can get on home. I'm sure you're pretty shaken up."

Ben nodded, and Jake clapped him reassuringly on the shoulder as Annie stepped forward with her hand outstretched.

"I'm the new game warden, Annie Heston."

Ben shook her offered hand.

Jake added, "Annie's going to take a look at those marks on the body."

Ben blew out a breath. "They're not pretty, ma'am."

"Understood." Annie turned to Jake. "You ready?"

Jake nodded and Annie fell into line behind the men as they started down the eastern fork of the trail at a pace just shy of a jog.

The thick morning fog had burned off into a fleeting hour of sunshine, but storm clouds had billowed up from the east, and now the wind was streaming in, bitter and steady around the mountain, directly into their faces as they hiked. Jake glanced over his shoulder and, catching Annie rubbing her arms briskly, slid out of his jacket and passed it to her without breaking stride.

They walked east for several minutes without speaking, Ben halting at intervals to peer down over the railing. Finally, he stopped and motioned them forward.

"Down there." He pointed, and over the sound of the wind, Annie could hear the tremor in his voice. "We're right over her; you can see her hair on the rocks."

Jake met Ben at the railing, leaning over to look, and Annie watched as Jake's shoulders dropped a fraction of an inch and his face fell. Grim, but not distressed. He turned to Ben and pulled a small, black recorder from his pocket.

"Let me take a quick statement from you, then you can get on home to the girls."

As Ben shared his version of events, Annie moved to the railing and peered over.

Her stomach lurched. A hundred dizzying feet down was the woman, lying on her stomach on the rocks. Even from so far up, Annie could see the clothing torn across her shoulders, and the long, dark hair billowing out over the cliffside like a sheet on a clothesline.

It was an insane distance, an unthinkable fall, and Annie could not imagine any sensible person climbing over this railing and risking such a plummet for any reason, unless they were forced . . . or desperate.

Annie searched the ground around her feet, looking for tracks, for a story told in the dirt, but the path here was too well-worn, dented with the prints of a dozen shoes, slurred and indistinct. Useless. There would be no telling what had happened from up here.

"Thanks, Ben," Jake said behind her, "you get on home. I'll call you later if I need anything else."

Ben left without another word, jogging back up the trail to his car, and Jake and Annie turned to each other.

"I don't know how we're going to get down there," Jake said.

"I think we can." Annie pointed into the woods. "If we head down on the western fork of the trail, then cut back across this way, we should come right out to where she is on the rocks. It'll be tough. It looks pretty steep, and there's no real trail to follow when we cut over, but I think it's doable."

Jake assessed her proposed path, eyeing the near-vertical hillside and the protruding rocks, then nodded. "Worth a shot."

Annie led the way down the steep western trail, estimating their distance as she went. She slipped once, her foot skidding over a root, and Jake caught her by the arm, hauling her upright again.

She cut left into the woods when she guessed them to be about parallel with the rock shelf where the woman lay. Annie gripped trees and rocks as she moved across the steep terrain with Jake scrambling behind her. After a few minutes, the trees tapered away into brush and shrubs, and they emerged into open air on the hillside.

The going was treacherous, and Annie's breath was shallow as she leaned into the grade, testing every step before she took it. The forest up here had changed so much in just a few weeks. Gone were the early-spring blossoms and tentative April wildflowers. Now, mustard-yellow buttercups and bright red Indian paintbrush were scattered across the slope in reckless abundance. The sight of those crimson flowers on any other day would have stirred joy in her, but today, they seemed like thick drops of blood littering the hillside at random. Heralds of the death ahead.

Here in the open, the wind was worse, tearing at her clothes and swiping tears from her eyes, sending them sideways into her hair as she moved across a slope that was ever steeper. She gripped the land with her hands, clasping at shrubs and stones as her feet fumbled for holds beneath her.

Slow and steady, Annie girl. Each move like you mean it.

Her father had first spoken those words to her as she scaled the dry bed of a waterfall in Bend, young arms trembling with fatigue—and countless times after.

The wind gusted again and Annie clung to the hillside, leaning hard.

"Hang in there," Jake called out, and for the life of her, she couldn't tell if he was making a joke or not, but just ahead were the protruding rocks, hemmed in on the cliffside by a few disheveled pines that had dared to take root on the precipitous ground. Annie edged toward them, growing overwarm in Jake's jacket as her muscles worked hard, straining to keep her stable. She kept her sights on the long expanse of bare rock that broke the plummeting fall from the ridge high overhead.

"I can see her," she called over her shoulder, "about fifty yards ahead."

Annie forced her hands and feet forward, like an insect clinging to the gully wall. Stretching her arms high, she clambered up onto the rocks. The shelf was narrow at the outset, only a foot wide where it jutted out over the drop, and with her eyes glued to her shoes, Annie inched forward, shuffling toward the dark hair dancing in the wind.

The rocks beneath her feet were smooth and precariously sloped. Risking a quick glance at the darkening sky overhead, she prayed that the rain would hold off. Wet rocks would be an absolute nightmare right now.

Foot by foot, the drop beneath her steepened into the vertical fall that was Lewis Ridge, and foot by foot, she edged nearer to the body. Fifty feet more. Forty. Annie blew out a breath as the shelf of rock beneath her feet widened, expanding into a trail of its own. Still, the ever-present plummet into the gulley kept her stomach balled up like a fist as she moved forward.

Another gust of wind ripped past, and Annie tensed, rigid on the rocks, but Jake was right behind her, pressing a steadying hand to her back.

"We're almost there," he said. "You can do this."

The woman was lying in a place where the shelf jutted out broadly, creating a wide, flat space, eight feet of standing room; the plateau that had broken her fall.

Annie moved forward in what felt like slow motion until she was standing over the body with her trembling hand at her mouth.

Blood darkened the rock around the woman's head, dried now in a clover-shaped shadow that was half covered by her hair. Her head seemed off in proportion, too small somehow, and Annie realized with horror that it was because the right side of her skull had been crushed against the unforgiving stone and now lay flat.

But worse by far was the absolute carnage inflicted by razor-sharp claws on the back side of her body. Annie had seen the carcasses of animals. Many times. Countless times. Deer and elk, left headless and skinless, their hides and antlers claimed as trophies and their flesh left to rot in the woods by the worst sort of men. But this . . . Her gaze traveled the length of the woman from head to toe and back again. Something had torn into her out here on the rocks, shredding the dark clothing to get at the body underneath—flaying it in long, deep gashes. There were dozens of marks, slashing down to the bone in places, and Annie let out a muffled cry at the sight of the woman's spine, white and knobby, exposed in one particularly vicious stripe.

Beside her, Jake muttered something under his breath that sounded like a prayer.

Annie took a step forward, but Jake's hand landed on her shoulder, pulling her back.

"Don't. I don't know what I was thinking. You don't have to do this."

"Yes, I do," she said without turning around.

"No." His hand was still on her shoulder. "I'll take pictures and you can look at them back at the station. Let's do it that way."

Annie turned to face him, shrugging out from under his hand. "I can help, Jake. Let me do my job."

After a beat, he nodded, and Annie turned back to the body, shoving the horror into the back of her mind as her training took over. There would be time later to process what she was seeing. Right now, it was time to work.

As Jake fiddled with his camera behind her, she took a knee on the rocks and zeroed in on a single mark breaking fabric and skin across the woman's back. She had seen the damage that different predators could do to human flesh, in pictures at least, in slideshows on classroom walls and photographs passed around in study groups, and she mentally thumbed through those images now, pulling them up one at a time to compare with the butchery in front of her.

They were impressive, these marks, sharp and deep, and she counted them, nodding to herself. There was a pattern, gashes together in groups of four, sometimes two or three, but never more than four. Never the five claw marks that she would have seen if a bear had done this, and they were too large to belong to any canid of these woods.

"I wonder how long she's been out here," Jake said behind her.

Annie lifted her nose, inhaling to catch any scent in the air, but there was no detectable smell of decay.

"Less than thirty-six hours." She pushed herself to her feet. "In all likelihood, I'd say it happened yesterday, but only an autopsy will tell us for sure."

Jake gave her a questioning look, and Annie's shoulders rose and fell.

"I've seen a lot of death in the woods. Not people, but plenty of animals." She met his gaze sadly. "There's no difference."

The startled look on Jake's face told her how callous the comment had sounded, and she quickly added, "As far as decomposition is concerned."

The wind howled through the gulley, whipping Annie's braid sideways and lashing her cheek with it as a few barely there drops of cold rain peppered the back of her head.

"We have to hurry," she said, and Jake nodded, raising the camera in his hands.

His face was colorless as he took several quick shots, and Annie stepped back when he moved around to the woman's other side, kneeling to brush the hair away from her face. The gesture was gentle, so tender that it was almost intimate, and Annie fought the urge to look away.

Jake lifted the camera and snapped several more pictures; each click of the shutter overloud to Annie as she stood waiting.

"There they are," Jake murmured, lowering the camera an inch.

He nodded toward the bruises, four blackish-purple marks running in an uneven line on the woman's pale skin like a necklace of shadow.

The rocks beneath Annie started to spin, and her stomach clenched. Ben was right. They *did* look like hands. Tight fingers that had gripped this woman's throat until blackness took over. How long had it taken for that to happen? How long had she suffered?

From some forgotten lesson of years before, Annie recalled the rule of threes. A human being could live for three weeks without food. Three days without water. Three minutes without air.

Annie stared down at the lifeless face with its bright brown eye fixed unblinkingly on the darkening sky above. Three minutes was an eternity.

Jake leaned in close, snapping another shot, then shuffled sideways to photograph the woman's back, the torn dark shirt, jeans, and sneakers. Annie wished she were the one behind the camera, keeping a degree of distance between herself and the dead woman.

Finally, Jake lowered the camera and sank back on his heels. He wore the same crumpled look he'd had speaking to Ben on the phone as he stared down at the woman's face.

"Who is she?" Annie asked.

He shook his head. "I don't know. She's not local. I've never seen her before."

He leaned over the woman and checked her pockets, one at a time.

"No ID." He looked away, scanning the valley unfolding below them. "Tourist season's almost here though. Out-of-towners from all over the country show up to hike the mountain during the summer, so she could be from anywhere, I guess."

Pity swelled in Annie's chest. This woman was a stranger in town, just like her.

Jake lifted his face, squinting as he scanned the top of the ridge where the wooden railing was barely visible. "Tourists almost never come out here alone though. It's always families . . . or couples."

Annie watched the train of thought as it unfolded on his face, his eyes tracking the downward drop from the ridge, the blood around the woman's head, and the marks on her body. He was running through the timeline, but Annie had already done the math.

The fall was not an accident. Someone who had lost their balance at the top would have fought for their life the whole way down, clawing at the hillside, lashing out with their arms and legs for a hold, any hold; twisting, scratching, scraping. And there was none of that. This woman had either jumped of her own volition or been thrown, already dead.

As for the gashes on her body, they were horrific, but there was some consolation in knowing that she hadn't felt them. They were clearly postmortem, deep, but clean. Her heart had not been pumping blood when the scavenger found her.

The bruises were the key, and the autopsy would either confirm or disprove the theory that was forming in Annie's mind. But until they knew for sure, she had to keep all possibilities open. She had to stop picturing it in one specific, horrible way—a man standing atop Lewis Ridge, holding this girl's neck in a vise grip until the life faded from her eyes. Dumping her body over the railing, watching as she fell down, down, down, until the dull thud when she hit the rocks below. An act of pure brutality. Unimaginably cruel.

"What do you think?" Jake asked, gesturing at the marks on the woman's back. "Cougar? Bear?"

For a moment, Annie didn't answer, but paced the rocks, searching, her braid wild in the wind, freed strands clinging to her mouth and cheeks.

There were little pockets of mud and earth on the hard, dented surface, and Annie searched them one by one until at last, in a smear of dirt behind the woman's shoes, she found what she was looking for.

"Cougar."

"You sure?"

Annie nodded, turning to face him. "I'm sure. It's the male I've been tracking."

Jake's eyebrows shot up. "How could you possibly know that?"

"Here." Annie beckoned him over and pointed to the print, placing her finger on the slightly asymmetrical dent atop the pad. A cat with a limp.

The heavens rumbled with a long, low peal of thunder, and Annie looked up at the sky. They were running out of time.

"And there's no way the cougar could have killed her?" Jake asked. "Maybe he fought with her at the top and followed her down when she went over? I mean, I know what the bruises look like, but could they be from the cougar pinning her down by the neck?"

Annie frowned. Cougars did sometimes pin animals down by the neck as they fed.

"I don't think so. If she was still alive when he got to her, she'd be covered in blood, and if they fought at the top and she died in the fall, I can't imagine him working his way down the ridge to get here, but I guess it's possible."

Jake nodded, twisting the lens of the camera back and forth in his fingers as he stared at the body.

"Do cougars do that? Scavenge? Eat something that's already dead?"

"They're opportunistic, just like any other predator." Annie nodded. "They need food, water, and shelter and will do just about anything to keep those resources at hand. Even scavenging, if it comes to that, just like the big cats on other continents. They prefer to hunt, but they'll sometimes claim kills that aren't their own."

Annie stepped around Jake, kneeling beside the woman and peering down at the bruises as thunder boomed behind the mountain again.

"In all honesty, Jake, these could be older bruises. Hickeys, even. They could have been there for hours before she died. Days, maybe, but there's only one way to be sure."

Jake screwed the lens cap on the camera. "Autopsy?"

"Autopsy." Annie nodded. "If the cause of death comes back as asphyxiation, I guess we'll know for sure what we're dealing with."

The rain was starting in earnest, tapping against the rocks, and Jake lifted his face to the sky.

"If they can manage to get her out of here today, Doc Porter said he'll be able to look her over first thing in the morning, so hopefully we'll have some answers soon." Jake lowered his chin, meeting Annie's eyes. "But for right now, I need you to not say anything to anyone. Not my parents, not anyone in town. Nobody. Until we know for sure what we're dealing with, we have to be careful how much information gets out."

Annie nodded. "Okay."

She understood. In a town this size, one whisper about murder could be the spark that set the whole house ablaze. For the time being, she and

Jake had to bear this burden alone, and the weight of it was like an anvil on her shoulders. It felt oddly personal. A dead outsider in a closely knit town. A woman with no voice of her own. No way to reveal what had happened to her.

"And, Annie?" Jake's voice was hard. "You better find that cougar. Just in case."

Annie nodded again. "I will."

The raindrops were falling faster now, pattering on the rocks with the cadence of a snare drum. There was no more time to lose.

"We have to go," Annie said, rising to her feet.

Jake hesitated, gazing down at the woman on the rocks. "I hate to leave her out here."

Annie shook her head as the rain fell between them. "We have to."

He nodded and turned to leave with Annie a step behind, following him toward the woods as the storm rose behind them.

Chapter 9

DANIEL

A woman screamed.

The sound ripped through the woods on the far side of the lake and echoed like a shock wave over the water to where Daniel stood on the dock, winding a spool of fishing line in the cool, twilight air.

His hand stilled, and the crawling sensation of goose bumps ran the length of his spine as he scanned the dense forest from where the piercing, guttural sound had come. The last echoes of the cry fell away into the forest behind him, and Daniel stared at the southern shore, his nostrils flaring with each shallow breath. Every hair on his neck and arms was standing at attention, every sense alert, but the sound did not come again.

A hiker?

No. Not this time of day. Not in such a remote patch of forest with less than half an hour of light left.

He waited, watching the woods for movement, for whoever had screamed to come sprinting through the trees, waving their arms and shouting for help—but there was only the violet calm of dusk and the shadowy firs across the water, tall and still.

He set the half-wound spool of fishing line on the dock and turned for the door. He should call Jake. Get him up here with his badge and take the boat across the water. If there was trouble, the last thing he needed was to be caught out there alone, with no one to prove that he wasn't the cause of it.

Daniel had one hand on the doorknob when the sound came again, longer this time, drawn out. It was terror personified. A death scream, the sound of a woman in the peak agony of torture, and he yanked open the door and ran for the phone.

He lifted the receiver from the wall, fingers poised to dial, when the small white card pinched behind the phone stopped him short. He had memorized the number on that card even before the taillights of Annie's Jeep vanished into the trees, and he hesitated now, his finger hovering over the buttons.

If you see any tracks or if you hear him, and believe me, you'll know if you do, give me a call.

Daniel shot a glance over his shoulder toward the open door and the lake beyond.

Was that it? He'd never heard a cougar's scream before. The only animal sounds that came at night were the chirping of insects, the haunting yips of coyotes, and the deep snuffling grunts of black bears who went nosing around the boathouse in search of food every once in a while. He'd read about the eerie vixen's cry made by the large cat that was often mistaken for a woman in peril, and there *had* been something otherworldly in the shrieking tenor of that scream, something both male and female that had made him want to sprint inside and lock all three dead bolts behind him.

Daniel deliberated, staring down at the buttons as the dial tone hummed softly through the earpiece.

He had one reason to call Annie Heston. Just one. But there were about a dozen reasons not to.

Daniel hung up.

If the cougar wandered closer to town, someone else would phone it in. It wasn't worth the risk.

He paced to the window and folded his arms across his chest, eyes fixed on the lavender lake beyond the dock. Night was falling, and before long, it would be too dark to see at all.

Call me right away if you hear the cougar. Day or night.

Daniel unfolded his arms, drumming his fingertips on the sill as he turned toward the phone again.

Much to his irritation, he'd caught himself replaying his one and only conversation with Annie over and over in his mind. Especially the moment when he looked up and their eyes met for the first time. He hadn't known it could be like that; that you could look at a woman and her eyes would blow right through the back of your head.

They had stunned him, those eyes. Caught him completely off guard, and ever since that night he'd been seeing them in his sleep. Deep and velvety and shrewd, a vivid shade of reddish brown, the exact hue of the eyes of the maned wolf he'd buried in the woods just before she showed up.

He had stood there at the gate, pretending to listen as she described the cougar's prints and the things he should be looking out for, nodding along as she spoke, but for all she said, she might as well have been speaking Latin. The words had gone in one ear and out the other as he studied her, fascinated.

She wasn't pretty, exactly, but there was precisely a zero percent chance she had ever been called plain. While her eyes were remarkable, the most extraordinary thing about her was the freckles. He had never in his life seen anyone with so many. Tiny spots spanned her face like constellations. Like God had dipped a brush in golden paint and flicked it over her face with reckless abandon. They didn't confine themselves to her nose and cheeks the way they did on most people, but speckled her chin and throat and what little of her collarbone he could see as well. They even ignored the boundaries of her mouth, dotting the corners and the bottom of her full lower lip, but he had cut his train of thought short when he started to wonder where else on her body they were gathered.

All in all, his general first impression of the woman was that if she were dropped into the Wild, Wild West with nothing but the clothes on her back and told to survive, she'd be just fine, but there was something soft about her, too. It might have been her straight, slightly snubbed nose, or her delicately pointed chin. It was hard to say, but something about her had given away a girlish spirit beneath the proud, womanly façade.

And yet, she was a threat, too. A serious threat, and technically a law enforcement officer, nosy and prying. Her curious glance at the boathouse and her comment about him hiding away up here for the apocalypse had rattled him so badly that his forehead and palms had gone instantly clammy, but it was impossible. There was no way she had recognized him. The picture they'd used on the news, the one every television-owning resident of the Pacific Northwest had been bombarded with for weeks on end, had been a snapshot taken when he was sixteen. A scrawny, bare-faced kid with wide, scared eyes. That was seven years and forty pounds ago. He had facial hair now, was five inches taller, and deeply tanned from the long days spent outdoors. She couldn't possibly have recognized him, but, then again, she was from Bend, less than twenty-five miles from Redmond, where coverage of the manhunt would have been the heaviest.

In the days after their conversation at the gate, she'd shown up a handful of times, parking the Jeep there and hiking around the lake, and each time Daniel had watched her from behind the windows of the boathouse, some part of him wanting to step outside and call out to her, to strike up another conversation just for the thrill of being face-to-face with her again, but his better judgment had kept him safely behind the glass.

Daniel walked to the phone, staring at it for a moment before turning away again.

He moved back to the window.

He drummed his fingertips on the sill, cleared his throat, and crossed the room again, pulling the phone from the wall and punching in the numbers on the card before the sensible half of his brain could stop him.

Chapter 10

ANNIE

The phone on the nightstand rang shrilly, and Annie twitched on the bed, startling herself awake. She sat up, dazed, and wiped a string of drool from her mouth, blinking at the window where faint light was tinting the sky beyond the fir boughs.

Was it dawn or dusk?

Dusk. The headache throbbing behind her eyes was proof that she hadn't slept nearly long enough. The lamp was on, and an open novel lay splayed across the bedspread where it had fallen from her hand. She hadn't meant to drift off, only to read for a little while before dinner, to try to distract her mind from the thing it kept spinning back around to again and again: the woman on the rocks.

Yesterday afternoon, a few hours after they found her, Jake had called with the update that the recovery team had decided to wait until the storm blew through before retrieving the dead woman from the cliffside, and Annie had lain awake all night as it poured, thinking of the poor girl out there alone, her body cold and lifeless and soaked by the rain.

The phone rang again, and Annie reached across the pillow for it.

"Hello?"

There was a pause, and then, "Ms. Heston?"

"Speaking."

Another pause—longer this time.

"I think I just heard the cougar. South side of the lake."

It took a moment for Annie's cobwebbed brain to catch up, to fill in the blanks.

"Is this Daniel?"

"Yeah."

She glanced at the cluttered corner of the room where her gear was heaped in a pile. "Are you sure it was a cougar?"

"Not positive, but I think so."

Annie stifled a yawn. "Did it sound like a woman screaming?"

"Bloody murder."

She swung her legs over the side of the bed and stood up. "I'll be there in fifteen minutes."

She hung up and stepped into her uniform. She'd felt helpless all day, holding the terrible secret of the dead woman in the woods. Jake was more stressed-out than she'd seen him in the month they'd worked together, calling the sheriffs of nearby towns to ask about missing women, with no luck. But at least the body had finally made it to the morgue and was awaiting an autopsy. Dental records would give them some clue as to her identity, and then he'd have somewhere to start. And now, at last, she had something to do, too.

Tracking down the cougar was *all* she had to do at the moment. It was the only task relating to the crime that fell within the boundaries of her job, and she clung to it. Without some sort of purpose, she'd go insane, and beyond that, she was fairly certain that the big cat was still limping. Plenty of maladies did not heal themselves in the wild, and without intervention, infection often walked hand in hand with death. If he was suffering from an open wound on his leg or paw, she was his only chance at survival, and her conscience would not let her rest until she saw the job through.

Annie retrieved her tranquilizer gun, tucked three darts into her shirt pocket, and slung her headlamp around her neck. There were two snares, a radio collar, and a small bottle of skunk oil, the scent preferred for trapping cougars, in the back of the Jeep already. She had everything she needed.

She drove slowly up to the lake, the engine humming low over the hills. The less noise she made, the better. There was no telling how long the cougar would stick around for, but if he was out for a night hunt, she might get lucky.

As her headlights swung around the last bend, Annie was surprised to find the gate unlocked and wide open, and she pulled right up to the boathouse, killing the lights before they swept across the lake.

Daniel was waiting for her, sitting on the dock with his legs dangling over the edge, and he lifted a hand as she climbed out of the Jeep, but said nothing in greeting, so neither did she. She moved around to the back of the car, opened the hatch, and pulled her gear forward.

The last of the day's light was settling down around the rim of the sky, and the lake was deeply indigo and smooth as glass. In minutes, the stars would be out, and the forest, alive already with the song of crickets, would be pitch-black. Annie pulled her headlamp over her head and flipped it on, bathing the inside of the Jeep with light, then loaded a dart into the tranquilizer gun and slid the snares over an arm before shutting the hatch and coming around to meet Daniel, still sitting on the dock with his hands pressed beneath his thighs.

"Thanks for the heads-up."

He nodded.

"Where did the sound come from?"

Daniel raised a hand to shield his eyes from the glare of her headlamp. "Can you lower that a little?"

"Sorry." Annie set the snares at her feet and reached up to flip the light off. "Normally for night tracking I'd use a red filter, but I don't have one with me. So, where'd you hear him? Was he close?"

"Straight across."

He lifted an arm and pointed toward the south shore. Annie followed his finger to where the dark water met the even darker tree line in the distance.

The violet light on the lake had winked out in a sudden eclipse of night shadow, and trying to navigate the overgrown trail around the lake would be treacherous this late in the day, with or without a head-lamp, not to mention noisy. Plus, the snares were heavy, and—

"I'll take you," Daniel said.

Annie turned to him. "What?"

"In my boat."

He nodded toward the corner of the dock where a small skiff sat in the water, bobbing gently up and down.

She eyed him for a moment. It was as though he had read her mind just then, but was she really stupid enough to put herself in the middle of a remote lake at night with a man she didn't know?

Annie studied him in the failing light. He looked somehow even younger than he had when they'd first met at the gate—perhaps because his face was cleaner than it had been then, his stubble shaved, and his skin free from the dirt that had smudged it that afternoon. He wore the same torn jeans, but tonight's shirt was a fraying, gray Mariners tee.

Again, Annie had the same overwhelming sense that she knew him from somewhere. The gnawing teeth of recognition were still chewing away at some forgotten memory in the back of her mind.

He dropped his gaze and Annie bent to grab the snares at her feet.

It was perhaps not the wisest idea, but he was watching her with the same sort of acute wariness she felt toward him, and in all likelihood he probably wanted to be out there alone with her on the water even less than she did.

"Okay," she agreed.

Daniel rose to his feet without a word and offered a hand to help her onto the dock, but Annie handed him the tranquilizer gun and one of the snares instead, scrambling up after with the rest of the gear.

Daniel stepped down into the boat first and Annie climbed in after, taking her seat on the bench facing him as he untied the rope and nudged the dock with an oar, sliding them out into the lake.

He rowed swiftly and steadily, the silence only interrupted by the sound of water breaking over the oars. His eyes stayed cast down at his lap as they left the boathouse behind, and Annie, catching herself staring at the coiling muscles in his arms as he rowed, turned to look at the dark woods instead.

A full moon was rising—broad and golden behind the trees. She gazed at it as they moved stroke by stroke farther out into the lake. The air was cooler up here, fragrant with the perfume of the pines that pressed in on all sides, and even as her eyes stayed trained on the forest, she felt Daniel watching her as he rowed.

They hadn't said two sentences to each other yet, and Annie was starting to feel the silence as it swelled between them like an over-inflated balloon.

She cleared her throat. "When we get close, I'll flip on the headlamp and see if I can catch eyes. On the off chance I'm able to see and shoot him from the boat, I'll collar him, but my guess is that he'll see us coming and take off, so I'll head into the woods and set up these traps before we go."

The oars dipped beneath the water again, sliding through and emerging with a little splash.

"All right."

Annie cleared her throat again and turned away. Fine. If he wanted silence, he could have it.

The southern woods were drawing near, rising up to meet them, and she squinted at the darkness beneath the trees, scanning for movement.

"How can I help?"

Annie turned in surprise, finding Daniel's gaze fixed intently on her face.

She considered him for a moment, his expression unreadable in the darkness, then she pulled her headlamp off and placed it on the bench beside him.

"You know how to flip a switch?"

His chest rumbled in a deep laugh. "Yes."

"Okay. Just turn the light on when I tell you and sweep it back and forth across the trees."

He pulled the oars twice more through the water before he spoke again.

"You need to swear me in for the line of duty?"

She blinked at him and saw the hint of a smile on his lips. He was joking. This man was actually telling a joke.

"Okay." She nodded seriously. "Do you solemnly swear to keep your mouth shut and not row away screaming if we see the cougar?"

He returned her nod. "I do."

"Congratulations, that's all there is to it." She smiled as she turned back to watch the shore.

Daniel slowed the boat as they approached the southern rim of the lake, and it glided on its momentum to the bank, beaching itself quietly on the soft soil. Annie glanced up at the wall of pines before them. The trees were so tall here, a fortress of black shadow. They could hide anything.

She held a finger in the air, warning Daniel to keep quiet as she strained to hear any out-of-place sound in the darkness. The shrieking screams that most people associated with cougars were far less common than their other noises; sounds that were sometimes mistaken for the chirping of birds, or the song of someone whistling in the woods. Unwitting hikers were sometimes even surprised by the throaty rumble of a purr.

"Watch the woods," she said quietly, lifting the tranquilizer gun to her shoulder and settling it there. "When you flip the switch, look for eyes between the trunks. Chest height. Go ahead."

Daniel flipped the headlamp on, bathing the nearest trees in anemic light. He swept the beam back and forth along the lakeshore and Annie followed it, searching the gaps between pine trees for a pair of glowing yellow eyes, but finding only darkness.

An animal, far too small to be the cougar, scampered into the undergrowth with the flick of a well-tufted tail, but other than that, all was still.

For several minutes, Annie kept her vigil, straight-backed in the boat, tranquilizer gun aimed and ready, swiveling her upper body with the slow rhythm of an oscillating fan.

"Anything?" she murmured.

Daniel swept the light across the trees again. "Nothing."

Annie lowered the gun into her lap with a sigh. "Okay." She took the headlamp from him and secured it back over her head with a snap. "I'll go get some snares laid down."

Daniel looped the rope around a felled log onshore as Annie stepped into the trees with a trap in each hand. A few meters into the woods, she found an indent in the undergrowth, a small animal trail weaving through the trees, and she left the snares there, about a hundred feet apart, spritzing each generously with skunk oil before heading back to the boat.

Daniel stood on the shore with a swollen moon rising behind him, water lapping at his heels.

"All set." Annie climbed back into the boat. "Do you think you could check them once a day?"

"I will," he promised, pushing the boat out into the water and wading in after it. He climbed in and rowed back the way they had come without speaking, and Annie sat with her hands in her lap, trying to embrace the silence that he obviously preferred.

Halfway across, her eyes were drawn to the stars on the mirrored surface of the lake as they danced in the ripples, thousands and thousands of them, reflected in tiny silver flickers, and she watched them, smiling, as they floated by.

And then, without warning, there was quick movement in the water, a brush of bright blue light that glowed for a moment where the oar split the surface. By the time Annie turned to look at it, it was gone, and she blinked at the dark water where it had been.

With the next dip of the oar, more blue light, electric and hazy, lit the black-velvet surface, and her mouth fell open.

She glanced up at Daniel to see if he had noticed, but he was watching her face.

"Did you see that?" she asked, incredulous.

He pulled the oars up out of the water and rested them across his lap. "Just wait." He tilted his head back toward the water.

Annie turned to look again. Among the reflected stars, blue flashes of light were appearing in multitudes now, sparking faintly, then vanishing, and far across the water, at the very edges of the lake where tiny waves lapped at the shore, thin blue streaks were rising and falling away. Awestruck, Annie turned a slow circle in her seat. The entire lake was rimmed in shimmering, vivid blue, and for a brief moment she wondered if she was hallucinating. Was she so sleep-deprived that her mind was conjuring up the magic before her?

"Annie."

Annie whipped her head toward him. It was the first time this quiet man had said her name out loud, and the word was a breath. A prayer. It was mist on the mountain, and she could not turn away as she met his gaze in the darkness.

"Watch." He dipped an oar into the water and dragged it in a slow circle that glowed like blue fire for an instant and was gone.

"What is this?" she breathed.

He stirred the water again, a figure eight of blue trailing the tip of the oar in the silken darkness, around, and around, and around.

"Bioluminescent plankton," he said quietly. "They exist all over the world in different places. Thailand. The Maldives. Some bays in South America. And here, for some reason, in a little lake in the mountains of Washington State. They show up around the start of summer, when the conditions are just right."

Somewhere in the back of her mind, Annie recalled a chapter on bioluminescence in one of her textbooks, but she had skimmed through it without the slightest expectation that she'd someday witness its magic.

Unable to help herself, she leaned over the side of the boat and dipped her hand into the water, swirling her fingers through it as her eyes danced with wonder. She trailed her fingers back and forth across the surface, watching the tiny streaks of blue lightning that followed in their path.

"That's why it's called Lake Lumin?"

Daniel nodded.

Annie drew her arm back and flung it forward, slapping the surface of the water and sending forth a shimmering blue splash, the drops rippling outward in cobalt rings.

Pure delight, deep and childlike, welled up within her and Annie laughed, the high, tinkling sound echoing out into the quiet darkness around them.

"This is amazing," she marveled.

"It is." He still dragged the oar gently back and forth in the water.

Annie looked up to find him smiling softly down at the blue glow.

There was a strange ache deep in her chest at the sight of that smile. He looked so young. He *was* so young. And with that flicker of joy in his eyes, she could see the boy he had once been in the face of the man he was now. The man who, for some reason she might never know, had chosen a life of isolation out here in the wild.

The oar stilled in the water at last, and he turned, his eyes seeking hers in the dark. Annie met his gaze, transfixed, her chest tightening around a realization that she could not deny.

He was beautiful.

Daniel Barela was beautiful.

The oars dragged across the surface, lighting up the water around them as the boat turned in a slow circle beneath the stars.

Who are you? The ache expanded, filling her chest. *Tell me who you are.*

Moments passed that felt like hours, and then Daniel began rowing again, looking away from her as he turned the boat around, back toward the north shore.

He did not speak again as he rowed them to the boathouse, and when they reached the dock, he climbed out first, offering Annie his hand.

This time, she took it, aware of every place that his skin touched hers. He lifted her up onto the dock where they stood mere inches apart. Annie took a breath, inhaling his scent of woodsmoke and pine, and his gaze dropped for a split second, half a heartbeat, landing on her lips before he looked down at the dock.

"Thank you," Annie said, tucking a loose strand of hair behind her ear.

He nodded, and lowered himself back down into the boat to retrieve the headlamp she had left on the bench.

"Here." He passed it up.

She lifted it from his hand, hesitating.

"I really do mean thank you," she said after a beat. "I know you're protective of your space up here. I was a little surprised that you actually called."

Silence fell after her words, lasting moments too long.

"I had to," he said at last.

Annie stood on the dock, searching his face as she waited for him to explain what he meant, but he didn't speak again.

"I should go," she said at last. "You'll call me if you hear anything else?"

He nodded.

She took a step back. "Good night."

She resisted the urge to look over her shoulder as she walked to the edge of the dock and jumped down onto solid ground.

Despite every single ounce of her better judgment, she wanted him to call out her name, to invent some reason for her to stay a little while longer, but she knew he would not, and in silence she walked to the Jeep, opened the door, and climbed inside.

Annie turned the key, and the engine rumbled to life. She sat still for a moment, the motor idling in the soles of her feet, then she backed away from the boathouse.

The beam of the headlights swept the clearing once, lighting up Daniel where he stood on the dock. His face was still unreadable as he watched her turn around and pull away into the night.

Annie stared at him in the rearview mirror, heart pounding, until she passed through the gate and the first curve of the road stole him from sight. Only then did she exhale, letting out all the air in her lungs.

What on earth had just happened?

It was impossible. Completely unprofessional. And yet, undeniable.

He had stirred something in her, that strange and quiet man of the woods. He had stirred something as alive and electric as those lightning-blue streaks she'd stirred up with her fingers.

Annie drove along the dark road in silence until, through the trees, she caught the lit window of her small room over the garage, winking bright with the lamplight she'd forgotten to extinguish on her way out.

She could not undo what had just happened, but she could leave it there. Chalk it up as a strange and beautiful dream, a onetime thing, and cut it loose. Forget all about it.

But as she rolled slowly down the last gravel hill, somehow still feeling the touch of Daniel's hand against her own, she could not manage to think about anything else.

Chapter 11

ANNIE

Annie slept late, overtired from her night on the lake with Daniel, and was surprised to find the station empty when she stepped in a few minutes before eleven.

She put on a pot of coffee and settled into her seat with a mug just as Jake's silhouette darkened the doorway.

"I've got it," he said, stepping into the station with a manila envelope in his hands.

Annie rose to her feet. "Autopsy results?"

"Yeah, Doc Porter's out right now, but he left it in the front office for me. I figured we should go over it together."

"Okay"—Annie nodded—"let's do it."

Jake held the envelope out like an offering. "You want to grab a bite at the Sky High? It's just about time for lunch and I could go for a sandwich. We could go over the results there."

Annie nodded. "Yeah, I could eat."

"Great." He held the door open with an arm. "Let's walk, it's nice out."

Annie followed Jake through the door, and they strolled together up the street and across the intersection to the café.

When they reached the Sky High, a quirky little place painted top to bottom with a mural of Mount St. Helens mid-eruption, Annie stepped up onto the curb and tugged at the door handle. It didn't budge, and then she noticed the sign with an arrow that read USE OTHER DOOR.

"Here, this way." Jake laughed, pressing a hand to the small of her back and guiding her around the corner to the restaurant's main entrance. As he lead her inside, Annie swatted his hand away playfully.

When they were seated at a window booth and served tall glasses of ice water with lemon wedges, Jake peeled open the envelope and pulled out the stapled stack of papers inside, scanning the first page as Annie waited.

A familiar forest-green Ford Ranger rolled past the window, and she followed it with her eyes, wondering if it was Daniel's. Probably not. There was a passenger inside that she caught a quick glimpse of as the truck passed the window, a young woman with long honey-blond hair.

When she turned back to look at Jake, his face had fallen.

"So?" she asked. He nodded without looking up.

Annie leaned forward, keeping her voice low enough to not be overheard by the older couple in the next booth. "Strangled?"

He passed her the paper. "Here."

Annie scanned the page quickly. Medical jargon abounded, but near the bottom, there it was.

CAUSE OF DEATH: Asphyxiation.

She glanced up at Jake, who looked as though he'd aged ten years in the last five minutes. Just as they'd feared, the young woman had been strangled to death and then dumped over the cliffside. This was no accident, no work of nature, nor the fault of any wild animal.

"What can I get you?"

Annie quickly flipped the sheet of paper over as the waitress appeared, a woman nearing thirty with brassy hair and a mouth full of metal braces—her pen poised over a pad as her eyes darted between Jake and Annie.

"Actually, Becca, I've lost my appetite." Jake slid the menu to the end of the table. "Can you just bring me a ginger ale?"

"Aren't you feelin' okay?" Becca frowned and placed the back of her hand to his forehead.

Jake batted her away. "I'm fine. I'm not sick."

"Work stuff?" She eyed the stack of papers beside his water glass.

Jake covered them with the torn envelope and gave her a pointed look.

Becca shrugged as she swiveled toward Annie. "You want anything?"

Annie shook her head. She'd lost her appetite, too.

"Flu's going around." Becca turned back to Jake as she tapped the pen against the pad. "Fever might not've hit you yet, but I bet you've got it."

"I don't have the flu." Jake sighed, but Becca didn't look convinced as she turned away with her eyebrows raised.

"And don't you go calling my mother," he called to her back as she walked toward the kitchen.

Jake looked at Annie and shook his head. "Becca," he said under his breath, as though the woman's name itself should suffice for an explanation.

Annie took a sip of her water and nodded toward the stack of papers. "Anything in there about dental records?"

Jake thumbed through the stack, flipping past the printed photographs of the woman's naked, maimed body on the stainless-steel table.

"Yeah, right here. Looks like he ordered them done. We should hear back in a day or two. Can't come soon enough, honestly. I need to find out who she is. I hate that somewhere out there her mom and dad are just waiting for their little girl to come home . . ."

Jake's words were choked with emotion, and he lifted his glass of water and took a sip, turning toward the window. He didn't look up as

Becca returned with his ginger ale, and Annie turned to stare out the window, too.

Cars passed. People passed. A boy with white-blond hair chased a black cat into a storm drain. On the other side of the glass, the town of Lake Lumin was going about its daily business. Tucked into these hills were men and women and families whose biggest concerns were which trees might fall in the windstorm forecast for the weekend, or how the Blazers would fare in the playoffs. This little village in the mountains had just been rocked to its very core, and only the coroner and two citizens in the Sky High Café knew it.

Chapter 12

DANIEL

D aniel twisted the copper lead wire around the nail three, four, five times, then tucked the loose end under the ceiling panel, careful to keep it away from the other wires spanning the exposed beams like a tangled nest of snakes.

It was an absolute mess up here. Whoever had done the original electrical work in the Lake Lumin General Store twenty years before had taken shortcuts and left loose ends, stringing down feed wires to the wrong switches, some that needed to be flipped down instead of up to turn the lights on.

When Daniel had arrived that morning, the store owner, Phil, a dead ringer for Morgan Freeman, walked him into the bathroom to show him a quirk that left Daniel scratching his head.

A hair dryer plugged into the outlet didn't work, but flipping the switch between low, medium, and high dimmed and brightened the fluorescent light over the sink. Daniel promised Phil that he'd figure it out and he had, tracking down a lighting and power circuit that had been mixed by mistake. Though it had meant an extra half hour of work, he'd gotten it done, and now he had just this last snarled knot of wires in the ceiling to deal with and he'd be home free.

Beneath him, in the eight aisles of the small store, a few people milled slowly through rows of packaged pastries and chips, overpriced Tylenol, and too many flavors of gum. They walked around Daniel's ladder without glancing up, as though he weren't here, half hidden in the ceiling, rewiring someone else's shoddy electrical work.

He didn't mind. He'd rather be ignored than antagonized. Twenty minutes earlier, Ian Ward and one of his many cronies had passed through the aisle where Daniel was working. The tatted-up friend had sniggered something under his breath that Daniel didn't catch, miming kicking out the ladder from beneath him, but Ian was a bit more obvious as he shouldered the ladder on his way back to the register for cigarettes; not hard enough to knock Daniel off his perch, but hard enough to let him know that he wasn't welcome.

Ian's parents were the richest couple in town with their stable full of racehorses, and they'd thought they could buy their son the position as the town's law enforcement officer when it was vacated, despite Ian's not having any prior experience or municipal education. The Proudys had stepped up and petitioned for Jake, who did have the qualifications for the job, and had gathered the signatures of nearly half the citizens in town to back him. Daniel's name was right at the top of the list, and Ian had naturally hated him ever since.

Daniel gave the last grounding wire a final twist and replaced the ceiling panel, climbing down the stepladder once a middle-aged woman clutching a bottle of Pepto-Bismol had ambled past. He tapped the notches between the rungs with a finger and folded the ladder together before lowering it to the floor.

"You done, Daniel?" Phil called from the front of the store.

"Yes sir." Daniel straightened up and nodded in his direction.

"Well, help yourself to a Moon Pie and come on up. I'll write you a check."

Daniel nodded over the tops of the chip bags and returned the tools wedged in his pockets and waistband to the open box on the floor.

There among the wrenches and screwdrivers was a stray fishing lure, orange feathered, and Daniel reached into the box, grazing it with his fingertips. A smile tugged at the corner of his mouth. The lure reminded him of fishing, and of the lake, which brought his thoughts back to Annie.

He hadn't been able to stop thinking about her all morning, lost in reliving the hour they'd spent together last night on the water. It had felt like a dream, that boat ride across the lake, but just as she had laid out those sharp-toothed traps in the woods, in dialing her number he had set out a snare of his own and then immediately stuck his foot into it like a buffoon.

He could pin it down to the precise moment, the exact second that the trap had snapped shut. It was the moment that Annie had drawn her arm back and hit the water with her hand, sending blue sparks out across the lake and laughing into the night air with a sound like wind chimes. Right then, he'd known it. He was a goner. A moth to the flame. Inexplicably drawn toward something that had the power to destroy him.

"Check's ready," Phil called, and Daniel pushed himself to his feet. He walked to the front of the store and nodded in thanks.

"Don't cash it until Monday," Phil called out behind him as he walked back to gather his tools. "Sheila went a little overboard at the boutique this week."

"Got it."

Through the window, the glint of sunlight on copper hair caught his eye, and Daniel stopped, his heart leaping into his throat. It was her, Annie, walking side by side with Jake up the street, their heads tilted together in conversation.

As though in a trance, Daniel moved toward the window, reaching out to rest his fingertips on the glass. At the front of the store, Phil was droning on, grumbling loudly about his wife's purchase of three pantsuits in different shades of blue when one would have done just as well for the Ladies Auxiliary meeting. Daniel made a noise of agreement, though his eyes stayed locked on Annie.

"She's draining me dry, Daniel," Phil said from behind the counter. "Slowly. Like a vampire. Remember that when the time comes for you to pick a woman. Be sure to check for fangs."

"Okay," Daniel agreed absently without turning around.

At the intersection, Jake and Annie crossed the street, Jake whistling at a car that zipped through the yellow light, but Daniel's eyes stayed on Annie.

Gone was the stiff olive uniform, replaced by a loose cream-colored blouse over casual jeans. She looked different. Her hair was still in its long braid, but it was woven a little looser today, with a few wavy locks hanging free, framing her face. From this angle, in side profile, that freckled, upturned nose looked even more delicate, and Daniel smiled.

They stepped under the awning of the Sky High, and Annie reached for the door, tugging it to no avail. The smile on Daniel's lips froze and fell away.

He was touching her.

Jake was touching her.

His hand was on the small of her back, his fingers dimpling the soft fabric of her blouse, and Annie was making no move to stop him. Daniel scrambled to reach a different conclusion from the one his eyes were telling him. Jake was a friendly guy. A touchy-feely guy. He often clapped Daniel on the back, sometimes hugged him, and once or twice he'd even rubbed Daniel's shoulders in a gesture of friendship, but as he stared out the window, Daniel could not explain away the tenderness of the touch. That was not the touch of a friend. It was the touch of a lover.

He felt sick, and he wanted to turn away, to look anywhere else, but his fingertips stayed glued to the glass, his eyes following Jake as he led Annie around the corner toward the main door of the restaurant.

Of course. How could he have been so stupid? They worked together. They spent every day together. What woman in her right mind wouldn't fall for Jake, with those bright blue eyes and that ready smile, his easy way with words, and the carefree attitude of a man who had never known the ugly bid for survival that life could be.

Daniel swallowed, doused by a cold wave of disappointment.

What he'd felt in the boat last night had been completely one-sided—all in his head, a figment of his love-starved imagination. And foolish moth that he was, he'd flown close enough to be badly, blisteringly burned.

"Excuse me?"

The voice behind him was high and feminine, and Daniel turned to find a vaguely familiar face with just a little too much eyeliner blinking up at him.

"Hi . . ." he said, flipping through the Rolodex in his head for the name of the girl standing in front of him, the Boyd girl who lived down the road. "Jamie?"

"Yep. And you're Daniel, right?"

He nodded.

She was almost shockingly pretty, this girl, except for her teeth, which were too small, crooked, and fading brown. But her bone structure more than made up for the ruined smile. Refined and almost feline with the high cheekbones and wide tropical-blue eyes of a Siamese cat—eyes that were fixed unblinkingly on his face as she tucked a lock of honey-blond hair behind her ear.

"You live up at the end of my road, don't you? Lake Lumin Road?"

Daniel nodded again, glancing back over his shoulder at the empty sidewalk where Jake and Annie had been.

"Do you think I could get a ride home?"

She made the request with such directness that Daniel turned back, blinking in surprise.

He hesitated. "Uh . . ."

He didn't know Jamie Boyd. Not really. Nothing more than a nod if she happened to be outside when he passed by in his truck. Up until this very minute, they'd never exchanged a word.

"Did your car break down or something?" he asked, giving the parking lot a quick scan.

Jamie shook her head. "Don't have a car yet."

Daniel shifted his weight. He wanted to ask how old she was, but the question wouldn't sound quite right voiced out loud. Improper. Or creepy, maybe. He lifted a hand and rubbed it across the back of his neck.

"I'm not sure your parents would be okay with me taking you home."

"I'm eighteen. Nineteen next week. I can decide for myself who I get in a car with."

Daniel considered her for a moment. She was older than she looked, this wide-eyed waif of a girl. And, fair enough. By the time he was her age, he had been living by himself in the boathouse for almost three years. She was technically an adult.

"Okay." He nodded. "I'm leaving now, though."

"Great." Jamie gave him a wide smile. "Just let me buy my gum and I'll meet you outside."

She bounced up to the register to pay for the pack of Juicy Fruit in her hand as Daniel gathered his tools and ladder. She was already in the passenger seat of the Ranger when he stepped outside, avoiding the urge to stare across the street at the café. He had no claim on Annie Heston. She was free to do whatever she liked with whomever she liked. This strange jealousy welling up in his chest was something he had no right to feel.

Daniel loaded the ladder into the bed of the truck and wedged the toolbox in beside it before climbing in next to Jamie. He hadn't noticed in the store, but she was spritzed with perfume: a sweet, cotton-and-lemonade scent that was borderline cloying, and he held his breath as he buckled his seat belt and rolled down the window.

The Ranger was old and the engine was loud, louder still with the window down, but for once, Daniel was grateful for the noise. It would keep conversation to a minimum.

He pulled out of the parking lot and turned onto Main Street, leaning back in his seat to keep himself from searching the window of the café for a glimpse of the couple inside.

Town was quiet, just a few people out on the sidewalks, strolling hand in hand in pairs or bending their heads over ice cream cones on benches. Daniel hung his arm out over the side of the truck, the metal toasty from the long hours in the sun. It was warming up now that summer was almost here, and before long the town would be bustling with tourists again, tourists who spent their weekends gawking at the lopsided mountain and the ravaged land behind it, then wandering into town to plunk down their dollars and cents on the countertops of businesses who depended on the summer tourism to stay afloat.

Daniel scanned the buildings of Main Street as he rolled past. Still, after all these years, it didn't feel like home, this blink-and-you'll-miss-it drive-by town that could quite literally be missed from the highway behind the wall of pines that outnumbered the buildings a thousand to one. It would never grow any bigger than it was now, and that was fine by him. It was a town where nothing ever happened; a place where nothing went wrong. That was why he had chosen it. Claimed it. Built his lie of a life here. There was no safer place for a man in hiding than a small town forgotten by the wider world.

Jamie waved through the window to a pair of teenaged girls walking arm in arm down the sidewalk, and they blew kisses in her direction while Daniel leaned farther back in his seat.

He took a left turn, and the buildings of town fell away behind them into the unbroken tunnel of forest that led up into the briars.

Jamie turned to face him. "I kind of have a favor to ask you."

Daniel's brows lifted. "Me?"

She nodded and Daniel glanced sideways at her. What could Jamie Boyd possibly want from him? "Shoot."

"Okay, so, I really, *really* want the lifeguard job at the pool this summer, but I have to pass this swim test to do it, and I was wondering if I could maybe practice in the lake."

Daniel pulled his teeth over his lower lip, fingers drumming the steering wheel. "Couldn't you practice at the pool?"

Jamie flumped back in her seat. "My dad won't drive me unless I have an actual job there, and I haven't saved up enough for a car yet.

That's why I need the work this summer. And I could just run right up to the lake if you say it's okay. It's only a mile and a half to jog there, and there's no weird fish or gators or anything like that, right?"

Daniel laughed. "No. No gators that I've seen yet."

"See? Totally safe. Is it true that the lake glows at night, or is that just made up?"

"Not every night, but sometimes. When the water's warm enough."

Jamie clasped her hands together beneath her chin. "So, can I? Please? *Please?*"

Daniel made the right turn onto Lake Lumin Road with another quick glance at the girl in the passenger seat. Could she really be just a few years younger than he was? She seemed so much younger. But maybe this was exactly what teenagers should be: hopeful and emphatic, every little thing either a wonderful excitement or a crushing disappointment. Maybe she wasn't young for eighteen. Maybe he was just way too old for twenty-three.

Daniel bought time by slowly rolling up the window as the dust from the road billowed thickly around the truck, opting for choking on perfume over choking on dust.

Of course, it was a terrible idea, giving someone he didn't know permission to walk onto his land anytime they wanted, but what harm could she do? It was just for a few weeks. Just until summer, and she was hardly the type of person who would analyze the place with the scrutiny of a detective, putting the pieces together and figuring out who he was.

She would have been just eleven when his face was plastered all over the news, probably absorbed in the highs and lows of early adolescence. And even if she had been paying attention to the news at that time, it's likely the story slid right off her mental plate as soon as something she deemed more important dropped onto it. A new crush, a fight with a friend, a part in a school play.

"I guess so," he agreed, turning his eyes back to the road. "Just until summer?"

"Just until summer," she said, smiling.

Favor granted, Jamie folded her hands in her lap and rode in contented silence the rest of the way to her house. Daniel didn't pull into
the gravel driveway, but eased the truck alongside the fence. As she
climbed out, he glanced through the trees uneasily, but there was no
sign of her parents in the overgrown front yard, and the only movement
was a striped sheet that flapped on a clothesline between two apple trees.

Jamie hopped around the front of the truck, giving a quick wave at
the windshield before bounding toward the house, her long hair flowing
out behind her.

Daniel pulled away from the fence and drove the rest of the way to
the clearing without seeing the road. Instead, he saw Annie over and
over, with Jake's hand on the small of her back as he steered her out
of sight.

Chapter 13

DANIEL

It was the belt this time. And not the leather strap, but the vicious silver buckle at the end that bit into Daniel's skin and tore it, leaving deep, purple welts that lasted for days.

Gary's face was red, the forked vein in his forehead a blue *V* against the skin as he raised his arm again, cracking the belt downward with a fury that split the air.

Daniel lay curled in a ball on the floor, his hands over his ears as the blows rained down. As with any beating, any storm, the best idea was to hunker down and not fight back. The tornado of his stepfather's rage would blow itself out. The anger would ebb away little by little with each strike. It always did. Or, Gary's fifty-year-old arm would tire, which amounted to the same thing.

Daniel stared at his stepfather's work boots as the buckle found its mark against his shoulder, his arm, and his ear—setting it ringing. Even from down here on the floor, he could smell the vapors escaping with each huff of breath. Jack Daniel's. He'd hate the sweet, sharp smell of the stuff until the day he died.

There was a sound in the hall behind him, the swishing hem of a skirt, and Daniel managed a single, small "Please" as his mother walked past the doorway with her head down. She hesitated for half a step, but did not stop, and the beating went on.

It was vicious, terrifying, and yet the pain was somehow far away. It didn't quite reach him, coiled there on the floor, or maybe he had drifted out of his head and detached from it completely.

The work boots took a step back as Gary reeled the belt high over his head for another blow. Daniel gritted his teeth, squeezing his eyes shut as the buckle came whizzing down and struck him squarely on the back of the head.

Pain; real, honest, searing pain tore through his skull, and he opened his mouth to scream, but no sound came out. He was trapped in his silence and the blood was pouring, pooling around his head.

Enough. Surely Gary had had enough. Surely his wrath was appeased now. But, no, he was raising the belt again, higher, higher—when, without warning, everything around Daniel went black.

There were three seconds of blind panic, then relief washed the feeling away. He couldn't see, but at least he was alone. Thank God, it was over, and he had somehow managed to regain his feet.

Through the darkness, his eyes were drawn to a bulky shape across the vast black room, tall and glowing and hissing steam. The furnace. The great red-bellied monster that had frightened him out of his wits when he was younger.

He was in the basement. The place where he had been sent as a small child and made to wait in the dark for punishment. The place he was tucked out of sight so that Gary could forget he existed for a few hours.

Water dripped onto the concrete floor beneath his feet, and Daniel looked down. Through the darkness, he could just make out the shallow puddle and the empty plastic water bottle beside it. He raised his left hand. In it, inexplicably, was his pocketknife, clutched tight.

Heavy footsteps creaked overhead. Someone was walking across the kitchen, toward the cellar door.

"Nico!" a voice called out, low and angry.

Daniel raised his right hand. In it were wires he didn't remember fraying, the sharp ends snapping with electricity. Live and deadly, just waiting for a bare foot, human skin, to act as conductor and executioner. The cellar door opened, white light spilled down the stairs, and Daniel cried out in his sleep, startling himself awake.

He sat bolt upright in the dark and scanned the room, wild-eyed, but quiet seconds ticked past, and he came back to himself, to the boathouse. He opened and closed his damp hands and took a slow gulp of clean, night air.

A nightmare. It was just another nightmare. Another terror ride through his subconscious that had left him drenched in sweat and breathing like he'd raced a mile.

It wasn't real. It wasn't real.

Daniel slumped back against his pillow, aware of a sound in the night, a sound his sleeping brain had translated as the sparking of electricity, but really, it was a scratching, dragging sound—the sound of restless branches tearing at the outside wall.

Daniel rose to his feet and walked to the kitchen.

Stiff wind was blasting the windows at the front of the boathouse, rattling the panes in their frames. The storm was here.

He filled a cup at the tap and drank it in the dark, then another, and set the empty glass in the sink. Without bothering to put on shoes or clothes, he unlocked the side door and stepped outside in his underwear, greeted by a mighty gust of wind as it tore across the lake.

The forest howled with it, the voices of the trees joining in one ceaseless rush, while behind him, the dock whistled as wind streamed through the old boards and water slapped at the pilings.

The tarp he'd tucked around the stack of firewood was already loose and flapping noisily, and Daniel secured it again before walking around the house to check on the trees.

The cherry tree at the back corner was flailing in the wind. Its limbs, laden with thin leaves and young fruit, attacked the outer wall, while behind it the alders danced for their lives—slender arms lashing in all directions.

Sharp pebbles nipped at the soles of his feet as Daniel walked to the center of the clearing, the wind whipping his hair around his face and peppering his bare torso with gravel and dirt.

He closed his eyes and threw his head back, letting the gusts buffet him forward onto his toes and back onto his heels.

He had always loved windstorms, even as a kid, but especially up here, when the forest moved and sang with the power of it.

Windstorms reminded him of the words he had memorized years before when he was ten. He had pulled down the never-opened Bible that lay gathering dust on the brick hearth of the Redmond house and flipped it open to somewhere in the middle, reading through forty pages in their entirety before deciding that the God of Abraham wasn't for him. But in those forty pages, he deemed one passage worthy of memorization, just one, from the book of Job, when a broken man cursed the day he was born and threw the injustice of his trials back into God's face. God himself answered, his voice bellowing out of a mighty windstorm:

Who is this who darkens counsel by words without knowledge?
Now prepare yourself like a man; I will question you, and you shall
answer me.

Daniel lifted his arms out to his sides in the moonlit clearing, welcoming the wind like a human embrace. He filled his lungs with air and cried out at the top of his voice, long and loud, the sound vanishing into the ferocious pitch of the wind, torn from his lips and whisked up and away, into bright, undiluted stars.

Can you bind the cluster of the Pleiades, or loose the belt of Orion?
Can you bring out the constellations in their season, or guide the
Great Bear with her cubs?

Jake, Sunday-school born and bred with his cross tattoo, could have the four walls of his church. This right here, this dark clearing in the middle of a windstorm with a cathedral of stars overhead, was the only place Daniel felt remotely religious.

From behind the boathouse came a terrible groaning and cracking. The sound grew louder. It was the whine of hardwood resisting the pull of gravity, the sound of a tree about to fall, and Daniel stared in dismay at the massive cedar standing tall behind the alders as it tipped and bowed and crashed sideways, its hundred feet of height and billowing branches plunging through the air, down, down, down, until it smashed through the back of the boathouse with a thud that shook the earth.

Another shout escaped his lips and Daniel leapt backward, his hands flying to the side of his head.

For a moment, he stood, pummeled by the wind in a pool of moonlight, his mouth open and his fingers in his hair, then he made his way around the back of the boathouse to assess the damage, staring in disbelief at what lay before him.

The entire back corner of the structure was obliterated, collapsed inward beneath the ton and a half of fresh cedar that had come through the ceiling. His bedroom was destroyed.

Daniel shook his head in dismay. This would take days to fix, weeks. He stepped forward, reaching out to lift a thick branch and gazing in disbelief at what was underneath. Glowing faintly with starlight, his mattress was upended between the boughs.

Daniel stared at it with his heart thudding behind his ribs.

The irony was not lost on him. Never in his life did he think he'd have something to be grateful to Gary Dunn for, but if he hadn't been startled awake by that terrible dream, he would have been fast asleep when the cedar came down.

That nightmare had saved his life.

Chapter 14

ANNIE

Y ou up there, Annie?"

The voice was Walt Proudy's, and Annie dog-eared the page of her novel before rising from the bed and crossing to the open window. Jake's father stood below in the driveway, one hand shielding his eyes from the late-morning sun.

"Hey, Walt," she called down. "What do you need?"

"Jake and I are headed up the road. Tree went down on the boat-house last night. We're gonna give Daniel a hand sawing it up. Jake's on his way here and he wanted me to ask if you'd like to come along."

Annie's heart surged in her chest as she leaned out, gripping the sill with tight fingers. "Is he okay?"

"Daniel?"

Annie nodded—her throat tight.

"He's all right. I'm sure he's shaken up, though. You know how to work a chain saw?"

She nodded again. "Of course."

"Well, come on down and we'll put you to work."

Annie's fingers fumbled through the pile of clothes at the foot of the bed. What should she wear? Pants, of course, while using a chain saw, but which shirt? She lifted two from the pile, a forest-green V-neck that complemented her hair and eyes, and a white tee from a Beastie Boys concert.

This was ridiculous. She was a twenty-eight-year-old divorcée behaving like a nervous teenager, choosing an outfit in the hope of being noticed by a crush at school. It had been five days since the moonlit boat ride on the lake, and Annie had been watching the phone ever since, telling herself she was only hoping he'd call with news of a cougar in the trap, but knowing deep down there was more to it than that.

Scolding herself sternly, Annie pulled the green shirt over her head and brushed her teeth. She jogged down the stairs and stepped outside just as Jake's cruiser pulled into the driveway. Together, they slid into the back seat of Walt's sedan, and Jake's father drove them up to the boathouse.

Annie's stomach was alive with butterflies as they rolled past the NO TRESPASSING signs, and when they pulled through the open gate, she caught sight of Daniel, carrying an armful of branches to a smoking steel drum down by the lakeshore. As Walt angled the sedan around the clearing, the damage to the boathouse came into view. The entire back corner was crushed beneath a felled cedar, and in almost comical unison, father and son whistled long and low in the car.

Walt parked the sedan and Jake jumped out first, leaving the door open behind him.

"Man alive," he called as he jogged toward Daniel. "That coulda killed you, brother."

Jake pulled Daniel into a tight embrace, but Daniel's arms stayed stiff at his sides, his eyes fixed on the sedan as Annie climbed out.

Their eyes locked as she shut the door behind her, and there it was again, that strange pull between them that set her heart thudding in her chest. Daniel looked away first, murmuring something to Jake, and Annie rounded the car to help Walt unload the tools from the trunk.

Together they carried two chain saws, a set of hedge trimmers, and a handsaw over to where Daniel and Jake stood perched on the apex of the destroyed back wall, staring down at the tree.

Daniel glanced over his shoulder as she approached, and Annie offered him a timid smile, but he quickly turned away. Behind him was the toppled cedar, resting peacefully in the midst of the havoc it had wrought.

What must it have been like, hearing it fall in the pitch black of night? The deafening crash that undoubtedly shook the whole clearing.

"Is that your *bed*?" Jake pointed into the heart of the tree where a mattress was ensnared in the boughs, sheets torn and tangled in the spindly branches.

"Yep." Daniel kicked at a splintered board near his foot. "I'm just lucky I was outside when it happened."

"Luck's one word for it." Jake hopped down onto a bowed section of the wall and crouched to stare into the branches. "What on earth were you doing out there in the middle of the night?"

"Just happened to be awake."

Jake turned to Daniel, arching an eyebrow.

"What?" Daniel asked.

"Oh, come on," Jake scoffed. "You gotta admit there was at least a little divine intervention."

Daniel heaved a frustrated sigh and shook his head, but behind Annie, Walt spoke up softly. "God works in mysterious ways, son."

Annie bit back a smile. Jake taught the boys' Sunday-school class at the church, and Walt was a deacon. Daniel was outnumbered here.

"Well"—Jake rubbed his palms together—"let's get to work."

For the better part of two hours, there was little talking as the chain saws buzzed, drowning out the chance for conversation. The going was slow as they shaved off the outer branches and carried them to the burn barrel to be consumed by the fire, but they worked steadily, and after a while the bare cedar trunk emerged.

As morning passed into afternoon, Annie stayed keenly aware of Daniel—of his movements, his proximity to her, and the rhythm of his body as he worked, but not once did he glance in her direction, and when he spoke at all, it was only to Jake or Walt.

"Let's take a breather, kids," Walt suggested as they carried the last of the boughs to the heap beside the steel drum. He took a seat on the pile of limbs and pulled a cigar from his shirt pocket. As he smoked, with Jake chatting away beside him, Annie took a long drink from her water bottle, her eyes fixed on Daniel, who was leaning against the felled trunk with the chain saw at his feet.

As though he felt her gaze, he glanced up for an instant, then looked away. Perplexed, Annie frowned and set her water bottle back on the ground.

Maybe he was waiting for her to break the ice. Well, she could do that. Though she'd promised herself things would go no further that night on the lake, there was no reason why they couldn't be friends. There was no reason for awkwardness between them.

Annie swiped a sweaty lock of hair away from her eyes and made her way toward him, but as soon as Daniel saw her coming, he stood and walked toward the lake, leaving her standing alone in the rubble behind the boathouse.

Annie blinked after him, speechless.

So, she hadn't been imagining it. He was avoiding her.

Jake walked up behind her, whistling, and came to a stop, leaning in close enough that their heads touched.

"I almost forgot," he said in a low voice, "I've got an update. Austin Smith called down from Landers. Apparently, a girl named Hannah Schroeder went missing up there. She left last Friday with her boyfriend and they came down to hike the mountain over the weekend. Her parents expected not to be able to contact her for a few days, but when she didn't make it back by Wednesday, they reported it."

Annie nodded along, but her eyes were on Daniel as he crouched beside the lake and splashed his face with water. "Did Austin give you a description of her?"

"Yeah, and it fit our Jane Doe to a T. We should have dental records back soon anyhow, but her parents are coming down in the morning to see if they can identify her."

Annie nodded. On one hand, it was sobering news, but on the other, at least it took some of the pressure off Jake's shoulders. "I guess that's good, right?"

"It is." Jake nodded. "If her parents give a positive ID, then the investigation moves up to Landers for the time being. Her boyfriend lives up there and he's the obvious place to start, but of course it's bad news for her parents. I can't even imagine what they must be feeling right now."

Annie nodded. It was a terrible, unthinkable brand of grief, and her mind wouldn't go there.

"I'm guessing you still want to keep it quiet for now?"

Jake shrugged. "I don't see any reason the rest of the town has to know, unless the boyfriend's ruled out and we have to start considering other suspects."

Jake turned, his gaze settling on Daniel for a few moments, and Annie turned, too, watching as Daniel shook sparkling droplets of water from his hair. As he swiveled away from the lake, he caught her eye and glanced between her and Jake.

"We better get back to work," she said, stooping low to gather an armful of the loose branches scattered across the ground.

She carried the limbs to the burn barrel and threw them in, watching as the hungry flames inside hissed around the damp boughs, sending up billowing plumes of smoke.

Behind her, Daniel had joined Jake, and they were discussing how to reframe the back corner of the boathouse and hang the drywall.

"Shouldn't take more than a week or two, but let's get the trunk sawed into rounds. You can chop them up later for firewood," Jake said.

"All right, but let's save a fifteen-foot section out of the middle. I'm gonna make a canoe."

Jake laughed. "A canoe? Why?"

"Why not?"

Annie turned to find Jake giving Daniel a three-fingered salute. "You got it, Boy Scout."

They all took turns with the chain saws, slicing the trunk into short sections that they rolled one at a time around the side of the boathouse. It was grueling work as the sun climbed higher, and the back of Annie's shirt was completely soaked through with sweat by the time she set down the chain saw to give her screaming forearms a break.

Again, as though pulled by some force, her attention was drawn to Daniel, and she found him frozen, staring at something across the clearing.

Annie followed his gaze, and her mouth dropped open. A young woman was jogging through the open gate as if she owned the place, as if the NO TRESPASSING signs were welcome mats and it was the most natural thing in the world. She wore a lime-green tank top and black shorts, and Annie blinked at her in astonishment. It was Jamie Boyd, from down the road.

Annie turned back to Daniel, confused. He was no longer looking at Jamie, but was rolling a section of the trunk toward the pile like it was the most urgent task in the world.

"Hey, neighbors," Jamie called as she jogged past, waving at Walt and Jake, who gave her identical head bobs from where they sat taking another smoke break. She ran straight toward Daniel, ponytail bouncing, and Annie wasn't close enough to hear what was said, but Jamie rested her hand on his arm for a moment and leaned in close to whisper in his ear. Daniel gave a quick nod and she bounded toward the lake, wriggling out of her shorts and shirt on the bank, revealing the orange one-piece swimsuit underneath.

Annie watched in mute disbelief as Jamie climbed up onto the dock and stepped to the edge, pulling her ponytail free from the scrunchie that held it and executing a perfect dive into the water, slicing the surface with barely a splash.

As her body arced in the air, the sun caught her loose hair for a split second, lighting it up like spun gold. Annie stared. It was the honey-blond hair of the passenger she'd seen riding in the Ranger.

It said so much, that ten-second interaction she'd just witnessed. Why else would Daniel let a woman have free rein of his land and lake? They must be together.

Jaw clenched, Annie turned back to the chain saw and yanked the motor to life.

Jamie was a stranger to her. And for that matter, Daniel was, too. The emotion in her chest was unwarranted, but she couldn't deny what she felt.

Betrayal. Hot, nauseating betrayal.

She could kick herself for being so naïve. Here she was trying to catch Daniel's eye all day when he was obviously with someone else. Someone a few years younger and a whole lot prettier. That strange pull she'd felt between them in the boat had been imaginary— a product of her lonely, aching heart, no doubt. It was pathetic to admit it, but she had wanted to look into a man's eyes and see desire there, and so, she had invented it. It was as simple as that.

"Well, well, well, Mr. Barela," Jake joked as Daniel returned for another round of the cedar trunk. "You got something you want to share with the class?"

Annie drove the humming chain saw hard into the trunk, drowning out Daniel's reply in the spitting of bark and dust.

Chapter 15

ANNIE

The mortuary was windowless, the wooden bench outside the door unadorned and perfunctory as it held Annie and Jake with their elbows on their knees, shoulders rounded in identical slumps.

The dead woman's parents had arrived thirty minutes before and quickly identified the body on the table as their daughter, Hannah Schroeder. Mrs. Schroeder had burst into noisy tears as she stepped out through the suctioned door of the morgue, burying her face into her husband's shoulder as his own went ashen. He seemed to Annie to be on the verge of fainting, and her instinct had been to look around wildly, wondering if there were smelling salts in any of the drawers, but Jake had jumped forward without hesitation, offering his own arms and shoulders for support as he guided the grieving parents to a set of chairs and took a knee before them, leading them in a prayer for peace.

Scolding herself, Annie had offered them paper cups filled with cold water from the cooler in the corner, and when they left with their arms tight around each other's waist, Jake used the phone in the office to notify the Landers police department. Sheriff Smith informed him that he and his deputies were already tracking down Hannah's boyfriend and would have more news soon, which left Jake and Annie free to resume business as usual. Neither felt like returning to the station right away, and they had been sitting outside in subdued silence ever since.

"You did good," Annie said, straightening her back and reaching out to rest a hand on Jake's shoulder. "What you did in there, for the Schroeders, it was good of you."

Jake nodded his bowed head. "Mom always says it's not the burden that breaks you, but whether or not you have someone to help you carry it. I sure do hope they find the guy and get some sort of confession out of him. Until then, those poor people are just going to be grieving over something senseless without answers."

"Hey there, Jake."

A tall man with silver at the temples of his dark face stepped up onto the curb, and Jake stood to shake his hand.

"Hey, Phil."

Phil leaned around Jake as though peering through a nonexistent window into the building. "Is the autopsy happening right now?"

Jake's mouth popped open, and he dropped Phil's hand like it was white-hot. "What are you talking about?"

"You know, that poor girl up on Lewis Ridge. Becca told me about it this morning at the Sky High."

"*Becca?*" Jake sputtered. "But . . . but I never said a word—"

"Course not," Phil said jovially. "Becca's niece is the same age as Layla Gannon, and Layla had a birthday party yesterday. The story made the rounds like chicken pox, and them kids carried it home to their parents. Was it true her head was twisted around backwards when you found her?"

"No!" Jake threw his hands in the air. "No, her head was not backwards, now get on out of here!" He pointed a stiff arm down the street, and Phil shrugged before ambling on.

A heavy sigh passed Jake's lips as he shook his head at the ground.

"I better go," he said. "If I don't start damage control, this thing's gonna get away from me. Now that the story's out, I might as well give them the plain facts."

Annie stood. "You want help?"

Jake smiled at her, but it was a sadder cousin of the happy gap-toothed grin she'd grown accustomed to.

"Honestly, Annie, you've been an angel. You've gone above and beyond to help me out with all of this, and if anyone deserves a day off, it's you. Go explore, or go on a drive or a hike or something. I'll see you at the station tomorrow, okay?"

She nodded gratefully and Jake gave her a half-hearted salute before turning on his heel and jogging down the sidewalk after Phil. Annie watched until he rounded the corner, then took a deep breath and looked around at the storefronts lining the street.

She hadn't spent much time exploring the shops of downtown yet, and it was the perfect day for it, warm and pleasant, with downy clouds ringing the summit of the mountain like a cotton halo, inviting her to put the morning's troubles behind her for a few hours.

First, she treated herself to a vanilla-bean latte and a marionberry-jam doughnut at Bigfoot's, then she spent the next two hours wandering up and down the row of shops lining the main strip of town. She bought a wind chime with a delicate glass hummingbird perched atop the hollow silver pipes, and a small pencil sketch of the mountain, hanging for sale in a store window with a label that boasted LOCAL ARTIST! She played a round of minigolf by herself on the wooded course behind the Lake Lumin Zoomin' Go-Kart Track and bought a black-cherry ice cream, throwing bits of the waffle cone to a pair of finches nosing around beneath the outdoor tables.

On her way back to the Jeep, she decided to make one last stop, ducking into the General Store for a bag of brown sugar. Laura liked to sprinkle it over their morning oatmeal and the bag was almost empty.

As she walked through the aisles of the store scanning the wares, Annie realized with a jolt of surprise that she was happy. Or, at least she wasn't miserable anymore, and that was as close to actual happiness as she'd been in a long time. After what had happened with Brendan, she'd gotten used to moving through the world with a sort of numbness. Things that should have made her glad utterly failed to do so, as though she were standing outside in the sun, knowing that she should be able to feel the warmth of it on her skin, but was followed around by a personal cloud that kept her shadowed—a cloud that had dissipated now, without her realizing that it was gone.

Food tasted good again. There was real, honest joy in a marionberry doughnut, a lucky hole in one through the snapping mouth of a plastic alligator, and the sight of a finch with a bite of waffle cone in its beak. A scab had formed over the wound and there was, once again, pleasure in being alive.

Annie found the sugar and carried a bag up to the front of the store, stepping around three men gathered at the magazine rack. At the counter, she exchanged a few words with Phil, who recognized her from outside the mortuary and pressed her for details about the body and the crime, all of which Annie deflected, echoing Jake's words and reminding Phil not to spread rumors.

She left the store and walked back up Main Street with her bags slung over her arms. She felt like whistling. Like humming. Like singing out loud. She felt somehow twenty pounds lighter than she had been when she woke up. And then, three blocks from the station, her heart stuttered in her chest.

She was being followed.

She could feel someone there, trailing her at the exact same speed at which she walked, but hanging far enough back to avoid notice.

Annie picked up her pace, using the stoplight to cross to the other side of the street, and in the reflection of a storefront window, she caught sight of them. Three men, crossing the street behind her. The same three men who had been clustered around the magazine rack in the General Store.

It could be a coincidence. It was entirely possible that they just happened to leave the store moments after she did and had intended to go this way all along, but when she picked up her pace again, moving at a brisk clip up the sidewalk, so did they.

Annie forced a deep breath. It was broad daylight. Other people were out on the sidewalk. Cars were driving by. Surely these men wouldn't be stupid enough to try anything out here in the open, but just as she was about to take the turn onto Hughes Street, one of them spoke.

"So," came the tinny male voice behind her, "you're the new officer in town, are you?"

Annie stopped walking and turned to find a thin man in his mid-thirties, flanked on both sides by younger men, each boasting tattoos on their necks, arms, and shoulders.

Heart thudding, she lifted her chin a fraction of an inch.

"That's me." She set the bags at her feet and stepped forward with her hand outstretched. "I'm Annie Heston, the new game warden."

"Ian Ward." He dropped his eyes briefly, distastefully, to her extended hand.

Annie lowered her arm back to her side. So, this was the infamous Ian Ward she'd been warned about, son of the Lake Lumin Wards, the only multimillionaires in the county, with their racehorse dynasty and sprawling stables south of town. He didn't look like much, certainly not the heir of millionaires, this sour-faced string bean of a man with a receding hairline and the fading tattoo of what must be his family crest visible over the collar of his shirt.

"Well"—he cast a glance over each shoulder at his companions— "I'm sure we'll all sleep a lot better at night knowing that even though there's a murderer on the loose, we've got the protection of Anne of Green Gables on our side."

His friends snickered, and a strange sound escaped Annie's lips, a bark caught somewhere between a scoffing laugh and a snort of disbelief.

"Excuse me?" she managed. The barb had broken the skin, a reference to the fiery red-haired heroine for which her mother had named her.

"No offense," Ian said, lifting his hands in an exaggerated gesture. "I'm just saying, pretty strange coincidence that we trade out one of our male officers for a female, and, lo and behold, we get our first murder in town."

Annie was so befuddled by the man's sense of logic that she simply stared at him in open-mouthed disbelief.

"You can't be serious," she said when she found her voice again.

Ian lifted his upper lip in what Annie supposed was meant to be a smile. "It's a pretty strange coincidence, is all I said."

Annie felt the indignation rising in her chest as his friends laughed again. *No. Tamp it down. That's just what he wants, to see you lose your temper so he can call you hysterical.*

She forced a smile. "Maybe it was more providence than coincidence. I'm not sure how many men could have hiked sideways across Lewis Ridge to reach the crime scene. You know, us *women* with our lower center of gravity and better sense of balance."

Ian laughed, throwing his head back to reveal molars studded with dark fillings. "Oh sure, better sense of balance. I'm sure you could take down a whole roomful of murderers with that. Ain't that just what this town needs, boys? A well-balanced lady cop?"

The last two words were sneered. An insult. A slur, and Annie squared her shoulders automatically. Her anger was just below the surface now, red and simmering, but she forced herself to keep eye contact.

"Ah, that's right"—she nodded—"you'd have done a better job than me if your daddy had been able to buy your way into the uniform."

Surprise flickered across Ian's features. He hadn't banked on her knowing this embarrassing bit of information about him, and with satisfaction, Annie watched the scarlet flush that rose on his cheeks. His friends went silent, their faces unsure, and Annie knew this was her moment to bow out, before they had a chance to react.

"Have a nice day, gentlemen," she said icily, grabbed her bags, and turned to walk away.

Ian and his friends immediately stepped around her, blocking her path forward, and Annie's stomach tightened like a clenched fist.

She could feel it coming, the pressure rising like mercury in a thermometer. Men like Ian Ward did not enjoy being put in their place and never surrendered the last word without a fight.

She could step off the curb and walk around them. There were no cars coming, but escape from the situation was secondary to what really needed to happen. Bullies didn't back down until they were stood up to.

"I said, let me by."

Ian leaned forward, and Annie felt his breath on her face. "You know . . . I don't think I will."

An unpleasant chill raced along her spine as she set the bags down again. There was a can of bear spray in her belt. With deliberate slowness, she slid it out and lifted it into view. Her Ruger was in the Jeep, but the small red canister was usually an equally effective deterrent.

"I said, let me by."

Ian stared at the spray, jaw clenched. "Rethink that move, Annie."

The world around her screeched to a halt, and Annie watched in what felt like slow motion as Ian reached a hand around his back, grasping for something in the waistband of his jeans.

A gun. It had to be a gun.

On instinct, Annie mashed her finger down on the trigger of the pepper spray, but nothing happened. She hadn't used it in months. It was clogged, or broken, or empty. She had nothing with which to defend herself, and she could see it now, the black grip of the firearm as Ian pulled it from behind his back.

A fraction of a second passed, and then, moving so fast she barely saw him coming, a man sprinted across the street.

Daniel Barela was a blur in her periphery, spry arms and legs and the quick flash of a white shirt as he barreled toward Ian. Lunging with impossible speed, he ducked at the last second and slammed his shoulder into Ian's chest with the force of a linebacker.

Ian went airborne with a shout and the gun he had pulled free flew up into the sky as he was knocked sideways. It skittered across the sidewalk, and both of his friends made a move for it, but Annie was faster and snatched it up. She flicked off the safety, held it high overhead, and fired a warning shot that made both men jerk backward.

"That's enough!" she shouted at Ian and Daniel, who were wrestling on the sidewalk. They kicked their way apart, each man rising slowly to his feet.

"Gimme back my gun." Ian glowered, breath ragged. His shirt was torn at the collar and his hair was a mess.

Annie didn't move. "No."

"Give it back!"

"I'm confiscating it." Beneath her uniform, her legs trembled with adrenaline, but her voice was steady.

Ian started to stutter a response but Annie cut him off.

"Look, I may not be a police officer, but I have the same power, privileges, and immunities that they do, including the power of arrest." She held Ian's seething gaze as she tucked his gun into her own empty holster. "And let me make one thing perfectly clear. If you ever, *ever*, threaten me like that again, I *will* exercise that authority. Do you understand?"

Ian's friends looked anywhere but at their leader as he finally dropped his head and nodded. She had broken him.

"Good," Annie said. "Then we're done here."

She shot a glance at Daniel. He was standing back, his features a perfect mask of indifference, though his chest heaved with breath and his lower lip was bleeding. When she caught his eye, he turned abruptly and crossed the street, walking back the way he'd come.

Annie grabbed her bags again, stepped past Ian and his friends with one more stone-faced glare and walked quickly around the corner.

The moment she was out of sight, she broke into a run for the Jeep.

Chapter 16

ANNIE

Annie roared up the hill to the boathouse, foot hard on the gas, tires spinning over the gravel. She was mad as a hornet—fingers white on the wheel—and the more she thought about it, the angrier she felt.

She'd gone straight home to cool down, but instead had paced back and forth in her room like a caged animal. How dare Ian Ward pull a gun on her in the middle of town. How dare he make those demeaning comments to someone in a position of authority. How dare his friends block her way when she tried to leave.

She paced for half an hour before deciding at last to pour some of her wrath out on Daniel. He was a civilian. A *civilian* who had thrown himself into the line of fire. And, yes, he had quite possibly saved her life back there, but he'd put himself in grave danger, then inexplicably walked away, like a brooding teenager. None of it made sense, and she was tired of leaving every interaction with him with more questions than answers. It was time for Daniel to talk.

At the end of the road, she was not surprised to find the gate closed, and she put the Jeep into park and jumped out, scrambling over the top and hopping down on the other side.

A fire was roaring in a circle of stones near the lakeshore. Beside it, Daniel stood over the long section of cedar trunk that he'd set aside, his bare torso gleaming with sweat and firelight as he lifted a hatchet high and brought it down over and over, bits of bark and dust flying up into the sunset air and catching the light like glitter.

"Hey!" she shouted.

He didn't look up, but the hatchet paused for a noticeable beat before he went on hacking.

"Daniel!"

Still nothing.

Annie came to a stop, facing him with only the width of the trunk between them.

"Why did you do that?" she demanded.

Her words were an accusation thrown at him rather than an inquiry, and with infuriating slowness, he looked up to meet her eyes.

For a moment, Annie thought he might not answer at all, but then he spoke so quietly that she barely caught his words over the spitting of the fire.

"I had to."

It was déjà vu, the second time he'd said those three words to her, and for the second time, she had absolutely no idea what he meant.

"You did not! You *chose* to. It was your choice to put yourself in the middle of that mess. I didn't ask for your help."

Daniel gazed at her with the same expression he'd worn in the boat, as if pleading with her to understand a secret he could not voice.

"He had a *gun*, Daniel!" Annie shouted, flinging her arms out to her sides. "A gun! You could have been killed!"

Slowly, Daniel laid the hatchet down inside the charred rut he'd created in the cedar trunk and came around to stand before her, sweat gleaming on his collarbones and in the hollow of his throat.

"I wasn't, though."

Annie's gaze dropped. His lip was split where Ian had hit him, right at the corner, and it was swollen, giving his mouth a slightly lopsided appearance.

She couldn't stop the tears that brimmed over as she stared at him, at that split lip and the grazed skin on his shoulder where it had scraped the sidewalk. All at once, her anger flickered out like a snuffed candle, and she felt only guilt over the price he had paid for stopping the fight.

"You're such an idiot," she whispered, voice choked with emotion as her hand moved without her permission, her fingers stretching upward to touch the broken corner of his mouth.

Daniel flinched in pain, but did not back away, and Annie moved her hand to the back of his neck and pulled his head down toward hers. Some dam of willpower in her had broken like a log in a fire, and for this one moment in time, she did not think about Jamie or Brendan or any of the consequences of what she was about to do. Instead, she closed her eyes and pressed her lips to his.

In the silence around them, the fire crackled and a hawk called to its mate across the water, and then Daniel responded, gathering her in his arms and pulling her to his chest with the tenderness of a first breath.

Chapter 17

ANNIE

Months ago, on a cloudless Thursday morning, Annie dropped her wedding ring into a street drain without a single ounce of regret. She'd listened to it ping against the grate on its way down before she continued on her way, vowing off men with a vehemence that felt permanent. The sewer could have it, for all she believed in love at that moment, but now, here she was—impossibly—on a first date once again.

The warm glow of sunset was eating steadily away at the late afternoon light as she angled the Jeep down the Proudys' driveway and turned left toward Lake Lumin, nervously assessing her appearance in the rearview mirror.

The mascara was all right, darkening her eyes ever so slightly, but the lipstick was too much, and she quickly swiped the back of her hand across her mouth.

Better.

In the master bathroom Laura had made a fuss over Annie's appearance, fluttering around the vanity like a mother hen. She'd sorted through hand creams, sleeping pills, and a bottle of milk of magnesia in the mirrored cabinet in search of an ancient tube of rose-colored lipstick, which she dabbed on Annie's lips before applying two quick swipes of mascara. As a finishing touch, she'd fixed a pair of small opal studs into her ears.

Annie hadn't been entirely honest with Jake's mother, saying that she was meeting a friend for dinner and wanted to look nice, but to her credit, Laura hadn't pressed Annie to find out whom she was meeting, or why.

Before she left, passing through the garage on her way to her room, Walt had glanced up from his table saw and chuckled.

"All right, Miss Annie," he said, eyes twinkling, "who's the lucky fella?"

Halfway up the stairs, Annie sighed and turned back. "How'd you know it was a date?"

"Those are Laura's date-night earrings."

Annie's face flushed and Walt shook his head.

"I won't ask who you're seeing, but . . . well, I'm happy for you, Annie. It's not easy to put yourself out there again after a broken relationship. Believe it or not, I have a little bit of experience with that myself."

Annie came down the stairs. "Honestly, Walt, it feels like a mistake. Like I'm just asking to get hurt again. It's probably way too soon."

Walt tilted his head, eyes full of the warmth she'd seen in her own father's gaze so many times.

"You mind if I give you a little advice?"

Annie nodded.

"Relationships are a bit like the briars, Annie. You know, those sharp little brambles that this neck of the woods is known for. They'll cut you up good before they give up their sweetest berries, but once you've got a pot of jam simmering on the stove and see those jars on your pantry shelves, you don't think much about the pain, do you? There's sweetness in life to be had, but sometimes you gotta get through the briars first."

Annie's eyes filled with tears as he spoke. "I'm glad you found some of that sweetness, at least."

"That I have," he said softly. "And you will, too."

One of the tears spilled over, racing in a quick path to her jaw.

"Oh, now, I'm sorry." He came around the table with another shake of his head. "I didn't mean to upset you."

"No." Annie swiped at the tear that had fallen. "You didn't upset me, it's just . . . I have a feeling that's exactly what my dad would have said if he was here."

Walt smiled and, impulsively, Annie gave him a hug and a kiss on the cheek. He batted her away with a wave, but looked pleased.

"Go on up now and finish getting ready before you ruin your makeup."

Annie nodded and raced halfway up the stairs before pausing to look back, her hand on the wall.

"You won't say anything to anyone? I just don't want to make something out of this when it might end up being nothing."

"Don't you worry," he said with a solemn nod. "I do most of my talking on the inside. But be brave, Annie. The sweetest berries are worth the briars."

"Thank you."

Walt nodded again, then went back to his work without another word.

At the top of Lake Lumin Road, Annie pulled the Jeep through the open gate.

The sunset was on full display over the western woods, the undersides of the low clouds blushing pink, silhouetting Daniel where he stood beside the painted lake, stoking the fire with a log in each hand.

Annie took a deep breath and stepped out of the car.

"Hey," Daniel called, watching her over the fire with a half smile on his lips.

"Hey."

As she neared the blaze, Annie caught the scent of roasting fish. A trout was suspended on a grill over the flames, sizzling in the heat, and the aroma made her mouth water.

"Wow," she breathed. "Smells good."

Daniel lifted half a lemon from a plate beside the fire and squeezed it over the fish, sending up a cloud of citrus steam.

"I grow parsley and dill in a little bed on the far side of the boathouse." He adjusted the fish on the grill with a metal spatula. "And there're wild onions in the woods. My favorite way to grill fish from the lake is brushing it with butter and fresh herbs, then dousing it with lemon when it's almost done. This place will feed you if you let it. You want a drink?"

"Sure." Annie dropped into one of the two Adirondack chairs that sat facing each other across the fire.

A spouted jar half full of amber liquid stood at his feet, and Daniel filled a glass and handed it to her.

"Homemade whiskey?" Annie joked, twisting the glass in her fingers with an eyebrow raised.

Daniel laughed. "Raspberry sun tea. My mom used to make it when I was a kid. You brew it outside all day in the warmth of the sun."

Annie took a sip. It was sweet and complex, tangy with the lemon slices floating in the jar and fragrant with the scent of fresh raspberries. Lifting the glass for a second drink, she watched Daniel take a knee beside the fire. He looked different. He wore the same torn jeans and fraying shirt, but there was an openness that had never been there before. He was smiling freely as he prodded the fish, eyes glowing with the embers. Their kiss yesterday had pulled back the curtain that he'd kept closed between them, and Annie had a feeling that this might be her first chance to get to know the real Daniel.

She nodded toward the fish that he was lifting onto a platter with two knives. "So, you can cook, too. I'll just add that to the long list of surprising things about you."

Daniel said nothing, still smiling as he topped her plate with a fresh slice of lemon.

"Snares still empty?"

"Yeah. Checked this morning."

"Thanks." Annie took another sip from her glass.

Daniel took his seat across the fire. "How's the case coming?"

Annie set her plate on the arm of the chair to cool. How strange it was to be up here alone with him, testing the waters with small talk about cooking, and the cougar traps, and work, when she was sure his mind was replaying the exact same moment hers was, their incredible kiss of the night before.

"Lake Lumin gossip reaches you way up here?" she asked with a laugh.

Daniel blew at the steam and took a bite. "It's all they're talking about down in town. Have they arrested anyone yet?"

"I don't think so. It's out of our hands for the time being, but I'm sure the sheriff up in Landers will let us know if they do." Annie took her first bite and closed her eyes, savoring the taste of fresh fish laced with bright herbs and warm butter.

Daniel cleared his throat. "Is anyone . . . has anyone said anything about me?"

Annie opened her eyes again. "What do you mean?"

His answering shrug was a bit too nonchalant. "I mean, this is the closest property to Lewis Ridge. I was just hoping no one had jumped to any conclusions or anything."

His face was still casual, but his body was tense as he waited for her reply.

Annie shook her head quickly. "Of course not. At least, not that I've heard. The sheriff up there thinks the boyfriend is hiding out somewhere, which all but spells out his guilt. My guess is everything'll be wrapped up in a bow by the end of the week, and the town gossips will move on to the next thing."

Across the fire, Daniel's chest sagged in relief, and he took another bite.

They ate the rest of their meal in companionable silence and set their empty plates on the ground when they were finished. Daniel topped off their glasses with more tea, then sat back in his chair, gazing intently at Annie across the fire.

Annie met his eyes as the logs crackled between them. "Tell me something about you. Anything."

Daniel's chest rose and fell. "You first."

Annie leaned back in her chair and thought for a minute.

"I'm afraid of horses. I got thrown when I was seven and broke my collarbone. I haven't been on one since." She paused. "More?" Daniel nodded. "My favorite color is green, and when I was in fifth grade, I shoplifted a pair of earrings and felt so guilty about it that I went down to the police station and turned myself in."

Daniel's mouth quirked upward. "Six to eight months?"

Annie retruned his smile. "A pat on the back and a Tootsie Roll from the sheriff."

Between them, a log snapped and sent up a fountain of sparks.

When they settled, Daniel said quietly, "Okay, now tell me something about you that nobody knows."

Annie opened her mouth, then closed it again as she stared into the flames.

"I hate my freckles."

Daniel's brows drew together. "Why?"

Annie waved a hand at her face. "You don't see women with freckles like these on the covers of magazines. They're from my mom's side of the family, and when I was little, I used to wish Dad had married some other lady with better skin."

The words tasted sour, spoken out loud, selfish and ungrateful, considering the age at which she'd lost her mom. Guiltily, Annie brought her gaze back to Daniel. He was smiling softly at her.

"Your face is a combination of two people who loved each other. And two people before them, and two people before them for thousands of years. If that doesn't make you feel beautiful, I don't know what will."

Emotion welled in her chest at his words and Annie looked away, toward the last of the purple light rimming the western horizon.

"Someday, I hope you have a little girl of your own with every bit of your freckles. Then you might see what I see when I look at you."

Annie couldn't breathe with him staring at her like that, saying those words that sank right through her skin to that broken place in her heart.

She shook her head and smiled. "Enough about me. It's your turn, tell me something about you that no one knows."

Daniel's smile faded and his gaze dropped into the fire. For a full minute, he stared at the flames without speaking.

"I don't think I can," he said finally.

The last of the light had left the sky, and the lake was murmuring in the darkness outside the circle of firelight.

Annie said Daniel's name, and he looked up, eyes wary.

"I want to know you. I have to know who you are if we have any shot at turning this into something."

There was pain in his eyes now, and they faltered again, staring down at the ground between his feet.

"I can't."

Annie waited. And waited. When Daniel looked up at last, his features were heavy with the weight of some decision, some inward wrestling match.

"Please," she said quietly.

Another minute passed, the air between them growing taut with his silence, and then he spoke at last.

"My name isn't Daniel."

The evening had been a sonnet, a slow and lilting melody, and with those four words, the first wrong note had been played, jarring and flat and tainting everything that had come before it.

Annie stopped breathing. "What do you mean?"

He wasn't looking at her, and Annie could feel the curtain falling between them again, swift and sudden, breaking the magic that had held her spellbound. Her throat tightened, heart rabbiting in her chest. She had come all the way up here to be with this man. Alone. And the plain fact was that she had no idea who he was.

"What do you mean?" she said again, a little more forcefully as she stared at him in the flickering light.

His throat bobbed before he answered. "I mean Daniel Barela isn't my real name. I changed it. I . . . took it. From someone else."

He looked up at her then, eyes glowing in the firelight, and Annie suddenly knew what it was to be an animal, lured into a trap by something enticing, only to discover the metal teeth a moment too late. Every ounce of her common sense had warned her to stay away from this man, with his silence, and his secrets, and his NO TRESPASSING signs, and yet here she was, at the moment of no return.

Make sure someone knows where you are, Annie girl. Always.

It was the very first rule her father had taught her about the wild, and right now, no one did. No one knew she was up here in the middle of absolutely nowhere with a man who was about to confess his darkest secret. No one but him.

She was certain he could see her collarbones rising and falling far too quickly as she stared at him, fear tainting the dark edges of the clearing that had just a moment ago seemed so peaceful.

"Why would you do that?" Her voice was deadly calm, the voice she used when approaching a frightened or wounded animal.

Daniel opened his mouth, closed it again, and cleared his throat.

"I had to."

She wanted to scream. It was the third time he'd used those words, but now they sounded sinister and utterly wrong.

Her first instinct was to bolt for the trees as fast as her legs could carry her, but she had no doubt in her mind that he'd be faster. She'd seen him sprint across a street like an Olympian, and he knew this clearing and these woods far better than she did. There was no way out.

"I want you to tell me who you are," she said, failing to keep her voice steady. "If your name isn't Daniel, what is it?"

She could keep him talking, keep him engaged while her mind whirled, grabbing at all the factors in play: the distance between her and the Jeep, the closest neighbor, who was too far down the hill to hear her scream, the two sharp kitchen knives resting on the circle of stones between them, and the heavy truth that whatever this man was hiding from her, it was bad enough to drive him up here all alone in the first place.

"It's Nico," he said quietly. The word sounded rusty with disuse.

He was watching her now with a curious mixture of apprehension and defeat, but whatever connection he thought she'd make at the sound of that name, it wasn't clicking into place. Nico. Nico who?

Annie didn't answer, offering him more silence, an opportunity to tell her everything, to be honest. When at last he spoke again, each word was heavy.

"I'm Nico Dunn, Annie."

His confession was met with more silence, but the fuse had been lit, and five seconds later, the bomb detonated. Annie's eyes widened in the firelight. She had the distinct feeling that the clearing was caving in around her. This was the horrible, sinking terror of tracking a cougar way up into the hills and suddenly whirling around to find the powerful predator standing in the middle of the trail, tracking her instead.

She had been exactly right when she thought she recognized him. She *had* seen him before. His face had been infamous, tied forever to the cold case that ripped through the Northwest all those years before. The sixteen-year-old Boy Scout from Redmond, Oregon, who had disappeared from his troop during a hike around Mount St. Helens; just vanished in the middle of the night from a circle of sleeping bags around a campfire. At first, search and rescue had assumed that he'd run away, but later, on a trail leading north, a torn piece of his clothing was found with blood on it, and then a shoe, and suspicion about an animal attack took over the headlines. But the thing that everyone remembered about the case, the thing that made Nico Dunn a household name, was the shocking turn of events after the bloodied clothing was found.

Gary Dunn, the boy's stepfather, had come forward and called a press conference, telling reporters that his stepson had made an attempt on his life and was running from the consequences, with a plea for Nico to come home and receive forgiveness. After that, the words ATTEMPTED MURDER were slapped beneath that famous school photo, becoming more a part of the boy's identity than the name Nico Dunn itself.

Wild theories abounded. Amateur sleuths became obsessed with the case, the young, wide-eyed, innocent-looking boy in the photo, the baby-faced felon who had escaped and brilliantly faked his own death, some assumed, to live life as a criminal off the grid. Fear spread, and the manhunt was massive, combing miles north of Mount St. Helens, the way they'd assumed he'd gone by the trail of breadcrumbs left behind.

Months had gone by. The leads dried up, and the news stations moved on to the next big thing, most people assuming that Nico had indeed met some grisly end out there in the remote wilderness. Eventually, his name faded into oblivion, but all this time . . .

"Are you really him?"

Another log popped in the fire, sending up a flurry of red sparks that lit Daniel's eyes for a moment as he nodded.

Annie had a decision to make. Right now.

On the one hand, there was what she *should* do, the thing she'd scream at any woman in this situation to do. *Run for your life. Do whatever it takes to get as far away from this man as you possibly can.*

Daniel was watching her, his expression unreadable.

Annie did not run. She did not scream. Instead, she leaned forward in her chair and met his eyes with every scrap of courage she could muster.

"Tell me everything."

Chapter 18

NICO

Nico trailed the group, lagging a few meters behind the rest as they hiked along the single-track trail toward the sound of rushing water. His pack was sitting uncomfortably on his narrow hips, and it was much heavier than the packs carried by the other boys.

Nico's was stuffed with as many freeze-dried meals, granola bars, and packets of oatmeal as would fit inside, plus first-aid supplies and tools far beyond what the troop's weeklong outing called for. There were also his drawing pad and the new set of charcoal pencils his mother had given him for his last birthday, and the most precious thing of all, hidden deep in a zippered pocket. A wad of bills bound by a rubber band. Every last dollar he'd scrounged for during the past year. Dozens of lawns mowed, dogs walked, and even babies sat. He'd busted his butt for that few hundred dollars, which would have to last him for as long as he could possibly stretch it.

Nico yanked on the straps of his pack to adjust the weight on his hips. He'd just have to get used to being uncomfortable. A lot more hiking was ahead of him in the days to come, but at least he'd be alone and could move at his own pace. Keeping up with the group had been a struggle for the last two days, but now even more so as the trail tilted upward toward the falls.

The sound of rushing water was growing louder by the second, and Nico strained to see over the heads in front of him. There, to the right of their troop leader, Mr. Sorenson, he spotted a metal sign.

RUBICON FALLS .2 MILES.

For the third time in five minutes, Nico glanced at his watch: 11:08.

They were early. Much, much too early.

He swore under his breath and quickly fished the itinerary out of his back pocket, opening it again as he hiked.

12pm. Lunch at Rubicon Falls

They were almost an hour ahead of schedule. Mr. Sorenson might decide to have the boys put in another few miles of hiking before they stopped to eat. They might pass right by the falls without breaking stride, and then this whole thing would be blown. They had to stop for lunch here. They just *had* to.

Around the next bend in the trail, the falls came into view: a snow-white wall of water tumbling over a slick dark lip of rock, churning up mist in the pewter pool below.

The troop crossed over a wooden bridge, boots echoing hollowly across the old boards, and Nico's hands balled into tight fists, fingernails digging into his palms.

Please . . . he willed Mr. Sorenson as the troop leader stepped off the other side of the bridge. *Please!*

A single, mossy picnic table sat below the trail in the mist off the falls, and Mr. Sorenson turned toward it.

Nico let out a breath of relief and unsnapped the front buckle of his pack.

"All right, men," Mr. Sorenson called, setting his pack on the ground and turning to face the gathered troop. "You have thirty minutes. Eat and filter water here, too. Make sure you're full up before we get going, we're not stopping again until we reach camp."

There was a gentle murmur of conversation as the boys pulled the packs off their shoulders and rummaged in them for lunch. Nico carried his pack to a shady spot beneath a feathery hemlock and dropped it there.

Glancing around to make sure no one was looking, he pulled out the single sneaker waiting in the top pocket and wedged it into the waistband of his pants, hiding it under his shirt. Then, he lifted the orange plastic trowel from the side pouch.

His heart was racing as he made his way through the boys to Mr. Sorenson.

"Watch it, loser," Bradley grumbled, catching Nico's shoulder as he passed. He stumbled, but kept moving forward and did not take the bait. He had no time to engage with Bradley or any of his basketball buddies, whose second favorite sport was pushing Nico around.

"Mr. Sorenson?"

The troop leader turned, both hands buried in his pack as he stared through his rectangular glasses at Nico.

"What is it, Nico?"

Nico's fingernails dug into his palms again. It was now or never. "Can I be excused for a few minutes?"

"Why?"

Nico lifted the plastic trowel in explanation, and Mr. Sorenson looked back down into his pack.

"Bury it deep," he muttered.

Nico walked back over the wooden bridge and down the trail, risking just one quick glance over his shoulder to make sure the eleven boys and Mr. Sorenson were all occupied before rounding the curve in the path.

The second he was out of sight; he broke into an all-out sprint.

It was three-quarters of a mile back to the remote Ingleside Trail, which led in a northbound offshoot around the summit, and he needed to make it at least a few hundred feet down that trail to plant the sneaker and the torn and bloodied piece of shirt tucked in his pocket. It was a mile-and-a-half round trip, and he had no time to waste.

He'd timed himself on the track after wrestling practice the week before, the same wrestling practice where he'd faked a bloody nose and snuck into the locker room to lift Daniel Barela's driver's license from his backpack. After practice, he'd hit the track behind the baseball fields for eight timed laps and discovered that he could run two miles in twelve minutes and fifty seconds. The trail he was running now was hillier and rockier, but with half a mile less distance, it should equal out.

Twelve and a half minutes to get there and back. Long enough to maybe raise an eyebrow at his absence, but not so long that he couldn't explain it away as an unfortunate bathroom delay.

Nico's legs were burning by the time he reached the Ingleside Trail and charged up it. He ran for another lung-busting half minute, then stopped, scanning the terrain for the best place to plant the evidence. A boulder jutted out from the forest, interrupting the path, which swung wide around it. A pine grew atop the rock with the roots exposed and dangling. Perfect.

Sucking in wind, Nico wedged the stained fabric under a root and stood back to inspect it. It worked. It looked as though he had scrambled up onto the rock and it had been torn from him there. Any casual hikers passing by would miss it, but someone who was looking carefully for signs of a missing Boy Scout would not.

Pulling the sneaker from his waistband, he hauled his arm back and chucked it hard into the woods behind the boulder.

Once they noticed the scrap of fabric, they would search the area thoroughly. They would believe he had left the trail and vanished into the wall of forest, chased by an animal, or wandering off by accident, dehydrated and lost.

Nico hesitated, his eyes on the rock. Was it enough? No. It was too neat. Too contained.

He didn't have time to waste. If he wasn't back in the next seven or eight minutes, questions would be asked and this little outing would be remembered, logged in Mr. Sorenson's mind when the timeline was gone over by searchers later.

Quickly Nico slipped the switchblade from his back pocket and flicked it open. Holding it over his palm, he squeezed his eyes shut and pulled.

Sharp pain exploded across the inside of his hand and Nico cried out, closing his fist around the blood that was pooling there.

He let a few drops fall onto the trail, then led them in a wavering path up and over the boulder. He climbed up after them and plowed through the woods in the direction he'd thrown the shoe, sweeping his hand back and forth to leave blood on ferns and bushes and a sizable smear on the slender trunk of a tree.

That was it. That was all he had time for. It would have to be enough.

Nico kept his fingers pressed tight to the thin gash across his palm as he raced back, giddy with adrenaline. That should do it. That should convince whoever came looking for him that he had gone west from the overnight spot, then north on the Ingleside Trail before running into trouble there, when in reality, as soon as everyone was asleep tonight, he'd pack up and head due east, then south for miles and miles to Warner Lake. After that, it would be as simple as hiking up and over Lewis Ridge, then dropping down to the forgotten little lake he'd read about in the tattered library book detailing the history of Mount St. Helens. Lake Lumin, home to strange bioluminescent plankton that glowed blue at night, the location of a pricey restaurant that had burned down decades before, leaving only a small boathouse behind on unclaimed land that no one had laid title to in years.

That's when the plan had clicked, when he'd read about the abandoned clearing that had belonged to a family with the last name Barela. It felt like fate, a beautiful coincidence, that the only student in Nico's school with that last name was a boy a year older than he was with a vague-enough resemblance, dark hair, olive skin, and muddy hazel eyes, that Nico was almost passable as the person in the driver's license photo, if he smiled widely and tilted his head the way that Daniel had.

That license was his ticket out, and there, in that abandoned boathouse, he would start over. Once the noise about the missing Boy Scout died down, he would pick up his new life as Daniel Barela. He would be free forever from Gary Dunn.

Nico reached the wooden bridge and slowed to a walk, forcing his ragged breathing back into a slow and steady rhythm as he rounded the corner and came upon the troop, still eating lunch.

Not one of them glanced up as he returned, taking his seat beneath the hemlock and opening his pack. Carefully, he smeared a dab of antibiotic ointment over the cut on his hand and closed his fist around it again.

He wasn't hungry. He was full to the brim with triumph, and he felt at this moment that he could live for days on this victory alone. Besides, it made more sense to ration every last bite of food in his pack, to eat only what was absolutely necessary to keep him moving forward for now.

Nico slid his uninjured hand into his pack and lifted out his drawing pad and one of his pencils. So far, there was only one half-finished sketch on the first page. Grace Dunn, as he saw her last, through the smudged glass of the school bus window two days before.

Nico brought the pencil to the paper and continued shaping her hand, held in the air in a wave of farewell. He'd started the drawing on the long ride up and had somehow managed to capture the look of regret in her eyes and the sad smile that barely lifted the corners of her mouth.

He met her charcoal gaze now, like she was staring right at him through the paper.

She had believed that the goodbye was for a week, but Nico had known. He had known that he would never see her again, and his heart had broken over it as the bus rumbled to life and pulled slowly away, his mother shrinking into nothing behind a black cloud of exhaust with her hand still in the air.

Chapter 19

ANNIE

The tin pail was heaped high with crimson cherries, and though Annie held her arm steady as she walked, more than a few rolled out, bouncing down the gravel road behind her as she trekked uphill toward the lake.

She had spent the last thirty minutes picking from one of the three wild cherry trees she'd discovered in the sloping wooded acre behind the Proudys' property and had a full bucket to show for her efforts—yet another advantage this place had over Bend. This wilderness, during the late spring and summer months at least, could feed a person all day long with its wild fruits and endless variety of berries in every shade of pink and purple and red. But today's harvest was not for her own enjoyment; it was a gift for Daniel.

He had his own cherry tree behind the boathouse, of course, but he had stripped it clean already, though it was only mid-June. Annie knew he was partial to the sweet red stone fruit, but more than that, she didn't want to walk into the boathouse for the first time empty-handed.

Daniel was unfolding to her in layers. It had been six days since their first kiss, five since his confession at the lake, three since the hike along Lewis Ridge she'd chosen for their second date, and today he had invited her to set foot inside his home for the first time.

The gate was open at the top of the hill, and Annie found Daniel waiting on the dock with his hands in his pockets when she strolled into the clearing, holding the pail high.

"Got about three pies' worth of cherries for you," she called as he hopped down from the dock and came strolling toward her.

He smiled as he approached, taking the bucket with a nod of thanks, and their hands brushed, the contact sending butterfly wings beating behind Annie's ribs.

She'd forgotten what a thrill a newborn relationship was, with its novelties and its unknowns. But her father had warned her about that, too, in a conversation she'd had with him at sixteen, waiting for a boy to come and pick her up for her very first date at the movies.

Keep your heart at arm's length, Annie girl. It's much easier to fall in love with what you don't know about a person than what you do know. Don't mistake mystery for worth. Remember that, Annie girl, build trust and take it slow.

Well, Brendan had sure done a number on her ability to trust, and as Annie followed Daniel to the side door of the boathouse, she took a quick tally of her broken pieces.

She no longer felt that quick flash of anger when she thought about Brendan. She didn't stretch out her arms in the night anymore, seeking the warmth of his body, or even slide her thumb over the empty place at the base of her third finger where she used to twist her wedding ring around and around out of habit. She was moving on, but her willingness to trust someone again would probably be the last thing to fully heal, and it would certainly have to be earned. She wasn't about to make the same mistake again.

At the door, Daniel hesitated with his hand on the knob.

"Just so you know, it's not much," he said quietly. "I was basically broke when I got here, and converting it was a lot of trial and error. The floor still creaks, and there's a draft from under the dock door. I furnished it little by little with what I could find cheap over the years."

He wasn't meeting her eyes, and Annie reached out, resting her hand on his arm.

"Show me."

Daniel turned the knob and held the door open. She stepped past him into a bare hall, rounding the corner into a cozy living area, dim from the awning overhanging the lake-facing windows.

Annie stopped. It was exactly right, perfectly suited to the man who lived here.

A stack of worn books on a scuffed coffee table.

A gleaming cast-iron skillet on a hook over a two-burner stove in the galley kitchen.

Low, exposed beams that ran the length of the ceiling, hung here and there with bulbs in blown-glass fixtures—lights that, Annie guessed, Daniel had wired and installed himself.

The lake was the focus of the room, the three tall windows at the front inviting the shimmering green light dancing off the surface into the boathouse and framing the forest that lived beyond it with a generous slice of topaz sky.

Turning around, Annie was drawn to the far wall by four pencil sketches in matching frames, the only decor besides a nautical clock and an old ship's rope, hanging in a neat coil. She crossed the room, staring at the drawings in wonder.

They were of the mountain in all its moods, snowcapped and majestic in the spring, bald and stony in the summer, ringed in billowing autumn clouds, and midwinter—a heap of whipped cream behind a frosted forest. In the bottom right corner of each drawing was a familiar signature, an uppercase *D* with an illegible squiggle after it, and Annie reached up to touch one, smiling in surprise and delight. When she turned toward Daniel, eyes dancing, he was clutching the pail of cherries in both hands, watching her with the apprehension of a defendant before a judge.

"What?" he asked.

"I bought one of your sketches." She laughed. "In town. It just said 'local artist' on it, no name. I hung it above my bed. I just . . . I can't believe you drew it."

Turning, Daniel set the pail of cherries on the narrow kitchen counter and rubbed the back of his neck with a hand as a pleased smile softened his features.

"Yeah, I . . . I draw a little when I have free time. I'm glad you liked it."

"I love it." Annie left the wall and moved around the space with an arm outstretched. She ran a hand along the back of the faded couch, around the base of a smooth-driftwood lamp, and drummed her fingertips along the torn spine of one of the books.

Daniel watched her silently, his posture tense, and Annie sighed as she turned to him.

"This is the first time you've had a woman in here, isn't it?"

He nodded.

For a few beats, Annie said nothing. This was difficult for him. Brand-new. And given his history, his trust issues were probably just as bad as her own, if not worse. He had been hiding out here for the better part of a decade without anyone knowing who he truly was. Inviting someone in to poke around his private sanctuary had to be setting off every alarm bell in his head, and sympathy pooled in Annie's heart as she gazed at him, standing stiffly in the kitchen.

Just like her, he needed time to open himself fully to someone else, though she sensed that he wanted to, badly.

"Come on," Annie said, moving past him to grab the pail on the kitchen counter. "These cherries aren't gonna eat themselves."

Out on the dock, Daniel pulled the Adirondack chairs close together and Annie took her seat with a contented sigh, kicking off her shoes and placing the pail of cherries between them on the wooden arm.

"I've been meaning to ask you," she said as he sat down, "now that I know the truth, do you still want me to call you Daniel?"

Daniel lifted a cherry from the bucket and popped it into his mouth.

"Nico Dunn is dead, as far as I'm concerned." He spit the pit into the lake. "Daniel's just fine."

"How about Danny, then?" she joked. "Danny and Annie?"

He shot her a sideways eye roll.

An hour passed, stretching into another, and the sun floated slowly across the lake, shimmering and hazy. They ate the fruit in easy conversation, laughing as they tried to outdo each other in launching the pits farthest into the water.

The shadows on the western shore were growing long, stretching dark, pointed fingers into the lake when Annie lapsed into a thoughtful silence.

"What are you thinking about?" Daniel asked as she gazed out across the water.

She turned to face him. "Honestly?"

He nodded.

Annie lifted another cherry from the pail and pulled the stem free, twisting it back and forth in her fingers.

"I'm wondering how it's possible that I feel more like myself with you in less than a week than I did in five and a half years being married to Brendan."

Daniel's answer was silent, a simple gesture that said more than words ever could as he reached for her hand and took it in his own, lacing their fingers together.

Annie gently squeezed his hand in return, smiling.

She *did* feel like herself.

More than that, she felt free, and younger, and bolder than she had in a long time, and when Daniel gave her hand a little tug, she rose wordlessly from her chair and joined him in his, sliding onto his lap and cupping his face in her hands as their lips met.

Chapter 20

DANIEL

Padding barefoot and bleary-eyed to the front of the boathouse, Daniel was greeted by wide puddles on the dock and a gloomy morning in the clearing beyond. The leaves and boughs drooped with moisture and thick fog rolled across the surface of the lake.

A heavy sigh passed his lips as he walked to the kitchen to start breakfast. It was less than ideal weather for what he and Annie had planned for today, but they'd figure out a way to make it work.

After a bowl of canned hash and eggs, Daniel donned a hooded sweatshirt and stepped outside to wait, leaning against the boathouse in the shelter of the awning as cold raindrops fell at his feet.

A few minutes before nine, the rumble of the Jeep's engine rose above the patter, and Daniel stepped forward as Annie rolled into the clearing, smiling behind the sweeping windshield wipers. Instantly, his worries about the weather vanished. Annie was a trooper.

She laughed up at the sky as she stepped out of the Jeep, then ran for Daniel, who wrapped her in his arms before they made a dash for the shelter of the thick firs on the lake's western shore.

"You sure you're up for this?" he asked as they approached a tarp-covered heap on the ground, and she nodded, brushing away the drops that had gathered in her hair. Daniel slid away the tarp that covered the canoe and folded it in a sloppy square, leaving it on the ground.

"Blessing in disguise," Annie said. "If we capsize, we'll be drenched anyway, so it won't matter."

She laughed again and Daniel's heart soared with the sound; his favorite in the world. This woman was a bubble in a bottle. No matter which way life tipped her, she would always find her way to the top. To joy.

"So, it's finished?" She nodded down at the narrow boat.

"Not quite." Daniel moved behind it. "I still need to sand and seal the inside, but she's seaworthy. Or 'lakeworthy,' anyway. Should get us across to the south shore and back so we can check the traps. Come on, I'll push, you pull."

Daniel crouched behind the canoe and pressed his shoulder against the wooden bow as Annie tugged on the stern. Despite its weight, it moved with surprising agility over the slick earth and slid easily into the lake. Daniel climbed in first and helped Annie aboard, then gripped the new wooden paddle he'd purchased in town and gently shoved the canoe away from the shore and into open water.

"It's a little different than the skiff," he said, stating the obvious as they teetered side to side. The canoe was long and narrow, and round underneath. Logs were built to roll, and though he'd done a fair bit of chiseling to steady it, it would be a miracle if they made it across the lake without tipping at least once.

Slowly, Daniel paddled forward, trying to get a feel for the craft as it wavered in the water. With each slight wobble, Annie threw her arms out comically, then gripped the sides, laughing in that infectious sort of way that drew out his own rumbling chuckle.

Daniel could no longer ignore the startling suspicion that he was falling in love with this woman. She was all the adolescent crushes he'd missed out on rolled into one, and though his days and nights and thoughts and dreams were saturated with her, it never felt like enough. He was falling for her goodness, her light, her laughter, and most of all for the way she made him believe that there could be more to his life than lonely isolation.

He'd been afraid for seven years. Afraid of people in town finding out who he was. Afraid of going to prison, or worse, of having to face down his past in Redmond. But Annie made him believe he didn't have to be afraid anymore. She was the first person who made him feel safe enough to show his true self—when he told her his story, and she didn't run.

After several strokes, Daniel got the hang of the canoe and paddled swiftly, slicing through the rain-puckered water in a determined rhythm.

Yes, his fear was lessening, but it wasn't falling off in pieces. It was like a snake skin; overtight and constricting as he wriggled slowly out, toward the sweet, open air on the other side. It was happening in small steps, and he was determined to keep taking them.

Annie had gone quiet as she watched the drops dancing on the surface around them, and Daniel felt a certain stab of conviction. Yes. Steps forward. He needed to come clean to Annie about the lie he'd told her.

Daniel paddled for a few more strokes as the guilt slowly inflated inside him. It had to be done. Perhaps he should tell her now. Being out in the rain was as good a time as any to come clean.

His paddling slowed, blade dragging in the water.

"There's something I need to tell you."

The urgency in his voice brought Annie's eyes to his face in concern.

"About what?" she asked, nearly shouting over rain that was thickening now, here in the middle of the lake, turning the surface percussive around them.

Daniel swallowed with difficulty and started paddling again. "About the attempted murder part of the story. Remember that night by the fire when I said Gary lied to the press and made it all up?"

Annie nodded.

"That wasn't . . . that wasn't entirely true."

A sharp pain twisted in Daniel's chest as he watched the color drain from her face.

The rain fell hard between them, streaking her cheeks and falling in drops from her jaw unnoticed as she stared mutely.

"You better tell me what you're talking about," she said above the torrent. "I swear, Daniel, you better tell me right now."

Daniel nodded, sweeping the wet hair away from his eyes with a soaked sleeve.

"I know. I wanted to tell you before, but it's . . . it's hard to talk about."

It was worse than hard. It was like tearing open an old wound that had never fully healed and exposing it to salt air. It felt impossible.

Annie said nothing, only stared with her mouth set, her hair dark with rain and plastered to her head and shoulders.

"The night before I ran away, I was down in the basement." He hated how loud the words had to come out to be heard over the downpour. "I pulled out some of the wires in the walls and severed them, then dumped a bottle of water on the floor to make a puddle."

The memory was coming up now in one acid gush, like vomit, and even as Daniel dipped the paddle into the water, he felt himself back there in the cellar, terrified in the dark.

"The human body is a conductor. Step a bare foot into water and touch wires with enough voltage running through them, it'll kill a grown man. Fairly quickly, too."

The color was coming back to Annie's face, two pink patches rising on her wet cheeks, but she offered no comment.

"When Gary came down the stairs, he flipped on the light and caught me down there. He thought the whole setup was intended for him, but it wasn't, Annie. I swear it wasn't meant for him."

Annie remained silent, but something new was dawning in her eyes. A realization. A question that he would have to answer.

"Ask me," he said, almost shouting as the cold rain worked its way past his inner T-shirt and bit into his shoulders. "Just ask me, Annie."

She didn't hesitate. "Who was it for?"

The snake skin was splitting, but it did not hurt.

"Me."

Daniel held nothing back as he told her the rest of the story, about how, in a moment of desperation, he had given up on his plan to run away and decided on another way out. The "easy" way out, as he'd thought of it back then. A puddle of water in the basement. A handful of live wires. A bare foot.

It would be so much faster than the attempted escape that he'd been planning for months. So much easier. And it came with a one hundred percent guarantee, whereas his odds of making it to the boathouse and surviving for the rest of his life without being recognized were slim at best. He'd just end up back in the house with Gary, and then it would be worse than before.

The prospect was unbearable, and he'd weighed it all out, finally deciding that suicide was the path that made the most sense. But before he'd gone through with it, his stepfather, drunk and reeking of whiskey, had found him down there and assumed the worst.

"He came charging across the room like a bull and slipped in the water. He knocked himself out. I don't know why, but seeing him on the ground like that brought me back to my senses. So, to make sure he didn't stop me, I tied him up and left him down there. My hands were shaking so bad, I barely managed to get duct tape around his wrists and ankles and over his mouth. Then I waited until the sun came up, and I woke my mom to have her drive me to the school for the Scout trip up to St. Helens."

The truth was, he told Annie, that he'd never know for sure if he would actually have gone through with running away if he hadn't tied Gary up and known what was waiting for him at home after the trip. He came to believe later that Gary's drunken intervention was some twist of fate or providence, some kink in the fabric of his destiny that meant he was supposed to go.

He'd never stopped believing that—even during that first year in the boathouse when he was starving and scrounging and hiding away while his story faded slowly out of the public eye. He had struggled, but at least he was free. And eventually, when enough time had passed and he worked up the courage, he went down to the county clerk's office with his face half hidden under the brim of a hat pulled low, Daniel Barela's driver's license in hand, and enough cash to pay the fee to file a claim on the clearing. The clerk had barely batted an eye, and Daniel was shocked when a letter arrived in the boathouse's battered mailbox telling him the claim had been accepted.

After that, he'd bought as many NO TRESPASSING signs as he could afford and posted them in every direction, and when he ran out of money a few weeks later, he'd started taking odd jobs around town as a freelance electrician and handyman. He was young, but he did good work, and folks in town began recommending him.

He was still bitter thinking about it, but work was the one thing he owed his stepfather for. Gary was a contractor. He'd built the Redmond house from the ground up, and Daniel, fascinated by the process, had paid attention as his stepfather wired the electricity.

And then, a stroke of good fortune when a client noticed his drawing pad and offered to buy the first charcoal sketch he'd done of the mountain. That had opened up another small source of income, and over time his meager savings grew.

Somewhere in the middle of the story, they had reached the southern shore, and the canoe sat half beached, Annie resting over solid ground and Daniel still in the water as the rain lightened.

"Why haven't you gone back?" Annie asked, completely soaked where she sat. "Now that you're an adult, and he can't hurt you anymore, you could at least let your mother know that you're still alive. Don't you think she deserves that?"

Daniel shook his head, droplets flying. "All of Redmond saw that press conference. Not just saw it, they believed it. Gary's a hero in that town, a special ops veteran, and they all think I tried to kill him. He knows how to fool people, Annie . . . how to win them to his side. He's one way in private, but around other people he knows how to keep a lid on it. He's really good at hiding who he is, and he's not the forgive-and-forget type. Going back now could land me in prison. Honestly, these last seven years, it feels like I've just been waiting with my breath held for him to track me down. To somehow find me and take revenge for what he thinks I did to him." Daniel shook his head again. "And then there's all the other laws I broke. I committed fraud and ran away from a federal manhunt. And besides that, what would I be going back to? It's not like he's holding my mom hostage. I miss her every day, but she chose him, and she chose to stay with him even after he turned violent against me."

Annie nodded, slowly.

Overhead, a single sunbeam pierced the clouds, bathing the tips of the nearest pines in filmy light.

"Say something," Daniel prompted when Annie made no move to speak or leave the canoe.

For another half minute, she gazed at him, her jaw working back and forth in the damp quiet, and then she spoke at last, in a voice he hoped he'd never hear again.

"It breaks my heart that you went through all of that, and I can't imagine everything it took just to survive . . . but you lie to me again, and this is over."

Chapter 21

DANIEL

The second day of summer broke misty and mild, and Daniel stepped out onto the dock with a mug of strong black coffee in his hands.

Closing his eyes, he pulled in a deep breath of cool air scented with pine and lake water, then took a quick glance at his watch, and another at the empty road beyond the open gate.

Jake was late, and he was never late.

He'd called the night before and confirmed eight thirty on the nose, he'd be there, ready to fish. Something important must have come up.

Daniel loaded the tackle box and the rods into the skiff, where they'd be ready to go, then took a seat on the dock to work on a half-finished sketch of Annie while he waited.

At eight fifty, the police cruiser came bouncing into the clearing, headlights glowing through the fog, and Daniel rose to his feet. Jake pulled right up to the boathouse and climbed out, leaving the engine running as he shut the door hard behind him.

Daniel tensed. Something was wrong.

"You all right?" he called as Jake approached the dock.

"You know that girl Ben found dead on the ridge last month?"

Daniel nodded.

"Sheriff Smith's boys finally found her boyfriend's rig this morning, in the woods east of Warner Lake. He didn't leave the state like they thought. He's hiding out around here somewhere. Justin Grimes. He's a hunter, knows how to navigate in the wild, and could have headed south. Tall guy, shaved head. You see anyone like that back in the woods?"

Daniel shook his head. "No. But I've only been back there to check Annie's traps off the south shore. No one's come sniffing around here as far as I know."

Jake nodded. "Well, keep your eyes open. They found some pretty incriminating stuff in the back of his Bronco. Zip ties, duct tape, a needle filled with something they're sending to a lab. They're thinking Hannah might just have been his first target when he snapped. There could be others."

Jake's face was paler than Daniel had ever seen it, his eyes darting around the misty clearing as though Justin Grimes might step out of the fog at any moment.

"Are you in charge of the search?"

"No." Jake shook his head. "This is the big leagues. Given the stuff they found in his car, they're calling in the state. Maybe even the Feds if they can't find him by the end of the week. The lake's right on the county line and his car was on their side of it, so headquarters will be up in Landers, but of course I told them I'd get the word out around here. I hate to scare people, but folks gotta know. He could be any-where."

Daniel glanced over his shoulder. The mist was rising off the lake now, showing just the lower halves of the firs around it.

"Sorry about fishing, but I gotta get to the station and start making calls. Keep an eye out, will you?" Jake turned to leave.

"I will," Daniel said to his back. "I guess I could tell people at the rodeo this afternoon if you need help spreading the word."

Jake stopped and spun on his heel, staring. "*You're* going to the rodeo?"

Daniel nodded, and Jake made a sound of disbelief.

"Brother, I've invited you to church potlucks, parades, and the New Year's Eve party year in and year out, and not once have you showed. What's up?"

Annie. Annie was what was up. She would be at the annual Ward Family Rodeo, the most anticipated event on the Lake Lumin social calendar, waiting for him with a blanket to share on the grass and two jars of his freshly brewed sun tea.

Daniel hesitated; his answer lodged in his throat.

Annie had told him that Jake was just a friend, nothing more, and he'd taken her at her word. He had no reason not to. But just because she only saw Jake as a buddy, it didn't necessarily mean the feeling was mutual.

Still, staking a claim on the same blanket at the rodeo was as good as a bulletin announcement in a town this size. It would be their first venture into town together as a couple, and Jake was bound to find out at some point. Going public was another big step, but Daniel was ready to take it. With Annie by his side, he might actually become a part of the community here, at last. But still, he didn't have to tell Jake right this second.

Daniel shrugged, but couldn't fight the smile tugging at his mouth.

Jake shook his head. "Seriously, man, what's with you? You're . . . giddy."

The smile was breaking free, a losing battle, and Daniel shook his head at the dock.

"It's nothing."

A scoffing sound came from Jake's throat. "I know that look, brother. It wouldn't have to do with a certain someone who lives down the road, would it?"

Daniel looked up to meet Jake's eyes. They were searching, but not affronted.

"It might. It's been going on for a couple of weeks now."

Jake's brows rose in mild surprise. "Well, I'm happy for you."

Daniel waited with his breath held for the other shoe to drop, but Jake looked genuinely pleased.

"Really?" he asked at last.

"Yeah." Jake nodded. "I mean it. It's high time you had a real relationship. This'll be good for you; it'll break you out of your shell. And, listen, I know there's a few years of age difference between the two of you now, but that won't matter as much later on. Truly, man, I'm happy for you."

Though it went against his nature, Daniel hopped down from the dock and wrapped Jake in a hug.

"Thanks, brother," he said into Jake's shoulder.

"Of course." Jake pulled back to look Daniel in the eyes. "I've always believed there's someone special for all of us. A soulmate. Who knows, she might be yours."

Daniel couldn't help the cynicism that rose up to meet Jake's claim. "I doubt fate has much to do with it. People lose their soulmates all the time."

Jake stepped toward the car and opened the door. "Finding them in the first place is the miracle. After that, every day is a gift, not something we're owed."

Daniel followed him to the car, smiling. "You know, one of these days you might spout your Sunday-school philosophy to the wrong guy and earn yourself a punch to the mouth."

Jake turned for a moment, lifting his arms at his sides, palms open to the sky. "Whom shall I fear, brother?"

Daniel shook his head, still smiling, and Jake climbed into the car and pulled backward, whipping the cruiser around in the clearing and roaring through the open gate.

Daniel spent the rest of the morning with his drawing pad on the dock. As noon approached, the fog lifted in earnest and the firs appeared around the lake, richly green and bathed in sunlight. A deer stepped out from the shadows on the western shore, and he watched as it approached the water, bending its graceful neck to drink.

"Hey!"

Daniel jerked his head to the right, startled. Jamie Boyd had materialized out of nowhere and was climbing onto the dock, her high ponytail swishing behind her.

"Hey." Daniel frowned as she stepped past him, pulling her hair free and letting it fall to her waist. "What are you doing here?"

"Thought I'd go for a swim."

Daniel's frown deepened. "When's the swim test, again?"

Jamie shimmied out of her shorts and let them fall around her ankles.

"Last week. I got the job at the pool, but it's closed for the rodeo, and I kind of had to get out of the house. My dad decided to start drinking early today. It's better to not be around when he does that."

She didn't look at him as she said it, but Daniel heard it in her voice, and he remembered all too well the desperate feeling of needing somewhere, anywhere, to hide.

"Okay. Don't swim too far out."

She pulled her shirt over her head, revealing a turquoise suit that perfectly matched her eyes. Daniel dropped his gaze back down to his drawing pad as she stepped to the edge of the dock and dove forward into the lake.

He should head inside.

He flipped the pad closed and stood, hesitating, remembering Jake's warning from earlier. He couldn't very well leave Jamie alone in the lake with a wanted killer wandering the woods. With a heavy sigh, he sat back down and crossed his legs at the ankles.

Sunshine was pouring freely from the sky now, and there was a steady wind from the south, the lake so bright with thousands of sunlit dimples that it hurt Daniel's eyes as he watched Jamie slicing her way across the surface with strong, clean strokes.

Quickly, he opened his drawing pad again and flipped to a blank page. He sketched straight dark pines and the rough outline of the lake. Jamie was still swimming powerfully, and Daniel's eyes flicked back and forth from the lake to the pad as he captured the scene.

Swiftly, he drew her, the curving outline of her body barely cloaked by the clean surface of the water, the strong, well-defined arm mid-stroke over her head, and the long fair hair sleek and smooth down her back.

His sketches of the mountain sold well enough in town, but he'd learned over the past few years that the highest prices were fetched by drawings with people in them. Jake mid-shout, his eyes hooded by the brim of his baseball cap as he reeled in a fish. Phil at the General Store, asleep behind the counter with his dark face lined in slumber, his chin resting on his hand. Those had gone for a hundred and fifty each, though the sketch of Phil had been bought by his wife, Sheila, and Phil later grumbled to Daniel about it, muttering that the woman could watch him sleep any doggone time she wanted without paying a small fortune for it.

Sketches with movement in them did well, too, like the one of the bald eagle soaring low over the lake, casting a long, distorted shadow on the water.

This drawing would tick both of those boxes. Two hundred bucks at least, if he could get the basic sketch done here, then copy it onto a larger canvas later on.

Jamie slowed in the water and rolled over, floating on her back with the sun kissing the front of her body. She spun in a slow circle and kicked her feet, propelling herself toward the boathouse in a back-stroke.

When she reached the dock, she righted herself and her head and shoulders popped above the boards, golden hair slick and gleaming in the sunlight. "Can you give me a ride down to the rodeo? I told my friends I'd meet them there, and my parents aren't going. Please?" She ran a hand through her wet hair.

Daniel cleared his throat. For a split second, Annie's face flashed through his mind—deep red-brown eyes filled with trust—and he swallowed hard. In a small town, people had a knack for making something out of nothing. The slightest rumor could explode into a scandal in the blink of an eye. What if Jamie was seen in his truck and someone misinterpreted what they saw? What if word got back to Annie?

"I don't know . . . you might want to call another ride. I'm not leaving yet. Not for another hour at least."

"That's perfect." She climbed up onto the dock and wrung her hair out onto the boards. "I'll jog home to shower and you can pick me up there, I'll wait out front."

Daniel sighed, weary. If anyone had ever learned how to say no to this girl, he'd sure like to know how it was done.

"Fine," he said in resignation.

True to her word, Jamie was standing at the end of the Boyds' driveway when Daniel drove down the hill an hour later, her hair still damp and her lips shining with pink gloss as she climbed in and buckled her seat belt.

"Thanks again. I swear this'll be the last time I ask for a ride. I should have enough for a car by the end of the summer, I think."

"It's no problem," he said as they pulled away.

Jamie flipped down the visor mirror and gazed at her reflection as she scrunched her hair with her fingers. "After I get a car, then I'll have to *really* start saving. I've got big plans."

"Oh yeah?"

"Yep, I'm going to college someday. It'll take a while to save enough, but when I do, I'll get out of here and head to some great big university with old brick buildings."

A smile lifted one corner of his mouth. "Old brick buildings?"

"Yeah. And new faces everywhere, and miles and miles of roads to run on."

"What will you study?"

Jamie flipped the visor shut and propped her chin in her hand as she stared out the window.

"Art," she said dreamily. "Dad says trying to be a professional artist is like trying to win the lottery, but I love painting more than anything in the world. I want to have my own studio someday, just a little loft with big windows in a city, where it smells like oil paint when you walk in."

Daniel smiled, but said nothing, and on the way through town, Jamie was happy to keep up most of the conversation with her endless stream of chatter until they finally turned left on a private drive and pulled through the wide, ornate gate with the Ward family crest emblazoned at chest height.

The long driveway led to a paved lot atop a grassy hill that sloped gently down to the stables and the corral where the rodeo would take place. The lot was full already, and a few dozen cars were parked on the grass shoulder of the drive. People were swarming the hillside like bees around a hive, and Daniel could feel his blood pressure rising already, but he calmed himself with the reminder that somewhere in the crowd was Annie, waiting for him.

"Can you let me out here? I see my friends."

Daniel slowed to a stop in the middle of the lot. Everywhere were families and couples and teenagers, all moving around them in a stream down toward the stables.

"Thank you *so* much."

Jamie unbuckled her seat belt and—faster than Daniel could react to it—slid across the seat and closed the distance between them. He turned toward her in surprise at the precise moment that she leaned in, and the kiss that was meant for his cheek brushed his mouth instead.

Jamie laughed and was gone, through the door and lost in the crowd.

Daniel sat with his hands tight on the steering wheel as the flow of people parted around his truck.

Had anyone seen?

Desperately, his eyes jumped from face to face passing by. People were laughing, talking, distracted. And then, standing in the shadow between two cars, he caught a familiar pair of bright blue eyes peering at him from beneath a Mariners cap.

Jake.

Chapter 22

ANNIE

Town was quiet, and Annie's Jeep was the only vehicle on Main Street as she drove with her eyes on the shuttered shops.

It was Sunday morning, and most of Lake Lumin's citizens were sleeping in or hungover from the raucous after-party at the rodeo, when the horses were put away for the night and Harrison and Tammy Ward brought in their traditional half dozen kegs to celebrate the occasion, as they had done since the sixties.

News of a killer on the loose had tainted the festivities, though, and neither Jake nor Annie had had the chance to enjoy the afternoon as they worked their way through the crowd, warning anyone who would listen to be on the lookout for Justin Grimes.

Annie felt terrible about leaving Daniel alone on the checkered blanket while she spread the word, and he had left early on his own, complaining of a headache. She'd need to find a way to make it up to him, and she smiled at the thought of setting up a picnic at their favorite lakeside spot, but that was for later. Right now, there was work to be done, even on a Sunday. There would be no weekends off until Justin Grimes was found and put into custody.

Annie pulled up to the curb and killed the engine. As she stepped into the station, the phone rang, and Jake, already seated behind the desk with an open map spread before him, answered.

"Hello? . . . Yeah, she just walked in, hang on."

Jake passed the phone to Annie.

"Hello?"

"Guess what?"

Annie smiled at the sound of Daniel's voice. "What?"

"We've got a cougar."

"You're kidding!"

"No, he's in one of the snares, I found him this morning. I won't be able to help you with him though. The Wards had so many lights and speakers going at the stable yesterday that something blew and they want me down there to fix it."

"That's fine, I'll take Jake, just leave the gate open."

She hung up, grinning, and filled Jake in.

Annie drove them up to the boathouse in the Jeep, heart pounding as she parked. Together, they loaded the gear into the skiff, and Jake rowed steadily toward the southern shore while she loaded the gun and checked the radio collar for a signal, limbs humming with adrenaline. It was always this way when coming face-to-face with something wild and deadly. It was truly the best part of the job.

The skiff slid onto the shore, and even before she set foot on the bank, Annie heard the cat in the woods, growling and hissing in frustration. Bright-eyed, she lifted the tranquilizer gun and walked into the trees to meet it.

She caught sight of his back first. Broad and golden, facing away from her as he curled around his ensnared foot in the shadow of the trees. Annie lowered the gun, gazing at him in awe. He was huge. The biggest cat she'd ever seen, muscles rippling as he worked at the trapped paw with his teeth.

Annie lifted the gun again and nestled it into her shoulder. She took a deep breath and let it out, stilling the muscles in her body as she took careful aim.

Pop!

The dart whizzed through the air and struck the cougar in the neck. A perfect shot.

The cat's ears flattened. His powerful golden body twitched violently, and a feral growl of annoyance rippled through the trees, sending a chill down Annie's spine.

For several seconds, he tried to swipe at the dart with his free paws, then angled his head downward to nip at it with his teeth, but it was too well placed under his jaw, and he was unable to free it.

Hauling himself to his feet, he hobbled in an unsteady circle around the snare, large yellow eyes hunting the trees. Annie stayed where she was. When he saw her, he froze, and they stared unblinkingly at each other for several seconds as the dart's sedative worked its way into his system. Abruptly, he stumbled on his feet, regained them for a moment, then slumped sideways onto the ground.

His limbs twitched as he fought the drug, then stilled at last.

Annie turned to Jake, who was waiting far behind in the trees. "He's safe."

They made their way to the snare, Jake trailing Annie as she came to a stop over the imposing predator.

He was beautiful. Well-fed and well-muscled, with a sleek coat and clean teeth. Young, but mighty; the king of these woods.

Annie knelt beside him and ran a hand over the tawny fur of his torso.

"Hey there, handsome," she murmured.

His eyes were half-open; massive irises the color of lamplight with dilated pupils that bounced her reflection back at her.

"I'm not gonna hurt you." She gently stroked his coat with her fingers before reaching up to scratch the spot behind his ear that all cats, no matter their size, loved.

"What's that?" Jake asked.

Annie smiled at the low, rumbling sound coming from the animal's chest. "He's purring."

"You mean he's *happy*?"

"No." Annie shook her head. "It just means his vocal cords are re-laxed. Even dying cats purr sometimes."

His breathing slowed, his eyes closed, and Annie reached out to lift one of his massive paws in her hand. A wound, badly infected beneath a tattered scab, marred the pad under his toes.

"That explains the limp." She rested the paw back on the ground.

Annie looked over her shoulder. Jake was standing back with his hands on his hips, staring at the animal with narrowed eyes.

"I can't just collar him and let him go. He needs to be transported down to the center in Portland to have this wound treated. They have a rehab-and-release policy. We'll give them our coordinates and they'll release him back up here, since he's claimed this valley as territory and isn't close to any neighborhoods or livestock. Come on, we'll take him in the Jeep."

Jake's mouth tightened, twitched. "How long will he be out for?"

"Six hours at least."

He looked doubtful. "You sure?"

Annie nodded.

"Better be." He stepped forward to join her.

Annie freed the cougar's foot from the snare, and she and Jake each took a fore and hind paw in one hand.

"I'll come back for the traps later," she said as they lifted the heavy cat and started back toward the shore.

Getting the animal to the boat took long minutes, with Jake and Annie resting the dead weight of his body on the forest floor several times. When they finally made it back to the lake, they loaded him into the boat and climbed in after.

Jake manned the oars and didn't take his eyes from the cougar for one second. Annie had to speak up twice when the skiff angled away from the boathouse, but they made it to the dock at last and slid the cat into the back of the Wagoneer.

Annie secured his paws together with a set of buckled straps, then climbed in beside Jake. She drove slowly down Lake Lumin Road, wary of jostling, though she knew even a meteor strike wouldn't wake the cat from his slumber. They were nearing the bottom of the road when Daniel's truck appeared, climbing toward home.

Annie sat tall in the driver's seat, watching for Daniel through the glass as a smile broke across her face. There he was, grinning just as brightly, his hand lifted as they passed each other on the gravel road.

"Will you just look at that smile," Jake said, laughing. "Man, I tell ya, I've never seen such a change come over someone in a month's time. You know he's seeing someone?"

Annie pressed her lips together as she turned left onto the paved two-lane road. She hadn't told Jake about the relationship yet. She hadn't told anyone, actually. The rodeo would have been the place to do it, but it hadn't worked out that way, and a small part of her was glad. Half the fun of a new relationship was the cocoon, keeping it a secret from the rest of the world.

"Is that right?" she asked.

"Yeah." Jake nodded. "Jamie Boyd."

A moment of silence passed between them. A moment when Annie was certain she must have misheard.

"What?"

"You know, Jamie?" Jake said as Annie turned to stare at him blankly. "The girl that came up to swim when we sawed up the cedar? From the blue house with the fence, Ronnie and Debra's daughter?"

Annie's heart dropped into her stomach. She dragged her eyes back to the road, growing lightheaded as a little laugh passed her lips.

"No"—she shook her head—"no, you're wrong."

"I know, I know." Jake lifted his hands in the air. "We talked a little about the age difference yesterday, but the truth is, she's nineteen now. She's an adult. And he's only twenty-three. My dad was eight years older than my mom when they met. It happens. Honestly, Annie, I'm just glad to see him happy, he's been isolated up there by himself for too long."

It was as though someone had filled her stomach with ice. Rock-hard, burning-cold ice. There must be some mistake. There had to be. This couldn't be happening to her. Not again.

"Are you *sure?*" Her voice, high and tense, didn't sound like her own. "You're absolutely positive they're together?"

"Yeah." Jake nodded. "Saw them kissing in his truck yesterday."

The Jeep swerved on the road, Annie's grip tightening so hard on the steering wheel that it squeaked under her fingers.

"Whoa, careful there." Jake laughed, but Annie couldn't breathe. She could barely see the road ahead as the trees rushed past in one long emerald blur.

It was happening again. She was once again being cast aside for someone younger and prettier, and Walt Proudy was dead wrong. The berries were not worth the briars. No amount of happiness was worth the moment of heartbreak when it was all torn away like a layer of flesh, leaving her raw and bleeding.

"Anyway, Jamie's a cute little thing," Jake said. "I'm not sure how serious they are about each other, but time'll tell."

Annie swallowed mutely.

She couldn't just stare ahead in stone-faced shock forever. She had to say something, but the words would not come, so she forced her head up and down in a nod instead.

"Gives you hope, you know? Seeing a guy like that find someone. Makes me feel like I might, too."

Annie didn't respond. Her fingers were still so tight on the wheel that they ached. She was fighting, fighting hard and losing against the lump welling up in her throat.

"Good for him," she managed, though she could hear her bitterness plain as day, and Jake must have, too, because his head tilted, and his gaze became searching.

"Hey," he said gently, "you'll find someone. I know you will."

Annie nodded. He had misinterpreted the resentment in her voice, and that was for the best. Let him think it was because she was lonely.

Let him think she was missing Brendan. That was far better than the truth, that a man she had only been seeing for a few weeks had already managed to mend her broken heart and shatter it again.

Jake turned away, moving the conversation on to the Justin Grimes case, and Annie stopped listening, staring instead at the green forest outside as it streamed by in a jeweled flow of light and shadow that blurred as her eyes filled with tears.

Chapter 23

DANIEL

Daniel woke to the sound of laughter, high and feminine, as it cracked through his dream-filled sleep.

Annie . . .

His eyes fluttered open and he pushed himself up onto his elbows.

A gentle night breeze, warm and fragrant, was stirring through the room from the open window in the hall, carrying with it the sugar-sweet scent of the rhododendrons behind the alders, just past their prime.

A silent minute passed, and Daniel stayed propped up on his arms in the bed as his muddled mind sorted dream from reality. In the distance, a faint rumble of thunder boomed, and the laugh came again, louder this time, and followed by a splash.

Confusion brought his brows together, and Daniel sat up fully, pushing aside the blankets.

He hadn't seen Annie since the rodeo, and she hadn't returned any of his calls in the three days since. He didn't know it with certainty, but he worried that word had gotten back to her about Jamie's kiss in the truck.

He'd called at least a dozen times yesterday alone, and the one time she'd actually answered, he had only managed to say, "Annie, listen," before the receiver slammed right back down. He'd tried, but at some point, he was just banging his head against a wall. The ball was in her court now, and when she was good and ready, she'd call him back. Or maybe she had decided to come up here in person and hash it out tonight instead.

Daniel pulled on a pair of jeans and walked to the front of the boathouse.

On the other side of the windows, the sky over the southern woods flickered with the lightning of a far-off summer storm. The lake glowed with plankton, the edges thin ribbons of electric blue, and there she was, just beyond the dock, facing away from him as she treaded water, her bare shoulders bobbing up and down in the moonlight.

Daniel's heart leaped into his throat, and he quickly unlocked the door and stepped out onto the dock, his eyes falling on the set of clothes heaped in a pile on one of the Adirondack chairs with a pair of sneakers placed neatly beneath them.

"Annie?" his voice broke the night stillness.

The woman turned in the water, and Daniel's breath hitched as he found himself staring into the dancing blue eyes of Jamie Boyd.

"Hey." Her voice was as casual as if they were passing one another on the sidewalk in town.

As a flash of dry lightning lit the far hills, Daniel stared at her, seriously entertaining the idea that he was still dreaming—but the woman in front of him was all too real, and a quick spark of anger flared to life in his chest.

"What are you doing here?" His voice was hard, but he no longer cared if he sounded unkind. Jamie Boyd had already caused enough problems for him and Annie.

Jamie's eyes widened. "I—I couldn't sleep, and I wanted to see if the lake really glowed in the dark—and look!"

She turned a slow circle in the water, beaming as the blue creatures lit up in a ring that burned brightly around her.

Daniel was wrestling for control of his racing heart. He was still waking up. He was still in total disbelief that this girl had jumped into his lake in the middle of the night, and he honestly couldn't tell if she was wearing a swimsuit.

Crouching down on the dock, he looked her dead in the eyes and spoke in slow, deliberate sentences.

"Listen. You can't be up here in the middle of the night. This is my property, my private land, and I didn't agree to let you show up here whenever you feel like it."

In the silence that followed his words, thunder rolled, low and booming, and Jamie blinked her cat eyes in the dark.

"Why not?"

She sounded genuinely surprised, and Daniel sighed, leaning back on his heels.

"It's not safe, for one thing. That guy who killed the woman on the ridge is still on the run somewhere around here, and for another, people . . . people are going to get the wrong idea about you and me."

Jamie rolled her eyes. "Exactly who are you worried about, Daniel? What people? I just broke up with my boyfriend, if that's what's bothering you."

Daniel rose to full height again.

"Go home, Jamie."

She stared up at him, making no move to swim to the dock.

"Look around." Her treading limbs stirred up a soft blue glow that lit her body faintly beneath the water. "No one's here. No one's watching."

She tilted her head as she gazed at him with those wide feline eyes, and when she spoke again, there was an invitation in her voice.

"No one's stopping you from joining me, either."

Chapter 24

ANNIE

G ray, again.

The world around her was gray, and dull, and flat, despite the wispy clouds scattered across a cornflower sky. Despite the lake shimmering with late-morning sunlight, and the forest in all its glorious summer hues of emerald, jade, and moss. It was all clouded over, and Annie sat stiffly in the skiff with her eyes on the mountain, ignoring the man who was rowing her across the lake.

"You sure you're all right?" Jake asked for the third time in as many minutes, and Annie nodded again without looking at him.

"I'm fine."

Her eyes were still faintly rimmed in red, but with any luck, he would chalk it up to allergies and eventually let it go.

She'd waited at the window of her room all morning until Daniel's truck rolled past, headed toward town, then she called Jake to ask for his help retrieving the empty snares they'd left on the south shore. She had no intention of running into Daniel anytime soon and would have preferred to go alone if Justin Grimes weren't still somewhere in the area, roaming the woods at large.

Jake rowed silently for another minute, then said, "You know, my dad used to take my mom up here when they were courting."

"Oh yeah?" Annie didn't take her eyes from the summit.

"Yeah." He nodded. "Back before the restaurant burned down. He'd take her out rowing on the lake after dinner. Said he spent his way through paycheck after paycheck, but he always saw the romance as a worthy investment in his future."

Annie met his gaze briefly, giving him a smile that didn't reach her eyes. "That's sweet."

Jake nodded and pulled the oars across the surface, water swishing with each stroke.

Annie turned in her seat. The southern shore was rising up to meet them, feathered with the sunlight falling through the firs, and the moment the bottom of the boat scraped dirt, she hopped out and started walking.

"Be right back."

"Wait, I'll come, too," Jake said quickly, scrambling out behind her and looping the rope around the felled log onshore.

Annie said nothing as she led the way under the trees, stopping to gather both snares and brushing off dirt and pine needles.

"All right, let's go."

She stepped past Jake, headed for the boat, then he called out behind her.

"Hey, wait a minute."

Annie turned back wearily. "What?"

"Uh . . ." Jake pulled a hand across the back of his neck. "It's nice out," he said after a beat. "Clouds are supposed to roll in this afternoon, and it's gonna rain for the next few days. What do you say we take advantage of the sunshine and go for a little hike since we're back here anyway?"

Annie sighed. "Jake . . ."

He took a step toward her.

"Annie, it's . . . it's just a hike. I just want to cheer you up. You seem a little off. Besides, it might be a good idea to look around in the woods for anything out of the ordinary since they haven't caught Grimes yet."

With another sigh, Annie set the traps on the ground.

"Okay."

They hiked south, then up and around the wide swath of briars that ran rampant on the eastern shore of the lake before angling east on an old, overgrown trail.

As they crossed the wide valley that lay in the shadow of Lewis Ridge, Jake kept up most of the dialogue while, during lapses, Annie's thoughts drifted, leaving him in silence. After a while, he conceded the conversation entirely, and they walked quietly beneath the ancient trees, alive with birdsong.

Jake veered off toward a cluster of velvety thimbleberries peeking out from beneath frilly leaves, picking some and offering them to Annie, who tried her best to smile as she took them from his open palm.

"Look, there's more over here." He stepped toward a thin vein of bloodred berries that broke the solid green thicket.

Annie left him to strip the bush and wandered farther into the trees. Why did it have to be so beautiful out? It was such a perfect day, flaunting its summer loveliness in the face of her misery.

She stopped walking and rested for a moment with her back against a tree.

"Look at that!" Jake called out excitedly from somewhere behind her. "I found the mother lode!"

But Annie didn't respond. There was something bright on the ground up ahead through the trees, right where the land began its upward slope toward the ridge.

Lying in a little sunlit clearing a mere fifty yards away was a heap of vivid color. Neon hues that did not belong to the woods: teal blue and brilliant orange.

"Jake . . ." she called, voice tight with alarm.

He was at her side in moments, and she pointed into the woods.

For three full seconds, he was silent.

"Oh no," he breathed, and broke into a run.

Annie followed, right on his heels as he sprinted through the trees, the clearing rising up to meet them. As they drew nearer, the heap of color on the ground took shape with the body beneath it, and as she had on the ridge, Annie fought against the bizarre sensation that her mind was floating up and away.

The orange and blue were a tank top and shorts. There was a woman lying on the ground.

Barreling ahead of Annie, Jake stumbled over an exposed root and staggered into the sunlight where the woman lay, her head and shoulders hidden behind a fir trunk.

"Stay back!" he shouted at Annie, but she ignored him, rounding the tree to find the woman with her head twisted away, long fair hair fanning over her face and the mossy ground around her.

Annie's hands flew to her mouth.

Jake stepped around the woman and knelt beside her, sweeping the hair away from her face.

All-too-familiar purple bruises ran the length of her neck, and a sound escaped Annie's lips, like that of a dog who had been struck.

Though she longed to squeeze her eyes shut, to turn and run, she could do nothing but stand and stare at the lifeless face of the woman Daniel had chosen over her.

Chapter 25

ANNIE

What a strange sensation it was, to be numb both inside and out. The hands in Annie's lap did not feel like her own, the feet in her shoes seemed miles away, and between her ears was only a cottony sense of disbelief as she sat in the passenger seat of the speeding police cruiser.

They flew down Main Street, sirens blazing and lights flashing—people on the sidewalk stopping to stare at the blur of color and sound. Annie met the eyes of some, envying their confusion and the ignorance that would be stolen from them soon enough, while Jake stared straight ahead, focused and silent as he gripped the steering wheel in hands clamped like vises.

The digital clock on the dashboard showed that fifty-five minutes had passed since they'd discovered Jamie's body in the woods, but it felt longer to Annie as she replayed the scene over and over in her mind, whirling through details she'd never be able to forget.

She closed her eyes and leaned her head against the cool glass of the window.

Jake had managed to flip a switch that she hadn't, forcing himself into work mode as he'd glanced up through the fir boughs shading Jamie's body, and asked the pressing question out loud.

"How long do you think she's been back here?"

Hours. The word stuck tight in Annie's throat, and she hadn't been able to answer. *Only hours.* After all, she herself had undoubtedly been one of the last people to witness Jamie Boyd alive, just the night before.

Annie had finally turned her lamp off at eleven thirty and was on the verge of drifting to sleep when she heard running footfalls on the gravel road through the open window. She'd made it to the sill and had searched the road beyond the yellow pool of garage light flooding the driveway, but she had been too late to catch sight of Jamie.

Still, she knew in her gut that it could have been no one else. Even her footsteps sounded peppy as she jogged up the road toward the boathouse. Toward Daniel. Jamie Boyd had been alive and well at midnight last night, and now she was dead.

"I have to get out of these clothes," Jake muttered, and Annie forced her eyes open, leaning her head away from the comforting cold of the glass. "Let's swing by my place. I'll change, then we can start making calls."

Annie nodded, searching Jake's face as he drove, wondering if he felt as numb as she did in this moment.

His shirt and shorts were damp and muddy. He had fallen into the lake when he shoved the skiff back out into the water, stumbling forward and submerging himself up to the chest before climbing in, dripping wet. It was understandable, given the circumstances. Annie had barely managed to keep her own legs from buckling beneath her as she clambered aboard.

Jake had rowed them back toward the boathouse with ferocious speed—the veins in his arms and neck bulging with effort—while Annie sat across from him, her muscles tensed as she tried to stop the uncontrollable shivering that persisted in her arms and legs despite the warm day.

Now, the shivering had stopped, but even with the miles between her and the gruesome scene in the woods, even safe in the cruiser with Jake, she already knew that she would remember those awful minutes in that little clearing for the rest of her life. That scene would land in the same mental file of nightmare material as the hiker in the tent and the woman on the rocks.

Jake yanked the steering wheel to the right and the cruiser revved up the steep grade behind the bed-and-breakfast. At the top, a small white bungalow peeked out over the hillside from a grove of black firs, and Jake screeched to a stop in the sharply sloped driveway.

"I'll be ten minutes," he said, unbuckling. "You can come in if you want."

Annie didn't hesitate, quickly unfastening her own seat belt and following him inside. She didn't want to be alone. She didn't want silence or space to think.

Jake jogged up the porch steps, peeling off his wet shirt as he climbed and slinging it over his shoulder. He held the squeaking front door open for Annie, who stepped inside ahead of him.

"I'll just be a minute," he said. "We've gotta move. Get word to the state that this guy's still active and get them back down here as soon as possible."

Jake strode through the kitchen, dropping his wet shirt on the counter before disappearing into a back room.

Annie glanced around. The place looked like Jake, tidy, but quirky, with old-fashioned swiveling barstools at the counter and an antiquated linoleum floor. Coffee mugs with various sports emblems were lined up on the windowsill, and a clock shaped like a black cat hung on the wall, its tail ticking back and forth with the passing seconds.

"Are there any messages?" Jake called from the back room.

Annie found the answering machine beside the sink. The red light was blinking with an unheard message.

"One," she called back. "Want me to play it?"

In the back room, a drawer opened and shut. "Yeah, go ahead."

Annie pushed the button, and a voice crackled through the speaker.

"Hey, Jake, Austin Smith here. State boys have been trying to reach you at the station all morning, but I guess you're not in today. They wanted me to give you a call at home and let you know they brought

Justin Grimes in last night. Got a confession out of him, too. They got lucky. He ended up hiking north instead of south, and one of their guys spotted his tent from the highway up past Rubicon Falls. Anyway, just wanted to let you know you can get back to business as usual down there. Have a good one."

There was a click as Sheriff Smith hung up, and Annie stood rooted to the floor, unable to tear her eyes from the small black machine as the recording ceased.

There was a sound behind her, and she turned to find Jake in the doorway, bare chested and wearing jeans that hadn't yet been zipped up. Annie watched as his face transformed, deep confusion creasing his brow as he stared past her at the machine.

"How far?" she asked, and his eyes found hers. "How far are we from Rubicon Falls?"

Jake shook his head. "Forty miles."

Too far. An impossible distance.

For a long beat, Jake and Annie stared at each other across the room.

That was the only word for it. *Impossible.* Justin Grimes couldn't have killed Jamie Boyd, and the same question racing through Annie's mind was clearly written on Jake's face as the lines on his forehead deepened in bewilderment.

Now what?

Chapter 26

ANNIE

Annie stared at the faded diamond pattern on the purple carpet beneath her boots.

Were she and Jake really back here? Back in the windowless mortuary with its dry, potted ficus and its watercooler that dripped with maddening regularity?

Yes. They were. Waiting for the results of yet another autopsy.

They had passed the twenty-four-hour mark since finding Jamie's body in the woods, but it still felt detached from the fabric of reality. Still just a bad dream.

"He's gotta be close to finishing by now," Jake said beside her.

Annie nodded, her eyes on the watercooler in the corner. The dripping seemed to be growing louder by the second, and she was going crazy with the *tap-tap-tap* of it.

Another minute passed, and she reached her limit.

Annie shot to her feet and strode across the room. She shook the appliance soundly and gave the base a kick with her boot for good measure, but it did nothing to stop the leak, and she returned to her seat defeated, sinking back into her chair with a sigh and resting her hands over her stomach. Her insides had been in knots since their fateful hike yesterday, and no amount of antacid tablets had put a dent in the nausea.

The minute hand on the clock swung past the four-o'clock hour and the rain came at last, the clouds opening their hatches with gusto. The sound was like applause on the roof and Annie closed her eyes, letting the noise wash over her.

Finally, the sealed door of the morgue opened, and Doc Porter stepped out, his mostly silver curls in frayed tufts at his temples where his glasses pressed into his hair.

"Jake," he said, beckoning him over with a finger, and Jake's chair groaned as he rose. "You're not gonna like this." The doctor lifted his clipboard and adjusted his glasses.

"There's nothing about this that I like, Doc, just give it to me straight. Strangulation?"

Doc Porter lowered the clipboard and peered over his glasses at Jake, silver mustache twitching as his mouth worked beneath it. It was a long moment before he spoke, and when he did, it was a single, unexpected word.

"Drowning."

For a minute, no one in the room spoke, and from her chair, Annie was certain she had misheard the man with the chart, his voice muddled by the sound of raindrops peppering the roof.

"Excuse me?" Jake said finally.

"That's right," Doc Porter confirmed with a head bob. "She was drowned sometime between one and three in the morning yesterday. Her lungs were full of water."

Jake stared mutely at the doctor.

"That's—that's not possible," he stammered. "We found her out back in the woods. I mean way, way back there at the bottom of Lewis Ridge, and she had the exact same bruises on her neck as Hannah Schroeder. How could her cause of death be drowning?"

"Well . . ." Doc Porter cleared his throat and hesitated, leaning around Jake to give Annie a pointed look, eyebrows raised behind his glasses. "You sure you want to be in here for this, ma'am? It's rather gruesome."

Annie opened her mouth to protest, but Jake spoke first.

"She's been through a lot worse than this since she got to town, Doc, she can handle it."

Jake waved Annie over then, as though he'd just noticed she wasn't beside him, and she crossed the room to join the two men.

"All right," Doc Porter said on a sigh, flipping the top sheet on the clipboard to pull free the polaroid beneath. "These bruises on her neck are consistent with hands, but she wasn't strangled. You'll notice they're positioned differently than the ones on Hannah Schroeder's neck, the thumbprints are around back instead of in front, here at C3. Now, my best guess is that someone held her head down in the water from behind until she . . . well, until her body forced her to breathe and she took all of that water into her lungs."

"So . . . so she was drowned and moved afterward," Jake said, glancing at Annie. "Why?"

"Isn't it obvious?" Annie nodded at the photograph. "Someone wanted it to look like a second Hannah Schroeder. Same area. Same bruises. They wanted it to look as similar as possible because they didn't know Justin Grimes had already been caught. They wanted to pin it on him."

Doc Porter's brows lifted in approval. "I'd say that's a fair guess."

Jake looked between them. "So, it had to be someone who knew about what happened to Hannah Schroeder."

Annie nodded.

"I'd say that limits your suspects to everyone in the whole town, then," Doc Porter offered with a wry glance between them.

Jake shook his head. "I know it."

"There's more." Doc Porter lifted a small plastic bag. "Wood shavings. From around the cuff of her shorts. And there was a smudge of something on her thumb. Dark gray. Ash, I'm thinking, but I can't be sure. I was able to scrape off a small sample. I'll personally drive everything up to the lab in Seattle to be analyzed. Quicker that way. They'll get the results back to you as fast as they can. All I have to say is that it's a good thing you two found her before the rain came, or all of that would have been washed away."

"I just—" Jake closed his eyes, and a pained expression crossed his face. "I can't understand the drowning thing. It makes no sense."

"Was she anywhere near water?" Doc Porter asked. "A stream, maybe?"

"She was due east of Lake Lumin," Annie said, "but at least half a mile, maybe more."

"It couldn't be the lake," Jake interjected. "There's that solid wall of briars on the eastern shore. Sharp as razor wire. It's impassable. Fifty feet thick at least and closer to a hundred in places. There's no way through, not without going all the way down and around the way we hiked, and that's at least two miles. No one would carry her that far in the pitch black of night. She had to be driven there on the ridge road. It runs just up the hill from where we found her. And that means she could have been drowned anywhere. A bathtub across town for all we know."

For a moment, no one spoke, then Annie asked, "Can you tell us anything about the water in her lungs?"

"Not for sure. Lab analysis will show more, but it looked fairly clear to me." The doctor paused for a moment. "She worked down at the pool, didn't she?"

Jake nodded. "Yeah, I think she did."

"That might be worth looking into, then. Or a good place to start asking questions, at least." Doc Porter cleared his throat and adjusted his glasses again. "But I'm straying into your line of work. Why don't you head on back to the station and let me take care of getting the samples to the lab?"

Jake nodded. "You tell them I want it expedited. I want every scrap of information they have the second they have it. I'm headed up to Ronnie and Debra's to give them an update now; you can reach me there if anything else comes up."

Doc Porter frowned. "You already broke the news to them, I imagine?"

Jake nodded again. "Debra took it pretty hard, but I think Ronnie's in denial."

Doc Porter placed a hand on Jake's shoulder. "Tell her folks I sure am sorry. There's no grief quite like the one they're facing today."

"I will."

With a pat on Jake's back, the doctor stepped back into the morgue and the door sealed itself shut behind him.

Jake turned to Annie again. He looked older, with dark circles beneath his eyes and unshaved stubble lining his jaw.

"Ronnie's kind of a loose cannon," she said. "Want me to come with you?"

"Yes," he said tiredly. "Thank you."

Ten minutes later, windshield wipers on full blast, the cruiser made the turn onto Lake Lumin Road and started to climb. Annie's stomach churned over the hills. She dreaded what was to come with every ounce of her being as, through the rain, the little blue house with the overgrown front yard appeared on the left.

Ronnie Boyd stood on the front porch behind a veil of water streaming over the broken gutter. His arms rested on the railing and his head was bowed between his shoulders, but at the sound of tires in the driveway, he looked up.

Annie wasn't sure if he could see them through the rain-streaked windshield, but his eyes tracked the cruiser as it parked. He reached down toward his feet, lifted a mostly empty glass bottle of caramel-colored liquid, and brought it to his lips.

He tilted his chin skyward, and the inch of liquid disappeared down his throat, then he stretched his arm back and let the bottle fly, hurling it out into the driveway where it shattered against the gravel in an explosion of glass just feet from the police car.

Annie's hands flew to her mouth.

Jake blew out a breath as he reached for his seat belt. "This isn't going to be pretty."

Chapter 27

ANNIE

The Boyd house reeked of rodents and strong liquor, and Annie held her breath as she followed Jake inside.

Ronnie's affinity for unusual animals had clearly not been quelled when she dismantled his exotic zoo. There was a foggy terrarium under a buzzing light beside the window, and three cages, acrid with urine-damp shavings, sat on the counter dividing the living room from the kitchen, their occupants curled into russet balls of fur in the corners where they slept.

Annie eyed the cages, the game warden in her trying to determine the breed of the animals inside. Ferrets, maybe . . . or weasels. Jake nudged her with an elbow, and she stopped staring, turning instead to the cluttered living room, where Jamie's mother and father waited. This was not the time.

Debra Boyd sat on the sagging couch, her face gray and drawn, the eyes she shared with her daughter vacant as blue sea glass in her pale face. Ronnie had retreated inside the house without greeting Jake and Annie from the porch and chosen the recliner in front of the television, where he now rested with his legs crossed at the ankles in the fully reclined position, giving his undivided attention to the tennis match on the screen.

"You mind turning that off for a second, Ronnie?" Jake asked, not unkindly.

Ronnie merely lifted the remote and turned the volume up.

"Okay." Jake strode to the set, reached down behind it, and yanked the cord from the wall. The screen winked off with a little puff of static, and silence fell, as thick and unpleasant as the smell in the room.

Annie couldn't see Ronnie's face from where she stood, but his voice told her enough about his state of mind.

"Whaddayawant, Jake?" The question was gravelly, nearly incoherent with drink.

"I've got an update." Jake stared down into the recliner. "Why don't you take a seat over there next to Deb and we'll go over it together."

To Annie's surprise, Ronnie complied without verbal protest, though he slammed his legs down to return the recliner to its upright position before rising unsteadily to his feet.

Jake caught Annie's eye, nodding toward the long coffee table in front of the couch, and Annie joined him there, taking a seat on the tabletop as Ronnie sank into the cushion beside his wife, coughing wetly with breath that reeked of bourbon.

Annie's stomach tightened. He was drunk. Completely, stone-cold drunk.

Jake folded his hands with a heavy sigh. "I think it goes without saying that I wish we were here under different circumstances."

Ronnie gave a bitter little laugh that turned into another cough.

"But," Jake persisted, "part of my job is to keep the two of you informed as we proceed with the investigation, and that's why we're here."

Annie sat beside him, fingers laced tightly in her lap and her eyes on the floor as Jake told Ronnie and Debra the unexpected results of the autopsy. When he stated that Jamie's official cause of death was drowning, Annie felt in her bones the anguished cry that passed Debra's lips, while Ronnie stayed silent.

Jake gave them the details of the autopsy with the least amount of emotion possible, and Annie knew it wasn't because he was being intentionally cold, but rather steady. Secure. Right now, the two people on the couch were lost in a riptide. Yanked into the sea of tragedy by a terrible undercurrent. What they needed were the facts, quick and clinical, and the chance to process them alone in peace.

Jake gave the Boyds what few assurances he had, promising them that the lab in Seattle was one of the best in the country and would be able to analyze every detail to provide information that would lead to an arrest, a statement that was met by a feverish nod from Jamie's mother, and a snort of derision from her father.

Annie caught Debra's gaze for a fleeting moment, but there was a hollowness in her expression that Annie could not bear, and she quickly looked away again.

Jake finished sharing what news he had, and Ronnie leaned forward to speak at last.

"Frankly, Jacob, I don't give two farts what the lab comes back with. Or what Doc Porter says. Or what you say, for that matter. Honest to God, I don't even care how the guy did it, I just want to know who he is so I can break his neck myself."

Annie risked a sideways glance at Jake, whose jaw had tightened.

"We only found her yesterday," he said evenly. "We don't have any suspects in custody yet, and I don't want you thinking about taking matters into your own hands. There's a right way to go about this and a wrong way, and I—"

"What about that creep who lives by himself at the end of the road?" Ronnie interrupted, voice rising in pitch. "You talked to him, yet?"

"Ronnie, please." Debra's eyes shone with tears as she turned to her husband. "We don't know if he has anything to do with it. Let's not point fingers before we have any real reason to."

Ronnie only shook his head, his bloodshot gaze falling to the stained carpet, where it stayed. "I got my reasons. Any numbskull in the world could put two and two together. He knows them woods. And Jamie went up there more than once to swim this summer. The guy's not right in the head and everyone knows it, but she . . . she trusted him. She trusted him."

Ronnie's hardened façade cracked as he repeated the last few words, and his eyes grew misty with tears that he hid by bowing his head to his chest.

Annie watched as his throat bobbed. He was right, or at least partly right, and she and Jake both knew it, though she had been actively trying not to think about Daniel since discovering Jamie's body. Her heart would not let her head broach the possibility.

Beside her, Jake's fingertips tapped together, and she knew that he was choosing his next words carefully.

"Let's focus on what we can do right now," he said. "Did Jamie do anything out of the ordinary lately? Were there any friends she'd had a fight with, or anyone she mentioned that might have wanted to hurt her?"

Debra's gaze slid to her husband, whose head remained bowed.

"We—we think she might have been seeing someone," she said, "but we don't know for sure. She didn't tell us. Jamie is . . . was . . . private about that sort of thing. At least with us. It must not have lasted long, because I heard . . ." Debra's voice trailed off and her eyes slid to the dark hallway that led into the rest of the house. "I was doing laundry, and Jamie's bedroom is on the other side of the wall. She's got a landline in there, and she was talking to her friend on the phone, the girl with the blue hair, Stephanie. She said something about breaking up with someone, but I turned the dryer on and didn't catch anything else after that."

It was an instinct, a reaction, the quick glance that Annie shot at Jake, but his eyes stayed locked on Debra's as he nodded.

"And when was that?"

"Two days ago. Before . . ."

"Okay," Jake said with a single nod, pulling out the small pad and pen that he kept in his shirt pocket. "Would you mind giving me Stephanie's number?"

While Jake took it down, Ronnie shifted on the couch.

"I need a drink," he muttered, pushing himself to his feet and brushing Jake's and Annie's knees in his path to the kitchen. Annie watched him go, clicking his tongue at the cages as he passed.

Jake leaned forward with his pen still poised over the pad. "Did Jamie ever sneak out of the house at night?"

"Once or twice. But didn't we all as teenagers? I know I did back when I first met Ronnie, and Jamie wasn't interested in partying or drinking. She was excited about her future. About painting, and working to save for college and a car . . . and starting a family someday. She wasn't the type to get into trouble."

Debra's eyes filled with tears again, and Jake set the pad down, abandoning his neutrality as he took her hand in both of his.

"I know this is hard, Deb, but you've gotta stay strong for me. Tell me about the night before last. Do you remember hearing anything unusual? Anything at all?"

"No." Debra shook her head adamantly. "Jamie went to bed when we did. Just after ten."

Annie's mouth popped open, the contradiction ready to be voiced, but she snapped it shut again. Saying aloud that she had heard Jamie running up the road at midnight would paint a bright red target on Daniel's back, when the truth was that there was plenty of room for doubt. She hadn't *seen* Jamie; she'd only heard running footsteps on the road and assumed that it was her. Hand on a Bible, staring down a courtroom, would she be able to say beyond the shadow of a doubt that the person jogging up the road was Jamie? No.

In the kitchen, the refrigerator door slammed, and Ronnie swore.

"We're outta beer, Deb," he hollered, and Debra glanced apologetically at Jake and Annie.

I'm so sorry, she mouthed.

Jake shook his head. "It's fine. Go on. Tell me what happened the next morning."

"Well, Jamie was gone when we got up, but she usually goes for her runs in the morning, so I didn't think much of it. We had breakfast, and I went outside to feed the chickens. She wasn't back by ten, but I still wasn't worried. I thought maybe she had run down to the pool, or to Stephanie's house. Jamie was independent that way. I don't think I truly would have started to worry unless she wasn't back by dinnertime. It was just a normal day until . . . until you told us the news."

Ronnie stepped back into the living room with a bottle of white wine clenched in his fist. He didn't bother returning to his seat on the couch, but stood swaying slightly as he stared down his nose at Jake and Annie.

Jake dropped Debra's hand and sat back, giving Ronnie a silent minute to speak, but when Ronnie merely gazed mutely at him, Jake cleared his throat.

"I want to thank you both for being willing to talk with me. And I promise, I'll give every waking hour to this case until—"

"Where's the state?" Ronnie interrupted. "They were all up in arms when that woman from Landers was killed, where are they now? Why don't they care about my little girl?"

"It's not that they don't care"—Jake stared up at Ronnie—"but once Justin Grimes was put into custody, this became a completely different investigation. Half of those guys got sent up to Wenatchee for an active abduction. They promised me more manpower down here when they can spare it, but they're not a limitless entity, and I've got the responsibility to head things up in the meantime. This happened in my town, on my watch, so for the time being I'm the one going after answers."

Ronnie lifted the mouth of the bottle to his lips and took a long swig before lowering it again. "You ain't good enough." He wiped his mouth on his sleeve.

Jake stiffened. "Watch it, Ronnie," he said, his voice low with warning.

"Come on, Jacob." Ronnie's eyes blazed as he gestured with the bottle, sloshing the liquid inside. "I know you. You ran through my yard in your pull-ups, remember? I picked you up when you flew over the handlebars of your bike out on the road there and called your pa when you hit a baseball through my truck window. I know you, and I've seen everything that goes on in this town, and you and I both know you ain't never faced nothing like this before. You're still a kid. Just a kid. And if you think you and Annie Oakley park ranger here can take on a homicidal maniac, then you're off your gourd."

Annie bristled at the insult, but kept her mouth shut. This was not a man who would listen to reason. This was a wounded animal backed into a corner, all claws and teeth and blind panic.

A silent half minute passed—Jake and Ronnie staring each other down without blinking. For a moment, eyes brimming with hostility and hands twitching at his sides, Ronnie looked as though he might lash out—might raise the bottle of wine and bring it down on Jake's head or slap him with his empty palm, but he didn't.

Annie glanced at Debra, whose eyes were flitting between the two men as though wondering which of them would snap first. Then, one of the cages on the counter rattled as the animal inside stretched, and Jake rose slowly to his feet. He was at least two inches shorter than Ronnie, but far sturdier as he squared his shoulders.

"Frankly, Ronnie, I'm all you've got."

Ronnie's nostrils flared, but instead of retorting, he lifted the bottle to his lips and took another drink.

"Come on, Annie," Jake said, turning to her, "let's go."

Annie rose quickly, avoiding the stares of husband and wife as she followed Jake across the room.

"That's right," Ronnie shouted as they reached the door. "Get out of here! And don't come back until you've got whoever killed my girl behind bars."

Jake and Annie kept walking, and footsteps thudded behind them as Ronnie followed.

"Do your job, Jacob! And if you can't, then I will!"

Neither Jake nor Annie looked back to acknowledge Ronnie's words as they stepped out onto the porch. He slammed the door behind them.

Jake blew out a breath as he shrugged out of his jacket, lifting it high to shield Annie from the falling rain as they walked side by side down the stairs.

Inside the cruiser with the doors closed, rain hammered the metal and glass relentlessly, and Jake's shoulders sagged as he let out a breath.

"That was rough," Annie said, heart still racing as she buckled her seat belt.

Jake shook his head. "It's not his fault. He's hurting worse right now than I've ever hurt in my life. He's just looking for someone to throw the blame at. And besides that, he's got a point."

She turned to meet his eyes. Jake's gaze was wary, and Annie braced herself for what was coming.

"You know what I mean. About Jamie and Daniel. And if she just dumped him, then you and I both know that puts him at the very top of the suspect list."

Annie said nothing. The seal had been broken, and there remained only the obvious move forward in the chess game of the investigation. Jake shifted into reverse and backed the cruiser up before pulling into the mouth of the driveway.

Annie prayed that he would turn right, back toward town, but not one bit of her was surprised when he turned left instead, toward Lake Lumin.

Chapter 28

ANNIE

The drive to the boathouse had never felt longer.

The twists and turns on the rutted road just kept coming, and Annie's stomach tightened around each one as they climbed through the rain.

"Cold, hard math," Jake said from the driver's seat. "First rule of any female homicide, you always start with the boyfriend or husband. Always. Nine cases out of ten, that's who did it."

Annie had a feeling he was saying the words more to convince himself than to sway her, and she didn't answer as she watched the windshield wipers swiping back and forth, clearing the gathering rain from the glass.

"I don't want to believe he's capable of something like this. I love him. He's like a brother to me, but the stats are overwhelming. I wouldn't be doing my job if I didn't at least rule him out."

Annie nodded to give Jake some sign that she was listening, but said nothing. *Overwhelming* was the perfect word for it. She was overwhelmed with sorrow for the grieving mother and father in that filthy blue house behind them. Overwhelmed with confusion as the details of Jamie's recent life and sudden death raised more questions than answers.

But mostly, she was overwhelmed, yet again, with doubt about the man who lived in the boathouse.

Daniel had lied to her before. Brilliantly. Smoothly. Convincing her that he was someone else entirely before revealing the truth about his past. Whether she liked it or not, she had been duped by him. Fooled. And a selfish, heartsick part of her wanted to ignore that he was the obvious suspect to start with.

Of all people, Daniel Barela was a man who knew how to live outside the boundaries of what society deemed normal. He had told her his version of how he had fled his hometown, but that's exactly what it had been; *his* version, and she'd taken him at his word. But what if Gary Dunn had been the one telling the truth at the press conference all those years ago? Daniel clearly knew how to lie. And he knew how to hide. Did he also know how to kill?

In the driver's seat, Jake cleared his throat, and Annie slid him a sideways glance. Daniel had fooled him, too, and if the investigation led where she feared it might, there would come a point when she would have to decide whether to betray Daniel's trust.

The familiar NO TRESPASSING signs appeared one by one, overbright against the rain-drenched tree trunks to which they were nailed. Annie's gaze jumped from warning to warning as they neared the gate that she already knew would be locked.

Who are you? she wondered, not for the first time as the signs flew past. *Who are you, really?*

The gate was indeed closed and locked, and Jake pulled right up to it, pressing a closed fist against the horn for several seconds. The door of the boathouse did not open, and Annie watched the windows for movement inside, but they perfectly mirrored the clearing, giving nothing away. Jake shifted into park and opened the door. Leaning out of the car with one foot on the ground, he cupped his hands around his mouth.

"Daniel!"

His shout echoed across the clearing, and when it was met with silence, he ducked back inside and turned off the engine. "I don't think he's here."

"He might still be down at the Wards' place. The stable's huge, it probably took more than a few days to figure out where the wiring went wrong."

Jake nodded, slipping his arms into his jacket before stepping out of the car. Annie followed, sparing a quick glance at the low clouds scraping the tips of the pines with mist.

The downpour had lightened considerably, and the firs around the clearing hung heavy with moisture, their lower boughs resting on the ground, higher branches shedding excess drops with a wet, tapping patter that filled the air.

For several moments, Jake stood in front of the gate with his hands on his hips, lower lip moving in and out of his teeth. He stared at the silver padlock that barred entry into the clearing, and after one long exhale, he nodded.

"Come on." He propped a shoe on the gate and started to climb.

"Jake." Annie reached for his arm. "We can't just barge in without a warrant, you know that."

Jake stared down at her, jaw working as the falling mist coated his hair. "I won't go inside the boathouse without his permission, but you and I both know that this isn't just cut-and-dried law enforcement anymore. I'm not only here as a cop, I'm also the guy who discovered Jamie's body, and I'm Daniel's best friend. The lines are blurry, Annie."

There was pain in his eyes. Pain and worry. He didn't want Daniel to have anything to do with this any more than Annie did. They had long since strayed from the black-and-white investigation of Hannah Schroeder's case and were deep into the gray area of Jamie's—where the distinctions between neighbor and victim and friend and suspect were harder to define.

Annie met Jake's gaze for a moment, then nodded, following him up and over the gate.

The boathouse was dark and shadowed where it sat tucked under the fringe of the dripping woods, and Annie was struck by how for-lorn it looked. In sunlight, the building was cozy and quirky, beloved for its shabby-chic furniture and its leaning stack of firewood. It was an extension of Daniel himself, damaged and rebuilt stronger, a stub-born survivor of the past that had burned down behind it. But there was something sinister about the sight of it now, sitting alone, with water streaming from the corner gutters and the lower wall stained with rain.

Annie trailed Jake to the side door, where he hesitated with his hand on the knob. He held it for a moment, then let go and knocked instead. Again, he called Daniel's name loudly, and Annie held her breath, lis-tening for sounds within, but the dripping of rain from the trees was too loud.

"Not home," Jake murmured, turning around to scan the clearing over Annie's shoulder. "Where do you think he keeps his canoe?"

"Over there." Annie turned to indicate the woods on the western shore. "He dug a little place on the embankment to slide it into the water. He hasn't sealed the inside yet, so he keeps it upside down under a tarp to protect it from the weather."

She'd said too much, and Jake looked at her curiously, but if he was wondering how she knew all of that, he didn't voice it.

"Show me," he said instead, and Annie led him to the spot where the canoe lay between two firs, covered by a blue tarp—dimpled with rain.

Jake slid the tarp away. "Help me roll it over."

They each took an end, turning the heavy canoe upright onto its hull. The rough wood was familiar under her hands, and Annie pushed back hard against the memory of her one and only voyage out on the lake in this vessel, a day that had started joyful and filled with laughter and ended with the unraveling of yet another lie Daniel had told her.

When the canoe was righted, Jake reached out a hand and ran it along the hollowed-out inside of the log, rustically chipped by the hatchet and still smelling sharply of pitch. When he lifted his hand again, Annie's heart sank. On his fingers were several small wood shavings, tiny, sharp little splinters, like those Doc Porter had removed from Jamie's shorts.

"I wondered," Jake murmured. "The second I saw those wood shavings at the morgue."

He turned to look at Annie in the weak light beneath the trees.

She nodded. "Could be," she said, though her mind was already spinning, explaining it away.

The wood shavings on Jamie's shorts could have come from anywhere. The fence that bordered the Boyd property, the lifeguard chair at the pool, even the diving board. The lab results weren't back yet. This didn't prove anything.

"There's nothing else, though." Annie leaned close to examine the inside of the canoe. "No blood or fabric. No hair or fibers or anything else that I can see."

Jake wiped his fingers on his pants. "That's true."

There was no hope in his voice, and when Annie looked up to search his face, he didn't meet her eyes. A change had come over him, a change that made her heart ache. The childhood innocence that had survived its way through to adulthood in his features had gone, and Annie felt instinctively that she would never find it there again.

"Come on," he said, "let's get it covered up."

Together, Jake and Annie rolled the canoe back the way they had found it and wrapped it with the tarp, then walked along the shore to the boathouse.

Annie followed Jake as he rounded the building, stepping past the waterfalls of rain that cascaded from the gutters. What he was searching for, she couldn't tell, but he examined the earth carefully as he walked, and when they reached the dock, he climbed up with a grunt, Annie followed after, avoiding the rain-soaked, wild-haired reflection staring back at her from the lake-facing windows.

"Look for anything out of the ordinary." Jake scanned the dock. "Anything that doesn't belong."

Annie nodded, but aside from the deck chairs and the propane tanks, the dock was empty. There were puddles gathered on the warped boards, and she stepped around them to the corner where the skiff was nudging the piling, the inch of water in the bottom of the boat sloshing gently. Nothing. There was nothing out of the ordinary. There was nothing at all.

She lifted her eyes. The lake was alive with the falling rain, thousands of tiny drops landing softly on the surface, setting it dancing with a sound like wind among leaves, and she couldn't help pausing for a moment to take in the haunting beauty of it. It was lovely. And if this rainy day had fallen earlier in the month, she'd probably have been curled up with Daniel on the other side of the windows, instead of standing out here on the dock.

Beneath the sound of the rain, an engine growled, and Annie whipped her head toward the gate. A vehicle was revving over the sloping hills, and she strained to separate the sound from the patter of drizzle around her, but couldn't discern whether it was the Ranger or not.

Jake stepped up beside her, searching the trees on the far side of the clearing.

Annie took a breath. "Should we—"

He held a finger in the air, cutting her off.

The sound grew louder, rising with a gust of wind that peppered Annie's face with cold raindrops, then tapered abruptly into a steady growl as the vehicle idled somewhere just out of sight.

She turned, sharing a long look with Jake as the sound went on and on, then the motor revved once more and the sound fell away. Whoever had come driving up the road had turned around to drive back down.

"Think it was him?"

Jake nodded. "Probably. I'll bet he saw the cruiser at the gate and got spooked. Although, it might have been Ronnie, coming up here to make good on his words."

A beat passed, and Annie asked, "Should we follow whoever it was?"

"No. Let's look around here for a few more minutes. I don't want to miss anything while we have the place to ourselves."

Annie glanced up at the sky. Afternoon was sliding away into evening behind the clouds, and the gray day would lose its meager light soon.

She joined Jake in looking around the dock and soon found Daniel's drawing pad tucked out of the rain between two of the propane tanks under the window, the outside edge damp where the drizzle had reached it. She snatched it up and flipped it open.

She'd looked through Daniel's work several times, always with the conviction that his art told her more about who he was than his words ever could. He brought pencil to paper with such confidence, such self-assurance, and all of the emotion that he never quite managed to translate from his heart to his mouth.

The sketches flipped past, one after the other, a black-and-white blur. There was the maned wolf, and the mountain, and Annie herself, laughing with her braid flipped over her shoulder. The book was nearly full, filled to the penultimate page, and as the paper flipped beneath her thumb, revealing the very last drawing, Annie's breath caught in her throat.

It was Jamie. Daniel had drawn Jamie swimming across the lake with her long golden hair plastered to her back. The sketch was beautiful in his sure, dark style, each stroke of the pencil deliberate and used to great effect, but there was something wrong with it. Something flawed. There, in the direct center of the drawing where Jamie's strong left arm met the water, her elbow bent gracefully mid-stroke, the sketch was smudged, as though it had been rubbed. Touched. As though someone had dragged a wet thumb across it.

The hair on Annie's arms lifted in a rash of goose bumps.

"Jake."

He crossed the dock, peering over her shoulder as she pointed to the smudge on the drawing.

"Charcoal pencil," she said.

It was audible, all of the air leaving Jake's lungs at once, and Annie could not turn to meet his eyes. She would bet a year's salary that the substance on Jamie's thumb had come from this pad.

Jamie had stood right here and touched this paper on the night she died.

Chapter 29

ANNIE

After a few hours of dreamless sleep, Annie woke to a dull morning and dressed quickly.

She splashed her face with cold water, which did nothing to help the circles under her eyes, and jogged down the stairs toward the house, stepping inside to find Walt and Laura already at the breakfast table. Laura invited Annie to the last of the scrambled eggs on the stove and a hot cup of coffee.

"Any progress on the case?" Walt asked as Annie sat down.

"Some." She rubbed at the corners of her eyes. "I'm guessing Jake filled you in on what's going on?"

"We haven't spoken to Jacob yet," Laura said. "We didn't want to be in the way on his first investigation, but, gosh, things sure aren't looking good for Daniel Barela, are they?"

Annie's fork stopped halfway to her mouth. "Who told you that?"

Laura leaned forward. "Oh, honey, after what happened with Ronnie Boyd last night, half the town is in an uproar about the case."

For a moment, Annie didn't reply, mouth hanging ajar as her eyes flicked back and forth between Jake's parents, their heads tilted identically as they gazed at her with twin lines of concern on their faces.

Finally, she returned her fork to her plate. "What happened with Ronnie last night?"

The phone rang in the kitchen, and Walt and Laura traded a look as Laura stood to answer it.

"Here we go again," she said as she stepped away from the table, and Annie turned questioningly to Walt, who shook his head.

"Apparently, after you and Jake left the Boyds' house yesterday, Ronnie headed straight down to the Wolf."

Annie groaned and took a bite of her eggs. She knew by now that the infamous Howling Wolf Bar and Grill was the only tavern for thirty miles in any direction. It sat just south of town, off the highway, mostly hidden behind a thick ring of arborvitae, as though announcing to the rest of Lake Lumin exactly what sort of patron was welcome within its stucco walls. Shady men. Sketchy men. Men who lived on the fringe. And Ronnie Boyd had long been its most reliable customer.

Walt stifled a yawn. "I guess Ronnie climbed up on the bar and started shouting about Daniel's guilt to anyone who would listen, then drank himself into a stupor and demanded that the men form a vigilante posse before he passed out behind the pool table."

A lukewarm piece of egg was stuck in her throat, and Annie forced it down with a gulp of coffee.

"And the guys who were down there? What did they do?"

"Well, they didn't exactly rally around him, if that's what you're asking. But they all went home to their wives and kids, and naturally the story spread like wildfire. Now everyone knows it wasn't that Justin Grimes guy, and the whole town has just about decided Daniel is the guilty party, what with the water in her lungs and her being found out in that clearing way back in his woods and all."

Annie closed her eyes against the headache forming at her temples. It hadn't even been twenty-four hours since the autopsy report, and already everyone in town had a detailed rundown of the results. Across the kitchen, she could just make out Laura's muffled half of the conversation as she chatted on the phone.

"Goodness no, honey," Jake's mother said, "I slept like the dead that night, didn't hear a blamed thing from the Boyd house, but there's been shouting over there for as long as I can remember, carries right through the woods . . . I know . . . Well, you're right about that, Ronnie's been getting worse for years. Now, I'm not saying he's capable of killing his own daughter, mind . . ." There was a pause, then a murmur of agreement. "Well, it's an interesting theory at least. I'll be sure to let Jacob know."

Annie realized with a fresh twist of anxiety that the phone was sure to be ringing off the hook at the station, too. They would be fielding calls all day from every busybody in Lake Lumin, phoning with what they deemed to be suitable theories and helpful information.

"I better go." Annie rose from the table and reached for her plate. "Things are going to be nuts in town."

"Good luck." Walt lifted his coffee mug in a salute of farewell.

Jake's cruiser wasn't in its normal spot when Annie parked along the curb of Hughes Street half an hour later, and the office was dark when she entered. She brewed a fresh pot of coffee, filling a mug when there was just enough in the carafe and carrying it to the desk.

As she sank into her chair, the phone rang, and it did not stop ringing for the next forty minutes.

Phil from the General Store called to say that Jamie had come in asking for beach towels in January, in *January*, and did Annie think that was significant to the crime? Another local who didn't give her name called in to say that she'd visited the community pool on the day after Jamie's murder and had felt a chill run from head to toe as she stepped into the water, which meant Jamie *must* have been drowned there, and Sally from the bed-and-breakfast phoned to bring attention to the fact that the nearest resident to the crime scene was a man who didn't quite fit in, an outsider who lived by himself up a dead-end road in a boathouse, and was "mighty peculiar," as she put it.

Annie took the tips in stride, scolding each and every one of the callers to stop speculating, reminding them that she and Jake were the ones who had to worry about catching the killer, and that spreading rumors would only amplify the fear already hanging over the town like fog.

She'd just hung up on the fifth caller when Jake appeared on the other side of the glass door.

"Cedar," he announced as he stepped inside, tossing a thin file onto the desk with a thump.

He fell into his chair and dropped his head into his hands.

Annie forced the words out. "The results are back?"

"Yeah," Jake muttered into the heel of his hand, slowly turning his head to catch her eyes. "The wood shavings were made of cedar. Just like the canoe. And the stuff on her thumb? Willow charcoal. The exact kind used in drawing pencils. The sample of water from her lungs isn't back yet, but even without it, this is more than enough evidence. Once the town finds out, they'll be calling for Daniel's blood. Heck, half of them already are."

"I know."

"I've never seen anything like it. This town has lost its mind. I walked to work today, and I must have been stopped seven or eight times. People are clustered together in little groups, talking over the details of the case like they're hashing it out in court. I finally had to disconnect my phone this morning so I could eat breakfast in peace."

He sounded angry, the barely subdued irritation in his voice raw and utterly foreign to the man who normally sat beside her at the desk.

"Were you able to track Daniel down?"

"No." Jake lifted his head from his hands. His hair was tousled, and his uniform shirt was one button off at the collar. "I went down to the Wards' place after I dropped you off yesterday, but they said he'd already left for the day, so I went home. Must have called the boathouse thirty times last night, but he never answered, so I drove back up there around midnight. Gate was still locked and his truck wasn't in the clearing. He's hiding, Annie, and he's not leaving me much of a choice about how to handle this thing."

The words only worsened the tight feeling in Annie's chest.

Hiding. It was what Daniel did best.

A shadow darkened the sunlight beyond the door, and they both looked up as Ian Ward appeared on the other side of the glass, pushing his way into the station with a cigarette between his teeth.

"Ian." Jake rose from his seat. "What can we do for you?"

Ian avoided Annie's gaze as he blew out a breath, twin plumes of smoke streaming from his nostrils.

"Thought I'd come by," he said around the cigarette. "I've got some information that may be useful to you."

"Oh?" Jake asked, his tone clipped.

Despite the wrinkled shirt and the hair slicked back from his receding hairline, Ian somehow managed to convey a sense of superiority as he stared down his nose at Jake and took another long drag from his cigarette. He freed the stub with two fingers and blew a cornucopia of smoke toward the desk, still ignoring Annie completely.

"That's right. I might have a bit of knowledge pertaining to the Boyd case."

Annie could read Jake's body language as well as anyone, and she didn't miss the impatient tapping of his fingers or the nostril flare of irritation.

"You might, or you do?"

Ian took one last drag of his cigarette and leaned forward to stub it out on Annie's nameplate, leaving the crumpled butt smoldering on the countertop.

"I do."

Annie resisted the urge to reach for her nameplate and brush the ashes away, but Jake made a show of lifting the butt from the counter with two fingers and dropping it into the trash.

"Well," he said, "you obviously came in to tell us, so go ahead and talk."

Ian rested his arms on the counter and took his time clearing the mucus from his throat before he spoke again.

"As you know, Jake, my family is . . . well-connected. We have our finger on the pulse of this town, and not much happens that escapes our notice."

The phone on the desk rang loudly, and Annie quickly lifted the receiver and slammed it down again. Ian didn't even seem to notice as he droned on.

"You'll know that the Lake Lumin rumor mill reaches the Ward estate first ninety-nine percent of the time, and the other one percent is when folks think we must have heard about it from someone else already."

Ian was enjoying this. Dragging it out. Dangling the information that he had like bait.

"If you have something to tell us, say it," Annie snapped, glaring up at him from her chair. "We've got a lot to do today."

Ian turned to her then, smiling, though his eyes remained cold and hard as ice. "I'm getting to it." He turned back to Jake. "Did you know Jamie Boyd worked down at the pool?"

Jake folded his arms across his chest. "Of course. So?"

"So, she had a little group of friends that gathered down there on the weekends, and you know how girls like to talk to one another. Sharing all the dirty details of their lives."

Jake's fingers were tapping rapidly against his arms now, and Annie could tell it was with great restraint that he was still behind the counter, and not on the other side of the desk, slapping whatever information Ian had right out of him.

"And?"

Ian pulled another cigarette from the pack in his pocket and wagged it between his fingers. "Honestly, Jake, here I was thinking you were smart. Who owns the pool?"

"Your parents," Jake said without inflection.

"I do," Ian said sharply, pointing a thumb at his chest. "I own it."

"Okay, your parents gave it to you. What about it?"

Ian ignored the jab and continued to flick the unlit cigarette back and forth. "Being the owner, I usually work in that little office around back, that room behind the lifeguard stand, and with my window cracked open, I can hear what goes on outside. Jamie's friends come down there almost every day, and the way them girls talk"—he laughed and shook his head—"it's like they haven't seen each other in years. They talk about boys, mostly. Their love lives. Heck, sometimes they even tell me directly if I'm out on deck. Kinda dropping hints here and there if they're available, I figure."

Annie barely managed to keep her face from folding into a cringe. She could just picture it, this man in early middle age sidling up to the teen girls beside the pool. There was a specific breed of man, a specific breed of snake, that specialized in mistaking the innocent conversations of young women for an invitation.

"So, you overheard something about Jamie's love life," Jake said, steering Ian back to the point at hand. "What was it?"

"Not overheard," Ian corrected. "Just heard."

"What was it?"

"Well, as of a week ago, Jamie was dating a guy from up on her road in the briars. Older than her, I gathered from the conversation. Jamie told her friend Stephanie that she was thinking of calling it quits on him; so, we've got us a dead girl and a spurned lover on our hands. I've seen enough *Law and Order* to know that's something worth looking into. Or, at least, I would . . . if I were you."

Jake dropped his gaze to the desk and shuffled the stack of papers there.

"We've been made aware of that already, thanks."

There was dismissal in his tone, but Ian didn't seem to notice.

"Now, she never said outright that it was Daniel Barela, at least not that I heard, but this *is* a small town, and there ain't many single men in it, am I right?"

"You're single," Annie pointed out, failing to keep the haughtiness out of her voice.

Something like surprise flickered in Ian's dark eyes, and one corner of his mouth twisted sourly.

"By choice," he retorted. "It's not like I couldn't have any one of those girls if I wanted to."

Jake's hands clenched into fists on the desk. "Be careful, Ian. Some of those girls you're talking about are minors."

"Jamie was nineteen." Ian turned for the door and pushed it open with a flat hand. Halfway out, he paused to look back over his shoulder. "And trust me when I tell you this: She was no child."

He was out the door and gone before either of them could respond.

"What a creep," Annie breathed as Jake sank heavily into his chair.

The phone rang again, and this time Jake was the one to lift it from the cradle and slam it down, yanking the cord from the back for good measure.

A full minute passed, Annie staring at Jake, and Jake staring at the phone.

"I need to go to Vancouver," he said at last. "That's the closest circuit judge from here."

Annie's brows drew together. "What do you need a circuit judge for?"

Jake turned to meet her gaze with eyes full of misery. "A circuit judge is the one who issues an arrest warrant."

Annie blanched, and for several seconds she could say nothing. She knew the indignation was unwarranted, but it welled up in her chest anyway, bursting out in a storm of words.

"You can't be serious . . . You're his best friend, Jake, you guys have known each other for years. He trusts you, and you're just going to waltz up there and slap a pair of handcuffs on him?"

Jake didn't look at her as the words fell like blows, and when she was finished, he merely shook his head.

"What else can I do, Annie? He's avoiding me. There's a reason he never went home last night. I know the guy. I know him better than just about anyone else does. Daniel's a turtle, he gets into his shell and there's no getting him out of it. I have to force him onto neutral territory. I have to put him into a situation where he has to answer questions. Where he has the fear of the law hanging over his head and can see me as something other than the guy he goes fishing with on Saturdays."

Jake was right, and there was no arguing it, but stubborn tears pricked at Annie's eyes anyway as her chest rose and fell in silence.

"If you have *anyone* else we should investigate, I'm all ears," he said. "But the fact is, you don't. You and I both know we have more than enough evidence for a warrant. And frankly, putting it off is not just stupid, it's negligent."

Annie sat back in her chair, suddenly worn-out and exhausted and a hundred years old. Why was she fighting back so hard against Daniel as the obvious suspect? Why was she clinging to the hope that Jamie's killer was someone else when Jake, who had known Daniel far longer than she had, was already willing to set his personal feelings aside in pursuit of justice. Jake, who didn't even have the full story. Jake, who still believed Daniel Barela was, in fact, Daniel Barela.

When Annie remained silent, Jake sighed again and rose from his chair.

"Can I take your Jeep? I left the cruiser at my place, and I don't feel like walking all the way back. I won't be gone more than a few hours."

"Sure." She handed him the keys. "Just be careful on the freeway, it's been stuttering a little bit over fifty-five."

Jake nodded and turned to leave.

He was halfway to the door when Annie's conscience got the better of her.

"Wait . . ."

He stopped, turning back.

Annie pushed aside her guilt. It was the right thing to do. And it was past time.

"There's something you should know."

He walked back around the desk. "I'm listening."

She could feel the words bubbling up, rising from the place where she had buried them. "Jake . . . Daniel isn't who you think he is."

Chapter 30

DANIEL

The paranoia was back, and much worse this time. Tangible and acute—impossible to shove into the far corner of his mind and write off as an overactive imagination. It surrounded him in the clearing, hunched in every flickering shadow, and sank into his skin with the sweet summer breeze.

Daniel raised the maul high over his head and brought it down on the splintered cedar round that waited on the chopping stump, cracking it halfway through. He swung again and again—tossing the quarters into the growing pile.

His sweat-soaked shirt lay in a forgotten heap behind him. The skin of his shoulders smarted with sunburn and his head throbbed with each swing of the maul. Even his eyes ached with fatigue, but he persisted.

Splitting the cedar rounds wasn't on his list of chores for the summer. He already had enough firewood to last the winter. Two winters, actually, but he couldn't sit still inside the boathouse for one more minute or he'd lose his mind.

It was torture, pure torture, just sitting and staring out the window with the door propped open and his ears tuned for the wail of Jake's siren. The sound of his imminent arrest.

After yesterday, he knew it was only a matter of time. The town had turned against him, and Jake was next. Now that Justin Grimes was out of the picture, whom else would Jake suspect? Who else knew the woods up here like the back of their hand? Who else had Jamie been seen with, friendly with, or *more* than friendly with, by Jake's reckoning?

The cards were stacked against him, so here he was, on exactly zero hours of sleep, chopping wood under a blazing-hot sun because he couldn't bear to spend one more restless minute inside. Physical exertion kept the demons at bay, the ones that had haunted him last night as he sat alone in the truck.

It seemed crazy, now, that he hadn't picked up on it at the Wards'. He hadn't thought anything of it when Tammy Ward handed him his check with her arm all the way outstretched, the slip of paper in her thin fingers pinched by the far corner. Even her head was drawn back far enough to wrinkle her neck, as though she were protecting every last inch of space she could put between them.

When Daniel told her there was one more breaker he wanted to get behind to double-check the voltage, she'd shaken her head quickly and said it wasn't needed; she'd call him if they ran into any more trouble. Odd, but still, he hadn't thought much of it, until he stopped in town on his way home, and there had been no way to miss the sense of unease. Sideways stares and furtive glances were leveled in his direction from every passerby—and a group of three women that he greeted with a nod instantly crossed to the other side of the street.

It was Phil who had said it outright, Phil who had checked left and right where he stood behind the counter, then leaned forward to warn Daniel to get on home before a mob formed around him, seeking justice for Jamie's death.

And sure enough, just outside the General Store, a group of people had noticed his truck parked in the lot and were gathered on the sidewalk a few meters from it, their voices falling away as one when

Daniel strode toward them with a cold bottle of Pepsi clenched in his fist.

There was fear in their eyes, and something else, something he hadn't seen leveled in his direction in three-quarters of a decade. Hate.

The whispers started as he fumbled with the key in the lock, growing louder and bolder until the voices blended together into one rumble of discontent. As Daniel climbed into his truck and reached for the door handle, one word slipped free, perfectly enunciated and unmissable.

"Murderer."

He didn't drive home. Instead, he sped straight through town and out the other end, flying west on the long, winding highway that led to the interstate and freedom.

The miles passed beneath the tires with his attention split between staring at the road ahead, and checking the rearview mirror for the sight of flashing lights in hot pursuit.

Not until he reached the on-ramp for the interstate did he slam on his brakes, skidding off the road onto the shoulder and juddering over the gravel.

With the engine rumbling, he sat stock-still in the truck, staring at the wide freeway ahead, cars zipping north toward Tacoma, Seattle, Bellingham, and beyond. Cities full of strangers where one more unfamiliar face would not be noticed.

He switched off the engine.

What was he doing? He had less than half a tank of gas and only twenty dollars in his wallet; and there was nothing but the set of clothes on his back and half a bottle of Pepsi rolling around under the seat to sustain him. He was hardly in shape to make a go at starting over again.

A bag of survival essentials had been stashed in the bottom drawer of his dresser for years. He could drive back home, grab it, then vanish into the woods like a shadow and just keep going, hiking east into the

Cascades, into the deepest, darkest wilderness in Washington State. He could let himself be driven out.

Or . . .

He could stay. Stay and own up to whatever came next.

Attempted murder and murder were two completely different accusations, and he knew full well what a conviction on this charge would mean, but running brought its own personal consequences. Running meant throwing away everything he'd worked toward with Annie, and though things weren't right between them at the moment, he believed with his whole heart that she was his future. She was worth fighting for. Worth doing whatever it took to make sure nothing got in their way.

Daniel caught his gaze in the rearview mirror and looked away again as a long-forgotten quote swam to the front of his mind.

At his best, man is the noblest of all animals; separated from law and justice, he is the worst.

He sat for a long time on the shoulder of the road. So long that the sky faded from blue to violet, and violet to black. Stars blinked to life at the top of the windshield and the cab of the truck grew cold.

At two in the morning, he drove back to the boathouse and spent the rest of the night staring out the window at the dark road beyond the trees, waiting . . .

Daniel lifted the maul and swung with all his strength, cracking the round down to a gnarled knot, where the maul lodged its heavy head and stuck fast. He wrenched the handle back and forth, but could not free it. He tried again, shoving the handle downward with his full strength, but stubbornly, it would not budge.

The misplaced rage that boiled up inside him was instant, and he took a step back and lashed out, kicking the side of the stump with his full strength as a feral cry of frustration and exhaustion passed his lips. The sound went on and on, flying up from the very bottom of his lungs and out through his mouth, loud and furious enough to frighten him.

The last echoes of his shout faded away into the wilderness around him, and in the silence that followed, Daniel heard the cruiser coming.

He sagged where he stood, depleted. He had come here for freedom. He had come here for peace. And now he was in far worse trouble than he had been all those years ago.

Jake was on his way. The engine grinding up the road was fast and steady, and there was no one else it could be. Not today.

Daniel's heart contracted in his chest, each thump marking the moment as it passed. He placed his foot against the cedar round, wrenched the handle of the maul with all his might until it popped free, and rested it carefully against the stump.

The car was close now, so close that he could hear the gravel popping under the tires, and in the moment before the vehicle appeared, a strange peace washed over him, a sort of surrender. Daniel closed his eyes and slowly filled his lungs with fresh forest air for what might be the last time.

Let him come.

The cruiser swung into view, tires splashing through the shallow puddles on the road, sunlight glaring off the windshield. Jake was hidden from view, but Daniel could feel the pair of eyes tracking him as he walked forward to meet his fate.

Inches from the gate, the car screeched to a halt and the engine died. The door opened, and the driver climbed out.

Daniel froze.

It was Annie, copper hair glinting in the sun as she practically high-jumped the gate, leaping over the top and walking toward him with long strides. Her face was white, her lips pressed into the thinnest of lines, and Daniel stood statue still, unable even to breathe as she lifted the pistol in her hands and aimed it straight at his chest.

Chapter 31

ANNIE

The Ruger was heavy as lead, but Annie's arms were steady as she strode toward the man standing alone in the clearing.

Daniel was shining with sweat, his bare upper body bronzed by the sun, eyes hooded in the shadow of his dark brows. His arms, lifted in surrender, rose and fell slightly with each breath like the fir boughs behind him, stirred by barely there wind.

Annie shoved back against the thought that always struck her when she stepped onto this land to meet him, that he was the beauty around them distilled into human form.

She stopped several meters short of where he stood, gun pointed straight ahead.

"Did you do it?" she demanded.

Her voice was strained, and there was no preamble, no ease-in. She would not give him time to think on his feet.

Slowly, he shook his head. "No."

"Did you do it?" she repeated, every word deliberate. An opportunity.

"No."

Annie stared at him, anger and doubt burning in her chest as her eyes flicked back and forth across his. Daniel did not look away and did not blink, meeting her gaze as she searched him for the truth.

"I didn't, Annie," he said quietly. "I didn't kill her."

Annie gathered her resolve. "Why should I believe you?"

Slowly, Daniel lowered his arms to his sides. "I know what people are saying. I know what they're thinking, but I had no reason to kill her. Listen to me, Annie, why would I?"

Annie did not lower the gun.

"Jamie was here that night," she said, her voice hard. "She ran up here at midnight. I heard her jogging by the house. And there were wood shavings on her shorts. Cedar, from the canoe, and charcoal on her thumb from your drawing pad, how can you possibly explain all that?"

"Look"—Daniel's gaze faltered, dropped to the gun for an instant— "all I can tell you is that I woke up that night and found her swimming in the lake. I asked her to leave and then I went back to bed. I don't . . . I can't explain the other stuff, but she must not have left. Someone else must have met her here. Whoever . . . whoever killed her."

"Who?" Annie said, voice rising into a shout. "Who else could it possibly have been? She was here. On *your* property. And Jake's right, ninety-nine percent of the time in a case like this, it's the boyfriend who did it."

Daniel stared at her as a cool wind dipped through the clearing, tearing a handful of leaves from the alders and tossing them into the air where they scattered.

"Jamie and I weren't together."

For a moment, Annie was too stunned to speak.

"You're seriously denying it?" she managed at last. "Right to my face, you're going to pretend like the two of you weren't involved?"

"We *weren't* together." His hazel eyes flashed. "She—she was interested, I think, but it was completely one-sided. And what Jake saw in the truck wasn't me kissing her, it was her kissing me." Daniel closed his eyes, chest sagging. "I swear to you, Annie, I never gave her a second thought. I never gave anyone a second thought after I met you. Jake . . .

he misinterpreted things. He has a bad habit of speaking up before he has all the facts."

Annie hunted for signs of falsehood, but there were none. His voice was steady and his posture sure. Slowly, she lowered the gun to her waist.

When she didn't speak, Daniel said, "You really think I killed her, don't you? You truly think I'm capable of that."

Annie stared back, willing herself to believe it, to follow the evidence with a hard heart and picture him holding Jamie down in the lake as she took that lethal breath of water into her lungs—but she could not.

"I don't know. I honestly don't, but I . . . I told Jake. I told him who you are. I told him everything."

Daniel took a step backward, face darkening.

"You told him?"

"What was I supposed to do? How could I hide something like that from him when I'm the one person helping him solve the case? Yes, I told him. And he's driving to Vancouver right now to get a warrant for your arrest. He'll be here in a matter of hours."

The look on Daniel's face shifted from disbelief to anger.

"So you're here to warn me? You're here to give a heads-up to the guy you think committed murder? Do you have any idea how stupid that sounds, Annie?"

There it was, the outrage she'd expected, and she raised the gun without hesitation, aiming it at his chest again.

"That's why I brought this."

Daniel's eyes did not drop to the weapon, but stayed fixed on hers.

"Why?" he demanded. "Why come up here and tell me? To give me a chance to run?"

Again, Annie could not answer. She could not explain her actions. Not to him, not even to herself, and as though dragged by gravity, the gun dropped back down to her side.

"I needed to know. Ask you myself. Part of me thought you wouldn't be here, that you . . . that you'd already run."

Silence fell between them until Daniel broke it with a sigh.

"I'm done running, Annie. I've made up my mind. I'm not doing that again."

Annie didn't respond, and after a moment Daniel shook his head.

"Where would I go? Start fresh in some new town? Do it all over—steal someone else's name? I'm tired of this. I'm tired of hiding, and I'm not leaving. Not when the one thing in the world I'm sure that I want is right here."

Annie's breath caught.

He was talking about her.

Facing him in the sunlight, in this beautiful place she'd come to love, she clawed against the truth . . . but it was no use. Daniel was the one thing she was sure she wanted, too. It was a rock-solid fact, and the knowledge was too deep, still branded on her skin in every place his hands had touched her. Believing in him now, deciding that he was innocent despite all the evidence to the contrary, was her choice to make, and deep inside her, a shift took place.

She knew this man, and he was not a killer.

"Then you have to fight your way out of this," she said at last. "You have to prove that you're innocent."

"How? I don't have enough time. I have hours. Just hours until Jake takes me in, and how can I possibly figure out who the murderer is from inside a jail cell?"

Annie turned away, her gaze lingering on the eastern shore of the lake where a pair of ducks were skidding to a landing on the surface.

He was right. There wasn't enough time. The end of the afternoon would bring his arrest, and if someone was going to untangle the threads of what really happened that night, it wouldn't be Daniel. It would have to be her.

"Can you think of anyone else?" she asked, turning to meet his eyes again. "Anyone at all who might have killed her?"

Daniel shook his head. "Believe me, I've taken just about every possible person I can think of and raked them over the coals in my mind looking for cracks, for motive, for the sort of twisted personality it takes to do something like this, but . . ." He turned to look out at the water. "I mean, there're guys who think they're above the law. Guys like Ian Ward and his friends, but I can't see any of them finding their way around the woods up here in the middle of the night." He hesitated, lifting a hand to rub at his jaw. "But Ian does work down at the pool, and maybe he drowned her down there later that night, then drove up to dump her body off the ridge road. It's possible, right?"

He turned to look at Annie again, brows lifted in question.

"Maybe." It was the most generous answer she could give.

They stared into each other's eyes for a long moment, then Daniel's gaze fell to the ground.

"And then there's the other theory," he muttered.

"What theory?"

Daniel hesitated, blinking at his shoes. "The one that makes me sound like a nutcase."

"What theory?"

"Gary."

Annie's brows shot up. "Your . . . your stepfather?"

Daniel nodded. "He was special ops before he became a contractor. He was smart and well-connected. If anyone could do something like this, it's him, believe me."

Annie was dumbfounded. It was too far-fetched. Too outlandish. Surely Daniel knew that, but his eyes were full of sincerity.

"But . . . but why? What possible motive would he have to kill Jamie?"

Daniel spread his arms out at his sides and looked around. "Wouldn't this be the perfect form of revenge? Tracking me down, making it look like I really did kill someone? It would dredge everything back up, put him in the spotlight again, and land me in prison for the rest of my life, which is what he wanted in the first place; a fitting punishment for what he thinks I tried to do to him."

For a moment, Daniel's eyes circled the clearing, as though his step-father might appear through the trees at any second, and Annie stared at him with her heart thudding behind her ribs. The idea was unhinged. Truly unhinged.

"You have to know how crazy that sounds."

Daniel turned back to her. "I do, but I'm telling you, Annie, you don't know the guy. He could be living out in the woods somewhere surviving off of squirrels and mice, that's the kind of person he is. He could pull something like this off just like any of the other crazy military missions he went on. He could have been scoping me out for weeks. Months. Honestly, a part of me feels like I've just been waiting seven years for something like this to happen."

Annie scanned the dark forest behind the boathouse. What Daniel was saying was unthinkable. And yet, twice, she'd come across unthinkable scenes out there in those very woods. Was the theory really crazier than anything else that had happened?

Her thumb twitched back and forth over the Ruger's safety as she contemplated the idea.

"You seriously think that's a possibility?" she said at last.

"I kind of have to. What's the alternative? That I somehow blacked out and killed her without meaning to?" Daniel lifted a hand and raked it through his hair in frustration. "I didn't do it, Annie."

Annie hesitated, wishing there were a way to see inside his head. But there was no litmus test for truth.

Remember, Annie girl, when push comes to shove out there, trust your-self. Have faith in your instincts and follow your gut, it's the best compass you've got.

Annie tucked the Ruger into its holster. "I better go. Pool should be open for another couple of hours. Maybe Ian's down there, or one of Jamie's friends I could talk to. You stay here. It'll be worse for you if you're gone when Jake gets back with the warrant."

Daniel blinked at her in what looked like genuine surprise. "You're going to help me?"

Annie nodded.

"Why?"

Silence fell again as she met his searching gaze.

"I have to."

She turned her back on him and jogged toward the gate, climbing up and over and ducking into the cruiser.

For the first time as she pulled away from the lake in the woods, Annie did not look back.

Chapter 32

ANNIE

Annie drove the miles between the lake and town with her foot hard on the gas, aware of every second that ticked by.

Time was precious. Minutes and seconds were all she had in the race against Daniel's arrest, against his being sent to trial, and after that, the unthinkable possibility of a lifetime in prison.

Annie knew next to nothing about murder trials. She had no idea if the evidence stacked against Daniel was enough to convict him, but if the reaction of Lake Lumin's citizens to the crime had been any indication, it was hard to imagine a jury finding him innocent.

As it stood now, she was his best hope, his only hope, and if he didn't kill Jamie, then someone else had. There was no such thing as a perfect murder. There was evidence out there somewhere, truth to be uncovered, and she was determined to try, not just for Daniel, the man she'd come to care for, but for sixteen-year-old Nico, who had been running for his life for far too long.

With the red and blue lights swirling atop the Crown Victoria, Annie sped through the town's lone stoplight and hit the speed bump before the pool with such force that she briefly left her seat. She whipped into the parking lot and mashed down on the brake, easing the cruiser around the lot with her eyes on the wooden lifeguard stand on the other side of the gate, once inhabited by Jamie, and now by a burly teenaged boy watching a couple of kids splash around in the water with a look of supreme boredom on his face.

Annie rolled by the gate, her heart surging up into her throat as she gazed at the turquoise water filling the massive pool. It rippled like satin in the bright sunlight, beautiful and lethal.

The lifeguard in the stand noticed the cruiser and watched it with mild interest as Annie backed into a spot facing the pool. She let the car idle for a minute as she gazed through the iron fence. A young woman was sitting on the edge of the pool, the dyed-blue ends of her hair draped over her shoulders as she stared down at her feet, swishing back and forth in the water. Annie stared, her mind replaying something Debra had said while Annie and Jake were at the Boyd house.

She was talking to her friend on the phone, the girl with the blue hair, Stephanie . . .

Annie switched off the engine and climbed out. The pool gate was unlocked, and she stepped inside. Three young boys were splashing one another in a shallow corner—their mother's face hidden behind a magazine as she lounged on one of the deck chairs—and in the middle of the pool, an elderly woman wearing a yellow swim cap and goggles was doing some sort of water aerobics.

Annie walked around the edge of the pool to the girl with her feet in the deep end and lowered herself into a crouch.

"Are you Stephanie?"

The girl lifted her face to look at Annie. Her heavy eyeliner was smeared beneath eyes that were swollen from crying, and her nose was pierced with a small silver stud.

"Yeah."

"I'm Annie Heston. I work with Jake Proudy over at the police station."

Stephanie looked Annie up and down as she took a cross-legged seat beside her.

"I want you to know that we're doing our best to figure out what happened to your friend Jamie. Would you mind if I asked you a few questions?"

"Okay."

Stephanie slowly withdrew her pale legs from the water, pulling her feet up onto the sun-warmed deck and wrapping her hands around her knees.

"I understand the two of you were close?"

The tears that sprang into Stephanie's eyes were instant, and two quickly spilled over in shining paths down her cheeks.

"We were best friends."

Annie nodded, offering a small smile, though her heart ached for the young woman beside her.

"And you shared details about your lives with each other? Secrets?"

Stephanie nodded and a third tear fell. "We told each other everything."

Annie wished she had a handkerchief or a tissue or even a long sleeve to offer this girl, but she didn't, and Stephanie ran her bare arm noisily under her nose.

"I know this is hard, but it's really important that we know who Jamie was close to, who she might have been spending time with in the weeks leading up to her death."

Stephanie looked away, staring into the pool as she thought, the rippling water reflected in her dark eyes.

"I mean, Jamie had just broken up with someone, like a day or two before she died. She had a boyfriend that her parents didn't know about."

Annie prepared herself for the blow. "What was his name?"

Stephanie shrugged. "I don't know. Jamie was weird about it. She wouldn't tell me. She said he made her promise. That he didn't want people to know because they might not understand their relationship with her being younger. She said he was a really private guy."

Annie nodded, trying not to let the emotion warring in her chest show on her face. *Private.* That was just about the number one adjective she'd use to describe Daniel Barela.

"Are you sure Jamie never mentioned his name? I know best friends sometimes share secrets with each other that they're supposed to keep. If Jamie told you who he was, I promise the best thing you can do for her right now is to tell me."

"She didn't," Stephanie insisted, dark eyes flashing. "I already told you, I don't know."

Annie turned for a moment, watching the three boys at the other end of the pool, one of whom was showing the others how to blast a stream of water through a foam noodle. Taking a deep breath, she turned back to Stephanie and forged ahead.

"Do you think it could have been Daniel Barela?"

Stephanie blinked at her. "That guy who lives at the end of Jamie's road?"

Annie nodded.

"No." Stephanie shook her head quickly. "I heard my mom talking about him on the phone and I know people think he did it, but . . ." She turned back to the pool, brows scrunching together as she thought. "I don't think he . . . he . . . actually, I don't know if he does."

Annie leaned forward. "If he does what?"

"If he has a tattoo." Stephanie turned to meet Annie's eyes again. "Jamie said her boyfriend had a tattoo. She went on and on about how much she loved it."

Annie's heart stuttered in her chest. Daniel did not have tattoos. Not one.

"Are you sure?" Annie leaned forward again. "Are you absolutely positive she said he had a tattoo?"

Stephanie nodded. "Yeah, I'm sure. She loved guys with tattoos."

Hope was stirring in Annie's chest. This was something at last. Something to go on.

"Did she mention what kind? Or how many?"

Stephanie pulled her lip into her teeth as she hunted through her memory, then her eyes flickered with some recollection, something dragged forward from her undoubtedly bottomless well of conversations with Jamie.

"At least two, I think. She said 'tattoos,' not 'tattoo,' I'm . . . I'm pretty sure. Not positive, but pretty sure. And I can't remember if she ever said what kind they were. She probably did, but I just can't remember."

"Okay." Annie nodded. "That's okay."

She reached out to lay a hand on Stephanie's back. "I know you're going through a lot right now, and I'm so sorry for your loss. If there's anything else you remember, anything at all that you think might be worth mentioning, big or small, I want you to come into the station or call and let us know, okay?"

Tears brimmed in Stephanie's eyes again at Annie's condolences, but they stayed in silver half-moons as she nodded and looked away, dropping her feet back into the water.

Annie stood to leave, casting one quick glance in the direction of the manager's office as she rose. The door was ajar, and inside, the cluttered desk was vacant. Ian Ward was not at work today. Ian, who had come into the station to make a show of pointing the finger at Daniel right off the bat. Ian, who had at least one tattoo.

As she walked around the pool on her way out, Annie gazed at the water, the azure of the deep end fading into the aquamarine of the shallows. For the first time, a new picture was emerging in her mind, a new version of what had happened that night, here, at the pool, where a tattooed man who thought himself a cut above the rest of the town—and certainly above being dumped by Jamie Boyd—had held her head down in the water until she died.

Annie's fingers were tingling as she strode toward the cruiser, and there was a strange spring in her step, as though the ground itself were propelling her forward.

At last.

At last there was a piece of evidence in her hands pointing at someone other than Daniel Barela.

Chapter 33

ANNIE

The station was empty when Annie unlocked the door and stepped inside.

She didn't bother flipping on the lights as she rounded the desk, her eyes on the landline where a blinking red number announced two unheard messages.

On the drive over from the pool, she'd run the timeline in her head, and it fit. It actually fit. Jamie had run up to the lake just before midnight. It had probably taken her a few minutes to strip down and get in the water, and not long after that, Daniel had stepped out onto the dock and asked her to leave. Twelve fifteen. Twelve twenty, maybe. With a time of death between one and three in the morning, that left plenty of time for Jamie to make her way down to the pool with Ian or someone else, and plenty of time for the drive up to the ridge afterward, where Jamie's killer had dumped her body in the hopes of blaming it on Justin Grimes.

In fact, it made *more* sense that Jamie's drowning had taken place in town, rather than up in the briars. If Jamie had been drowned in Lake Lumin, the easiest thing for the killer to do would be to leave her body there and let Daniel take the blame for it.

The more she thought about it, the more convinced Annie became that the lab results would prove Jamie had drowned in the pool, and that's what had brought her back to the station, the hope that Doc Porter had called with results from the lab in Seattle.

Breath held, Annie pressed the play button for the first recorded message.

"Hi, this is Paula Rizzo for Annie Heston. I'm with the Northwest Wildlife Rehabilitation Center in Portland, and I wanted to let you know that the cougar you brought in has been treated and released back into his territory with a new radio collar at the coordinates you gave us. The wound wasn't as deep as we first thought, but he does have a few stitches that will dissolve on their own within the next week or two, and a light bandage to keep them clean in the meantime. Thank you again for bringing him in, and please don't hesitate to call us if you have any questions or need anything in the future. Thank you."

Impatiently, Annie clicked the arrow for the next message.

"Annie, are you there? It's Jake, pick up . . . pick up . . . guess not. So, listen, good news and bad news. The good news is I know why the Jeep's been stuttering on the freeway, but the bad news is you need a new head gasket. It blew out on me when I was heading back from the courthouse. I called a tow truck, and I'm at a garage in some tiny town called Hockinson, about twenty minutes from Vancouver. I told the mechanic I'm on police business so he bumped me up to first in line, but it's still half a day's job. No idea when I'll be back, but probably way later tonight or early tomorrow morning. I don't wanna spend the night down here with Daniel being such a flight risk and all, so I'll be back up as soon as I can to get him into custody. If you need me in the meantime, here's the number for the garage . . ."

Annie grabbed a pen and took down the phone number he rattled off, shoulders sagging with relief. It wasn't much, only a few extra hours, half a day at the most, but one bad gasket had bought Daniel a little more time before his arrest.

Placing the pen down, Annie reached for the Rolodex on Jake's side of the desk and flipped it open. When she found the number she was hunting for, she punched it into the handset and lifted the phone to her ear, listening as it rang once, twice.

"Hello?"

"Hi, Doctor Porter, this is Annie Heston. I'm sorry to bother you in the middle of the workday, but I'm calling to see if the results have come back from the lab yet . . . results from the water in Jamie Boyd's lungs, I mean."

The doctor chuckled. "Your timing is impeccable, Annie. As a matter of fact, I was just about to give the station a call. The results came in a few minutes ago. Is Jake around to hear this?"

A wave of blood surged past Annie's ears, making her lightheaded.

"No, he's out for the day, but I'm happy to relay the message."

Annie heard the rustling of paper as an envelope was peeled open and pages pulled out.

"One second here, let me find my glasses . . ."

Come on! she wanted to shout as her fingers tightened around the phone. *Come on!*

The phone was set down, then lifted again, and paper rustled once more as a page was turned.

"Well?" Annie asked, breathless.

"Ah, here we are . . . Goodness, it's uh . . . it's remarkable, really. You'll never guess what they found in the sample of water, still living, still swimming around in there."

Annie's face went slack. She knew.

She knew what they'd found. And she forced herself to say the words out loud.

"Bioluminescent plankton."

"That's right. Seems there's no question about it; Jamie was drowned in Lake Lumin."

Chapter 34

ANNIE

It was torture for Annie, lying in bed with the window open, listening to the soft song of crickets outside, knowing that Jake could drive past at any moment on his way to rip Daniel from his home. It was torment, watching the sand in the hourglass run out.

Jake hadn't given much weight to the tattoo theory when Annie called him at the garage to give him the update. Stephanie was a troubled kid, he'd told her, unreliable, one of the teenagers who regularly skipped school and made up stories when he caught her smoking pot. And besides that, he'd pointed out, now that they knew with certainty that Jamie had been drowned in Lake Lumin, they had every reason in the world for Daniel's arrest.

Annie rolled onto her side to stare at the minutes passing by in ruby light on the face of the digital clock: 11:47. 11:48. 11:49. 11:50.

Even if Jake didn't buy into what Stephanie had said, Annie did. The trouble was that there were simply too many young men in town who had tattoos. Ian and every single one of his friends, for starters, and plenty of other guys she'd seen down at the rodeo of the rugged, truck-driving variety. Even Jake had that tattoo of a cross on his arm.

Annie sighed in frustration at the endless circling of her thoughts as the minutes ticked past: 12:02. 12:03. 12:04.

It would have been right about now that Jamie ran past the driveway on her way up to the lake that fateful night. What had she thought about during that jog? Daniel, or someone else? Or had she simply enjoyed the cool night air on her skin, completely unaware that it was the last run of her life?

Annie tried to close her eyes, but they stayed stubbornly open. There had to be something else up there in the briars. Something she'd missed at the scene of the crime.

Five more minutes passed, and Annie gave up, pushing the blankets aside. She'd never find sleep tonight, and if she was up anyway, she might as well make use of the hours.

She was a tracker. That's who she was, so that's what she'd do.

Switching on the lamp, Annie rose from the bed and changed quickly into leggings and a T-shirt, then found the old pair of running shoes she'd tossed in the back of the closet and slipped them on, knotting both tightly.

Plucking her headlamp from the nightstand, she left the room and stepped lightly down the stairs into the night forest beyond the garage.

It was quiet outside, the trees tall and black as a chilled breeze whispered through their boughs. Annie started to run, the cool night air burning her lungs as she jogged up the first hill in the dark.

For a minute or two, she was barely able to discern the edges of the dirt road from the ferny little ditches that lined it on both sides, but slowly, her eyes adjusted to the blackness, and she kept her headlamp off. If Jamie had run up to the boathouse in the dark, so would she.

Far back in the trees, a bullfrog chanted, and Annie whipped her head toward the sound, goose bumps rising on her arms. This forest, the most beautiful place in the world by daylight, was terrifying at night. It could hide anything and anyone, but it hid her, too, and on she ran.

After fifteen minutes of climbing, the first NO TRESPASSING sign appeared, glowing orange in the filtered moonlight, and Annie passed it, huffing with effort. A few minutes later, she reached the closed gate and the clearing beyond it, silent as a tomb.

She slowed to a walk and stopped at the gate, placing both hands on the cold aluminum as she watched the boathouse for any signs of life, just as Jamie must have done on the night she died. This was tracking, putting herself in the head of the creature she needed to understand and retracing its movements, one at a time.

Carefully, quietly, Annie climbed over the gate and stepped onto Daniel's property.

She didn't need to go to the dock. She needed to figure out what had happened next, once Daniel had gone back to bed after he told Jamie to leave. What had she done after that?

The wood shavings on her shorts had come from the canoe, and the water in her lungs from the lake. It made the most sense to start there.

Annie walked to the western trees where the covered canoe waited, dark and formless. She lifted a corner of the tarp and pulled it away, unsheathing the rustic boat beneath.

It took most of her strength to roll it onto its hull, then, moving behind it, she crouched, bracing her feet against the soft earth. The canoe was heavy, and her shoes slid in the mud as she shoved her weight against it, driving it toward the water with all of her might.

Inch by stubborn inch it moved, easing its way over the dirt until the bow slid soundlessly into the lake and the rest followed—lighter and easier as the water held more of its weight.

At last, it floated completely on the surface, and Annie grabbed the wooden paddle lying in the dirt and carried it into the water, wading in up to her knees before clambering into the canoe.

It was strange, being alone in the vessel. She could feel its weight beneath her, and the power of each pull of the paddle as she moved slowly out toward the center of the lake.

She drew even with the boathouse and stilled. The water glimmered with starlight, silken and lovely. Out here in the middle, in the quiet and the dark, Jamie and her killer would have been far enough from shore that a muffled struggle would not have been heard by the man sleeping inside the boathouse.

Annie leaned out over the side of the canoe, peering into the dark depths of the lake—the last thing Jamie would have seen as her head plunged beneath the water. Closing her eyes, she imagined it, the awful minute of struggle, and the horrible, impossible truth that would have dawned in Jamie's oxygen-starved mind as she tried to raise her head. The man holding her down in the water was too strong, and too powerful. She was going to die.

Annie tensed at the thought of those final seconds of strain, everything inside burning and bursting and crying out for air—and then the breath. The betrayal. The compulsive expansion of her lungs that pulled cold dark water into her body and stopped her heart.

And then what?

Annie sat back in the canoe, frowning.

Why hadn't the killer simply left Jamie's body in the lake?

Daniel was the only person who had a reason to move her, to tuck her body back in the woods in the hopes of the murder being blamed on Justin Grimes. Anyone else would surely have left the body in the water and let Daniel take the fall, unless . . . unless the killer knew Daniel and cared enough to protect him from blame.

Annie turned toward the southern shoreline as she ran both scenarios in her mind.

No. If Daniel had been the one who killed her, he would have had the luxury of privacy on his side. He could simply have dug a grave by daylight the next day and buried her somewhere along the shore where her body would never have been found. Why would he have hiked all that way around the briars to drop her in the woods or taken the trouble to load her body into his truck and drive it up by way of the ridge?

Annie turned toward the eastern wall of firs that bordered the lake. Beyond them, cloaked in darkness, were the briars.

There was something gnawing at her, something tugging at the edge of significance in her mind, and as Annie sat bobbing gently up and down in the canoe, she realized what it was.

The creek . . .

On one of her woodland ramblings, she'd come across a small stream behind the Proudys' property, spilling downhill with a sound like hushed laughter. That stream was undoubtedly fed by this lake. It was an outlet, and if there was an outlet, there had to be an inlet as well, water flowing down from the eastern mountain that kept the lake full. Wherever that creek was, wouldn't there be a natural break in the briars? A short path through to the other side.

Heart thudding, Annie picked up the paddle again and dipped the blade into the water, propelling herself east. When she reached the shoreline, she beached the canoe quietly and climbed out, stepping past the low-hanging boughs of the pines to walk in darkness alongside the thick wall of brambles.

They were monstrous—four, five, even six feet tall in places, marching almost to the shore in lethal coils just behind the first row of trees. Annie could smell the berries, sour and underripe as she edged the thornbushes, looking for the break where fresh mountain water emptied into the lake.

She heard the creek before she saw it, a soft, trickling sound, and came upon it suddenly, her sneakers sinking into the soft earth and filling with cold water.

Annie jumped back, shoes squelching. The water was fanned out along the bank, sliding noiselessly beneath the trees and into the lake, unnoticeable, surely, by anyone who didn't already know it was here.

She turned toward the briars where the stream cut through, tumbling down the gentle hillside in little cascades only inches wide in a much-larger creek bed that spoke of spring flooding, four or five feet across. It was a path—a tunnel that the brambles did not breach, could not breach, any adventurous little seedlings being washed away with every substantial rain.

Annie stepped into the black corridor, clicking on her headlamp for the first time as she carefully worked her way through the passage, shoes sliding in the mud as she ducked beneath the stretching arms of thorn-bushes eager to reach their cousins on the other side. Step by step, she analyzed the path. Yes, it was narrow, but it was certainly wide enough for a person to pass through. Even a person carrying a dead body in their arms.

The footing was slick, and the creek thinned in places, hollowing into little currents that Annie splashed through with her soaked shoes—but it never shrank to the size of impassability.

The deeper into the briars she walked, the more certain Annie became that this was it. This was the path by which the killer had carried Jamie's body from the lake to the woods.

Everywhere she looked were tracks and signs left by someone passing through with a hundred and thirty pounds of deadweight in their arms. The slender, thorny shoots encroaching on the path had been stomped down and broken, and though any shoe prints had been washed out, there were plenty of indents in the distinct pattern of human step, leading straight on toward the dark woods beyond the briars.

Annie stopped suddenly. Something gleamed in the mud beneath her feet, right in the center of the path, a quick flash of silver that caught the beam of her headlamp.

She reached for it, fingers sliding through the muck before closing around something small and solid.

Holding it up in the light, Annie's stomach plummeted.

It was a lighter. Cheap and ordinary, made of orange plastic—the exact type and color that she'd seen in Daniel's hand countless times as he ignited the edges of newspaper pages balled up for bonfire tinder.

Annie shoved the implication aside, even as her mind connected the dots. After all, lighters like this were a dime a dozen. It could belong to someone else. Some other man who had struggled to carry a body up the slick, wet trail—the shuffling of his feet causing enough jostling to wriggle a lighter loose from his back pocket and drop it to the ground, unnoticed.

It was coated in slippery mud, and any hope of fingerprints was surely lost, but she'd bet a year's salary on it. This lighter belonged to the person who had killed Jamie Boyd.

Annie slid the lighter into the narrow pocket of her leggings, and forced herself to walk on.

Just keep moving. Just keep tracking.

A minute later, the briars fell away all at once, and she stepped past them into the dark forest beyond, open and stark in contrast to the claustrophobic tunnel she had just passed through.

Annie's eyes jumped from giant to giant of the pines standing tall beyond her weak circle of light. The woods were hauntingly still by night, and far too quiet. This was where Jamie's killer had brought her, and with the shortcut through the briars, it would not be a long walk to where her body had been left.

Annie started forward again, but a small, chirping sound in the trees above stopped her in her tracks.

Slowly, she raised her chin, and, one foot at a time, the circle of light from her headlamp illuminated the lower half of a sprawling Oregon ash—and a sight that made her blood run cold.

Peering down at her from the lower arms of the ash was a cougar. *The* cougar, his limbs draped languidly over the branches, one paw still bandaged and both eyes gleaming like lanterns.

A muted cry passed Annie's lips, and she took a backward step.

The cougar blinked once, its head tilting as though assessing what sort of creature this was, what sort of threat. What sort of meal.

Annie's hand slid automatically to her waist, but she was not wearing her belt. She had no bear spray with her, and no gun, tranquilizer or otherwise.

Don't run, came the voice in her head. *Make yourself bigger. You are not prey.*

Fear wrapped itself around her, but Annie raised her arms high and puffed up her chest. She needed to make noise, to yell at the top of her lungs, but there seemed to be no connection between her brain and her vocal cords, and silently, she backed away without taking her eyes from the cat's jeweled gaze.

The briars were at her back now, the tunnel through which she'd emerged opening to her, and Annie retreated into it slowly. When the thornbushes cloaked her again and she could no longer see the lamp eyes in the dark, she turned and fled, racing as quickly as she could down the path, stumbling twice and catching herself in the dark, the encroaching brambles tearing at her arms and face as she half ran, half slid back down to the lake.

When she emerged through the other side of the briars, she sprinted for the canoe, shoving the vessel back into the water, and climbing aboard.

Still blanketed in terror, Annie paddled hard toward the western shore, the blade dipping beneath the surface and rising again. In less than half an hour, she'd be safe in her bed. In less than thirty minutes, she'd be home.

Just once, she turned to look back over her shoulder at the briars, and when she did, dragging the paddle through the water for a split second too long, the canoe wavered in its course, dipping precariously to the left. Too fast, she overcompensated, leaning hard to the right and thrusting the paddle into the water as the cedar log rolled beneath her.

Annie flew out with her arms splayed, hitting the cool surface of the lake with a splash that echoed through the night. Water shot up her nose, filled her ears and shoes, and for three panicked seconds, she didn't know which way was up. She floundered in the darkness, and her shin slammed into the canoe.

Annie cried out, bubbles escaping her mouth as her body contracted around the pain.

She kicked instinctively downward with her legs, and as she shot up, the top of her head struck wood with a crack that ignited silver sparks behind her eyes. The pain was instant and blinding, and for one horrible second, she felt her consciousness wavering on the edge of blacking out. She couldn't breathe. She couldn't think. She had to get out from under the canoe before she drowned.

She thrashed wildly, kicking sideways, out and away from the log as the pain in her head dulled. Then a long-forgotten lesson from a survival course kicked in and she went limp as a rag doll, trusting that the remaining air in her lungs would send her bobbing up to the surface if she just stopped struggling.

Her body stilled and rose, and fresh night air broke across her back. Annie threw her head up and gulped in oxygen, coughing and sputtering as she filled her lungs. The burning in her chest eased, but her head and shin throbbed as she swam back to the canoe.

With difficulty, she rolled the cedar log in the water until it was righted again, then heaved herself up onto it and lay draped over the side, dripping and depleted.

For long minutes, she did not move. The crown of her head ached sharply with each pulse of her beating heart, and her shin would be badly bruised, but that was all. She was alive. When she was certain she had the strength, she slowly reached a hand down to pat her pocket. Miraculously, the lighter was still there.

For another minute, Annie lay motionless as the canoe drifted in a slow circle, and then the shivering set in, starting between her shoulder blades and spreading outward into her arms. Inch by Inch, she lifted her head. An eerie silence had settled over the lake in the aftermath of her splash, and even the crickets had ceased to sing.

She forced herself to sit up. The night was not cold, but cool enough to make hypothermia a real threat, sopping wet with a steady breeze that chilled her skin through her soaked clothes. She needed to get dry.

The paddle was floating a few feet away, and Annie retrieved it with a foot. She dug the blade into the lake, her arms half useless with fatigue and cold. Stroke by stroke, the canoe moved across the water, and the movement brought warmth to her limbs again.

Not until she was even with the boathouse did she notice the lamplight, pale yellow in the three lake-facing windows and pouring out over the dock. The sight was as inviting as a Christmas card—or would have been but for the silhouette that it lit from behind: Daniel, standing still as a statue, watching her from the dock.

Chapter 35

DANIEL

It was the second time he'd woken to the sound of a woman in his lake, and for the second time, Daniel stepped outside and was startled by whom he found in the water.

He waited on the dock, his bare arms brushed by the cool night breeze as Annie angled the canoe in his direction and paddled forward. It didn't take a genius to figure out what she was doing here, but why hadn't she woken him first? Asked for his help, or at least his permission, to hunt around for clues in the dark?

Stroke by stroke, she drew nearer, until at last she veered the vessel away from the dock and toward the gently sloped northern shore.

Daniel almost raised a hand, almost called out to her, but something stopped him short. It was the stiffness of her body as she paddled. The way she was avoiding looking at him where he stood on the dock. The way she wasn't calling out to him first. It was all wrong.

The canoe drew near to the shore and Daniel walked to the edge of the dock, jumping down as she brought it up onto the bank.

"Here, let me." He reached for the bow.

"I've got it," Annie snapped, and Daniel took a step back, tensing at her tone.

She still wasn't looking at him and said nothing else as she clambered out of the canoe, splashed around to the back of the log, and shoved it forward, straining against the weight.

Though it pulled against every one of his natural instincts, Daniel stood back at a distance and didn't offer his help again.

It took Annie several minutes to beach the canoe, minutes during which she did not meet his eyes, but when it was properly aground and rolled over to drain, she blew out a long breath, looking up at him as drops of water fell from her sleeves and hair and the hem of her shirt.

Daniel shook his head. "Seriously, Annie, what were you thinking? You could have drowned taking the canoe out by yourself. I was right here, right inside the boathouse, why didn't you wake me up? I could have gone with you. Helped you find whatever it was you were looking for."

Annie stood silent as a statue while the lake lapped at her heels.

"Well?" he asked.

"I . . . needed to do this on my own."

Daniel waited, but apparently it was all she had to say.

"That's it?" he said, incredulous.

Daniel searched the eyes that had once looked into his with something close to love, but were now guarded and unreadable.

A night wind brushed the surface of the lake and met them onshore, and Annie's hands flew to her arms. Even in the dark, he saw the trembling in her lower lip. She must be freezing.

"Come on." He turned for the boathouse. "You can't stay in those clothes."

"Wait," she called out behind him, and he stopped, turning back.

"Let's build a fire." She nodded toward the dark ring of stones on the ground. "I can hang my clothes on one of the chairs to dry."

Daniel hesitated. She was watching him strangely, her face full of an anxious anticipation that didn't match her words, and he had the distinct feeling that he was being tested, that whatever he said in response would be carefully weighed in the balance.

Slowly, he nodded once. "Okay. Let's build a fire."

She returned his nod, but her eyes did not clear as she said, "I'll grab a few logs. You go get your lighter."

Daniel half turned back toward the boathouse, his gaze lingering on hers for a moment. "Okay. You can wear something of mine in the meantime."

Annie followed him inside, choosing clothes from his dresser and shutting herself in the bedroom to change while Daniel waited in the living room. When she emerged wearing his white T-shirt and boxer shorts, he stood from his seat on the couch, throat bobbing.

She looked angelic, straight out of a dream, and he couldn't fight the surge of desire that flooded him at the sight of her wearing his clothes—hair loose and flowing over her shoulders like something from the Sistine Chapel. With effort, Daniel kept his eyes on hers.

"Are you going to tell me what you were looking for out there? Risking your neck in the dark."

Annie held out the wet pile of clothes in her hands. "Let's start that fire. Then we can talk."

Daniel nodded and walked past her to the kitchen, where he pulled open the drawer beside the sink and grabbed the box of matches that lay inside.

"Let's go."

He walked to the door and pushed it open, but Annie did not follow him.

"Daniel . . ."

She had never said his name like that before, and it stopped him cold. Daniel turned to look at her, but Annie was staring at the box of matches in his hand like it was something venomous.

"Where's your lighter?" she asked, her face oddly drawn. "Where's the little orange lighter I've seen you use to start fires every time I've been up here?"

Daniel blinked at her in confusion as he held the box of matches in one hand and the open door with the other.

"What are you talking about?"

"Where is it?" she said, voice rising. "Where, Daniel?"

Something strange happened as he stared at her, something other-worldly. For a split second, bright light filled the living room like a silent streak of lightning, illuminating Annie where she stood, staring at him like he was holding a smoking gun instead of a box of matches—and then it was gone, and a horrible realization crashed over him like an ocean wave.

Headlights. Someone's headlights had just swept across the clearing.

This was it, and he hadn't even heard it coming.

Daniel whipped his head toward the open door and stared into the two bright lights of the vehicle that had just pulled up behind the gate, high beams, blindingly white, that stayed on as the driver stepped out and slammed the door.

A dark figure climbed over the gate and came striding across the clearing with quick steps.

"Jake," Annie breathed behind him as the figure drew near, and Daniel shifted where he stood, closing the door halfway with some instinctive surge of protectiveness, blocking the view into the boathouse as Jake approached.

The shoulders Daniel had seen strain under the weight of a fish on the line were straight and squared now, the body of the only man in town he had ever called friend rigid with purpose as he marched straight to where Daniel stood in the doorway, the pair of handcuffs he held jangling with every step.

"Little late for fishing," Daniel said, his voice low and humorless.

Jake came to a stop before him. "You know why I'm here."

Daniel said nothing and Jake met his eyes steadily, the white light framing him like an eclipse.

"I don't want to do this, brother, but it's my duty."

For a moment, Daniel did not move, and then, slowly, he dropped the box of matches and lifted his hands, presenting his bare wrists.

Jake slipped the cuffs on, the cold metal biting at Daniel's skin, and slid them closed until they clicked into their locks. When they were secured, he gave each a stiff tug for good measure, and a hot surge of anger flooded Daniel.

He'd sworn he wouldn't let it get the better of him, but it was rising, lifting its horned head and sniffing at the injustice in the air.

Jake cleared his throat. "You're under arrest for the murder of Jamie Boyd. You have the right to remain silent. Anything you—"

"Anything I say can and will be used against me in a court of law," Daniel snapped, cutting him off. "It's me, Jake. Talk to me like a human being. Talk to me like the man you've known for five years."

A tense moment passed between the two men, a flicker of something barely checked in each of their eyes, and then Jake said, "If I had any other choice, I'd take it, brother. My hand to God."

All of the outrage Daniel hadn't let himself feel, all of the resentment and anger he'd shoved deep down somewhere beneath his heart broke over him now in one terrible wave, and his fury outgrew him as he glowered at the man who had come bearing a warrant for his arrest.

"Don't." His voice was hard as iron behind gritted teeth. "For once in your life, Jake, don't. God has nothing to do with this."

Jake leaned in until their noses were an inch apart. "There's an easy way to do this and a hard way. Don't make the mistake of thinking I won't use force if I have to. I swear to you I will."

There was a click at his waist, and Daniel looked down, eyes narrowing at the firearm Jake had silently removed from his holster.

Slowly, he looked into Jake's face again.

"Why don't you ask me outright if I murdered Jamie," he said, voice deadly calm. "Go on, ask. Would it kill you to have a conversation without handcuffs or guns, or are you that afraid of what might happen without them?"

Jake's entire body stiffened, and anger the likes of which Daniel had never seen in his friend's eyes burned there now.

"Ask?" Jake shot back. "And then what, you'll tell me the *truth*? Just like you've been telling me the truth all these years, Nico?"

The name was a slap across the face—swift and painful—and Daniel made a decision he knew was wrong, shifting where he stood, moving his foot to nudge the door open wide and give Jake a clear look at what was inside.

Jake's gaze slid past him and caught Annie where she stood in the living room, wearing Daniel's underwear and T-shirt. A brief flicker of confusion crossed his face, then something like distress. Behind Daniel the floor creaked as Annie took a step forward.

"Jake . . ." she said quietly, "I can explain."

But Jake's face had hardened, and he turned away, his blue eyes burning as they found Daniel's again.

"Since you already know your rights, it's time to go."

Without waiting for a response, Jake closed his fingers around Daniel's wrist and yanked him out of the doorway, pushing him into the clearing, where he wedged the cold barrel of the gun between his shoulder blades.

Daniel stumbled forward, feet scuffing on the gravel.

He wasn't ready. He wasn't prepared to say his farewell to this place, but farewell was upon him now. This was the last time he would see his home. The last time he would ever be beside the lake or hear the wind in the pines, but when he turned to look back over his shoulder, there was only one thing he latched on to.

As Jake led him away to meet his fate, Daniel held fast to the sight of the woman standing in the doorway.

Chapter 36

ANNIE

It was the hottest morning of the summer by far, and the sunlight was bright and glaring. It blazed down over the pines behind the community pool and burned through the windshield of the Jeep, where Annie sat with her hands twisting in her lap.

No breath of wind stirred the tree boughs, no clouds broke the endlessly blue sky, and the temperature inside the car was close to smothering as she waited, the parking lot filling slowly around her with pool patrons eager to escape the heat.

Annie glanced at her watch for the dozenth time. She'd been sitting here for an hour and a half, and it was nearing ten in the morning, but the man she was waiting for had not yet arrived to work.

She needed to get to the station. Needed to clear the air with Jake and get their working relationship back to normal after what had happened last night. It still made her face burn to think about the state Jake had seen her in and the thoughts that must have crossed his mind in that moment, but stronger than the shame she felt was the hollow, gutted feeling of knowing Daniel was in custody.

She hadn't gotten the straight answer she wanted from him about the lighter, but there was still a chance, still a distinct possibility, that it belonged to someone else, and that Daniel honestly had nothing to do with Jamie's death. He was still innocent until proven guilty, at least in her mind if not in Jake's, and after a few restless hours of sleep, Annie had woken more determined than ever to see the investigation through to its end—whatever that might be.

Yes, she'd deal with the fallout with Jake as soon as possible, but first, this. Another fish to fry. A slippery little fish named Ian Ward.

At ten fifteen, a black SUV with wide, custom rims rolled into the parking lot and took the spot marked MANAGER ONLY. The driver angled the vehicle in a deliberately crooked diagonal that far overshot the painted white lines, and inside the Jeep, Annie rolled her eyes.

Definitely Ian.

Two minutes after he climbed out of the SUV and disappeared through the gate, Annie followed, rounding the pool and storming into his office without knocking. She left the door open behind her as she crossed the room and seated herself facing him at the wide, cluttered desk, enjoying the gaping astonishment on his face.

Intent on keeping him off guard, she deliberately swept aside a crumpled pile of receipts, sending several fluttering to the floor, then folded her hands on the desktop as she leveled a cool gaze in his direction.

"Good morning, Ian."

"What are you doing here?" he sputtered, rising from his chair.

Annie directed him back down with a pointed finger. "I'm here about Jamie."

Ian fell back into his seat. For five full seconds, his mouth hung ajar, then he seemed to recover his senses and snapped it shut.

Slowly, a change came over his features. The mask she was accustomed to seeing on his face fell into place, superior and full of contempt. He rose from his chair and came around the desk.

Moving past her, he shut the door and slid the lock into place with a click that made her stomach clench, then returned to his seat.

"Privacy. Them kids walk right in without knocking sometimes."

A warning bell sounded in the back of her mind, the same siren that blared whenever she found herself at a disadvantage on the job, downhill from some predator she was tracking, or in too isolated a spot while confronting a belligerent poacher or fisherman.

Always have a way out. A plan of escape. It was a necessity for a woman in this line of work, and the golden rule of all those her father had taught her about the woods. But, the morning was warm, and plenty of people were splashing in the pool already, all within earshot through the window that was cracked open. Surely Ian wouldn't be stupid enough to try anything in here.

"I need to ask you a few questions."

"Drink, Annie?" he interrupted, gesturing at a minifridge behind the desk. Annie quickly shook her head, but Ian opened it anyway and withdrew a can of Sprite for himself, popping the top loudly.

Annie cleared her throat and started again. "Ian, we need to talk about Jamie."

"So you said." Ian lifted the fizzing can to his lips and took a long, noisy sip.

Annie couldn't keep the scowl from her face as she stared at him across the desk. There was more than one way to skin a cat, but with Ian, the direct approach was best. Present the evidence and let the obvious conclusion hang in the air.

"I've recently learned that the man Jamie broke up with just before she was killed had tattoos, and given that you've spent the last several weeks in close proximity to her here at the pool, well . . ."

Annie sat back, sweeping a hand in front of her to indicate the obvious.

Ian gave a breathy laugh that concluded in a burp.

"Isn't that convenient." He traced a dirty fingernail around the rim of the can. "Lo and behold, Ian Ward has tattoos." He shook his head at her, chuckling as though they were old friends. "Oh, Annie . . . you must be in serious trouble if I'm the best suspect you've got."

Annie didn't bat an eyelash. His condescension was infuriating, but it would only derail her if she let it.

"You are," she said without inflection. "The fact of it is that you interacted with Jamie almost every day in the weeks leading up to her death—and, yes, you have tattoos. I'd be stupid not to suspect you."

Ian tilted his head back, appraising her down his nose. "Does Jake think I did it, too?"

"That's none of your business."

Ian's gaze slid briefly to the window beside the door, then back to Annie.

"Fair enough." He nodded once. "Yes. Clearly, I have tattoos. Three of them to be exact, but guess what, Annie Oakley? So do a lot of other guys."

"Not that many."

"Twenty-seven percent of the male population, according to last year's census."

The frown on Annie's face deepened, and Ian lifted the Sprite can in a sort of salute.

"I like statistics."

Annie gazed at him for a bewildered moment, then, for the first time since walking in, she took a good look around the room.

The small bookshelf beside the window was lined with novels that were tattered in a well-read sort of way. *Moby Dick*, *War and Peace*, and *Lolita* sat side by side on the shelf. Beneath them on the floor was an untidy stack of magazines that ran the gamut from motorcycle accessories to high-end equestrian. The potted plants on the windowsill seemed watered and healthy, and on the desk itself, beside an ashtray overflowing with orange and white butts, was a calendar with several dates penciled in, in neat, narrow cursive.

Annie read through a few of the dates on the calendar upside down, her confusion and surprise only deepening. The man was impeccably organized. In the corner of each square were his work hours for the day, and several appointments had been jotted in as well, including a scheduled root canal and even an eye checkup with an ophthalmologist.

Who *was* this guy?

It dawned on Annie suddenly that Ian Ward was not the low-life buffoon he portrayed himself to be. It was a façade, and underneath it was a calculating man who took himself very seriously.

Quickly, she scanned through the calendar squares until she landed on the date of Jamie's death, and there, in Ian's tidy writing, were four words that made her mouth go dry.

Meet at the lake

Annie's heart stuttered.

It was right there. Scheduled into his plans. Ian's intent to meet Jamie at the lake on the day of her death.

The sweat that rose on her palms was instant and clammy, and Annie fought the urge to bolt, to turn and run for the door as Ian sat watching her, spinning the cold can of Sprite in the same hands that had held Jamie Boyd under the water.

Slowly, Annie looked up to meet his gaze.

"Where were you on the night Jamie died?"

The confidence had left her voice completely. She was a game warden, not a cop, and they both knew that she was out of her league. Ian watched her carefully, his dark eyes dancing with an unnerving mixture of amusement and disdain.

"It wasn't me, Annie."

He was enjoying this. Entertained by her discomfort.

"Where were you?"

Ian leaned forward in his chair, the corners of his mouth twisting upward.

"With a woman."

He was taunting her, goading her, and she couldn't let it show on her face that it was working.

"Who?"

Ian raised the Sprite to his lips and drank without breaking eye contact. He drained the can and crumpled it in his fist, then sent it in a flying arc toward the corner trash bin, missing by a mile.

"Doesn't matter who. She wasn't Jamie, and that's all that counts."

Forcing steadiness into her trembling hands, Annie reached out and touched the calendar, pressing down hard on the words he'd written.

"Then how do you explain this?"

Ian didn't even look down. "Lake Chelan. My family owns a summer house up there. Sorry to disappoint."

"Lake Chelan?"

Ian rolled his eyes. "Yes, Lake Chelan. Up by Leavenworth." He leaned forward, pronouncing every word with deliberate slowness. "Seven hours from here. I took a girl up there for a day of fishing and we spent the night. Didn't get back until the next afternoon, and by that time the whole town was buzzing about Jamie's murder."

Annie felt the dead end rising up to meet her, but she forged stubbornly ahead.

"Can you prove it?"

As though he'd had it prepared, Ian slid open the center drawer of the desk and pulled out a single, wrinkled receipt. He handed it to Annie and she scanned it. It was from a Lake Chelan liquor store, and time stamped for 11:02 p.m. on the night of Jamie's death.

"We had dinner late that night, then picked up that bottle of Tanqueray on the way back to the house to make gin and tonics. Even if I'd driven straight here after leaving the store, I wouldn't have made it back in time to kill Jamie."

Annie stared at the slip of paper in her hands. It was proof. A solid, airtight alibi, but she couldn't let it go. She couldn't just get up and walk away. Ian Ward was the one suspect she had tethered her fraying hopes to. Maybe . . . maybe the receipt was forged, or he was rich enough to charter a private plane to get here in time, or . . . or something. Her thoughts floundered for several seconds, collapsing in and tumbling over one another like grains of sand gripped in too tight a fist. If she let go of her theory now, she'd have nothing left. Nothing but Daniel.

Annie sat back in her chair. There was an open pack of cigarettes beside the calendar on the desk, and she nodded toward it. "Can I have one?"

One of Ian's sparse eyebrows lifted in surprise, but he said nothing as he pulled a single cigarette from the pack and passed it across the desk.

Annie took it and held it up. "Light?"

Ian reached around to his back pocket, fishing there for a moment before withdrawing a silver lighter. It was large and monogrammed with an elaborately embossed *W*, the ends of the letter curling and twisting around each other.

"That's fancy." Annie touched the tip of the cigarette to the flame. "You had it long?"

"Since Christmas." Ian pulled out another cigarette and lit it for himself. "A gift from my father. Real silver."

Of course it was. Ian was the exact kind of person who would have a summer home on Lake Chelan, and custom rims, and a monogrammed silver lighter. The cheap plastic variety was beneath him.

For appearances' sake, Annie touched the end of the cigarette to her lips and took a shallow breath. Blowing out a cloud of smoke, she rose from her chair.

"Am I cleared, then?" Ian asked with another self-satisfied smile.

Annie took one more puff of the cigarette and mashed the end into the ashtray.

"For now."

She turned to leave, disappointment crumpling her face the moment she twisted away. Ian was not Jamie's killer.

Crossing to the door, she slid back the lock and pulled it open.

"You should have listened to me in the first place," Ian called when she had one foot out the door. Annie turned back.

"About what?"

"I told you." His cigarette smoldered in his fingers. "Jamie said she was dating a guy from her road, more likely than not someone she grew up with. Heard it plain as day."

Ian reached a hand across his chest and pressed a fingertip to his forearm, the very same place where Jake had a tattoo of a cross.

"Maybe it's time you start looking a little closer to home."

Chapter 37

ANNIE

It was absurd. Ridiculous. There was no way Annie could entertain the possibility of what Ian had suggested, but as she climbed back into the sweltering Jeep and drove the half mile to the station, the idea would not leave her head.

Jake was the one who had told her that Jamie and Daniel were together. And if Daniel was telling the truth that he was never involved with Jamie, then Jake had lied. One of them was lying.

Had Jake been deflecting on purpose? Going out of his way to drop those seeds of doubt in the soil of Annie's mind before committing the crime? It would have been too easy, planting the idea that Jamie and Daniel were seeing each other—an idea that would later sprout and grow into hideous vines of doubt once Jamie was dead.

Jake had also been the one to suggest the hike, then steered her through the remote woods to the exact place where Jamie's body had been dumped mere hours before. What were the odds?

Despite the heat inside the car, a chill broke out across Annie's shoulders.

The notion was diabolical. Evil. And Jake was the kindest, most decent man she knew. What possible reason would he have for killing

Jamie Boyd, a neighbor girl he'd grown up with? Even if they *had* been secretly involved, as Ian implied, Jake seemed like the last person on earth who would commit murder over a mere breakup.

. . . And yet, wasn't that what friends and neighbors always said about someone after they'd been caught for murder? That they never saw it coming. That the killer was a perfectly pleasant guy and a model citizen? The last person on earth who would do such a thing. Even Ted Bundy had his coworkers fooled into thinking he was a nice, normal guy.

Annie shook her head to clear it. She was losing her grip. Barely sleeping. Questioning everything.

She pulled in beside the cruiser on Hughes Street and forced a deep breath into her lungs.

Ian was messing with her head. That's all this was, but her hands were still trembling as she climbed out of the Jeep and shut the door behind her. Clutching her keys so tightly that they dug into her palm, she stepped into the station.

Jake was behind the desk, scribbling away at a stack of forms, and didn't glance up as she came inside. Two voices warred inside her head as Annie looked at him. The one who knew Jake Proudy to be a good man, and a good cop—and the other, who repeated in a whisper the words that Ian had said in his office.

"Hey," Annie said, taking a step forward.

It took all of two seconds to realize that Jake was giving her the silent treatment. He was stone-faced and sullen, his pen flying across the paper.

Annie rounded the counter.

"Hey," she said again, standing over him, and he gave the subtlest of nods. She set her keys on the desk with a sigh. "Jake . . . look at me."

He swiveled in his chair to face her. His eyes were bloodshot from lack of sleep, his jaw lined in fine stubble, and Annie's words of defense died in her throat.

There was a terrible well of pain in those eyes, deep and gut-wrenching.

From his perspective, what he'd seen last night must have looked like an utter betrayal. He had caught her in the enemy's camp on the eve of battle.

Maybe she should have told him before all of this that she was seeing Daniel, but she hadn't, and now that decision was blowing up in her face.

There was too much to explain, and Annie didn't quite know where to start, so she sank silently into her chair instead, bringing her hand to her temple.

"Where is he?" she asked quietly, and Jake turned back to his paperwork.

"There's a holding cell in the basement of the church. The building used to be a courthouse before they built a steeple on it in the forties."

Annie balked. "You put him in a *basement?*"

Jake turned slowly to look at her again. "It's better than the cell he'll have in real prison."

She couldn't tell if he was saying the words to wound her or not, but they hit their mark and her anger flared.

"For your information," she said icily, "I took the canoe out on the water last night to see if I could piece things together by re-creating the crime. On my way back, I capsized it and soaked my clothes. The splash woke Daniel, and he offered me something to change into. Nothing else happened."

Annie stopped short, leaving the *so there* implied, and Jake blinked up at her, surprised.

"I thought . . ."

"I know what you thought. And we weren't . . . but . . . but we . . ." Her bravado faltered and broke. The truth was written on her face, she was sure of it, and Jake must have found it there, because he nodded slowly and leaned back in his chair.

"I see . . ."

Annie met his gaze for another moment, but the hurt there was too deep, and she looked away.

"I'm going to see him," she said, standing again.

"Fine." The etching of his pen picked back up.

Annie turned her back on him. If he wanted them at odds, so be it. She didn't have time to waste sitting around the station bickering.

When she reached the door, she remembered and turned back, smoothing her features into casual nonchalance.

"Oh, before I forget." She reached into her pocket and pulled out the lighter. "Is this yours?"

She held out her hand, and for a moment, half a heartbeat, she saw it, the spark of recognition in his eyes as Jake stared at the lighter. And then it was gone.

He shook his head. "No."

Annie waited, keeping her arm outstretched for a few moments.

"Why?" Jake asked.

Annie stepped forward and set the lighter down on the desk, hard enough to make him flinch in his seat.

"I found it last night on a path that cuts through the briars from the lake to the woods. The path Jamie's killer used when he dumped her body."

She turned and pushed through the door, leaving the words hanging in the air behind her.

Chapter 38

ANNIE

The church was empty and silent, except for the two fans on the ceiling that creaked in slow circles, swirling warm, stale air around the room.

Annie scanned the sanctuary, with its polished wooden pews and its imposing pulpit. The eight windows that punctuated the long walls were darkened by the thick patch of forest into which the building was nestled. Leafy bough tips bent against the panes and overgrown rose-bushes crept up from beneath the sills. The only piece of stained-glass in the room was a small, round window above the baptismal tank that showed a pair of hands, folded in prayer.

"Daniel?" she called out.

Annie walked down the center aisle, her footsteps echoing on the wooden floor. There was a door to the right of the baptismal, and she pulled it open with a screech that reverberated around the sanctuary. It led to a narrow hall with a kitchen the size of a closet, an office, and another closed door at the far end, which Annie reached for in the hope of a way down into the basement.

Behind the door, musty air met her at the top of sagging wooden stairs, badly in need of repair. The steps disappeared into a darkness below that smelled damp and fetid, and Annie's pulse started to hammer as that childish pull to turn and run from unseen monsters gripped her.

"Daniel?" she called into the darkness.

There was the muffled sound of someone moving around below, and then a voice called back.

"Annie?"

She took the decrepit stairs as quickly as she dared, sticking to the edges and avoiding the sagging middles. Halfway down, the banister ended abruptly, the lower half lost to termites or some other malady. Only when she reached the bottom did she risk lifting her eyes to look around.

At first, she saw nothing. It was so dark in the recessed room; only one small window high in the far corner that let in choked light. And then she found the cells lined against the wall.

Annie's hand flew to her mouth. Three rusted metal pens about eight feet tall and deep sat side by side, and Daniel lay curled on the floor in one of them, his form vague in the darkness.

Annie ran to him, nearly tripping on the uneven dirt floor under her feet.

There was no cot in the cell, no chair, and nothing but the earthen floor on which to rest. It was a cage.

With a sob rising in her throat, Annie knelt and stretched her arm through the bars to touch his shoulder.

"Are you okay?"

Slowly he sat up, one cheek dusted with dirt from where he'd rested his head. "I'm fine. Just sleeping." He turned to look at the hand on his shoulder and Annie let it drop.

"We need to talk."

Daniel lifted his eyes to hers and smiled tiredly. "You can't break up with me. We sort of already did that, remember?"

Annie's heart cracked at the sadness in his voice, and she raised her hand again to brush away the dirt on his face.

"We're running out of time," she said. "I need you to tell me the truth about that night. All of it. Anything you left out. I need to know what really happened up there."

"I told you. I found Jamie in the lake and asked her to leave, then I went back to bed."

"There has to be something else. Something you're forgetting. Think."

His gaze faltered and fell.

"Tell me."

Daniel did not look at her as he answered. "When Jamie climbed out of the water, I . . . my drawing pad was right there, and I . . . I showed her the drawing I'd done of her swimming in the lake. She loved art. Wanted to study it, actually. I thought she'd appreciate seeing the sketch, and I asked if she was okay with me selling it. She said it was fine. I told her she could have it, since I'd already done the outline on the bigger canvas, and she touched it, just reached out and brushed her thumb over it for a second. I think that's where the charcoal came from."

"But she didn't take it?"

"No. She wanted me to keep it." Daniel hesitated. "She said she wanted me to think about her every time I looked at it. I didn't want to hurt you by telling you before, but I think we're past that now."

Annie nodded. They were way past hurting each other. All that mattered now was finding the truth.

"And the wood shavings on her shorts? Did you take her out in the canoe?"

"No." He shook his head firmly. "Her killer must have done that. She jumped down off the dock and walked into the dark, but I didn't stick around to make sure she climbed the gate and started back toward home. I just assumed she did, but she must not have."

Annie wrapped her hands around the bars. "And your lighter. Why did you go for that box of matches when I asked you to build a fire? Where's that little orange lighter I've seen you use all summer?"

Daniel frowned. "What does that have to do with anything?"

Annie's grip on the bars tightened. "Just tell me."

"It's in my bedroom. In the nightstand. I rewired the electricity after the tree came down, and lately I've been having issues with it. Sometimes the light shorts out back there. I keep a candle and the lighter in my nightstand just in case. You can go up and check if you don't believe me."

Annie sat back on her heels. She *would* check. As soon as she left here. She had to be sure. So much hinged on it.

She deliberated for a moment, then quickly told him about finding the lighter in the woods, and about her interaction with Ian. Then she leaned forward, hesitating, her face almost touching the bars. Her next words would come as a shock.

"I'm wondering if it could have been Jake."

Daniel's mouth fell open, and he coughed the word:

"Jake?"

Annie nodded, and Daniel stared at her as though she'd just suggested that Christ himself had taken human form again to commit the crime.

"Annie, come on . . . of all the men in this town, Jake is the *last* person who'd be capable of something like that. And then to lock me up for it?" Daniel shook his head with conviction. "No . . . no, he wouldn't do that. We may be at odds right now, but that's only because he's a good cop, and a good man. He . . . cares about me."

"Exactly." Annie leaned close. "Why would anyone else move her body? Jake wouldn't want you to be blamed for it, and he knows the lake like the back of his hand. He knew he could get her through the briars and into the woods where it would look like Justin Grimes had killed her, and he brought me straight there on a hike the next day to find her body."

"But didn't he know Justin Grimes had already been caught?"

"He didn't find out until afterward. I was with him when he got the message. He seemed stunned, just . . . frozen. And I can't help but wonder if part of that reaction was because his plan had just gone out the window. He only took you in when he realized there were no other suspects left."

Daniel's gaze fell to the dirt floor, eyes roving back and forth as he thought. After a long moment, he sighed and shook his head again.

"No, Annie. Jake isn't one of those people who pretends to be a good person. His faith is genuine. He's a good, decent man, and there's no way you could convince me he's capable of something like this."

Annie sat back on her heels, staring through the bars into the bleak cell where Jake had locked his best friend.

"Really?" She waved an arm around at the dark, dank surroundings. "That man just sent you to hell without blinking an eye."

"Hell?"

To her great surprise, Daniel laughed, then sank into a silence through which he smiled softly.

"I've been to hell, Annie," he said, shaking his head. "This isn't it."

But Annie could not move past the darkness, and the earthen floor, and the bitter smell of mice.

"How can it even be legal to lock you up somewhere like this?" she said, voice rising. "There are standards, laws."

Daniel shook his head. "He had nowhere else to put me. Besides, it's just for today. He said I'll be transferred down to Vancouver tonight to wait for the trial."

Annie sat back, blinking at him. "I don't get it. Why aren't you angrier?"

Slowly, Daniel reached an arm through the bars and took the end of her braid in his hand, running the copper strands through his fingers. Annie did not pull away.

"I was angry last night. Really angry, but . . . it's out of my control now," he said with his eyes on the fine ends of her hair. "And I realized that no matter what, even if this is my fate, even if this is how my story ends, it still can't take away what you've given me."

Annie swallowed, and the hand holding the end of her braid moved to her cheek, stroking her skin.

"You gave me my freedom."

Annie stilled beneath his touch, staring into his eyes.

"I never really came back," he murmured. "For seven years, I was still that kid in the basement, standing there paralyzed with fear, ready to end it all. I was hiding. I was surviving, but not really living. I didn't truly come back to life until I met you."

Tears filled Annie's eyes, and she let them fall.

"Don't give up," she whispered. "This isn't the end of our story."

"Even if it is, I regret none of it. 'It is necessary to have wished for death in order to know how good it is to live.'"

The words landed somewhere far back in her memory and she pulled them forward. They belonged to *The Count of Monte Cristo*, her father's favorite novel.

Annie turned her head, kissing the palm of Daniel's hand, before rising to her feet.

"Dantès made it out of his prison cell," she said, looking down into his eyes. "And if I have my way, you will, too."

Chapter 39

ANNIE

Annie dipped her head into the sink and took in a mouthful of water, swished, and spat. Looking up, she caught her gaze in the mirror and stared at her reflection in dismay. Who *was* that woman? She looked terrible. Gaunt and exhausted, with eyes that were red from crying all the way home from the church, and dark circles that spoke of serious sleep deprivation.

All in all, she'd averaged maybe four or five hours of sleep a night since this whole ordeal started, and it was definitely taking a toll, but hopefully the walk up to the boathouse would help.

Without bothering to smooth her wild hair, Annie quickly took the stairs down to the garage and nodded at Walt, who was tinkering with the separated pieces of a leaf blower on the workbench.

"Hey there, Annie," he called as she stepped quickly past. "You all right?"

Annie gave a brief nod. "I'm fine."

The threat of tears was still in her voice, and Walt came quickly around the table.

"Come on, now, what's wrong?"

Everything.

"Nothing." She shook her head. "I was just . . ." She angled a thumb vaguely at the road. "I need a walk."

Walt tugged off his work gloves and flopped them over the sawhorse behind him. For a moment, Annie thought he would wrap her in a hug, and she knew the tears barely held at bay now would never survive it, but he clapped her gently on the shoulder instead.

"I'll go with you," he said quietly. "Whatever's on your mind, the woods will help, come on."

Annie fell into step beside him as they walked down the driveway and turned left up the dirt road.

After several minutes of silence, Walt spoke.

"Forgive me if this is an obvious question, but is it the case that has you so upset?"

Annie nodded. "It is. It's got me questioning everything."

Beside her, Walt murmured, "It's more than that though, isn't it?"

Annie glanced sideways at him, and he gave her a knowing look.

"Everything's all wrapped up in one horrible knot that I can't seem to untie. I'm caught between two people that I care about, and I can't figure out who to believe." Her eyes fell to her shoes as they walked up a steep incline. "I just can't trust my instincts right now."

Walt's head bobbed. "You're torn."

"That's an understatement."

He stopped walking and turned to face her for a moment. "May I offer you an outsider's perspective?"

Annie nodded and Walt started walking again, the dappled sunlight falling in patches on his salt-and-pepper hair.

"I hope I'm not presuming too much, and stop me if I'm way off base here, but maybe the reason you're fighting so hard against Daniel's guilt is because he's the one you've chosen in your heart, and you can't bear to face the truth."

Annie turned to him, the look in her eyes a silent confirmation of what he'd said, and Walt smiled sadly.

"Honey, Laura and I care about you. We want to see you happy after everything you've been through." He chuckled softly. "Selfishly, I was hoping that you and Jake would fall for each other so I'd have you for a daughter-in-law, but you can't force love. The heart wants what it wants."

Annie had no idea her love life had been so transparent in Walt's and Laura's eyes, and she was flattered that they'd privately been hoping for something to happen between her and their son.

"It's not that I don't care about Jake. I do. A lot, actually. But with Daniel, it's . . . different." Annie shook her head. How could she explain it? "It's like there was something about him that called out to me the first time we met. I don't know exactly what it is, or how to put it into words, but I've never felt it with anyone else."

Annie stopped talking, embarrassed by the emotion she'd just laid bare, but Walt merely nodded and neither commented nor pressed her for more.

"You wanna turn back?" he asked after a quiet minute.

Annie looked up, surprised to find that they'd made it all the way to the NO TRESPASSING signs. "No. I . . . I left something at the boathouse. I need to grab it."

Walt nodded and they walked on.

The signs didn't matter. The locked gate didn't matter. The guardian of this clearing was not at home. It was time to check Daniel on his words. Time to test his claim of innocence.

When they reached the gate, Annie climbed up and over quickly while Walt followed behind, more laboriously.

"Haven't been up here since that day we sawed up the cedar." Walt dropped down onto firm ground with a grunt and gazed admiringly around the clearing. "Mighty pretty this time of year with the woods all filled in and the lake lit up like that."

Annie nodded, but her eyes were on the boathouse. All of a sudden, she didn't want to do this. She didn't want to walk into Daniel's bedroom and look inside that nightstand. One way or the other, whatever happened in the next few minutes could alter the course of her future forever.

"Wait for me on the dock," she said, "I'll be just a minute."

Annie jogged ahead, limbs spry with adrenaline, and slipped in through the side door. It was quiet inside, and the place already felt abandoned, the hall dark and much cooler than the warm summer day outside.

With her pulse surging in her throat, Annie stepped into Daniel's bedroom and crossed to the nightstand. The drawer was ajar and she took a deep breath as she wrapped her fingers around the handle. With one hard tug, she pulled it open, and her heart sank.

There was no lighter inside.

All that the drawer contained were a small stack of novels, a hunting knife in a leather sheath, and a tapered candle, half burned.

Annie lifted out the books and tossed them onto the bed, then pulled out the knife and the candle. She yanked out the drawer with a jerk and stared into the hollow space it left behind, but there was simply no lighter. Desperate, she dropped to her knees and peered into the black and cobwebbed space beneath the nightstand.

She stretched an arm into the gap, hand patting around on the dusty floor as her heart raced. Then, just as she was about to pull her hand away, her fingertips brushed something small and smooth, and she grasped for it.

Annie drew it out—and opened her hand.

It was an orange lighter, wreathed in wispy cobwebs from where it had fallen unnoticed behind the nightstand.

She closed her eyes and let her head fall forward. A sound, half exhale, half laugh, passed her lips, and she clutched the blessed lighter to her heart.

"Thank you," she offered in the briefest of prayers, and rose to her feet.

Walt was outside on the dock, seated on the edge with his shoes beside him, bare feet dangling in the water.

"Find what you came for?" he asked, turning to look at her.

"Yep." She held up the little orange lighter jubilantly, turning it back and forth in the sunlight.

Walt gazed at it. "Huh . . ."

"What?"

He flicked a finger toward her. "Oh, nothing, it's just funny. I lost mine, too. Can't find it for the life of me. Had to pick up a new one in town this morning."

A strange sensation crawled the length of skin from Annie's tailbone to the nape of her neck as she stared at him, but Walt seemed not to notice as he turned back toward the lake, pulling his feet out of the water with a contented sigh.

"We better get on back," he said, reaching for his sneakers.

But Annie couldn't breathe, couldn't move, and time itself seemed to slow as Walt wedged his feet into his shoes. One at a time, he knotted the laces with little twists of his hands as she stared at his wrists, at the tattoos from his military days that she had seen a hundred times and thought nothing of.

SEMPER on one wrist, FI on the other.

Always faithful.

Chapter 40

JAKE

Jake sat slumped in his chair behind the desk, his forehead resting on the stack of empty forms.

They were a prop, nothing more. Blank citations that he'd been scribbling away at when Annie came in for the mere appearance of having something to do, when the honest fact of it was that he'd been too ashamed to look her in the eyes.

What a mess. This whole investigation was a lousy, rotten, knotted, miserable mess, and all he had to show for it were the deep sets of crow's-feet around his eyes that hadn't been there before.

Jake turned his head, gazing at the clock on the wall as his lids grew heavy with impending sleep. Reluctantly, he let them close.

Somehow, in the span of mere days, he'd managed to lose his best friend and alienate his work partner, too.

Daniel and Annie.

He sure hadn't seen that one coming, but greater than the personal resentment he felt over Annie's hiding their relationship was the unsettled knot it left in the pit of his stomach. The entire case he'd built against Daniel revolved around his relationship with Jamie, a relationship that Annie claimed never existed. Was it possible that he had mis-interpreted what he'd seen in the truck?

There was a sudden thud against the glass door and Jake snapped his head up to find the dusty imprint of a wing left behind by a bird that had collided with the pane.

For the first time in days, a smile tugged at the corner of his mouth.

It was a fitting metaphor. He was the bird and last night was the glass. The moment Daniel opened the door to reveal Annie standing there in the living room . . . *Smack.*

Jake's eyes dropped to the lighter, still lying where Annie had slammed it down on the desk with the claim that it belonged to Jamie's killer.

He was sure he'd seen it before, but where?

He reached for it and turned it over in his fingers, eyes drawn to an imperfection in the plastic. Yes, it was that little nick near the bottom that was triggering something in his mind, something that had instantly sparked when Annie first held it out in her hand, though the recollec-tion it evoked had been faint and fleeting, and he hadn't quite been able to drag it out of the fog.

His thumb found the starter, and absently, he flicked the lighter once, twice, three times. On the third attempt, a flame flickered brightly to life, and with it, a memory—searing, lucid, and devastating.

He was back up at the boathouse, sitting on a stump beside his fa-ther. The air smelled of cedar pitch from the log their chain saws rested against, and Jamie Boyd had just jogged into the clearing. Jake watched his father, Walt's green eyes lingering on Jamie as he flicked his orange lighter once, twice, three times, before it lit. As he pulled the cigar away from his mouth and exhaled a cloud of smoke, his fingers fumbled with the lighter, and he dropped it. Jake reached down to pick it up, the plas-tic freshly nicked.

The heat from the flame was burning his thumb, the room was start-ing to spin, and Jake was out of his seat, chair tumbling behind him as he flung the lighter away, sending it skittering across the desk.

"No!"

The world was caving in beneath him; the firm ground on which he'd dwelled a minute ago no more solid than shifting sand.

It wasn't possible. His father could not have murdered Jamie Boyd . . . but . . . but the way he had stared at her across the clearing with that cigar between his lips . . . and what were the odds of the killer dropping another such lighter, identically colored and nicked in the exact same place?

Impossible. They were impossible odds. The lighter belonged to his father, and there was only one reason why Walt Proudy would have been back in those woods.

Jake was around the desk in an instant, through the door of the station, and leaping off the sidewalk for the cruiser. With shaking hands he managed to yank open the door on his second try and fumbled with the key in the ignition until, at last, the engine turned over and he shot backward out of his parking space, roaring toward Main Street and praying through his panic.

"Please," he whispered. "Please let me be wrong."

Chapter 41

ANNIE

Annie?" Walt was staring at her curiously, one shoe untied, the laces stilled in his hands. "What is it?"

Annie could not answer. She had no voice. Tight, suffocating fear had stolen it. Just whisked it away, along with her ability to move and think. The lighter was still in her raised hand, her mouth hanging open as Walt waited for the words that would not come.

She had to speak. She had to answer him. Every second that ticked past in silence was confirmation that she'd figured out what he already knew. Walt was Jamie's killer.

He did not rise from where he sat on the dock, but steadily met her gaze, his green eyes hooded. Slowly, he brought his hands together and knotted his shoelaces into a bow.

When far too much time had passed and the only sounds were the lapping of water and Annie's heart beating wildly in her chest, he turned away and stared across the lake.

"Say it," he said to the water.

Annie's hip nudged the sill behind her as she took a backward step.

"Say it," he said again, louder this time.

Annie's mouth was dry as dust, her voice a hoarse whisper that did not belong to her.

"It was you?"

He turned to her again, and nodded, and the fear that held her became panic.

Pieces of the puzzle that had confounded her were flying into place, the full picture emerging at last as Annie stared at the man who had been under her nose this whole time. How had she missed it?

She remembered now, how she'd moved to the window that night at the sound of jogging footsteps, searching for Jamie in the yellow light spilling out through the open garage door. Walt had been in the garage. Still awake. Still working. He had seen Jamie run by that night, and he had followed her. Walt, with his tattoos and his penchant for cigars that necessitated a lighter in his back pocket wherever he went. Walt, an older man from her road, just as Ian had heard Jamie describe him.

She should have known that first morning at breakfast, when Walt said people in town were suspicious of Daniel because Jamie was found in a clearing in his woods. She had never mentioned the word *clearing*, not to anyone. No one but Jake had known that detail, and Jake hadn't yet spoken to his parents about the case. There was no other way Walt could have known unless he'd carried her body to the clearing and left it there.

"Why?" she asked, but even as the question left her lips, Annie knew the answer.

Walt gazed at her for a moment, then lowered his eyes to the dock. Shaking his head, he muttered something that Annie could not make out beneath the sound of the lake gurgling around the pilings.

"I'm a good person, Annie." He lifted his face to hers. "A good father and a good husband. Jamie was an indiscretion. A mistake. I let temptation get the better of me that day we were up here sawing the cedar, and she was willing, but when it ended, she didn't have the maturity to keep it quiet. I only followed her up here that night to talk to her, to try to reason it all out, but she wouldn't listen."

He turned to look out at the water again, and anger burst through Annie's fear like a fist. This man had damaged every single person that she cared about in this town.

"Laura's tired spells," Annie said to the back of his head, "she's been having them for weeks. She said on the phone that she slept like the dead that night. Was that you? Were you drugging her with those sleeping pills in the bathroom? Were you drugging your wife so you could sneak out at night and meet Jamie?"

Her voice was taut with accusation, but when Walt turned to look at her—there was no emotion on his face. For a moment, he simply watched her, then, without a word, he rose to his feet.

How had she never noticed how tall he was? This meek middle-aged man who preferred the quiet solitude of tinkering in his garage to conversation. The father who sat with hunched shoulders at the breakfast table, smiling at his wife over his mug of coffee. The former marine who was still every inch of six feet and sinewy with strength.

Annie's eyes darted around the dock, but there was nothing with which to defend herself. The only objects at hand were the three propane cans lined beneath the window, too large and heavy for her to wield effectively, and the two Adirondack chairs, useless for the same reason.

"Listen to me, Annie." Walt raised one hand in a gesture she supposed was meant to calm her. "I only wanted to talk to her that night, only to talk. What happened after that was her fault, not mine. I never intended to kill her."

Annie's anger swelled. He believed it. He honestly believed that Jamie's murder had somehow been deserved, and the calmness with which he spoke the words infuriated her.

"I don't care what you intended," she shot back. "Jamie's dead, and this town is broken because of it. Because of you."

Walt took a step toward her, and Annie matched it with a sideways step of her own. There were less than fifteen feet of space between them on the dock, and every muscle in her body went rigid with anticipation.

She was a deer in the woods, poised for the inevitable end of this, a flight through the trees for her life.

"I only meant to scare her into keeping quiet, I didn't mean to kill her."

Annie bristled at the lie. "No. You knew exactly what you were doing when you took her out in the canoe, and where you'd carry her body through the briars. You know this lake. Jake told me you used to take Laura rowing up here at night back when the two of you were dating."

Walt stilled where he stood, and Annie could see the deliberation in his eyes. He was deciding what to do next. How to best eliminate the threat that she posed.

"Why did you move her?" The question still burned, needing an answer, even as Annie inched closer to the edge of the dock and the three-foot jump down to the gravel where she would break into her sprint toward the gate. "Why not just let Daniel take the fall right from the start and leave her in the lake?"

Walt tilted his head, brows lifting as though the answer were obvious.

"I'm not an evil person, Annie. I didn't want Daniel to take the fall for this any more than you did. That's why I took the trouble to move her body out into the woods. In a perfect world, it would have been blamed on Justin Grimes the way it was supposed to, but that's not how the cards fell. The fact that Justin had already been caught was bad luck, but when all's said and done, Daniel's the outsider. He never would have truly fit into this town, and it's better for him to take the blame for this than for it to land on my shoulders and destroy my family. I'm a deacon, Annie, a deacon of the church and a pillar of the community. Do you have any idea what it would do to this town if the truth came out?"

This man was a sociopath. A narcissist. A wolf in sheep's clothing.

"Jake trusts you. Laura trusts you. *I* trusted you. How could you do this?"

She had reached the end of the dock, and her heels teetered over the edge. Just one quick twist and she'd be down on the ground, running for her life.

"You're right, Annie." He nodded slowly. "My family trusts me. This town trusts me. And they'll go on trusting me once all this is over and done with."

His voice was calm, his face stoic, and Annie knew it then. Knew it with a certainty that filled her veins with ice. Walt Proudy was going to kill her.

For one last moment, they met each other's gaze, both unblinking, both full of defiance, then Annie turned and threw herself from the dock.

She hit the gravel hard and stumbled forward onto her hands, skinning her bare knees as her feet slid for traction. Behind her, the old boards creaked as Walt lunged across the dock, but he was too late, she was already back on her feet with her sights on the gate gleaming across the clearing like a beacon of safety.

One of the propane tanks rattled as Walt lifted it from the dock, and Annie broke into a sprint, not daring to look back.

She heard it coming.

Heard it parting the air behind her, the very particles singing as the heavy can came sailing toward her, and she offered up a wordless cry for deliverance a moment before the tank slammed into the back of her skull and everything went black.

Chapter 42

JAKE

The tires spun over gravel, spitting sharp pebbles out behind the car with a sound like falling rain as Jake sped up the hills of Lake Lumin Road.

"Come on, come on, come on," he urged the cruiser, foot hard on the gas.

It had never taken so long to reach home, and the twisting fear in his gut told him he was running out of time. Annie was smart. And fiery. And impulsive. If she had managed to put it all together, she would confront Walt by herself, Jake had no doubt of that, and there was no telling how his father would respond. Jake knew better than anyone else that Walt was stronger than he looked, ex-military, and if backed into a corner, he was capable of anything. If Annie had figured it out, then she was in danger.

The Proudy house appeared on the left, the home of his childhood, serene and lovely where it sat in dappled sunlight beneath the pines, the place where his best and earliest memories had been formed.

It would not register. It would not sink in, and Jake had sense enough to know that he was probably in shock, but he would deal with the emotional fallout later. There was no time to think, only to act.

As he whipped the cruiser left into the driveway, he slammed the heel of his hand into the center of the steering wheel, blaring the horn until the front door opened. His mother appeared, her face lined with confusion as she took in the sight of the police car, lights whirling as it skidded to a halt in front of the house.

Jake jammed the cruiser into park and threw open the door, stepping out with one foot on the ground.

"Where is he?" he shouted. "Where's Dad?"

She pointed an arm up the road. "He went for a walk with Annie. I saw them heading that way about an hour ago. What's wrong?"

Jake allowed himself one more breath before delivering the news no one should ever have to receive.

"He killed Jamie, Mom. Dad killed her."

Laura's face went blank as stone, completely expressionless, and with everything in him, Jake wanted to go to her, to wrap her in his arms and offer her the comfort that they both needed, but there was no time.

"Stay inside," he shouted, pointing at the house. "Lock the doors and windows and don't let Dad in if he comes back, no matter what he says, understand? I called Austin and he's on the way with backup."

Jake left her where she was, wide-eyed on the stoop, and tore out of the driveway.

The woods blurred past as the cruiser shot uphill toward the clearing, every passing second ratcheting up his urgency, and when the first NO TRESPASSING sign appeared, he reached for the loaded Glock waiting on the passenger seat and flipped off the safety.

Ahead through the trees, the lake waited, bathed in sunlight and sparkling blue, but Jake's eyes were on the boathouse—on the flash of movement there on the dock.

The gate was rising up to meet him, but it was his father that Jake watched, his heart stuttering in his chest as Walt rolled Annie's limp body over the edge of the boards and into the water.

Jake floored the gas and smashed through the gate. Free from its hinges, it flew end over end through the air.

Walt's head whipped toward him, and Jake slammed on the brakes, watching in horror as his father kicked the heavy propane tank he had tied to Annie's ankle over the edge of the dock and into the water, dragging her body down beneath the surface with it.

Jake jammed the cruiser into park, leapt out, and charged.

"Get down!" he shouted.

Walt turned and jumped easily off the dock, striding across the clearing with his eyes on his son.

"Put that gun away, Jake," he called, lifting a hand in front of him.

"I said get down!"

Walt did not break stride, and a part of Jake seemed to float up and away, looking down with mild surprise as he aimed the gun and fired.

Walt jerked backward, spinning on his feet before he fell to the ground. A rosebud of blood blossomed at his shoulder, and he clawed at it as Jake sprinted past and threw himself into the water in a splashing dive.

The lake swallowed him whole, and for a moment, he could see nothing, only pale green water and translucent bubbles as he kicked downward, and downward again, in what he hoped was the right direction.

He was certain he had less than a minute to reach Annie before she drowned, but where was she? The shore fell off steeply behind the dock, a natural shelf, and the water around him grew dark as he descended, lungs already begging for breath.

Please, he prayed. *Please!*

In the corner of his eye, there was a glint of copper where a lance of sunlight caught floating hair, and Jake kicked toward it furiously.

Annie was floating beneath the water as though standing upright, her face serene as her hair swirled around it, eyes closed, lips parted, and Jake prayed with everything in him that she was just unconscious, not dead. *Please, God, not dead.*

The rope joining her to the sunken propane tank was knotted tightly around her ankle. Lungs burning, Jake swam down to untie it.

He tore at it with his fingers, but couldn't loosen it fast enough. The thin rope was triple knotted, and it slid beneath his fingers as every alarm bell in his head went off at the same time. Second by second, he fought against the growing urge to kick to the surface for air as he struggled with the rope.

The first knot gave, and the second, and his body began to convulse. *Come on!* he screamed inside his head.

The third knot slipped beneath his fingers, his vision darkening at the edges.

No!

And then he had it, Annie was free, and he kicked upward with what little strength he had left, wrapping his arm tightly around her waist and dragging her with him as he moved toward the light.

For a desperate moment, it seemed he would never breach the surface, and then air broke against his face at last and he took a great, heaving gasp of it as he swam toward the shore, encumbered by the weight of the woman in his arms.

He dragged her up onto the dirt, still gasping, and spared his father a half-second glance to find that Walt had lost consciousness. The sleeve of his shirt was soaked through with blood, but Jake had seen worse. He'd live.

Quickly, Jake tilted Annie's head back and covered her mouth with his, giving her the breath in his lungs, once, twice. He placed the heels of his hands on her sternum and pushed hard, counting thirty compressions.

"Come on, Annie," he rasped. "Breathe . . . Breathe!"

He pinched her nose and blew into her mouth twice more, but she stayed motionless, utterly still.

"Come on!" Tears blurred his vision as he jammed the heels of his hands into her sternum and pumped over and over. "Come on, Annie!"

Water, cold and violent, shot out of her mouth and into his face as she coughed. Her eyes flew open, locking on his with raw terror, and Jake gathered her into his arms.

"You're okay," he said into her wet hair. "You're okay now."

Annie sagged in his arms, losing consciousness again, but her chest was rising and falling without his help. She was breathing on her own, and a sound Jake had not made since he was a boy escaped his lips.

In the distance, he heard it, faint but growing—a song on the wind. The high and mournful wail of sirens.

Jake blew out a breath of relief, leaning forward until his forehead rested against hers.

"Thank God," he breathed.

Chapter 43

DANIEL

On the floor of his cell, Daniel slept light and often, dreams coming to him like strange ships passing by.

The egress window in the far corner was only a dim wedge of light at its brightest, and so far away that he was half certain his eyes were playing tricks on him and it was not there at all. There was no way of knowing how much time had passed, but when enough of it had gone by without Jake coming to haul Daniel from his cell and take him to await trial elsewhere, he could not ignore the faint stirrings of hope.

Lying on his back with his hands behind his head, unsure whether his eyes were open or closed, he allowed himself to wonder if Annie had actually done it—managed to chase down a killer as elusive as morning mist, and he drifted off again.

The jangling of keys woke him, and Daniel sat up in the dark.

There were footsteps on the stairs. Familiar footsteps, but not Annie's.

He searched the blackness until Jake emerged, walking quickly across the basement with his head bowed low. There were keys in his hand, and they were in the lock before Daniel could scramble to his feet. The door swung open and Jake stood back, holding it wide for Daniel to pass through.

"I'm sorry," Jake said before he had a chance to speak, to ask the first of a hundred questions exploding across his brain. "There's a lot to say, but I owe you that much first. I was wrong. About all of it. I'll tell you everything, but come on, let's get you out of here."

Daniel followed in silence, one part of him weak with relief, another part bursting with curiosity about who or what had proved his innocence—but most of him was tempted to throw his fist into Jake's back as he strode across the basement.

Why not finish what they started up there at the boathouse? It was beyond ridiculous that Jake thought he could waltz in with a two-sentence apology and expect Daniel to forgive and forget everything that had passed between them.

He followed Jake up the stairs to the sanctuary. Though the room was dim with late-afternoon light, it was still bright beyond what Daniel's eyes could bear after so much darkness. He blinked, vision clearing as he followed Jake around the altar and down the center aisle.

"I'm free?" he said, voice croaking. "Just like that?"

"You're free." Jake stopped where he was between the pews and turned to face Daniel in the light.

Daniel's next question died in his throat.

There were tears in Jake's eyes, tears on his cheeks, and it looked like he hadn't slept in a month. Jake was broken, and Daniel realized instantly that this was bigger than the two of them. Much, much more was going on here.

"Who did it?" he asked quietly.

Jake's head fell. His shoulders shook, and Daniel barely made out the words as Jake told him what had happened in the clearing.

He accepted the news rigidly. He thought he'd feel relief, or perhaps righteous indignation, or at the very least some sort of vague satisfaction when Jamie's killer was caught. But as Jake choked out a single sob that echoed in the empty sanctuary, Daniel felt only exhaustion.

He wanted to see Annie. After the harrowing ordeal she'd gone through, he wanted to see her for himself, to watch her chest rise and fall and know that she was breathing and alive and okay.

And he wanted to go home.

Jake sank into a wooden pew and rested his forehead on the back of another, breathing deep as he gathered his composure. Daniel did not offer him any words of comfort. Anger still burned within him—live coals smoldering long after the fire had died—and he stood mutely in the aisle, staring down as Jake's shoulders heaved and fell.

"Listen," Jake said without lifting his head. "You have every right to be mad at me right now, I know that, but I'm still asking for your forgiveness, even though I don't deserve it."

Daniel looked away. The light behind the single stained-glass window at the front of the church was pink and worn, and he blinked at the fading mosaic of hands folded in prayer as he took a seat of his own in the pew across the aisle.

If Annie had taught him anything this summer, it was to let go. To move on from the past. To stop holding his life in a painfully tight fist and open his hand. After all, everything could be taken from him in an instant. His freedom. His home. His very life. What good was holding tight to it when, ultimately, he had no control anyway? He had vowed to loosen his grip, to let go of past wrongs, and now it seemed that fate had seen fit to give him a chance to make good on that promise. To let go of a bitter anger that would poison only him in the end.

He turned to look at Jake, and as though Jake sensed it, he lifted his head. There were new lines around his eyes, and a heaviness that hadn't been there before as he waited for Daniel's answer.

It was his choice. Burn with it, or let it go.

Daniel extended his hand across the aisle.

Jake took it and shook.

"Brother," he said, and Daniel nodded.

When he turned to look at the stained-glass window again, the light had gone.

Pew creaking, Daniel rose to his feet.

"Take me to her."

Chapter 44

ANNIE

The world was shadow and fog, and Annie lingered in the mist between waking and sleep, where time was stretched and thought had no anchor in reality.

She dreamed often, falling into nightmares and fading out again, until a dream as lucid and terrifying as any she'd ever had shot her to the surface of consciousness.

In it, she ran for the trees, even as they receded, shrinking away into the distance, her stubborn legs refusing to turn over any faster as she lumbered across the vast gravel plain of the clearing.

She was trying to make it to the forest. Trying to get away, but the man behind her was too fast, and so close that she could feel his breath on her neck. She couldn't make it to safety, and she screamed as his strong, sinewy hand closed around her upper arm and squeezed tight.

Annie's eyes flew open. There was a blood-pressure cuff around her arm, constricted to the point of pain. She stared at it, heart pounding as it slowly released again.

Where was she?

She sensed someone in the dark room with her, but did not have the strength to turn her head and search the blue glow from whatever machine had her tethered to the bed.

Somewhere behind her, a monitor beeped with every beat of her heart, and a half-drained IV bag hung in the corner beside a window that showed weak, salmon light through the blinds—though sunrise or sunset, she couldn't tell. Annie closed her eyes again. It felt as if someone had taken a sledgehammer to the back of her head.

Through the open door, she heard an elevator ping. She must be in a hospital somewhere. Maybe Vancouver. For a minute, she waited, listening for someone, anyone, to make their presence known and tell her what was going on, but her mind was sluggish and heavy, and silky unconsciousness wrapped itself around her once more. Reluctantly, she gave in, sliding back into sleep.

When she woke again, it was to the sound of hushed voices in the hall, low and male. She knew those voices. Jake and Daniel. Annie tried to sit up on the pillow, but her body felt like lead, and it took every bit of her strength just to turn her ear toward the door.

"You sure?" Daniel murmured.

"I'm sure," Jake said. "Go on home and get some sleep, brother. I can stay so she won't be alone if she wakes up."

"You'll call if there're any updates?" Daniel sounded anxious, and Annie wanted to go to him, to call out, but she had no command over her voice or body.

"Of course. They said her vitals are good. They'll only keep her until she's ready to be up and about. Knowing Annie, that'll be about five minutes after she wakes up."

Daniel chuckled. "I'll head back then. Honestly, I could probably sleep for about a week right now."

Annie closed her eyes, her tired mind easing her back into the darkness.

When she woke again, a hand was holding hers. A hand she had never held before, with strong, calloused fingers, the thumb running back and forth over her own.

She opened her eyes, finally feeling truly awake, and found the room bright with sunlight. Jake was leaning back in the chair beside the bed with his eyes closed, the sun catching the fine blond hairs on his jaw like dandelion silk.

"Jake," she said, her voice barely there.

He lifted his head.

"Hey," he whispered, eyes bright with relief as he released her hand to brush the hair from her face.

Annie turned to look at the window, the small movement sending shooting pains across the back of her skull.

"My head hurts." She squeezed her eyes shut.

"I know."

Speaking took a tremendous effort, and the monitor beeped half a dozen times before she tried again.

"Where are we?"

"Portland."

Annie licked her chapped lips and attempted to raise herself from the bed. "Walt . . . he . . ."

Jake pushed her gently back down into the pillows. "I know. He's in custody. They got a full confession out of him, and he'll be put away for the rest of his life."

Jake told her then what had happened after her world went dark, and Annie listened with strange detachment, feeling only a faraway sense of dismay when she realized how close she'd come to death. She could hear it in Jake's voice, the disbelief, the sadness. He was still processing it all.

"Are you and Daniel okay?"

Jake nodded. "We will be." He yawned and stifled it with a fist. "He's been here for two days. I finally sent him home for some sleep last night."

"That's how long I've been out?"

Jake nodded, reaching out to brush her forehead again.

"I'm so sorry, Annie. About everything. I was so bullheaded about this whole thing. Certain I was right. Never in a million years would I have thought . . ."

His voice trailed away, and Annie tried to nod but couldn't quite manage it. Instead, she gazed at him from the bed as his blue eyes filled with tears.

"You deserved a better father than him."

They lapsed into a long silence, and Annie took his hand again.

"Thank you for saving my life. You're a hero, Jake."

Jake closed his eyes and his head dipped as he shook it. "I don't feel like one. My life's been turned upside down and I . . . honestly, I don't know how I'm going to face the days ahead."

Annie squeezed his hand gently. "It's not the burden that breaks you. It's whether or not you have someone to help you carry it."

They stared into each other's eyes for a long moment, and something in Jake's face changed, a peace dawning there that she had not seen since that awful day in the woods. With a small smile, he let go of her hand and rose from the chair.

"I'll go tell the nurse that you're up. And I'll give Daniel a call, too. He'll want to know you're awake."

"Wait. Don't call him yet. There's something I need you to do for me first."

Chapter 45

DANIEL

In the peaceful stillness of late afternoon, Daniel walked up Lake Lumin Road.

Pinched under his arm were the nine NO TRESPASSING signs that had lined the quarter-mile stretch leading up to the clearing, and tucked in his back pocket was the hammer he'd used to wrench their nails free.

As he stepped into the clearing, he stretched out a hand to brush the jagged, broken hinges attached to the fence post. The gate was gone, and the gap it left behind continued to catch his eye like a missing tooth, but, somehow, he knew that he'd never replace it. He was done barricading himself from the rest of the world. Done barricading his heart, starved of love since his youth.

He carried the signs to the bonfire he'd left roaring in the circle of stones and dropped them into the flames, then hopped up onto the dock and reclaimed his seat in the Adirondack chair. Smiling, he reached for his sketch pad and flipped it open to the drawing he'd been working on since sunrise.

It had come to him in the basement of the church, and it was the first time in his life he'd sketched something he had not seen. Something imagined. Something he hoped would one day be.

It was Annie, older than she was now, with her hair loose around her face, standing beside the lake, looking back at him over her shoulder with a smile on her lips. A vision. A dream. A future.

Daniel etched fine lines of patience and determination into her features and shaded with soft shadow, but his gaze kept sliding up past the top of the paper to the lake beyond, the silken surface pearled with late-afternoon light.

He'd almost lost her. He'd almost lost Annie to this very lake, and he would never be able to repay Jake for saving her life, though they had about fifty years' worth of fishing weekends for him to try.

The light on the lake dulled as the sun dipped behind the treetops, and Daniel set down the drawing pad at last and went inside to warm a pot of soup on the stove. As he stirred, he glanced at the clock.

He was itching to see Annie now that she was awake and recovering, but on the phone from the hospital, Jake had told him to stay where he was, that Annie had insisted on coming to him when she was ready, and not the other way around. That was two days ago, and time was absolutely crawling as he waited, ear constantly attuned for the sound of a rumbling engine on the road.

He couldn't wait to see her. Couldn't wait to sit across the fire from her and speak as they once had, without the investigation hanging between them.

Daniel ate his soup with his eyes on the clock. When he was finished, he rinsed his bowl in the sink and settled into the corner of the couch to wind down the early evening hours with the novel he'd started yesterday, but just as he cracked the cover, there it was—the telltale growl of a motor outside.

The book slipped from his fingers as he lunged to his feet, flying across the room to the window. With his fingertips pressed to the glass, he waited and watched the trees. The sound rose with the hope in his chest, and then, just behind the pines, he caught the flash of beige and wood paneling.

It was her.

Sudden nerves flooded him, and Daniel darted to the back room to check his reflection in the mirror, running his fingers through his hair a few times as anxious butterflies erupted in his stomach. Outside, the sound of the engine rose to a pitch as the Jeep pulled into the clearing, then fell away.

A few moments passed, then a knock sounded on the side door, and Daniel moved to answer it.

What should he say to her? What should he do? After all they'd been through, it was impossible to know where to start.

Breath held, he opened the door.

Annie did not hesitate, but stepped inside and threw her arms around his neck, clinging tight. The dam inside Daniel broke and he kissed her over and over and over. He pressed his lips to her hair, her cheeks, her mouth, saying her name between every kiss as though the word itself was the breath in his lungs.

"I love you," he murmured without forethought, kissing the tear that had slipped down her cheek. "I love you, Annie."

She clung tighter to him, crying steadily now as he said the words again and again, until at last she said them, too.

"Come on," he said, bringing her farther into the house, and she shook her head.

"Wait, I . . . I have to tell you something."

With great effort, Daniel released his grip on her, and she stepped back, breathless.

"I asked Jake to do something for me," she said, swiping at the tears that had fallen. "I sent him down to Redmond."

Daniel stilled, staring at her as his throat constricted, but Annie shook her head quickly.

"I had to know. And you should, too. Gary died of a heart attack a year ago."

Daniel's blood seemed to stop flowing as the words landed, and he searched her eyes for truth.

"Are you sure?"

She nodded. "It's over, Daniel. You're free."

Daniel gathered her into his arms again, hands trembling. The last chains of fear binding his heart had been cut in one fell swoop, and the broken links were falling to the ground in pieces.

"Thank you," he whispered into her hair, and led her inside by the hand.

Later, as a weary sun slipped violet light through the western pines, Daniel and Annie sat on the dock with their hands joined in the space between the wooden chairs.

Crickets sang softly in the alders behind the boathouse, and overhead a single star pierced the darkening dome of the sky.

Daniel tracked a dragonfly as it chased its mate across silver water, then turned to Annie, who was watching him with a tender smile on her lips.

"What are you thinking?" she asked.

Daniel met her gaze and did not look away. "That this place has never felt more like home."

Annie's smile widened, and her chin dipped in a single nod. "You read my mind."

Daniel lifted her hand and pressed his lips to her fingers, then turned back to the water.

The lake was smooth as glass in the palm of the forest that held it.

Quiet had come to the woods again.

ACKNOWLEDGMENTS

My deepest thanks to Laura Brown, editor extraordinaire, whose golden touch could make a masterpiece out of a grocery list.

To Kimi Cunningham Grant and Allison Nance, dear friends and gifted writers. I am honored to walk beside you in the triumphs and heartaches of this rather splendid day job.

To Jane Dystel, whose support and tenacity made a career out of a pipe dream.

To Ali Hinchcliffe, Dayna Johnson, Natalie Argentina, Jessica Laino, and the rest of the team at Simon & Schuster who keep the wheels turning.

To Lindsay Sagnette, who believed it should be Annie's story in the first place.

To Guthrie Hood, whose knowledge of the wild saved me from many an embarrassing blunder.

To Michael, my idea man, now and forever.

And to Charlotte and Emmy, who will one day be delighted to find their names in the back of this book.

ABOUT THE AUTHOR

S ARAH CROUCH is the *USA Today* bestselling author of *Middletide* and *The Briars*, literary thrillers set in the Pacific Northwest, where she was raised. She is also known in the world of athletics as a professional marathon runner.

ATRIA BOOKS, an imprint of Simon & Schuster, fosters an open environment where ideas flourish, bestselling authors soar to new heights, and tomorrow's finest voices are discovered and nurtured. Since its launch in 2002, Atria has published hundreds of bestsellers and extraordinary books, which would not have been possible without the invaluable support and expertise of its team and publishing partners. Thank you to the Atria Books colleagues who collaborated on *The Briars*, as well as to the hundreds of professionals in the Simon & Schuster advertising, audio, communications, design, ebook, finance, human resources, legal, marketing, operations, production, sales, supply chain, subsidiary rights, and warehouse departments who help Atria bring great books to light.

Editorial
Laura Brown
Natalie Argentina

Jacket Design
Claire Sullivan
James Iacobelli

Marketing
Dayna Johnson

Managing Editorial
Paige Lytle
Shelby Pumphrey
Lacee Burr
Sofia Echeverry

Production
Annette Pagliaro Sweeney
Vanessa Silverio
Steve Boldt
Jill Putorti

Publicity
Alison Hinchcliffe
Jessica Laino

Publishing Office
Suzanne Donahue
Abby Velasco

Subsidiary Rights
Nicole Bond
Sara Bowne
Rebecca Justiniano